A SERVING OF SCANDAL

ALSO BY PRUE LEITH

Leaving Patrick
Sisters
The Gardener (originally published as *A Lovesome Thing*)
Choral Society

PRUE LEITH

A SERVING OF SCANDAL

First published in Great Britain in 2010 by

Quercus
21 Bloomsbury Square
London
WC1A 2NS

A CIP catalogue record for this book
is available from the British Library

ISBN 978 1 84916 169 5 (HB)
ISBN 978 1 84916 170 1 (TPB)

10 9 8 7 6 5 4 3 2 1

Typeset by Ellipsis Books Limited, Glasgow

Printed and bound in Great Britain by Clays Ltd, St Ives plc

For Daniel and Emma

ACKNOWLEDGEMENTS

Ever since my first novel had my hero fishing on the Scottish bank of the Tweed on a Sunday and a surprising number of fly-fishermen had the pleasure of pointing out my mistake, I've been neurotic about factual errors. I check all sorts of things that really don't need to be accurate in a work of fiction, but I can't help it.

I am no habitué of the Westminster village, so am grateful for help with the protocol and practices of government departments from Lords Malloch-Brown, Hurd and Chadlington, from Danny Kruger, Derek Wyatt, MP and Anne Power.

Sarah Seabright gave me help on antique Yemeni jewellery; Jo Darke and Philip Ward-Jackson on the sculptures on Hyde Park Corner; Katherin Townsend on the etiquette involved in vaulting on horseback; Helen Smith on the Wolseley Restaurant; Nat Moser on Russian expressions; Jo Jennings and Charlotte Arnold on the furnishings and layout of Hampton Court Palace; Vivien Bedford on commercial flower buying at New Covent Garden; Hilary Knight on how much a newspaper might pay for a juicy kiss-and-tell; Pelham Ravenscroft and Martin Chown for locating an Anthony Trollope quotation about politics; Jonathan Sankson for how banks lend money, and Paula Hudson on pre-teen culture such as the likelihood of ten-year-olds saying 'Don't get your knickers in a twist'. (Answer: they wouldn't.)

And then, once again, I must thank Jane Turnbull, my agent,

for liking my writing and putting energy and commitment into selling it, and my editor Jane Wood for excellent suggestions on improvement which I hate getting but end up acknowledging as dead right: e.g. 'Your favourite word is "O" (which by the way should be spelt "Oh") and at least fifty per cent of them should go.' And I want to thank Lucy Ramsey in advance, in the hopes that she will do as brilliant a job on publicising and marketing this novel as she did on *Choral Society*.

Enormous thanks too to my PA, Francisca Sankson, who has read the book like a policeman doing a finger-tip search. She's the one who tells me that so-and-so's eyes where brown in Chapter X, so how come they are blue now; that if it's June, why is it snowing? Writing without Francisca's intelligence, beady eye, and general confidence that all will come right in time would be very hard.

A SERVING OF SCANDAL

CHAPTER ONE

'Are you waiting at table then? You can hardly do it in chef's whites.'

The voice was not friendly. Kate turned from the sink to see Dennis, the Foreign Office butler, lips pursed, and eyes narrowed behind his designer frames. Hell, she thought. Why him? Why couldn't I have had Tom, or Rodrigo? Dennis was the head butler and a pain. Reaching round her back for the dishcloth tucked into her apron to dry her hands, she said, 'Hello, Dennis, I didn't know you were here. It's only a working lunch isn't it?'

'This *is* One Carlton Gardens,' he replied, 'and the official residence of the Foreign Secretary. We have standards to maintain.'

Kate, knowing she must work with the man, said evenly, 'And *I* will not let you down, don't worry. But I did clear my waitressing with Julian, and I'll wear a black apron over the top. It'll be fine.'

Dennis gave his head a little shake of disapproval. He did not like the facilities manager, to whom they all reported.

Kate said, 'Of course if you want to do it, that would be wonderful, but as it's such a tiny job I said I could manage on my own.' Better lay it on thick, she thought, and added, 'I'm sure you've got much more important stuff to see to.'

'I have, as it happens, though I do not like to leave the Secretary of State unattended, even for a small working lunch.'

She shrugged, pulling her mouth down in an ironic *moue*.

'Everyone, even the government, is trying to save money. The budget is so tight, I'll be lucky if I cover my costs. Julian seemed to think I could do it for the price of the food.'

'What do you mean? You make a fortune.'

'I wish. I do OK, but not on a job for four. If it was anyone other than the Foreign and Commonwealth Office I'd have turned it down, but I've got to impress the new boss.' She picked up two sauté pans and shoved them upside down onto the pot rack.

Dennis, leaning against the fridge, was inspecting his nails, which irritated Kate. She'd have liked him out of her kitchen. Only it wasn't her kitchen.

'You won't get the catering contract here, you know,' he said. 'We have our own chef and he's *really* good.' He shrugged and turned to study his reflection in the shiny chrome fish kettle. 'Only he's sick today, so needs must.'

Kate had to make an effort not to rise to this. 'Dennis, come on . . . you know all I'm after is keeping my place on the approved list of party caterers for the department. Oliver Stapler has a reputation as something of a foodie and he might just have a pet caterer of his own. I don't want some Chelsea girl with connections shoe-horning me out.'

Dennis gave a dismissive little snort. 'That's all gone now. Government jobs have to be awarded after a proper selection process. You were lucky you got in before the rules changed.'

Thanks very much, thought Kate. But she kept her tone pleasant as she laid out her starter plates on the worktop and switched the subject back to practicalities.

'Are you doing the drinks or do you want me to? The starter and pud are cold, so I can easily manage it.'

'No, of course not. A sommelier's job can't be done by any Tom, Dick or Harry.'

What a tosser, she thought; they'd only drink water anyway, but she was determined not to give him any ammunition so she smiled and said, 'Well, at least I am none of those.'

'I'm more concerned about you doing the waiter's job,' said Dennis.

'Since you've decided to do it yourself, I'm prepared to run you through the do's and don'ts.'

Kate would have liked to punch his self-important paunch, but said, 'It's fine, Dennis. I was a waitress long before I was a cook, and I can still carry a row of plates up my arm – *and* serve from the left and clear from the right. Don't worry, I won't let you down.'

She watched him glide out of the kitchen with an almost imperceptible sway of his hips, his nose very slightly in the air and his hands held a few inches away from his body. He wore the regulation butler's uniform but always managed to look infinitely smarter than the others: his striped worsted trousers perfectly cut, starched white cuffs just visible under his tailored jacket, the tie of thick black silk, shoes (even the heels) polished like new. And he always smelt expensive.

I bet he shaves that bald head, thought Kate. And wears silver hoops in his ears – she'd noticed they were pierced – when off duty. She had a sudden vision of Dennis dancing in a gay club, kissing the neck of a young lad. She shuddered. Well, at least there was no danger of his pushing her up against a storeroom door.

Kate walked confidently and purposefully about the kitchen but she was anxious. As she ground coriander into the spiced potatoes, and turned them carefully in the pan, her mind stayed on Dennis. She really did not like him, and she was unused to disliking people. Also, she was made uneasy by Dennis's obvious dislike of her. Why did he try so hard to get up her nose? Surely it was easier and pleasanter to get on with your colleagues? He was charm itself to the clients, nothing too much trouble: Yes, Sir; Certainly, Minister; At once, M'lady. And he was very good at his job, which no doubt accounted for his rise to head butler. But below stairs he was poison, a master of drama. His staff never quite knew if they were in favour or out, and he certainly had it in for all outside contractors – especially the females.

All she could do was take no notice, tread carefully, and give Dennis no cause for complaint. She was as conscious as he that one word from him to the facilities manager and she would not be hired again.

Very soon, in the stress-free enjoyment of such a simple job, Kate had forgotten all about Dennis. She laid the table with care. The silver, china and linen were provided by the Foreign Office and, to Dennis's credit, everything sparkled. She was pleased with herself for bringing a bunch of snowdrops as a centrepiece. The department did not run to extra flowers for internal or inter-departmental events, and though the main rooms would have flowers or plants, the dining table would not. That she and Toby had been out in the garden last night, picking the flowers, was a thought that cheered her. It had been almost dark, but the snowdrops had glowed bright white and the five-year old had dashed from clump to clump, filling his plump hands.

The raw peeled beetroot for the goats' cheese starter went through the Robot Coupe in a single long push, and the fine red julienne strips snaked into the bowl below like magic. She sprinkled them with lemon juice and sea salt. She'd have liked to add fresh mint but it was January and, over the years, she'd become ever keener on sticking to seasonal produce. She made four neat piles of beetroot in the centre of each plate and surrounded them with chunks of goat's cheese and fresh walnuts, then garnished each with a few young beet leaves (poly-tunnel grown, but at least English). All they needed now was a drizzle of good olive oil before serving.

Rather than risk disturbing the look of her salads with plastic wrap – which she hated wasting in any case, as well as feeling guilty that it was non-biodegradable – she covered each plate with an upended soup bowl and left them on the side. She wanted the cheese to soften slightly to develop its flavour.

Kate liked cooking on her own. She was fast and methodical, constantly wiping her boards as she used them, washing up as she went along, putting things away. She swung round the kitchen now, tossing debris into the bin, stirring a pot here, flicking salt into a pan there, slamming the bread rolls into a hot oven. She cut deep slashes through the skin of the sea bass fillets, noticing with approval how fresh and thick they were. The fish was wild and had cost a bit, but it was worth it; farmed sea bass were so often skinny and tasteless. She lay the fillets on the greased grill pan. Once she'd got the first course in front of the diners, she'd brush them with melted butter, salt them and bang them under the blazing grill. Seven minutes should do it, then she could whip them off and let them settle while she cleared the first course.

The leeks were cooked and delicious, the spiced potatoes ditto, the plates warm. The dessert was finely sliced pineapple with a thin dusting of five-spice powder and castor sugar, and the thinnest of ginger thins, made to her grandmother's recipe. No cheese, just coffee, and exactly four perfect chocolates, filled with brandied cherries. Her friend Talika made those and they cost a fortune.

The Secretary of State was late, of course, but they sat down straight away. Dennis unfolded their napkins and laid them reverently on their laps (a carry-on that always amused Kate – surely grown men could open out their own napkins?) and she went round with the hot bread rolls, then put the beetroot salads in front of them.

She had time for a good look at the new Foreign Secretary. He had presence, no doubt of that, and he was good looking in an elegant old-fashioned way. 'Patrician' the press called him. He sat straight in his chair, very still, his hands in his lap, and yet he looked as relaxed as his colleagues who leant on the table or lounged back in their chairs. He did not acknowledge her.

His hair was prematurely grey – at forty-five he was one of the youngest members of cabinet – but it suited him. She could see why the tabloids had him down for a snob and a toff in spite of his Labour credentials. His stillness and silence were unnerving. He listened, nodded, seldom commented, and when he picked up his knife and fork to eat his first course, or his glass to take a sip of water, he did so with no unnecessary movement. His stillness made Kate notice how the other guests pushed their food about the plate, ran their fingers up and down the goblet stem, shifted back and sat forward in their chairs.

When Kate served the Foreign Secretary's sea bass, it struck her, as it so often did, that well-brought up people with apparently impeccable manners could not spare the time for a quick glance or a thank you when their food was put before them. Besides, she thought crossly, that fish dish was faultless: the skin was crisp and brown, the flesh plump, moist, glowing white through the cuts in the crusty skin, the fillet sitting on a perfect round of chopped young leeks in a cream sauce. And to the side, a delicate castle (she had used a mould to get a perfect shape) of crumbly, golden, spicy potatoes. And it smelt like heaven. Even he, living off the fat of the land, could not get lunch that good every day. You'd think he'd not seen the plate before him, but since he promptly set about eating it, he obviously had.

Dennis deigned to serve the coffee but disappeared as soon as the guests had gone, leaving Kate to clear away and wash up alone. She didn't mind. If it had been one of the other butlers she would have liked the help and the chat – butlers always knew all the political gossip, true and false – but she'd rather have no help at all than that of the petulant Dennis.

By three o'clock everything was done, grill and cooker-top cleaned, floor mopped, rubbish bagged. As Kate picked up her handbag, a smartly suited young man with dark hair and glasses appeared in the kitchen doorway.

'Kate McKinnon? I'm Sean, PPS to the Foreign Secretary. He sent me to have a word.'

Kate's heart sank. 'Was something wrong?'

'No, no, not at all. He was delighted. He said to tell you he has seldom had a better lunch, and do you do private dinner parties?'

'Whew, that's a relief.' She fished in her bag for a business card. 'Yes, of course I cook private dinners. Love to.'

'Well, he's got a dinner arranged for next Thursday at his own house in Lambeth, but the chef here was to have done it and, as you know, he's ill. I was about to appeal to Government Hospitality to find us another, but since he likes your food . . .?'

Kate nodded, 'I'd be happy to step in, but I'll have to check my diary. I'm pretty sure it will be OK, though.' It will have to be, she thought.

Sean looked at her card. "Nothing Fancy." He smiled. 'He'll like that. I'll be in touch.'

Kate picked up her handbag and ran her eyes over the kitchen one last time to make sure there was no smudge of grease or crumb on the floor that Dennis could complain of. Then she hurried down the corridor to the cloakroom.

She stopped at the sight of herself in the mirror, unused to the black apron. She usually wrapped a white chef's apron round her middle, its multiple folds round her waist giving her a dumpy look. At five foot three and nine stone plus she would never be tall and thin, but the long black apron down to her calves and wrapped tightly round her waist made her look slimmer and taller than she was. And the white of her jacket set off her Celtic colouring, right now heightened by the kitchen heat. She did not wear a chef's skullcap or toque because it was a struggle to stuff her mop of dark curls into them. She knew she was meant to, but no one had ever challenged her and, as yet, no customer had found a hair in the soup. Her other non-regulation touches were her gold earrings, chunky little hoops which she wore all the time, even in bed or the bath.

She gave her reflection a brief nod. Bravo, she told herself, a very good day. Everything worked, cooked lovely food, managed not to fight with the poisonous Dennis, impressed the boss.

Best of all, I'll be home in time for Toby's tea.

Chapter Two

Oliver was irritated with himself. He had fallen asleep in the train from Euston, and the thought of his Queensmead constituents seeing their elected MP snoring was horrible. What if someone used a mobile phone to take a shot of him slumped and open mouthed, and sent it to *Private Eye* or posted it on YouTube?

He caught the eye of Jim, his detective, sitting opposite him. He rose and stretched for Oliver's overcoat in the rack above his seat. Oliver picked up the slightly battered 'red box' that told the world he was a cabinet minister. He sometimes thought he should use an ordinary briefcase or one of those wheelie things, or even a backpack carried over one shoulder as his younger officials did. But he was proud of his position, and the red box was a badge of honour. No one, he told himself, should be ashamed of being a politician. Anthony Trollope was right to believe that 'to sit in the British Parliament should be the highest object of ambition to every educated Englishman.'

They stepped from the First Class compartment onto the fume-filled platform at Birmingham New Street and hurried to the taxi rank, hoping to beat the queue. But, as usual, it curved the length of the pavement in front of the station. Damn, a good fifteen-minute wait.

Of course, as Foreign Secretary, he could be driven from Whitehall to his Staffordshire door in a comfortable Government

Jag, the uniformed Debbie at the wheel and the detective beside her. But on a late Friday afternoon that would have taken a good two and a half hours, and, anyway, he considered it his duty sometimes to travel as ordinary citizens did. Not, he thought ruefully, that First Class, with a detective in tow, a driver at one end and a taxi at the other, all paid for by the taxpayer, was exactly slumming it.

Jim kept the taxi to return to the station. His replacement, a copper seconded from the local nick, was already at the Stapler front gate.

As Oliver stepped into the kitchen (they seldom used the front door) and called out Ruth's name, he secretly hoped she would be out. He would dearly like a quiet quarter of an hour in front of the television news with a whisky in his hand and Obi-Wan Kenobi, their Jack Russell, lying across his foot.

But Ruth emerged from the boot room, still wearing her Barbour and scarf, with her jeans tucked into thick socks. Her muddy wellies were dangling from one hand. She padded across the tiles to the sink, pausing on the way to offer her cheek for a kiss. She began washing the boots under the tap.

'You're early,' she said.

'And you're out very late aren't you? Darling, you're not mucking out or riding in the dark?'

'I've been lunging one of the yearlings in the school. We floodlit it, remember? So I could work at night?'

He had forgotten. He wasn't really interested in Ruth's ponies, except that they kept her busy and moderately happy. She was a much respected breeder of Welsh cobs, with buyers from all over the country and often from abroad. Yet, though she let the old hay barn to a saddler and two of the paddocks to a neighbouring farmer, and ran the yard as economically as she could, the business lost money more years than it made any and the maintenance of farm buildings, stables and land was a worry.

When the girls were very little, both competing in local gymkhanas and going to Pony Club camp in a field half a mile away, he took more interest. He shared with Ruth the pleasure of seeing how many of the ponies being lovingly groomed by their young owners – chequerboard patterns brushed into their gleaming rumps, manes tied with little ribbons, tails plaited, hooves oiled – had been bred by Ruth. She could name them all, and they would sit on a hay bale together watching the jumping, and chalking up 'their' rosettes.

But once the girls got really serious about their riding, Oliver had begun to feel excluded. He did not ride himself and couldn't spare the time to travel miles to see his daughters compete in three-day events or horse shows. Sometimes he felt his only role in the family was to write cheques for more horses, new saddles, bigger horseboxes, endless vet's bills.

'I'll light the fire,' he said. 'Shall I get you a drink?'

As soon as they had sat down in front of the fire, whiskies in hand, and Obi had taken up his favourite position on Oliver's left foot, the girls clattered down the stairs and erupted into the room. Neither looked at their father.

'What's for supper, Mum?' asked Andrea as Mattie said, 'Mum, Can I have a beer?'

Ruth just shook her head at this, but Oliver said, 'Of course not. You're only fourteen.'

'Nearly fifteen.'

'. . . And you don't even like beer.'

Ruth said, 'Leave it, Oliver. She's only doing it for effect.' She turned to Andrea, 'It's bangers and mash. And salad. But nothing's cooked yet.'

'But Mum, we're starving! How long till supper?'

'Depends if I get any assistance. How about helping? That would speed things up.' Ruth's voice had an edge of sarcasm to it that made Oliver long to intervene, but he knew better than to inflame her. 'Like cook the sausages?' she persisted. 'Or make the mash? Or make the salad? Or lay the table?'

'OK, OK, we get the message,' muttered Mattie.

I could do without this, thought Oliver. Ruth was plainly exhausted and grumpy. He said, 'Look, girls, sit down and join the conversation, or go away and we'll call you when it's ready.'

The girls sloped out of the room and thudded upstairs again.

Ruth looked at him, faintly hostile. 'You, I suppose, had a delicious lunch, served by a flunky in white gloves?'

Oliver pretended she was teasing, and said with a smile. 'No white gloves, sadly. Delicious lunch though, some new cook. Nice girl. She seemed to be the waiter too.'

'Three courses? Wine? Chocolates? Liqueurs?'

He could not go on ignoring her tone. 'Ruth darling, don't be snarky. It's been a long tough week, in spite of the ministerial perks you object to so much.'

'If we are to compete on tough weeks, darling Oliver, I think I win hands down.'

He took a slow sip of his whisky and said evenly, 'I'm sorry. What went wrong?'

'What didn't? Neither of those two mares we put to Welsh Dragon at that stud halfway to bloody Scotland are in foal. It pissed with rain all week so the only work I could do was in the covered school. Little Nonny is lame, and the sale of the chestnut, Ruby, fell through. Oh yes, the cost of feed has gone up from the first of next month by four per cent which makes it eleven per cent up on last year. Is that enough to be going on with? And please don't tell me I should give up the ponies.'

'I wasn't going to. You've made it very clear you want to stick with it.' He stood up, fetched the whisky bottle and poured her another half-inch. His free hand on her shoulder, he said, 'It's just sad that it's giving you so much grief and no pleasure.'

She looked up at him, suddenly contrite and said, 'I'm sorry, Oliver. I'm tired, the girls are driving me nuts and I haven't made the supper. And I want a shower.'

Relieved, Oliver sank back into his chair and smiled. 'Darling, don't worry. I read somewhere that for most couples the risk of flare-ups is highest when one of them walks through the door. He wants slippers and pipe and cosseting, and she wants appreciation.'

'Do you want slippers and pipe?'

'Do you want appreciation?'

'Yes, too right I do!'

Oh God, thought Oliver, she's going to take off again. I'm too tired for this.

She went on, 'I work bloody hard, mostly on my own, and do all the domestic stuff. So when you swan in looking sleek as an otter, I guess it gets up my nose.'

'Would it make you feel better if I told you I fell asleep on the train, and no, that wasn't due to a boozy lunch, I never drink at lunch. It's because I went to bed at three a.m. last night because I had to finish my boxes when I got back from an extremely tedious dinner at the QEII Conference Centre. And that the PM is not finding me as pliable as he'd hoped and I fear we will not agree on West Africa. And the Chancellor told us today that he wants fifteen per cent out of everyone's budgets because we are in deep shit on the debt front—'

'OK, OK. I concede that grave affairs of state outrank mere domestic problems.'

Oliver stood up abruptly. 'Ruth, this is not a competition. Look, why don't you go and have your shower. I'll watch the news.'

After half an hour Ruth was not yet down. Oliver walked into the kitchen and yanked open the fridge. There were two packs of sausages – good butchers' ones, he was glad to see. He tipped them into a roasting pan and used the scissors to separate them, then slid the pan into the top oven of the Aga.

He found the packet of frozen mash in the freezer, stabbed the bag with the tip of a knife and put it in the microwave. While he waited for the blocks to thaw he heated the milk and butter.

He liked cooking. It was calming. He stood quietly stirring the mash until it was smooth, then ground some black pepper into it, suddenly wondering if that jolly little cook with the plump round face ever stooped to frozen mash.

By the time he had tossed the salad the girls had reappeared and the sausages were almost done. He flipped them all over to brown them evenly, and put them back in the oven. Then he rummaged around in the cupboard for the onion marmalade, which he and Ruth liked, and the ketchup without which the girls didn't seem able to swallow anything.

'Andrea, go and call your mother, will you? And Mattie, could you lay the table? Knives and forks, big plates, the salad servers, two lots of serving spoons. And glasses, some paper napkins and salt and pepper. Got that?'

'Do I have to?'

'If you want any supper you do.'

Oliver wanted to tell Mattie to take her earphones off, and concentrate on the job in hand. She failed on the salad servers, napkins, and pepper and salt, but Oliver lacked the energy for a confrontation. Eventually the table was laid and the food was on it, looking good and smelling delicious. Oliver fetched a bottle of wine and a corkscrew and the three of them sat down at the table.

Ruth had still not appeared, but Oliver resisted the girls' demands to eat without her. No, he said, this is a family meal, and we need to have it together. But he was tempted to just dish up.

Why did his wife have to be so awkward? It had only taken him twenty minutes to put the supper together, which surely she could have managed hours ago. Because she hadn't, it was now nine-thirty and they were all hungry and cross.

He sometimes thought Ruth was still fighting the good feminist fight, which had largely been won before she was out of primary school. Daily, or at least weekly, she proved that she did not have to do what he wanted.

Of course, her waywardness was what had attracted him in the first place. He had loved the fact that she – beautiful, intelligent and rich – was scornful, even outraged, at the preoccupations of her generation. In those days she never wore make-up, she ripped the power shoulder pads out of any jacket or suit she bought, and she loathed the Spice Girls and Mrs Thatcher with equal venom.

She'd disapproved of the rampant money-centredness of eighties Toryism, and when they married she had refused her father's offer of a big marquee wedding (he was High Sheriff of the county and a Labour life peer – a reward, according to Ruth, for his largesse to the party). Instead, she had insisted he give the money he would have spent on their nuptials to Refuge, the battered wives' charity.

But now Oliver found her little gestures of independence, like not making supper or refusing to attend any political or business functions with him, petty and sad.

Oliver chose not to see Mattie sneak her fork into the bowl of mash and eat a mouthful. Poor girl, they were all very hungry. He got up and fetched the bread and some butter. He cut the girls a slice each. 'Here,' he said, 'eat this. Mum will be down in a minute.'

'What's for pudding?' asked Andrea.

'God knows. I've no idea,' he replied, and realised that it was the first time he had been deliberately disloyal to Ruth in front of the children. His tone had plainly said, 'Ask your mother. Her responsibility. Which she's failing at.'

Then Ruth appeared, looking more cheerful and dressed in a much-washed black and white kaftan that hugged her slender body. She had her fair hair scraped back with a comb, exposing her fine eyes, straight nose and long neck. She had never needed make-up to look good. All she needed, thought Oliver, was to smile.

He tried to get some conversation going, but Ruth seemed distracted, Andrea answered questions about school without enthusiasm and Mattie complained, 'Dad, why do we have to talk at supper? It's boring. Why can't we just eat and go, like other families? And why do we have to have supper in the kitchen anyway? Jason's family eat in front of the telly. It's cool.'

Sometimes I wonder why I come home at all, thought Oliver. Ruth is clearly unhappy and the girls have nothing to say to me. So much for the fruits of success.

CHAPTER THREE

Kate had her hands in the water, scrubbing mussels, and Talika was mashing parsnips to a purée in the Robot Coupe, when a child's loud wail cut through the noise of the food processor. Kate looked up to see her son stumbling away from Sanjay, the red plastic cricket bat in his hands, and Sanjay with his skinny arms in the air, emitting a second cry of protest.

The women looked at each other, silently agreeing that the cries weren't serious, more indignation than pain, and that they belonged to Sanjay, so Talika would deal with it. Talika stopped the machine and, with an apologetic shake of her head, walked through the little ante room – once a scullery, now a clutter of boots, toys and catering equipment – and into the garden.

Watching her friend through the window, Kate noticed, as she so often did, how thin and graceful Talika was – even in jeans and an oversized shirt, presumably Amal's. And how calm. She walked quickly but without hurry, taking the same small steps as when she was all dressed up in a tightly wound sari. She dipped her knees to scoop up Sanjay, who, at five, was hardly heavier than a toddler.

From where Kate stood Sanjay looked all skinny arms and legs, like a monkey clinging to his mother's hip. Talika bent to talk to Toby, who was clutching the cricket bat behind his back. Kate couldn't hear what Talika said, but Toby was sufficiently mollified to take her outstretched hand, although still gripping the bat in his free hand and truculently dragging his feet. Sanjay's wails diminished to grizzles as he sunk his head into his mother's shoulder.

She brought them into the kitchen. 'How about we park them in front of the telly for an hour? They're getting tired and tetchy, and it's cold out there. Toby's hands are freezing.'

'Good idea. It's about time for *Ben 10*.'

Kate crouched to help Toby out of his wellies and into his trainers. 'So what happened, Toby? You didn't hurt Sanjay, did you . . .?'

Talika looked up from tugging off Sanjay's boots, 'No, don't be silly. In true Indian tradition, Sanjay was disputing Toby's "Howzat!" and regarded confiscation of the bat as an outrage.'

'I got him out, Mum! I hit his legs. That's lbw.'

'You didn't!' protested Sanjay. 'I wasn't in front of the wicket. And the ball hit the bat, not my legs!'

Once *Ben 10* had worked his instant magic the women got back to work. They were preparing for the dinner Kate was doing at Oliver Stapler's house in Lambeth. She liked to prep as much as she could at home, especially if it was the first time she was cooking for a new client or in a new kitchen. Mr Stapler's assistant had told her it was an important dinner and the Prime Minister would be present. The dinner should be delicious and unusual, but not costly, and the ingredients must be mainly British. Her boss had a horror of showing off or making the food the main focus of the evening, she said. And, Kate might like to know, he was knowledgeable about food, having been a minister of it in Defra.

Kate smiled at the memory. 'Do you know, 'Lika, our Foreign Secretary was once a minister of food? His PA says I need to be aware of that.'

'What difference does she think the info will make to our cooking?'

'I guess she thinks it will scare the hell out of us and we'll try harder. She also told me that he believes dinner parties are for intelligent conversation and serious debate, not primarily about food, so nothing fancy.'

'Maybe we should give him baked beans and chips.'

'Pompous prat,' said Kate. She hated scrubbing mussels. The stringy 'beards' were difficult to remove, and you had to stay alert and make sure you discarded any that wouldn't shut when tapped in case they were dead and poisonous. But cleaning the things was their only drawback. They were relatively cheap, delicious in classic moules marinières, added oomph to any seafood dish and made the best soup in the world.

Kate scooped the cleaned mussels into her biggest saucepan, added a splash of white wine, a cupful of chopped shallots and another of chopped parsley, and set them over the heat, the lid of the pan clamped on firmly. For the next few minutes, she gave the pot an occasional shake, then she opened the lid and peered inside. Good, all open, she thought, breathing in their heady aroma and registering every ingredient: mussels, wine, onion, parsley. Together they made your mouth water.

As Kate set the whole pan in a sinkful of water to cool, with the lid on to prevent the mussels steaming dry, Talika's husband, Amal, walked in the back door.

'Great smell!' He lifted the lid of the mussel pan and inhaled deeply, then replaced the lid and turned to kiss Kate.' What are you going to do with them?'

'Mussel soup.'

'Mmmm. Yum yum. Then what?'

'These,' said Talika, nodding at the oven tray of pigeon breasts neatly wrapped in the thinnest of bacon. She was brushing them with a fine coat of melted butter. 'How come you're early? I thought you were meeting the EHO?'

Amal and Talika had a restaurant, a very good one, and they were having a battle with the local environmental health officer about their newly tiled kitchen. The man had a preference for seamless plastic walls, which Amal would have installed had he known tiles were no longer flavour of the health department month. But now he was reluctant – in fact he'd flatly refused – to junk the tiles and start again.

'Met him. He's gone.'

'And?'

'The bastard has now added half a dozen other things to his requirements. There must be separate probes for raw meat, cooked meat, etc, even though they get a sterile wipe every time we use them. The outside bin cage must have locks fitted to keep the foxes out, which is nonsense because the foxes can't get in anyway. Can you imagine? If it's a padlock the cooks will lose the key, and if it's a code they will forget the numbers! And the bin men will smash the locks for sure.'

'Why don't you ask the council for wheelie bins? The lids are pretty good and I put a breeze block on top of mine, which works fine,' suggested Kate.

'Because they won't let me put them out on the street, and the rubbish cupboard isn't big enough for wheelie bins and they won't let me enlarge it. I told him to shoot the bloody foxes but he said they couldn't do that. The residents would object.'

'Toby would certainly object. There's a family of foxes in that scrubby land beyond our garden and in the spring they come and play on our lawn. Bold as brass. We watch from the kitchen. Toby loves them.'

Talika put her tray of pigeon breasts, now covered in clingfilm, into the fridge and gave her husband a kiss. 'Cheer up, darling, you will win him over in the end. And we've got the cleanest kitchen for miles around.'

Amal shook his head. 'I know, and what's more they know it too. Why don't they go pick on that doner kebab joint? That guy has nowhere behind the counter to wash his hands, the place is filthy. Or why don't they harass the ice-cream van at the park gates? Doubt if they ever clean that machine. It's encrusted with weeks-old mix. Poor Sanjay can't understand why he's the only kid on the block not allowed to buy the stuff.'

'He and Toby,' said Kate, 'but it's the junk that goes into the ice-cream I'm scared of, rather than the bugs.'

Kate pulled together a scratch lunch for all of them: she boiled some linguine and added chopped chicken and ham left over from a pie she had made for a customer yesterday, some cherry tomatoes and garlic, and a sprinkling of grated cheese. Then an endive salad, made more acceptable to the boys by the addition of tangerine slices. It took her less than ten minutes, while Talika washed up from the morning's work and Amal prised the children away from the telly and got them to wash their hands.

Talika laid the big table in the kitchen. It was work-top height and they sat on stools. As Kate doled out the pasta, she felt that familiar wash of pleasure at feeding people. Especially people she loved. And, she thought with a little thrill of pleasure, soon Mum and Hank will be here. Toby will have his adored gran around and we'll be a family for a couple of weeks.

But Amal and Talika were her best friends and she could not do without them. They helped her with her catering business and she occasionally helped them in their restaurant. And they looked after each other's children, although, thought Kate, since

I'm a single mum and in greater need than she is, Talika gets the worst of that deal.

Kate looked at her friend and noticed the dark eyes and slightly drawn look. Talika and Amal worked hard. Their flat was over the restaurant, where Talika served behind the bar and acted as cashier every night, a baby alarm in the plug behind her. And Kate knew they had been trying for a second child for four years, and her failure to conceive was getting to her. Kate said, "Lika, I don't have to pack the van until five. I'll have the boys till then, and you can get some sleep. You look a bit peely-wally.'

'What's peely-wally?' asked Toby.

'It means not looking or feeling well. My Scots grandmother used to say it.' In an exaggerated Scottish accent, Kate said, 'Ye bairns are looking reet peely-wally. Eat up your porridge and get oot in yon bonny fresh air.'

When Amal and Talika had left, she took the children to the park. If anything, it was even colder than this morning and the swings were deserted. While the boys romped about, chasing and shoving each other, climbing things and running from one piece of equipment to another, Kate sat on a slightly damp swing, huddled in her quilted coat, and allowed her thoughts to drift back to those Scottish holidays. She wished she could give Toby summers like that.

We were a proper family then, she thought, with Grandad taking us out on the loch in his old rowboat, Mum and Dad hiking with us along the lower slopes of the Monroes, Grandma making girdle cakes for tea which we ate hot, with butter and honey running down our chins. If only Toby could have something of that life.

Kate missed her family. Her grandparents were dead, and so was her father. He'd smoked eighty cigarettes a day and emphysema had killed him in Arizona where he and her mother had gone, they said, for his health.

But that was an excuse. The truth, Kate believed, was that they wanted to be with her brother Arthur and his family. Or her mother, Pat, did. Arthur's wife, Sheila, didn't have a mother, and each time she gave birth to another child, Kate's parents would be there, her mum to help, her dad there because her mum was. As more children arrived – they had three now – they'd stayed longer and longer and Pat had become more and more indispensable to the family. Or so she'd said. Kate had suspected her mother was falling for Sheila's father, Hank, a senior policeman in Tucson and a widower.

And sure enough, after Kate's dad died her mum had married Hank. With indecent haste, Kate thought.

Kate told herself that of course her mother had spent more time with Arthur than with her. Arthur had three children years before Toby was born, and the family needed help. Plus her father breathed more easily in Arizona and the hospitals were better. I probably never even told them I minded, she thought.

And in truth she knew that she only minded intermittently. At that time she'd been young, single and ambitious and only too delighted to be left in sole occupation of the family house, the beneficiary of Mrs Thatcher's policy to sell off council houses cheaply to their occupiers. How else, she thought, would I have afforded a place big enough to run my catering business from.

And anyway, by the time Toby was born, Mum had already married Hank.

But somehow she did feel, though she'd never said so, even to Talika, that everyone abandoned her, sooner or later. Her dad died, her whole family decamped to Arizona, Toby's father scarpered for Australia as soon as she'd told him she was pregnant. How much further away could they all get?

Because this was a private occasion rather than an official government dinner, Kate had hired Joan, her favourite waitress. She and Joan had worked together for years, and it was a relief not to be working with Dennis, the Foreign Office head butler.

The Stapler kitchen, in a pretty terraced house in Lambeth, wasn't brilliant – a bit poky and cluttered – but bearable. There were signs of someone interested in cooking. Kate saw a heavy omelette pan, decent sized board, chef's knives, and a well-used food processor, but it also told of a man living mostly on his own and never eating in. The freezer wanted defrosting and the fridge needed a good clear out: there were two large pillows of now manky supermarket salad leaves, a fermenting box of orange juice, a rock-hard lump of cheese, and a jug of God knows what under a furry blanket of mould. Kate hadn't time to tackle the freezer, but before Joan arrived, she sorted the fridge and swabbed it with bleach, then stacked the wine and water in it.

The dinner went like clockwork. Both mussel soup and pigeon dish were perfect and she followed the main course with an endive salad like they'd had at lunch, with the addition of a handful of chopped walnuts in the dressing. No pudding. Just some mature Montgomery cheddar with her own plum chutney and the American-style hot biscuits she'd prepped at home and baked while the main course was being eaten.

The guests were gone, Kate was washing up the coffee things and Joan was counting the silver into the drawer in the dining room when Oliver Stapler came into the kitchen, a bottle of red wine in one hand.

'Hello, you must be Kate.' He was smiling so he must be pleased.

'Yes. Was the dinner all right?'

'All right? It was perfect, just exactly what I wanted. Not fussy, not too much, but delicious. You are a very good chef. And you might like to know the PM ate everything.'

She shook her head, suddenly embarrassed by his charm. She indicated the bottle in his hand. 'Did you want me to decant that?'

'No, I came to offer you a glass. And it doesn't need decanting anyway.' He reached into the cupboard for two glasses. 'You would like one, I hope?'

He was much less stiff and formal than she'd expected. She said, 'I'd love one. Thank you.'

He poured them both a glass and said, 'You know, in the middle of a cabinet meeting this morning I suddenly realised that you would be faced with the horrors of my fridge. I very nearly dashed back at lunchtime to empty it, but then I decided you would have seen worse.'

'Much worse! But surely you have a cleaner. Doesn't she chuck stuff out?'

'Yes, but after she threw out a whole pound of that Stinking Bishop cheese because it stank, and a jar of Beluga caviar, just opened, because she thought it had "gone black", Ruth decided to do the chucking out herself.'

Kate laughed. 'Don't worry, I like sorting stuff out. But you must use the fridge for something. A bottle of white wine? Or milk for your tea?'

'No, I seldom drink white wine, and I have my tea without milk. I only noticed it was full of horrible things when I was getting some ice for a friend's drink, and I could hardly have a go then. And then I forgot.'

'Well, your secret is safe with me.'

'I hope so! My reputation is now in your hands. Just think

how that would look in the Londoner's Diary. "Minister Grows Deadly Bugs in Home Fridge".'

They were both laughing when Joan came in and Kate was pleased, and surprised, when he immediately put out his hand and said, 'I must apologise for not introducing myself when we have spent the whole evening in the same room, but I was deeply embroiled . . .'

'Sir, please don't worry,' said Joan.

'What is your name? I'm Oliver Stapler.'

Joan, who was old enough to be his mother, or almost, was perfectly relaxed as she said, 'Yes, Sir, I know. I'm Joan. I hope everything was to your satisfaction.'

'It certainly was. I was just saying to Kate that the food was delicious and I must say to you that the service matched it. Thank you.' He produced a folded tenner and handed it to her.

Kate was rapidly revising her opinion of the Foreign Secretary. He tipped the waitress, for one thing. Few government ministers ever tipped. And he was friendly and funny. And she liked his hair – that premature grey, she had to admit, looked good. But he did have a ramrod back and a way of looking at you down his patrician nose.

By the time Kate got back to the Taj Amal, the restaurant was almost empty. She looked through the windows to see if Talika was still in the bar, but only Amal was there, bowing goodbye to the last few customers. She passed the restaurant entrance and used her key to let herself into the flat. She and Talika had keys to each other's houses – it dated from the time when the boys were babies and sleep was so precious you snatched what you could when the children slept. It meant the babysitting mum and the babies would not be disturbed by the bell as the other mum came in.

Of course Talika would be awake now, she'd have only just

cashed up. But in fact the flat was silent and in near darkness, only the single light from the hall faintly illuminating the passage to the bedrooms.

As Kate passed Talika and Amal's room she could see the hump of her sleeping friend lit by the reading light on Amal's side of the bed. Poor girl, she must be exhausted, thought Kate. I shouldn't have asked her to help this morning, I could have easily managed.

She tiptoed past to Sanjay's room. Both boys were fast asleep, Sanjay small and neat, properly tucked in, Toby sprawled across his bed, his duvet thrown to the floor. No wonder, thought Kate, he still has his woollen dressing gown on.

His curly head was tousled, his face was absolutely still, lids closed and lashes laid on his cheek like those of the doll she'd had as a child, which opened her eyes when you sat her up, closed them obediently when you laid her down. Toby's mouth was open a fraction, the plump pink lips tender as a baby's. Kate felt the familiar, never fading, crump of absolute love.

She steeled herself to wake him up and face the complaints and grumpiness; he was now really too heavy for her to carry safely down the stairs, into the car, and up the stairs of her house into their bedroom. If she was feeling strong she still did it, but tonight she would be sensible and wake him.

The thought crossed her mind, as it frequently did, that she should sacrifice her office and give Toby his own bedroom. She could put bunk beds in it, one for Sanjay. But the truth was she loved her boy in her bed. And he was only five, damn it. Since they both liked the warmth and company, why not?

She found his slippers and put them on his feet. 'Toby, darling,' she said, 'wake up.'

Chapter Four

Oliver leant forward to speak to his driver.

'Pull over somewhere could you, Debbie? I need to read my brief.'

Debbie met his eyes in the rear-view mirror. 'We could park right outside Lancaster House, in Stable Yard, Sir. We won't be moved on.'

Sean sat in the front with Debbie. Sean was an up-and-coming young MP who was cutting his teeth as Oliver's personal private secretary. Next to Oliver in the back sat Jim, his most usual detective and ever-present shadow. They sat in silence, but for the purr of the Jaguar's engine, as the heater kept out the February chill.

Oliver opened his folder. On top was a copy of the invitation that had been couriered to the embassies and high commissions. It was a large, thick white card with gold edges, the Foreign Office emblem embossed on the top.

The Rt Hon Oliver Stapler, MP
Secretary of State for the Foreign and Commonwealth Offices
requests the company of

....

to a dinner to mark the 2010 Prime Minister's Conference

He couldn't prevent a small thrill of pleasure at the quality

of the thing. He had already held two secretary of state port-
folios, first Transport and then Education, so he was used to
the little trappings of power, like parking in reserved spaces.
But there are trappings and trappings, he thought, tipping the
card so its gold edges glinted. The black lettering was so shiny
the ink looked wet.

None of his previous positions had given him the chance, or
the right, to host lavish dinners in wonderful places. Indeed, he'd
hosted very few official dinners at all. Conferences, yes, or occasional suppers to motivate his junior ministers, and endless
working lunches. They were necessary, sometimes even interesting,
but the pleasure of playing host did not enter the equation.

And food, he thought, was not a strong suit at the Department
for Transport. They'd mostly eaten finger food: sandwiches of
indifferent quality, onion bhajis, sausage rolls and doughnuts,
all deep-fried a long time ago and delivered cold. At Education,
since they were trying to reform the diet of the nation's school
children, he'd decided they should set a good example, so fruit
rather than biscuits appeared with coffee, and out went the Kit
Kats and mini Mars Bars. This nearly caused a strike, only averted
by turning a blind eye to half the department taking time off
to patronise the snack shop across the road.

Oliver ran his finger over the highly embossed seal and elegant
black lettering of the invitation card. His previous jobs had not
carried rights of access to a clutch of the grandest houses in
England. Now some of them were for his, or his department's,
exclusive use. Like Lancaster House, the great Victorian pile with
rooms the size of tennis courts and almost as much red plush
and gold leaf as Buckingham Palace. It was under exclusive
Foreign Office control and access to it was jealously guarded.

And then there was the extraordinary Durbar Court, a
grandiose piece of the British Raj in the heart of the Foreign

Office, said to have been rebuilt at the behest of Queen Victoria, where the splendour of sweeping staircases and painted ceilings took Oliver's breath away. And then there was the Foreign Secretary's town house at the end of Carlton House Terrace, with its own large garden, made to appear even larger by backing onto the gardens of the great Pall Mall clubs. Oliver didn't entertain there much, using it more as a private office and for working lunches. The truth was, he would have liked the family to move in, but Ruth had said, a little unkindly but realistically, that he was unlikely to be in the job long enough to justify the move from Lambeth.

More important to him was the Foreign Secretary's country estate, Chevening in Kent. He and Ruth could have chosen to live there if they'd liked, and Oliver would have loved that. At the very least he'd wanted to spend, say, every other weekend there. It was a glorious place, way beyond anything they could remotely afford as private citizens. Oliver was not, as the press liked to portray him, a patrician grandee from the landed gentry. He'd grown up, it's true, on a Shropshire estate belonging to an earl, one who'd fallen on hard times and been forced to let most of his property. The Staplers rented the old rectory. Oliver's father was an accountant and his mother a dental nurse, both working in Chester. He was an only child and his parents had scrimped to send him to a minor public school, their sacrifice paying off when he won a scholarship to Cambridge.

Maybe growing up in a Georgian house, close to a magnificent, if crumbling, stately home, followed by the beauty of Cambridge, had given Oliver his leanings towards gracious living. To him, Chevening represented the chance of a lifetime. Damn it, he had earned this privilege by dint of his commitment and skill, so why on earth not accept it?

But Ruth thought the whole idea of freebies for ministers

distasteful, if not actually corrupt. She had not yet deigned to spend a single night there, and he could scarcely go without her, but it was early days and perhaps he could persuade her. To deny the girls those memories for the future would be mean-minded. They would never forget a housekeeper or maid making their beds, a cook in the kitchen, and maybe their first grown-up dinner party in the dining room, waited on by a butler . . .

Oliver glanced at his watch and pulled his thoughts to the matter in hand. Tonight's dinner. The guest list brought a return to reality. Grand surroundings and the best food and wine did not prevent these occasions being pretty dull. Interesting conversations with the wives of heads of state or of senior officials were rare as hens' teeth. If Ruth only realised it, she would get the best of the bargain during his tenure as Her Majesty's chief giver of posh parties. She might be sandwiched between such mavericks as Berlusconi, Sarkozy or Gaddafi. The people the government required him to do business with were sometimes unsavoury, but seldom boring. Which could not be said for their wives.

At least most of the Asian wives had been to university or school in England or America, and he could get along in French, Italian or German with most of the Europeans if, which was rare, they did not speak English. But of course you couldn't talk to them of their country's woes, or relations with Britain, or discuss their husbands' chances of survival. The inevitable catalogue of their children's achievements was seldom riveting.

Tonight's guests, a pan-African delegation, had been here a week and he had already had one dinner with them in Downing Street, hosted by the Chancellor. It had been dire. Few of the wives of the potentates, despots, villains – and occasional honest politicians – who led that benighted continent spoke any English and talking through an interpreter whispering in your ear from behind was a nightmare. Tonight would be the same.

He pulled out his speech for after dinner, which he had not yet seen. It had been written by Sonia, who was good but as yet unfamiliar with his style. And he had never learnt the trick, mastered by nearly all his colleagues, of saying someone else's words as if they were his own.

'Sean, have you got a highlighter?'

He marked a few key words on each page, scribbled a couple more and said, 'If you could find a card and jot these words down so I can read them, and get it to me before I have to stand up, I'd be grateful.'

He felt fleetingly sorry for Sonia, who had obviously tried hard. She had all the main points, properly marshalled into a coherent whole, and she knew he liked his speeches double spaced, in bold, font size 12, printed on half pages and fastened with a Treasury clip so he could easily handle them without a lectern. But he'd speak from a few words on a card.

Sean would almost certainly tell her he had not used her speech. Oliver resolved to make a point of congratulating her on the content and suggesting she read some of his published speeches to get his tone. He used, he thought, a more measured, musing style, as if he were proposing solutions or ideas rather than banging a soap box.

Oliver leaned forward to Sean. 'Sean, wait for me, will you? I'll just ring Ruth and the children. I won't be long.' He opened the car door and climbed out, followed by the detective. Jim was an old copper, a little slow, but reliable. And discreet. He stood just out of earshot as Oliver made his call, but Oliver knew his eyes would be constantly on the alert, with himself at the centre of Jim's vision. Poor man, thought Oliver. Imagine having to be permanently on the look-out for something with almost no likelihood of happening. But someone had done the risk assessment and Foreign Secretaries were deemed a possible terrorist target.

Mattie answered the call. Ruth was out in the yard, talking to Ben, the man who mended their saddles, but both girls were there. Mattie was doing her homework and seemed distracted. Oliver wondered if she was watching a game or movie on her computer while talking to him, but he had the good sense not to ask.

Andrea was her usual uncomplicated self. He told her he was standing outside a grand house in London and just about to go and have dinner with a lot of prime ministers from lots of other countries. And that he had a detective keeping watch as he made this phone call. And all the guests would have detectives too because they were so important.

'Is the detective like on the TV? Solving crimes and stuff?'

'Well, mine is more like a policeman or a security guard.'

'Oh, I know.' Oliver could picture her face, bright with recognition. 'Mum said that you have a policeman looking after you all the time. Like the one that comes to our house?'

'Similar. He's also a policeman but more senior. You've met him. The big fellow, Jim. He came home with me last Friday, remember? He had tea with you in the kitchen and then went and looked at the horses.'

'He wasn't a *policeman*.' Andrea's voice was loud with scorn. 'He was just ordinary. In ordinary clothes. Like a school teacher. He didn't have proper policeman's clothes.'

Oliver rang home every evening between six and eight if he possibly could. Sometimes, when the children were tired and didn't want to be asked boring questions about school or their ponies, or Ruth was busy and brisk, he wondered why he was so religious about it. But he knew the dangers of being away from home and he did his best to remain part of their lives, a proper father. Though sometimes he felt he was more like a weekend visitor.

But tonight Andrea had been lovely. He snapped his phone shut with a smile and set off for the front door of Lancaster House, closely followed by Sean and, more discreetly, by Jim. Debbie would wait in the car, or park it and join the other drivers for a gossip. Three public servants to look after one politician. It seemed a little ridiculous, but at the same time (though he'd never have said it) he did think it was somehow his due.

In spite of his dread of incomprehensible dinner neighbours, Oliver walked into the cavernous hall of Lancaster House feeling a sense of ownership, or at least boss-ship, and cool satisfaction at the sheer grandeur of it. He mounted the wide, shallow stairs with his straight-backed easy stride, walked along the balustraded gallery and into the Gold Room.

Tonight he would entertain the group of sixteen delegates and their wives to pre-dinner drinks in this room, and then they would dine in the State Dining Room. Both rooms were far larger than the number of guests strictly warranted, but the intention was to flatter, certainly to impress, maybe even over-awe them. The splendour of the high ceilings, heavy paintings and rich carpets, and the views onto the garden, Mall and park were a treat, even in the dark.

The Foreign Office head butler greeted him with a formal dip of his head. Not quite a bow, but almost. 'Good evening, Secretary of State.'

'Hello, Dennis. All in order?'

'But of course, Sir.'

'Are the caterers here? Are they any good?'

'I hope so, Sir. Mr Hobhouse, the head of Government Hospitality, engaged the young woman you told me to suggest. She did that little lunch at Carlton Gardens, you remember?'

For a moment Oliver was baffled. Then his face cleared and, pleased, he said, 'Oh, yes, of course. Kate something. She did an excellent private dinner for me too. But that was for six people, this is for thirty something.'

Dennis's face was not reassuring. There was a hint of a shrug, and his mouth went down.

'You said to tell him you wanted her for your next official dinner, Sir, so I did. I confess I had my doubts, but I believe Mr Hobhouse checked her out and she has done some bigger jobs. She's an amateur, of course—'

Oliver cut in coldly, 'And what is a professional, do you think?' It irritated him that Dennis was hedging his bets, making sure that the decision to use Kate could be all his if it was a triumph and all someone else's if it was a disaster. He went on, 'Some of the food I eat in government departments is unspeakable, presumably made by professionals. She makes her living at it, doesn't she? Does that not make her a professional?'

Dennis knew when to back off. 'Yes, Sir, I am sure it does.'

Oliver checked the placement in the dining room, Dennis respectfully at his heels.

'I would be glad if you would hurry things along, Dennis. I don't want to be here a minute beyond ten o'clock if I can help it.'

'I will do my best, Sir. Of course the kitchen . . .'

'Yes, I know. You can't help it if Kate is slow. Just make sure she isn't, then.' He looked at his watch, turned on his heel, and walked out to greet his guests.

He was in luck. The wife of the Prime Minister of Zaire, on his right, had been to Cape Town University, was a practising lawyer, and delightful. On his left was the very large but beautiful wife of the Nigerian Prime Minister. She was in national dress, lime green cotton swathed over a glittering headdress of green and orange, both stylish and jaunty. Her great arms and shoulders rose bare out of the matching wrappings of her ample body. She was as loud and jolly as she was fat, and her cackling laugh alone banished any pretension and formality.

The African women were either very thin, chic and dressed in Western designer fashions, or simply enormous and in African costume. But all the men, with the single exception of the Prime Minister of Nigeria, were big. Not necessarily obese, though some were, but tall and heavy, with enormous arms and big hands. Interesting, thought Oliver, does the weight come as a result of the power, or the power as a result of the intimidating size?

The first course was the same beetroot and goats' cheese salad that he had had for lunch in his office. He remembered now. When Sean had shown him Kate's suggested menus, this was not on any of them, so he had specially requested it.

They had a Montrachet with the starter, and it was perfect. Enough power to hold its own with the garlicky beetroot, the little kick of acidity at the end, the full flavour still filling his mouth long after he had swallowed it.

The Nigerian wife, whose name he knew he would never master, liked it too. She drank it like Coca-Cola, in long draughts that quickly emptied her glass, which was promptly refilled, but with no visible effect.

He asked her about her children and was astonished to hear her describe her two boys as villains.

'One has a taxi business in Czechoslovakia. In Prague. They drive tourists all around the town instead of straight to where they want to go, and when they can't pay, they take them to a cash point to extract all their money. Aiyeee! He was always a bad boy, that one.' And she cackled with affectionate pride.

Oliver, amused and, in spite of himself, impressed by her insouciant attitude, asked, 'And the other boy?'

'He's in jail.' Her great round shoulders moved up and down: whether laughing or shrugging with indifference, he couldn't decide. 'Embezzlement,' she said. 'Very stupid boy. You do not try to steal from your father's company, do you? Especially if your father is a clever, clever' – she strung out the word: cle-e-e-e-ever – 'old hyena and he will catch you.'

Oliver was enjoying himself. He looked across the enormous and elaborately laid table at the said 'old hyena', the one small man in the room. He was talking to Margaret, one of his senior officials who was standing in for Ruth. He looked more like a clerk than a prime minister.

'And did he catch him?'

'Sure. Of course. He just tell the police, and they put poor boy in jail.'

'That must have been hard for your husband, shopping his own son. And for you.'

'No, no, he's safer in jail.' She laughed with her head back and Oliver had a good view of perfect white teeth in a large deep pink mouth. It made him think of a hippopotamus. He quickly banished the thought which was unkind, probably racist.

'Fathers always afraid of the young sons. Or nephews,' she said. 'They so ambitious. And in big, big hurry.'

Oliver did not think this a time for a discussion on the rule of law. 'Well, I am sure he did the right thing,' he said, and changed the subject.

Well trained by years in politics, Oliver politely divided his attentions equally between his two neighbours. The time went fast. The sea trout with braised fennel was delicious and quickly eaten.

This was followed by a champagne sorbet, to Oliver's slight irritation. He did not remember ordering it and he hated being given things he had not ordered: things that came with 'Chef's compliments' – 'amuse bouches' or extra little courses.

He assumed this sorbet was a trou Normand, that archaic interlude meant to aid digestion and ready the stomach for more food to come. Oliver looked at his watch. God, if we still have the main course, pud and coffee to go, we'll be here till midnight. Maybe Dennis was right to have doubts about Kate.

There followed an unconscionably long wait. When both his neighbours were engaged with *their* neighbours and turned away from him, he caught Dennis's eye, and was rewarded with an almost imperceptible shrug. I told you so, it said.

This angered Oliver, who at once signalled for Dennis to come to him. Dennis did so, walking swiftly and bending obediently to his ear.

'What the hell is happening out there?'

'I had a little contretemps with the young lady because she wanted to serve something that was not on the agreed menu, and we cannot have that, can we? But it is all sorted now, and coffee will be right out.' Dennis's voice was intending to be soothing, but the emollient tone irritated him further.

'Coffee?' Oliver was having difficulty keeping his voice down. 'What about the main course and the pudding?'

Dennis put his lips close to Oliver's ear, and whispered, 'The sea trout was the main course and the sorbet is the dessert.'

Oliver could not believe it. It was ridiculous. The UK Government could not serve short rations to the largest collection of men ever seen together in a Mayfair dining room. These men could eat an ox single-handed. Besides, in his short experience, African politicians were even touchier than Arab ones. They could make a diplomatic incident out of this.

He glanced to right and left but his guests were all enjoying themselves, apparently unaware of the long wait for more food. He leant first to left, then to right, murmuring 'I'm so sorry, I won't be a minute.' And he walked quietly into the kitchen, followed by Dennis.

Two butlers were lined up with coffee cups and saucers ready laid out on trays, waiting for the waiters to slip into place behind them with the pots of coffee, the cream and sugar.

Oliver put a hand up and said to them, 'Hold it a second, will you?' He looked across the still-room section to the kitchen proper where Kate was busy tipping biscuits from a serving basket into a biscuit tin. She had her head down and did not see him.

Oliver strode round the pass. 'Kate, what on earth is going on? You cannot feed full-blooded Africans like Kensington ladies at lunch! It's a bloody disaster.'

She looked up and he saw at once that she had been crying. But she brought her chin up and said, 'I know. I told everyone. Hobhouse, your office, Dennis. No one would listen.'

'But for God's sake, Kate. You are the one who proposed the menu. You knew what the occasion was. Why on earth did you come up with a salad, a piece of fish and a sorbet? They are all sitting out there expecting two more courses!'

To Oliver's astonishment, the woman took a step towards him, eyes shiny, face flushed, her chin up. 'Foreign Secretary, I did not choose that menu. You did. I sent you three menus, and you insisted on the beetroot, which wasn't on any of them, and you picked the sea trout which I had proposed for a starter, not as a main course, and the sorbet which I had as a light ending to the heaviest of the menus, the butternut soup and roast beef of old England . . .' Her voice was rising as she said, 'I knew it was all wrong. I told everyone, and I tried to change it.' Her voice was near a shout now. 'But everyone is so fucking frightened of you they didn't dare tell you.'

She met his eyes. Her plump round cheeks were red and her eyes were flashing, whether from crying or anger, he could not tell. 'Sorry about the "fucking", Sir. But it is so frustrating. Your officials haven't the guts to challenge you, and of course they wouldn't let me speak to your secretary or to Sean, never mind to you! Only your immediate underlings are allowed to speak to the Secretary of State!'

Absolute silence followed this. Kate put her hand up to her mouth and kept it there, her eyes wide and shiny above it. She looked as though she might weep again and was holding her lip steady with her fist.

Oliver took a breath and said, icily calm, 'Let's do the post-mortem later. Right now, is there anything we can do?'

Kate looked across at Dennis, and gestured to the biscuit box in front of her. 'I wanted to serve some cheese and fruit. I brought some just in case but Dennis refused . . .'

'We cannot serve things that have not been agreed and that are not on the menu. It's printed,' said Dennis.

But Kate was already tipping the biscuits back into the silver basket, and reaching for the cheeses.

'Dennis,' said Oliver quietly, 'I think it more important that the guests don't go home hungry, don't you?'

'And while they're eating,' said Kate, 'I could do Scotch Woodcock for everyone. I brought the eggs and anchovies too – in the hopes I could get you guys to see sense.'

Oliver did not like being lumped with Dennis in the 'you guys' and he was generally taken aback by Kate's tone. No one spoke to secretaries of state like that. He turned on his heel and went back into the dining room.

Later that evening, while Oliver was being driven home, he put his head back against the leather and surveyed the evening. In the end it had all been rather good. And, warmed by the Montrachet and an excellent Volnay, he could see the funny side of the menu drama. That feisty little Kate had certainly stood her corner – and saved the day.

Maybe cheese followed by a savoury was not the most balanced end to a meal, but at least they didn't go home hungry, and it was all satisfyingly British and old fashioned.

Poor old Dennis had had the worst of it. Oliver smiled at the thought. The man was such a jobsworth. He'd had to have the last word, it was pathetic. As Oliver was leaving the building, the butler had thrust a menu into his hand saying, 'You see, Sir, I could not let it go. The menu is printed here, clear as daylight. No cheese on it ... no savoury. You had not authorised ...'

Oliver, feeling well fed and content, had said, 'Never mind, Dennis, sometimes we have to be flexible. And I did authorise it in the end. And you did very well to come up with that excellent Volnay for those two last courses. More of the Montrachet would not have done.'

And Dennis had simpered, glad to be forgiven.

CHAPTER FIVE

Kate snapped the Velcro across Toby's trainer and stood up.

'Come on, darling, or we'll be late. We don't want poor Granny and Hank arriving without us there to meet them, do we?'

She grabbed her coat and Toby's and hurried him into the car.

As they joined the traffic heading for the M25, he asked, 'Why is he called Hank? That's not a real name, is it?'

'I don't know, darling. I think it's a real name, or a nickname. Lots of Americans are called Hank.'

'Is he American?'

'He is. He's a policeman.'

'Does he have a gun?'

'Oh dear, I expect he does. I think all American policemen have guns. You can ask him.'

'I'll ask him if he shooted people.'

'Shot people, not shooted. I'm sure he hasn't. He is a nice, gentle man. You'll like him.'

Toby was soon head down, absorbed in his Super Mario and Kate turned on the radio. James Naughtie and some think-tank woman were speculating about the possibility of a cabinet reshuffle. The Chancellor was wildly unpopular for bailing out the banks and for raising taxes. There was talk of replacing him, though everyone knew this would not change the policy.

'The brightest tool in the box is undoubtedly Oliver Stapler,' the woman said. 'He's got the brain power and the judgement for the job, and he is very, very ambitious. But he's only just arrived at the Foreign Office so I'm sure the Prime Minister will not move him now.'

Very, very ambitious. And brainy. And wise. Mmmm, thought Kate, I got the impression he was mostly cool and laid back. Her thoughts drifted idly round Oliver, thinking how aloof and grand he could be – the press had him boxed in as a right toff – yet at his house in Lambeth he had been friendly enough, and at Lancaster House he had been diplomatic with the ghastly Dennis. And he could have slaughtered her for being so rude, but he'd not said a word. I would never have had him down as ambitious, she thought, more like indifferent. I wonder what his family is like . . .

The plane was late and Kate and Toby ate hot porridge from a cardboard carton at Souper Douper. They had been in such a hurry they'd missed breakfast and only had an apple in the car. Kate ate her porridge in the Scottish manner, with salt. As Toby opened a third packet of brown sugar for his, Kate again regretted the loss of her Scots grandmother's influence. But at least he was eating porridge, not Kit Kats or crisps, which most of his school friends seemed to have for breakfast.

When Pat and Hank finally emerged through the great sliding doors, pushing a trolley of luggage, they looked round blankly, unable to locate Kate and Toby in the crowd. Kate was shocked at how old and tired her mother looked. But then, as Pat noticed her daughter's frantic waving, her face instantly broke into the familiar, ageless image of her mother, happy, loving, pleased. God, I've missed her, thought Kate, suddenly close to tears. It had been over two years since she'd seen her, and though Toby believed he remembered her, Kate thought that was because of the photographs and telephone calls.

When Pat put her arms round Toby in a giant hug, exclaiming at his size, Toby bore it, standing stolid as wood. Kate, seeing his turned-away face, screwed up and rigid with disgust, burst out laughing.

'Pat woman, let the lad go,' said Hank. 'He's a big fella now. Doesn't want to be drooled over.'

Pat released Toby, who shot Hank a look of gratitude.

Hank, who had not been with Pat on her last visit and had not seen Toby since he was a babe in arms, put a big hand on his shoulder and said, 'My, but she's right, you are a big boy. Are you strong enough to carry this for me?' He handed Toby a shoulder bag. 'Here, let me shorten the strap.'

Kate watched Hank push the trolley before them, Toby at his side, proudly carrying the bag and looking up at him, instant friends. Her son could do with a man around for a bit, she thought, as she put her arm through her mother's and followed them.

Pat and Hank dumped their cases on the long blanket box at the end of Kate's big bed.

'This is lovely,' Pat said. 'You've changed the curtains. And you've repainted, haven't you?' She looked round, impressed. 'But where will you sleep, darling?'

'I'm fine. I'll be on the sofa. I can sleep anywhere.'

In truth she was nervous about the arrangement. Tonight Toby would sleep on the camp bed in the office and it would be the first time he'd slept the whole night anywhere but with her. She had never mentioned to her mother that her son shared her bed and had done so since he outgrew his cot. She didn't want to hear Pat say, which she inevitably would, that she was babying him.

And then, because she'd moved Toby into the office so that

he could get to sleep (she hoped) at a reasonable hour while she and the others were still in the sitting room, and because she often did her admin or accounts in the evenings, she'd then had to move desk, printer, fax and assorted office stuff into the sitting room – where it seemed to take up a third of the space.

Before they'd even had a cup of coffee Pat insisted on leading Hank round the house with a proprietorial air. Kate had rather wanted to show them the changes, but she reminded herself that it was still her mother's house, not hers.

Pat and Hank ooh'd and ah'd satisfactorily at the changes to the house: the big new kitchen made by knocking her brother's old bedroom and the kitchen together; her teenage bedroom now an office, the garden shed she'd enlarged and turned into a storeroom and outside larder with walk-in fridge and freezer, and the front garden paved to take the delivery van.

'You must be doing well,' said Hank.

'Not bad. I'm busy, but it's hard work. All day prepping and planning parties, mostly held in the evenings and at weekends. That's why I prefer the City lunches and the government work. They tend to be in the week and in the day.'

'But isn't it the big parties that make the money, when you can sell lots of alcohol? No one drinks at lunchtime any more, do they?'

'Not a lot. But I wouldn't get to supply the drinks very often anyway. Even private clients usually provide their own.' She shrugged, smiling. 'Can't say I blame them. They go to Boulogne with a van and buy the lot at a third of what I'd have to charge them. Even Oddbins and Majestic are cheaper than me and they provide free glasses, which I can't afford to do.'

At six o'clock, Amal and Talika came in to meet Pat and Hank and to offer to have Toby for the night.

'Darling, why don't you do that?' Kate suggested. 'It would be fun to sleep all night at Sanjay's instead of me shaking you awake as I usually do.'

But Toby, excited about his 'new room', refused, and Kate thought they would probably both end up having a restless night on her sofa-bed. She knew she would be unable to make him go back to the camp bed if he crept in beside her.

And indeed, Kate barely slept on the squashy cushions. Not because Toby climbed in – he didn't – but because she was so aware of the lack of him. Meanwhile, he slept in the office without stirring, only appearing at six a.m. Then, half asleep, he did crawl into her arms and she felt a wash of gratitude that he had come. She held him close, her body wrapped round him. Oh, she thought, I wish he would never grow up. Five is just perfect. I'm still the centre of his universe, and he's so unself-consciously affectionate and outgoing, so fearless, happy, confi-dent, no suspicion of slings and arrows to come. How will I bear it, she thought, when he prefers his friends, or his teacher, to me?

When they had been with Kate for a week, Pat and Hank went out for the day to visit friends and do a bit of shopping, and Kate felt her body relax and her spirit lift with the freedom their absence gave her. She loved her mother, but having to seem carefree and friendly when she longed to shoo everyone out of the house so she could get on with her job, was a strain.

Hank had been on her computer and it took her a while to find her papers under his printouts of *Places to Go* and pages from *What's On*. But once she was absorbed in costing a dinner dance for a twenty-first birthday, and sending a few polite, and one or two terse, reminders to late payers, she forgot about her guests, and about Toby.

At lunchtime she walked round to the Taj Amal. She and Talika sat at a window table in the early March sun and ate fresh cucumber sticks dipped in lassi, and hot naan bread straight from the tandoor oven.

The restaurant was almost empty and Amal came over and sat with them. 'Don't you want some proper food? Rogan gosht is just made, and it's good.'

'No,' said Kate. 'I'd resolved to confine myself to the cucumber and lassi, but the smell of the naan was too much for me.' She squeezed the flesh of her midriff. 'Why have I no will power at all when it comes to food?'

She leant over and tried to squeeze Talika's middle. 'And why do you have to be so slim, damn you?' Talika was thin as a wraith and Kate couldn't get a grip on her flat stomach. Talika shrunk away, slapping Kate's hand down.

Amal said, 'She's too thin. She's a bag of bones.'

Kate noticed the sudden hurt in Talika's eyes before she lowered them quickly. Talika said, 'I'll have Toby today, won't I?' She looked up, smiling, 'You've got some function tonight, haven't you?'

'Yes, but I won't be long. It's just a chicken casserole and rice, English style, with salad and a trifle to follow. Everything's ready, and I only have to deliver it, not serve it or wash up or anything. So I won't be late.'

'Shall I fetch the boys?'

'Let's go together, 'Lika. I don't have to deliver the stuff till six-thirty, and my mum and Hank are out. We could take the boys to the park.'

At five o'clock, they came back from the park, and Toby went home with Sanjay and Talika while Kate went back to work. She wasn't able to lift full catering boxes on her own, so she put two big empty ones into the van, and carried the food out to the boxes. She packed one of them with large shallow roasting trays of cooked rice, plastic boxes of washed and dried salad and a jar of French dressing. She tucked a couple of wooden spoons and a clean apron into a corner. Good, she thought, everything nice and snug: won't tip as I bump over the wretched 'traffic calming' humps.

Kate went back for the coq au vin. The two big stainless steel saucepans would just fit into the second box. She opened the fridge in what had once been the garden shed. She tightened her jaw and closed her eyes briefly, trying not to mind that the middle shelves were stacked tight with beer for Hank, Coke for Toby and white wine for her and Pat. She was irritated. This fridge was exclusively for the business, the small one in the kitchen was for her and Toby.

OK, she could see it was too small for American quantities of chilled drinks. And Hank was only trying to be kind, to spoil her and Toby. She should be grateful. After all, the wine was better quality than she could afford, and it wouldn't kill Toby to drink a few Cokes while they were here. And since she had completely failed to buy any beer for Hank, how could she feel miffed at such a minor invasion of her space? She was becoming a control freak.

She stacked the drinks on the floor as she unpacked the fridge, looking for the coq au vin. But it was in big saucepans and she soon knew it wasn't there. Where on earth had Pat put them?

Oh hell, she thought, anxiety tightening her throat. I bet it's in the freezer. It will be a solid block and won't ever thaw in time. And the texture will be ruined, especially the mushrooms. But the saucepans weren't in the freezer.

As she turned distractedly, she tripped over a six-pack of beer, which knocked over a couple of the wine bottles, one of which smashed on the hard concrete floor. Kate forced herself to put the drinks back in the fridge, get the dust pan and brush and sweep up the broken glass. The pool of wine could wait. She had to find the chicken casserole.

She looked at her watch. Quarter to six. She should be leaving now, but if she was a little late it wouldn't matter. They weren't eating till eight-thirty. Plenty of time.

Back in the kitchen, she looked in the domestic fridge, even though she knew the big pots would not fit on the shelves, and she couldn't imagine Pat transferring all that casserole into shallow dishes.

And indeed the fridge, though unusually stuffed on account of last night's leftovers and the supermarket pizza and pecan pie that Pat had been unable to resist, contained no coq au vin.

She hurried into the sitting room, dug her phone out of her handbag and dialled her mother. It went straight to voice mail. They had gone to Tate Modern, not the theatre, so why had she switched off her phone?

What was Hank's number? She scrolled down the list without much hope of it being there. She always rang the house, or her mother. Never Hank. But maybe his number was on her computer.

Kate went to her desk and booted up her laptop. It seemed to take for ever. But the number was there and Kate dialled it on her mobile, silently willing him to answer. He did.

'Hank, please, it's Kate. Can I speak to Mum? It's a bit urgent.'

'Sure, baby, but she's gone to the washroom. She won't be long.'

Kate screwed her face up in anguish, but kept her voice calm. 'OK, Hank, do you know where on earth Mum put my two big pans of chicken stew?'

'Chicken stew?' He sounded completely confused.

'Yes, that I cooked for the function tonight. I am meant to be delivering it right now, and she's moved it from the big fridge to make room for all your beer and stuff. I'm going mad here.'

'Ah. I see. Hold on a moment. I'll go find her.'

Kate looked again at her watch. Almost six. No panic. She would just have to ring Joan, that was all. The wine, the ice, and all the hired stuff, was already there, so they could start laying up.

While she waited for Hank to extract his wife from the Ladies, Kate used her free hand to check her handbag, making sure she had Joan's and the waitresses' wages and the stack of numbered cards advertising the catering services of Nothing Fancy that they always gave to guests as cloakroom tickets. Still hanging on for her mother, she walked out to the van and put her handbag on the passenger seat with her coat on top of it. Then she locked the van. Not a good moment, she thought, for her handbag, or indeed van, to be nicked.

As she slipped her keys into her pocket, her mother came on the phone. She was laughing,

'Darling, this had better be good! Hank stood in the washroom door yelling for me!'

'Mum, didn't he tell you? Where the hell have you put my coq au vin? The two saucepans—'

'Darling, I am so sorry. I meant to tell you. I put them behind the shed. I figured it was quite as cold outside as in the fridge and I needed—'

Kate interrupted, 'Thanks, Mum,' and pressed the off button. She ran along the path down the side of the house to the garden and round the back of the shed, and stopped dead.

One of the saucepans was upside down under Toby's trampoline, the other on its side. Both lids were lying on the ground a few feet away.

Foxes! Kate, her hand to her mouth, her stomach in a knot of apprehension, walked slowly forward. The saucepans were licked clean, not a bone, mushroom or shallot undevoured.

She stood over the empty pans for a second, then sprang into action. She picked up one of them and ran with it into the kitchen. She put it into the sink and turned on the hot tap. Then she ran out for the other one and the lids. She washed everything in near boiling water with a super-squirt of detergent, dried her hands, and dialled Amal.

As she waited for an answer her mind was racing, but without panic. There was no time to start again: even if all the raw ingredients for coq au vin were here, ready to go, it would be a mighty struggle. She had to get the food to the house by seven forty-five or she would clash with the arriving guests and panic the Coleridges. She had to leave here in an hour and a quarter, max. Somehow she had to shop for and cook coq au vin for forty in that time.

'Amal, can you help me? I've got a bit of a crisis here. Can you lend me anyone, a pair of competent hands, for an hour, right now?'

'Sure,' he said, 'I'm on my way.'

'Thank God for that. Wonderful. Have you got any shallots?'

'Only onions.'

'Fine, can you bring half a dozen over here, chop them up and sweat them in half butter/half oil. And could you boil down two bottles of red wine, I'll leave them out for you. I'm going shopping.'

'Take your mobile.'

'Thanks, Amal. I'll explain later.'

Kate stuffed her mobile in her pocket and ran out of the front door to the van, fishing for her car keys as she ran.

As she drove fast down the high street she made a mental list. Chicken, mushrooms, bacon, garlic, stock.

In the supermarket car park she took a pound from her stash of coins in the ashtray, unlocked a big trolley with it, and practically ran with it to the deli counter.

To her relief they were still roasting chickens. There were a total of ten portions of jointed chicken – eight legs and two breasts – in the tray, two whole cooked chickens ready for sale and eight chickens on the rotisserie.

'Can I have those ten portions, the two cooked ones and all of the chickens on the rotisserie?'

'What, all of them?'

'Yes. Please. I'm afraid I'm in a huge hurry. Don't worry about foil bags, just put them all in a big carrier bag, that will be fine.'

'I'm sorry, Madam, I'm only allowed to sell you the cooking ones.' She didn't look sorry. She looked smug. She parked her ample bottom against the back counter. 'Health and Safety, you see.'

'Oh God.' Kate looked around. 'Do you think you could ring for the manager?'

The woman shook her head. 'He's in a meeting. And anyway I know what he'll say. He'll say we can't sell half-cooked chickens to the public because they may not be safe to eat if they are not cooked through.'

'Look, I am a professional caterer and I know about salmonella and food poisoning. These chickens will be cut up and reheated in boiling sauce which will kill any bugs. I understand the rules, they are sensible, but surely you can see that in this case . . .'

'That is all very well, Madam, but rules are rules. They are there for your protection.' She stripped off her latex gloves, dropped them in an invisible bin behind the counter and pulled two more out of the box behind her. 'Do you want to take the cooked ones?'

'Not unless I can have the ones off the rotisserie too.' Kate was beginning to feel frantic. She said, 'Look, this is getting us nowhere. Would you please call the manager?'

'I am sorry you feel that way, Madam, but I wouldn't be able to sell you all the chickens even if they were fully roasted. We have a policy to look after our regular customers, and we can't let caterers clean us out of all our stock at once. It wouldn't be fair, would it? The limit, unless ordered in advance, is three chickens. So you can see, Madam, I cannot help you.'

Kate's temper was now rising fast. 'You mean you will not,' she snapped. 'I insist on seeing the manager, right now. If you don't ring for me, I will just lift my voice and yell for him, and that would be embarrassing for all of us, would it not?'

'You had better go to customer services at the front of the store, Madam.'

Kate ran to the front of the store and, forcing herself to stand still, waited while a customer got a refund on a dodgy avocado pear. Then the young assistant turned to her and smiled. 'How can I help?'

Kate explained the situation, saying she understood the company's rules, but she needed to ask the manager to make an exception.

'Poor you!' said the assistant, 'I'll get him now. I'm sure it will be fine.'

Hope beginning to calm her panic, Kate said, 'Great, would you mind if I ran round your store getting the rest of the ingredients while you call him? I have no time to lose at all.'

'Yes, OK, that's fine. I'll come and get you as soon as he's here.'

Kate pushed her trolley rapidly round the shelves. In the fresh section she picked up chestnut mushrooms and fresh parsley; in the deli six packets of rindless streaky bacon, a tube of so-called fresh garlic paste and two jars of concentrated chicken stock; in the grocery section, five tins of baby onions and five glass jars of red wine sauce by some chef or other. And she threw in half a dozen tins of cooked mushrooms too.

When she got to the checkout there was still no manager to be seen and Kate's stomach once more contracted with anxiety. It was now nearly quarter to seven, and if she did not get those chickens almost instantly, she'd be sunk.

Leaving the checkout girl pushing her things through the scanner she ran to the customer service desk.

'Here,' said the young woman. 'Mr Evered said it was fine. He used to be in the restaurant trade, he said, and he knows what it's like. So I went and got them all packed up for you.' She dropped her voice. 'I didn't think you would want to go back to Shirley. Grumpy old cow. We all hate her.'

As they dumped the chicken on the moving belt, she cut off Kate's thanks with, 'You did want all eight chickens off the grill, the two cooked whole ones and the extra ten portions?'

'I did. And you have been just wonderful. What's your name?' Kate looked at her name badge. 'Sisi! Well, Sisi, I hope they make you a store manager one day soon, because you deserve it.'

On the short drive home Kate rang Amal and said, 'Can you make a space on the worktop with boards for jointing cooked chickens, and we've still got to fry bacon and mushrooms. Could you get a couple of pans ready? The whole job only needs another ten or fifteen mins. One of us can fry while the other joints.'

As Kate deftly split and quartered the hot chickens, trimmed off the extra bone, skin and untidy bits, and laid the neat pieces in the bottom of the two saucepans, Amal fried chopped bacon and quartered mushrooms. Then they scattered the contents of his pans, and the onions he had previously fried, over the chicken.

Both pans were sticky with brown bacon and onion residue and Amal swiftly deglazed them with the reduced wine, then said, 'OK, now for the sauce. What are we using?'

Kate laughed, 'Let's just bung everything in. Can you open these tins for me and then make some *beurre manié* while I do the sauce?'

She tipped the contents of both frying pans into a saucepan and added, in quick succession, half the tube of garlic paste, the tinned mushrooms and baby onions, the contents of the stock and red wine sauce jars, the rest of the reduced wine and a jug of water.

Meanwhile Amal melted half a block of butter and stirred two teacupfuls of flour into it. He smiled across at Kate. 'You're enjoying yourself, aren't you?'

It was true. It was satisfying and exciting working fast to get out of a crisis. 'Of course. Isn't that the best bit of catering? Working fast and furiously with people who know what they are doing?'

'Maybe. But I'm not sure tinned mushrooms and reheated chicken are part of my vision!'

Kate's mixture seemed to take for ever to come to the boil, but once it did, Amal whisked half his *beurre manié* into it, and watched it thicken.

'Bit more, I think,' said Kate. Some juice will run out of those half cooked chickens, which will thin it a bit.'

The sauce did not taste too bad, but Kate added a hefty squeeze of tomato paste and a handful of chopped parsley.

'Tomato paste? In coq au vin?' Amal cocked an eye at her.

'Bet it's delicious!' She divided the sauce between the two

saucepans, and gave them each a shake to get it flowing round all the chicken pieces. She slammed on the lids, and she and Amal carried one each to the van.

As she went back for her phone and keys, Kate kissed Amal and looked steadily at him for a second. 'What a fantastic friend you are.'

'I know, I'm marvellous,' he said, handing her a plastic pot with a lid.

'What's this?'

'Chopped parsley for the top – to disguise all inadequacies.'

Kate arrived at the Coleridges' a few minutes before the guests, and hoped her face, beetroot from anxiety, exertion and excitement, would not give her away.

'Hello, Mrs C. I hope you weren't worried about us. Did Joan tell you . . .'

'Yes, she did. Joan's wonderful. Everything is ready. She said you would be heating the coq au vin at your place to save us room on the stove. How very thoughtful.'

As soon as she had left the kitchen Kate said, 'Thanks for the cover-up, Joan. You're a good woman.'

'No problem. I knew you'd turn up.'

'We'll put the rice in the oven and the chicken on to simmer now. It still has a bit of cooking to do, but keep it very very slow, won't you.'

'Yes, boss.'

'And give me a ring tomorrow. I want to know if anyone rumbled us.'

CHAPTER SIX

Oliver was in the kitchen reading the papers, with overweight Obi lying in his favourite position across Oliver's foot, when he heard Andrea jumping down the stairs. He looked up as she burst into the kitchen. She was in some sort of turquoise costume, skin-tight and printed in scales like a mermaid. She was barefoot.

Andrea did an excited twirl, arms out. Obi waddled across to her, eager for attention, but she pushed him away with the side of her foot and said, 'Look, Dad.' For a second she stood still, steadying herself, and then slowly curled over backwards, bending her knees, thrusting out her pre-adolescent ribcage, her outstretched arms seeking the floor behind her. As she put her palms down close to her heels, she transferred her weight to her hands and lifted first one leg and then the other into a handstand. She scissored her straight legs once or twice, then brought them together and jumped to her feet.

Oliver looked at her in amazement. 'Good Lord, Andrea! That is astonishing. Where did you learn that?'

'That's nothing. I can do it on a horse. And while he's cantering!'

'You can't! Isn't it dangerous?' Oliver felt suddenly uncertain, aware that his children were doing things that he had no part in. Or didn't approve of. Like hunting. They both hunted with the Meynell and he had been unable to persuade Ruth that it was a bad idea, expensive and dangerous and with the potential of grief for all of them. And political embarrassment for him.

'Not particularly. Mum says it's less dangerous than hunting, or polo, which Mattie does.'

Oliver blinked, confused. Mattie was playing polo? Surely not. Women and children didn't play polo, did they? 'Mattie's playing polo?'

'Sure, she's going on a weekend course to Cowdray Park.' As she spoke Andrea stepped onto a chair and then onto the pine breakfast table, moving the teapot out of the way with her foot. Standing about two feet from the end, she said, 'I can do it up here too. Watch, Dad.'

'No, Andy!' Oliver jumped up, but Andrea had already bent over backwards so her palms came down on the table edge. She did her backwards handstand again, this time fast. She landed lightly on the floor and straightened up, grinning with triumph. 'That's the cool way to dismount.'

Oliver put his arms round his daughter. 'God, girl, you scared the life out of me!' He steered her to a chair and said, 'Sit down and explain it all to me. Why are you wearing this extraordinary costume?'

'That's the best part. You don't have to wear boots and hacking jackets and ties and stuff. We wear sexy stuff, like cat suits and pumps.'

'Sexy?' Oliver was beginning to feel a hundred. His daughter was ten years old.

'Yes, our team has two kinds. The pink ones with silver wavy lines are really cool. They're my favourite, but Scilla says we all have to wear this one today.'

'Scilla? Who's Scilla?'

'Our teacher. She teaches us vaulting.'

Vaulting? Oliver felt like an idiot, understanding so little he could only repeat words in the hope of enlightenment.

'Andrea, for God's sake, explain! From the beginning. What is vaulting? When do you do it? Why? What for?'

Andrea laughed happily, 'Oh Dad, you're so useless. Vaulting is gymnastics on horseback. We have a team. Some of the girls are from school, and some from the village and we're all learning. It's fun. Sometimes we compete with other teams.'

'And today?'

'We're going to do a display at the Queensmead Spring Fête. You should come. It'll be cool.'

When Oliver announced that he would go, Ruth looked at him narrowly. 'Why the sudden interest? You turned down opening the fête, remember?'

'I want to see Andrea's display.'

'Really? But you never watch the girls riding any more.' Her voice was neutral, but Oliver knew at once he was in dangerous territory.

'I know,' he said. 'That's just it. Mea culpa. I didn't even know about the vaulting or whatever it's called. I knew all three of you would spend all your waking hours on horses if you could, but I didn't know the girls were doing circus riding.'

'It's not circus riding. Vaulting is different,' Ruth said. 'Well, if you are coming, it would be great if you could bring the trailer. I've got the horsebox full with four, and I'd really like to take Zoro too.'

'Five horses! I thought only Andrea was doing this.'

'No, there's a gymkhana and a little horse show, and both girls are competing, so they need their jumpers. And I want Andrea to give one of the new ponies a tryout with crowds around, and we've promised to do pony rides for the fête so we need a couple of plodders for them. Zoro and Tufty.'

Oliver had to agree, but he couldn't help a flush of irritation. He felt he was doing his bit by going at all, and he'd hoped to drive to the fête, catch the display and skip home again. And maybe, if he got through his papers, he'd reward himself by watching the rugby. Now he'd have to get there early, hang around while his wife gave pony rides, and then God knows how much longer until his daughter did her bit.

But he did want to watch her. It was a constant source of subterranean anxiety for Oliver that he saw his daughters so little. Of course, he told himself, many fathers worked long hours, and modern children led their own lives of school and friends and ballet or tennis classes. But horses! They were such a full time occupation. If it had been swimming or volleyball, it would be all over after the match or the session and his girls might have hung about the house and leaned over his desk, or asked him to help them with something. But they seemed to spend every waking moment they could grooming and feeding, stroking and loving their wretched ponies.

In the event, wearing his Barbour and wellies, and with Obi trotting at his heels on a lead, Oliver enjoyed himself. The committee chairman was delighted he'd made such an effort to come after all, and Oliver knew he was earning brownie points by being out and about among his constituents. 'Building relationships', his political agent called it. At least a dozen people came up to tell him they agreed with him on Afghanistan, or Iraq, or Zimbabwe. Oliver was too polite – and too astute – to ask testing questions. He knew they probably had no more idea of his stance on these matters than his daughters did. They were just pleased to see him and discover he was not as chilly and aloof as his reputation. And they adored Ruth.

He had to admit it. Ruth was one hell of an asset in the constituency. She seldom left it, and she was in the thick of any co-operative effort, whether it was funding a village bus, campaigning to keep the post office open, or getting hooligans out of the playground and into the community centre.

He watched Mattie in the grown-up show ring jump two elegant clear rounds to win her class, and yet another silver cup. Then he and Mattie watched Andrea in the gymkhana, first on the new pony whose idea of the bending race was to barge through all the poles, and then on Toppy, who garnered her usual bridleful of rosettes.

When the vicar, acting as compere for the day, announced the 'Dazzling Display of Equestrian Excellence' Oliver walked through the village to the far side of the green where a small crowd had gathered round the roped-off area about twenty metres across.

Andrea stood just inside the improvised ring, with seven identically (and scantily) clad girls, shivering in the spring breeze. They ranged from maybe nine to fourteen and Oliver felt a twinge of anxiety for his daughter, one of the youngest. But at least, thought Oliver, she is on her own pony. According to Ruth, Toppy was the safest Welsh cob in the country.

A tall young woman (Scilla he supposed), carrying a carriage whip and leading Toppy, strode into the ring as music sputtered unevenly out of large speakers in the back of a van, its back doors open. She stood in the middle of the circle and shook the reins to set Toppy walking round in a circle.

Toppy had had a lot of spit-and-polishing. Her hooves were oiled black, her mane and tail brushed and her coat gleaming. She had no saddle but there was a wide girth with two half-hoop leather handles, one each side at the top. As Toppy passed the entrance to the ring, a dumpy girl, perhaps ten or eleven, peeled off the row of girls and walked beside the pony for a few paces and then, with surprising agility, sprang onto her back, using the handles to pull herself up. She swung her leg over to sit astride the cob. Then stretching her arms wide, she twisted and turned, lay back on Toppy's bottom, and sat up again, more or less in time to the music. It was briefly interesting, but repetition quickly dulled the spectacle.

Oliver was suddenly conscious of Ruth beside him. It pleased him and he said, 'Hello, darling. How nice. I thought you were doing pony rides.'

'Thought I'd take a break to see Andrea.'

They watched for a minute or two, then Oliver whispered, 'This isn't very exciting. Andy does more glamorous stuff on the breakfast table.'

'Give the poor girl a chance. She's only been vaulting for a fortnight. And it gets better, you'll see.'

Not a lot, thought Oliver, as one pubescent girl after another jumped onto Toppy and went through a series of manoeuvres and then jumped off again. They all wore skin-tight turquoise catsuits like Andrea's and what looked like white ballet shoes. Their hair was variously done in tight plaits, buns, or laced with ribbons, neat as a pin and off their faces. All of them had glittery painted eyes, and cheeks dotted with sequins. No wonder Andrea likes this, thought Oliver, she must feel like the fairy on the Christmas tree.

It got better once Toppy was cantering, and the acrobatic skill standard went up with the experience of the girls. Some of them spun round, at a canter, so they were briefly riding backwards. Still, mostly they just seemed to pose like synchronised swimmers as Toppy kept a slow steady pace. Oliver sneaked a look at his watch. The display was advertised as a half-hour show and he was sorry to see they were only halfway through.

The tempo of the music hotted up and the riders became more daring, jumping on and off the horse from both sides, kneeling or standing briefly on her back.

Oliver wondered if he found it boring because they made it look so easy.

At last it was Andrea's turn, and Oliver could not take his eyes off her. He had had no idea she possessed such control, or could ride with such agility and grace. His fear for her vanished in admiration.

'Is she a million times better than the others,' he asked Ruth, 'or am I just an infatuated dad?'

'Maybe both?'

Andrea closed the show with a rolling backwards somersault off Toppy's tail. She landed as acrobats do, bum out, knees together, neatly, hands out to steady herself. Then she ran to Scilla, who had gathered up the long lunge rein and stood holding Toppy. She and Andrea bowed together. Then the rest of the team joined them and they all bowed again.

Oliver, clapping and shouting 'Bravo!' put his arm round Ruth's thin shoulders. Hugging her to him, he said, 'She's amazing, isn't she?'

Ruth laughed at him, but it was a friendly, happy laugh. 'They both are,' she said. 'You should see Mattie. She's absolutely fearless. If we could afford the horses, she could be a champion.'

Oliver did not like the idea of a serious professional rider for a daughter, and was relieved that Ruth didn't expect an answer. She had walked over to collect Andrea's pony, being fussed over by a group of girls.

That night at supper all the talk was about horses: shows, jumping, dressage, hunting, polo. Andrea was highly indignant that Scilla had not let her do her backwards handstand dismount, or even the forwards one. 'She's so mean. Why couldn't I do it? I've done it before! Loads of times.'

'But the somersault was wonderful, darling,' said Oliver.

'And "loads of times" was mostly on the barrel, or the gym horse, not on Toppy,' said Ruth. 'How many times have you done it on Toppy?'

'Besides,' said Mattie, not waiting for her sister to answer, 'you'd have hogged the show, and it's meant to be a team effort. You're such a show-off.'

It was good to see them all so animated, but Oliver could not maintain much interest in the marvels of Marjorie Someone's state-of-the-art horse box, or the sad fate of some pony he'd never heard of. His few attempts at changing the subject were a failure. As he cleared the plates and brought the pudding he wondered ruefully how he'd managed to marry a horse breeder and beget a pair of horse-mad daughters.

He looked across at Ruth, wondering if she ever felt the unease he so often did. It had been a good day. What had he to complain of? He could not say he was disappointed with his life. He was in the Cabinet, damn it, in a top job. They had a lovely house and enough money to live in middle-class comfort. He had a beautiful wife who cared for his healthy daughters. All were doing well, happy with the life they had. No one was depressed, on drugs, rebellious or sick. He had it made. Who knows, he might even get *the* top job one day.

The girls chattered on, unconcerned at his lack of interest. Perhaps that was it, he thought. He wasn't interested, and they didn't mind his lack of interest, but *he* minded that they didn't mind.

Oh really, he thought, I'm just tired and grumpy. I'm not an excluded pariah in this family. They like horses. I don't. It's hardly the end of the world.

Oliver continued to study Ruth, thinking how little she had changed. They had met when they were both at Cambridge. He'd been blown away, he remembered, by Ruth's *cleanness*. Her unmade-up face looked newly scrubbed, and her thick blonde hair always smelt as if it had just been washed. She mostly wore it tied back with a rubber band, or held off her high forehead with an Alice band.

She was nineteen when he first saw her but she'd looked much younger. They'd both been invited to tea in the garden of his tutor's house. Oliver watched her handing round cake and was struck by how natural and carefree she looked, how long her legs were, how her hair shone in the sun. She was wearing an open-necked white shirt neatly tucked into jeans, the sleeves rolled up to expose lightly tanned, slightly freckled arms. No rings, no bracelets, not even a watch.

Oliver was captivated by her, though he tried to hide it. He assumed she was about sixteen and told himself she would be silly and giggly. And it would be beneath his dignity, if not illegal, to hit on a schoolgirl. But then she came over to him with a plate of cake.

'Hi,' she said. 'There's chocolate or lemon.'

He shook his head. 'Thanks, I won't. Did you make them?'

Her eyes widened and she laughed, showing even, pearly white teeth in healthy pink gums, like a toothpaste commercial.

'No chance. I can't boil an egg.' She nodded towards his tutor's wife. 'Mrs Rafael made them, I think.' Then she said, 'Are you a tutor? You don't look like an undergraduate.'

'No, I'm neither. Post grad. PhD at Emmanuel. And you?'

'PhD?' She sounded impressed. 'What on?'

'Maynard Keynes. And you? What are you up to?' Maybe she wasn't at school. Too assured. Yet close up she looked, if anything, even younger.

'Maynard Keynes. Really? Bretton Woods and all that?'

He was impressed. She must be at a very good school if she'd heard of Maynard Keynes.

'Your turn,' he said. 'You can't just ask questions and not answer any.'

'Sorry! I'm reading sociology. Girton. I love it.' She put down the cakes and folded her arms, hugging her chest, and Oliver had to force his gaze away from the soft swell of her breasts under the thin cotton. She made him think of hayfields and daisies.

Now, more than twenty years later, Ruth still looked years younger than she was, still mostly free of make-up, still slim and lithe, with not a single grey in her thick blonde hair. What was he complaining of?

Oliver stood up, walked round to his wife's side of the table. He kissed the top of her head. She looked up, surprised. 'I'm off, work to do,' he said. He hugged the girls. 'Night, you two. Well done, Andrea.'

At the door, he turned back to Ruth, 'Give me a shout before you go to bed, won't you, darling? With luck I'll be done by then.'

She nodded, but he didn't miss the tiny cynical smile. She's probably right, he thought. I always aim to go to bed when she does, but I nearly always fail.

The following Wednesday, Oliver hosted an informal dinner at their Lambeth house for the Governor-General of Australia, Tom Attley, a blunt but jovial Aussie who had just chaired a Commonwealth trade conference, and who was in town for a few days. Oliver had read a pile of positioning papers and briefing notes from his Australia experts but he wanted to get a bit of lowdown, unfiltered, from those in the game. Tom had been a big mover and shaker in Commonwealth politics for years and would give it to him straight.

Oliver had also invited the last British High Commissioner to Australia, now in the House of Lords. His third guest was a renowned historian and political journalist, particularly good on Australia.

Kate was cooking the dinner. He'd now used her for another lunch at Carlton Gardens – the chef was still off sick – and also to do some canapés for a cocktail party, against the advice of Hobhouse, the head of Government Hospitality. Hobhouse had heard, from that snake Dennis, no doubt, about Kate's outburst in the Lancaster House kitchens and had wanted to strike her off the approved list of caterers. But Oliver had insisted she stay. Kate was not, he said, to blame. Between his interfering with her menus, no one in the department listening to her and Dennis stoking rather than dousing the flames, she'd been powerless.

Wednesday night's dinner was, as usual, exactly what it should be, delicious but unostentatious. And the wine, Australian and chosen to flatter his guest, was excellent. Hobhouse could be sniffy about New World wines, but when Oliver had insisted, he had trawled the Foreign Office cellar stocks and come up with a top of the range Penfolds, and had declared it superb.

Oliver was feeling relaxed and expansive when he walked into the kitchen at eleven-thirty. He had a bottle in one hand and two glasses in the other.

Kate was on her own, and on her knees, wiping the inside of the oven.

'Hello, Cinderella. Why didn't you bring some help?'

Kate stood up. 'Waste of taxpayers' money.' She looked impish, he thought. Her round face was flushed and her eyes flashed merrily at him. 'There were only four of you, after all.'

He poured the wine. She pulled off her gloves and took his offered glass.

'Ah,' she said, her eyes closing for a second as she swallowed. Then, in an exaggerated Irish brogue, she said, 'And here was I just thinking a glass for a working girl was exactly what the doctor ordered, but I wasn't sure, at all, at all, she'd be getting one.'

'I always give you one!'

'I know.' She dropped the Irish and said seriously, 'It's much appreciated too, I promise you. But the present is not a guarantee of the future, is it? There's no reason why you should give me a glass of red every time. I might come to expect it as my due.'

'It is your due.'

'Have your guests gone?'

'Yup. Everyone has to be up for breakfast meetings. Politics isn't what it used to be.'

'You mean there used to be long summer hols, late mornings, lots of eating for your country and port after dinner.'

'Well, all of that, I suppose. And it's not all changed. Plenty of eating and drinking still goes on, which you must be glad of. The big change is the paper load. It's crazy. Even if you could read everything in your boxes every day, there's no time to think about them.'

'Mmm.' She tipped her head slightly to the side and looked at him quizzically. 'Maybe that's all your fault. If you guys in government keep passing more legislation, you need more people to write it all up, get it through parliament, revise it, implement it, police it . . .'

'Whoa, whoa! It's nearly midnight and my brain is off duty . . .'

But Kate was in full flow. 'Of course there's more paper!

There's more bureaucracy, which means more people, who earn their living writing more stuff.'

They drank their wine and mulled over the need for good law and the insatiable demand of the political machine for over-legislation. Then Kate put her glass down with another 'thank you' and went to fetch her van, which she'd had to park a block away. She left Oliver sitting on the kitchen worktop, still drinking his wine. I should go to bed, he thought, but he didn't. He poured another glass, topping Kate's up at the same time.

He enjoyed talking to Kate. She didn't have a brilliant mind, but she was unafraid of him and she said what she thought. It was refreshing. His civil servants rarely gave their real opinions. He had the feeling that they were telling him what a whole ladder of committees in the department had concluded, but that none of them were really committed to the line.

Kate's interest in everything was refreshing too. Over just a few brief late-night chats in this kitchen, or the one at Carlton House, they had talked a lot about almost everything – including politics. Oliver generally avoided casual political discussion, espe-cially with women. He was wary of strident Tory women preaching at him, or earnest Blair babes getting steamed up and shrill, but with Kate it didn't feel like political discussion. She had a knack of making political points lightly and conver-sationally as though she were chatting at a bus stop, whether about health and safety in restaurants, or the illogicality of banning hunting but not fly fishing, or the extravagance of planting garish annuals in the public parks. Last time, they had got onto to the subject of prison, and the madness (Kate's word) of sending women to jail.

'OK, I agree you can't just let off a murderess, but nearly all the women in prison are there for debt or aiding and abetting their blokes who do the real hard stuff. If a woman is in debt, why not give her some lolly? It's got to be cheaper than locking her up, don't you think?'

'But what if she just spends it and gets into debt again? You'd be rewarding irresponsible behaviour.'

'Sure,' she'd said, 'it's a risk. But there's a risk of her coming out of prison a drug addict or a real criminal, and that *is* expensive. So is keeping her kids in care, which will screw them up good and proper and maybe fit them for a life of crime too. And most of the women in clink are there because they can't pay their TV licence or their debts to some loan shark.'

Oliver smiled at the memory. He and Ruth hardly ever talked politics at home, and his daughters groaned and sang, 'Boring, boring,' if he raised anything remotely political. Or they listened politely, then slid out of the room.

He and Ruth had grown apart politically. She was the daughter of a Yorkshire pig breeder who had started life as a farm labourer and pig man and ended it as a millionaire producer of pork products, still a staunch Labour supporter. Ruth had adored her father. She wasn't exactly old Labour, but she hated New Labour's championing of the City, and the 'privatisation by the back door' of public services.

Oliver suspected that Ruth instinctively disapproved of people in 'high places', of which her husband was now one. She had inherited a good bit of her dad's no-nonsense attitude. And of his obstinacy, thought Oliver. Oliver was privately convinced that had the old boy still been alive, he might have supported the Tories, or at least New Labour, but he had died in the early nineties, leaving his daughter in charge of his political affiliations, and she had decided he would never have voted for Blair and what she now called 'your lot'.

Until his conversations with Kate, Oliver had not realised that he missed the good-tempered debate he and Ruth had enjoyed in their early years. Before she lost her sense of humour, he thought. She would probably say before he got the power bug.

Kate reappeared and picked up her glass. 'Thank you. This is rather more than my due. It's wonderful. It's Australian, isn't it?'

'Yes, it is. How did you know? Don't tell me you're a wine expert as well as a brilliant cook.'

'I looked at the label.'

He laughed, and she said, 'Actually, I did recognise the wine. My ex-partner is Australian, a chef, and a bit of a wine buff. He came from the Hunter Valley and he introduced me to it.'

'Tell me about him. Is he the father of Toby?' He was pleased with himself for remembering Toby's name.

She told him how she and Chris had fallen for each other in a hot restaurant kitchen and lived together happily for two years.

'And then suddenly I was pregnant, and Chris fled as though the fires of hell were at his heels.'

'That must have been a truly horrible time.'

'It was, but I'm glad now, and I'd hate him to resurface. But there's not much chance of that. He's back in Oz and married with a baby of his own, so Toby doesn't exist for him.'

'So you're not in touch?'

'No fear. I only know about him because I saw his photo – with wife and baby – on a restaurant magazine website.'

'But he could find you the same way, couldn't he? Or on Facebook or something?'

'That's precisely why I'm not on Facebook!' She laughed. 'Or anywhere else. It is also why I work for myself, and call my business Nothing Fancy rather than Kate's Kitchen or McKinnon and Co, or something else obvious. And why I don't have a website.' She drained her glass and reached for his empty one. She put them into the sink and turned on the tap.

'You don't have a website? But how do you manage? Get business I mean?'

'Word of mouth. The old fashioned way. It's not bad.'

'But Kate, are you sure you're not worrying needlessly?'

'No, I might be. I'm probably paranoid. Chris isn't violent or anything, he's actually a nice guy. Just weak. But I could not bear him muscling in on Toby, though now he's got his own child, I guess there's no real danger.' She washed and dried the glasses, put the bottle into the box with the other empties, and took off her apron.

She's very disciplined, thought Oliver. Anyone else would have left a couple of glasses for the maid to deal with, but she cleans the oven, and takes away the rubbish and the empties.

Kate had previously refused Oliver's help with carrying her catering boxes to her van, but tonight, since she didn't have Joan, she accepted. As they loaded the boxes of ingredients and equipment into the back of the van, and followed them with the empties and the rubbish sacks, Oliver said, 'Who will help you the other end?'

'I'll manage. It's only when there are crates and crates of fresh food to go in the chiller, full cases of wine, boxes of dirties and umpteen bags of rubbish that I think a man might be a useful addition to my life.'

Suddenly he wanted to know. 'Is that the only reason, Kate?'

She had her head and shoulders in the back of the van and she straightened up to look at him. The street lamp lit her face, close to laughing.

'Well, I do miss the rumpy pumpy of course. Celibacy isn't any fun at all.'

Oliver was shocked, though of course he would never show

it. Women, in his experience, joked about sex but didn't admit to any personal desire. He had no idea how to respond, and felt he'd stepped into territory he should have stayed right out of. What if she thought he was making a pass at her? But she grinned and said, 'But that's all most men are good for, I guess. Humping boxes and women.'

She slung the final rubbish bag into the back and slammed the doors. 'Besides,' she said, 'I barely have time for Toby. Couldn't possibly fit a man in too.'

Relieved the conversation was back on safer ground, Oliver said, 'I could never do what you do. The hours must be killing: long and anti-social to say the least.'

'Sounds like politics,' she said.

CHAPTER SEVEN

The Indian party in the famous Durbar Court of the Foreign Office was set for June, not for another eight weeks. But it would be in the thick of the party season and Kate wanted to get her hire orders in. Exotic things: hot buffet dishes with lids like Eastern temple domes, Benares brass platters, gilded Champagne glasses which would be in short supply. But to plan the hire, she needed to plan the menu. And she needed to get her prices in to Julian Hobhouse. Until he had agreed them, she didn't have a contract.

Amal frowned at the long list of dishes.

'The point is,' said Kate, 'since this is to be a sort of British Raj banquet, we have to have both Muslim and Hindu food, don't we?'

Amal shrugged. 'Sure. The Brits were always happy to bastardise anything Indian. If you can have kedgeree for breakfast and a chicken tikka sandwich, why not?'

'Don't be such a snob! As long as it tastes and looks terrific, that will do. And it will if your guys cook it.' Kate plonked a big book on the kitchen worktop, and started to page through it. 'Let's think about the look of it all.' She stopped at a picture of a market spice-seller, his spices piled high in perfect pyramids on dishes laid out on the pavement. 'I want this sort of rich, multi-coloured look. Lots of brown, orange and saffron, yellow and ochre.'

'OK, OK, I get it. The advertising equivalent of authentic.' He hugged Kate round the shoulders and said. 'Only teasing. It will be great. Only don't call it British Raj.'

'Why not? Nostalgia is the big thing now.'

'Maybe for the Brits. Maybe not for the Indians.' He shrugged. 'Anyway, we can lend you some Indian stuff: I've got those two big elephants, you know the ones, covered in mosaic and mirror. They'd look good on the buffet. We could hire silver thalis for the guests to eat off, and Talika has a chestful of Indian fabrics, saris and silks. Great colours.'

'Thanks, Amal. This has got to be the best Indian party ever seen in the famous Durbar Court. I want to pull all the stops out and impress Oliver.'

Amal looked at her, his eyes narrowing. 'You think a lot of our grandee Foreign Secretary don't you? Fancy him, do you?'

'Of course not!' Kate punched his arm lightly. 'But I like him. He's great, not a bit like he looks and he's not a grandee at all. Last time, he helped me carry the rubbish out to the car at midnight.'

'Maybe he fancies you.'

Kate burst out laughing. 'Not a chance. He's got a wife and two horsy daughters that he simply adores.'

Pat and Hank were finally going home after Easter, and Kate could hardly wait. She loved her mother and knew she'd miss her once she'd gone, but she spoiled Toby so. The boy had begun to believe he was the centre of the universe and Kate was forever biting her tongue to avoid an argument about sweets or toys.

But more than that, Kate wanted her house back. She longed for her old office, with no Hank on her computer, and for the ordered separation between domestic and professional catering that she had managed before her mother invaded her kitchen. And she wanted Toby to sleep quietly beside her again.

She reminded herself daily that the house belonged to her mother and that she and Toby were lucky to have it. For two weeks she had managed to repress her protests, or most of them, and to concentrate on the pleasures of a proper family to feed, and on the luxury of affection and company and help around the place. But now she just wanted a return to their old life.

One day Pat was dusting the sitting room while Kate was trying to work at her makeshift office.

'Kate,' said Pat, 'I'm sorry to go on about it, but *why* won't you come to Arizona in the summer? You know you could do with a holiday and Toby could get to know his cousins.'

It was an ongoing discussion, but Kate could not resume it now. She closed her eyes briefly to dispel the irritation. This was the third time her mother had interrupted her this morning, once to enquire about the whereabouts of the furniture polish, once to show her photos of Toby at the zoo, now this. It was hard not to complain. It wasn't only having to start again at the top of the list of figures she was adding up, but her mum's persistence about the Arizona holiday got to her. She was like a terrier with a bone.

Kate looked up and said, her voice as relaxed as she could make it, 'Mum, we agreed to talk about this at the weekend, didn't we? I've got to finish this in fifteen minutes and then I'm out of here. I've a meeting. I told you. Remember?'

Pat put both hands in the air, her yellow duster waving like a flag of surrender. 'OK, OK, I'm so sorry, darling.'

Before dawn on the Thursday before Easter, Kate crept out of the house and into her van. As she turned the ignition she thought, please don't break down now, it's three in the morning and I haven't had any coffee.

Happily, on the second attempt, the engine coughed into

life and Kate set off for the flower market at New Covent Garden. She was buying for a big wedding party on Easter Saturday. As the flowers were to be simple pots or jugs of spring blooms, Kate, in a flush of enthusiasm, had decided to do them herself rather than subcontract to a professional florist. Why not, she'd thought, it's hardly difficult, and I could do with the money.

Now she thought she must have been mad. The catering for this wedding would provide quite enough stress without this. She negotiated the market barriers, paid the attendant, parked her car and made for the main warehouse.

Still feeling half asleep, and desperate for coffee, she bought a paper cup of some not-altogether-disgusting hot drink from the café and carried it into the enormous market where, as always, the scent of millions upon millions of the freshest flowers hit her like a blast of heaven.

Suddenly wide awake and glad she'd come, Kate walked through the aisles doing a preliminary recce: she'd too often made the mistake of buying the first flowers she liked, only to find something more inspiring or radically cheaper later. Since the flowers had to stay fresh till Saturday, she would buy everything in bud. The weather was warm for April and she didn't want her tulips extravagantly open or the narcissi drying at the edges by the time their big moment came.

One of the stalls selling florist's supplies of ribbons and wrapping paper, tubs, vases and buckets, also had a stack of cheap straw hats. Puzzled, Kate asked, 'Why beach hats? And it's a bit early for summer, isn't it?'

'Nah. Them's Easter bonnets. Kids decorate them at school and stuff.'

Not at Toby's school, she thought, but what a great idea, we'll do it at his birthday party. She bought a pile of the hats, a collection of ribbons and some narrow buckets for holding her flowers until needed.

Kate walked rapidly, darting from stall to stall selecting tulips, jonquils, flat-faced narcissi, hyacinths and giant snowflakes, multi-hued primulas and polyanthus. She bought a few extra of each for Toby's party.

She had forgotten how much she liked the flower market. It wasn't just that it smelled so good, but the stall holders were full of banter, calling her 'Darling' or 'Princess' which, though she knew the words were meaningless, nevertheless made her feel merry and attractive. It was a lot more fun than shopping in the Cash and Carry.

But it sure wasn't quick. If she wanted very little from one stall, say a single box of jonquils, she would pay for it and then carry it all the way to her van. But mostly she paid for her purchases and asked the stall holder to keep them while she found a porter with a barrow. Then they'd do the rounds, up and down the aisles, Kate studying her shopping list and receipts and praying she wasn't forgetting anything. They'd load up the barrow and trundle the boxes to the car park. Maybe, she thought, florists deserved what they charged.

By the time she was on her last trip, some of the stall holders were packing up and the area immediately outside the big shed was strewn with odd bunches of abandoned flowers. Kate watched a huge van drive over a perfect bunch of purple anemones. She winced at the thought of the delicate petals being smeared into the dirt. On an impulse she darted forward, dodging moving vans as she ran over to scoop up two bunches lying undamaged next to their squashed neighbour. She cradled them in her arm, pleased with the success of her mercy dash and the fact that she'd got two free bunches.

*   *   *

Saturday dawned bright and sunny and the wedding reception went well. Kate's arrangements of mixed spring flowers, lightened by tiny twigs of yellow-leafed spring willow, were a big hit. She had bought small, cheap, deep-blue teapots, stuck gold heart-shaped stickers all over them and then filled them with a mix of all the flowers. There were three pots to a big round table and they looked charming.

At the end of the reception, Kate, as usual, offered the flowers to the hosts, the guests, her staff, anyone who wanted them. She hated the thought of fresh flowers being junked because no one could be bothered to carry them home.

But there were still a lot left over, which she rescued for herself. She would add them to the flowers she'd saved for Toby's party.

The Easter Monday sky was a pale cloudless blue. Kate had chosen Kew for their outing, an occasion that was to double as Toby's birthday treat and a farewell treat for Pat and Hank, who were going home to Arizona immediately after Easter. It would be a chance to show Hank picture-book scenes of English spring.

Kate was glad to see Hank so impressed. Kew was at its glorious best, with clouds of cherry blossom just out and swathes of tulips in the grass. The trees were in tiny shiny leaf and the grass so bright in the sun it made you narrow your eyes.

Toby had invited six of his friends. Talika came too, and it took all of them to carry the picnic boxes, rugs, coats, boots, flowers and straw hats to their chosen picnic spot. By one o'clock they had staked their claim and spread two thick picnic rugs on the slightly damp grass. Kate stayed behind to sort out the lunch while the others set off to explore. As the three grown-ups walked sedately together the children ran excitedly in all directions, never going too far, always returning to safety before setting off again. Like puppies off the leash, she thought.

They had party crackers and paper hats, and lunch was entirely hand-held. There were tortilla chips, biscuits, strips of naan bread, and crudités to dip into or spread with taramasalata, cream cheese, hummus, pesto, peanut butter and fish paste. There were also mini sausages and fingers of cheese.

'Kate, when did you do all this?' said Pat. 'I could have helped you.'

'I didn't, the whole lot came from Ocado. Ordered online and delivered. I decanted everything out of their containers and into dishes this morning. I couldn't quite bring myself to lay out a picnic in packets and plastic tubs.'

'Eureka!' Pat turned to Hank. 'I do think this is the first time my daughter has ever bought ready-mades!'

'Well, I owe my conversion to you,' said Kate. 'If you hadn't fed the foxes with my coq au vin, I might never have realised that most of the world can't tell the difference.'

After ice creams and coffee, both bought by Hank from the café, Kate laid out her boxes of flowers, hats, ribbons, sticky tape, and scissors. 'OK, then,' she said, 'we're all going to make Easter bonnets and I've got prizes for the best ones. What you have to do is help yourselves to any of these flowers and ribbons, and decorate one of the hats with them. Any way you like.'

She cut a length of elasticated ribbon, tied it round a hat and tucked a little bunch of primulas into it. 'Like that,' she said, 'only I'm sure you can do it better.'

Pretty soon all of them, adults included, were industriously decorating hats. The children loved it, and Toby, who had groaned and complained that Easter bonnet making was boring and too girly, changed his mind and squabbled happily with Sanjay over who got the red polyanthus and the bright blue hyacinths. With a bit of help from Hank, Toby produced a hat circled in concentric rings of red, white and blue.

Kate was enjoying herself. An afternoon with three generations of family was, she thought, the sort of life she longed for Toby to have.

When everyone had done a hat, Pat took photographs of them one by one to email to the parents. She got a passing stranger to take a picture of them all together, wearing their completed bonnets, standing under a white cherry tree.

Then Hank and Kate did the judging, making sure each child won a category: funniest bonnet, prettiest bonnet, most original bonnet, etc. Toby won most patriotic, which had to be explained to him.

Hank and Talika took the children off to the Xstrata Treetop Walkway while Kate and her mother cleared up the mess of cut ribbons and paper hats, of discarded anoraks and caps, and made two trips to carry everything back to the car.

Walking back to meet the others, Pat said, 'Darling, have you thought about Arizona?'

'Mum, I just cannot afford it.'

'But darling, it will cost very little. If we buy the tickets now, we'll get good deals and you'll be staying with us . . .'

'I know, Mum. I can afford the tickets, but I cannot take the time. I can't afford to have no income, and not be here to land contracts. Nothing Fancy has only really been going five years and I don't dare turn down anything. It's still too fragile to trust it to other people. That's the problem.'

Kate watched her mother's eager face change to anxiety and then fall, making her at once look heavier and older, defeated. Pat dropped her gaze to her shoes, saying nothing.

Suddenly Kate could not bear to disappoint her.

'Maybe Toby could come to you on his own,' she suggested. 'I could travel with him, maybe stay the weekend, then leave him with you?'

Pat's face lifted as rapidly as it had fallen a few seconds before. She looked deeply into Kate's face, smiling, close to tears.

'Darling, that would be so wonderful. We'd give him such a great time.'

As Kate looked over the shoulder of her mother's enveloping hug, she thought, Oh God, what have I done? How will I survive without him?

At four-thirty they were all at the Victoria Terrace Café for tea. The table was decorated with balloons and the centrepiece was Toby's birthday cake, made by Talika in the form of a long green snake with black eyes and forked tongue. Pat was busy taking more pictures when a man wearing the blue uniform of Kew Gardens appeared.

'Which of you is in charge here?' He looked across the table to Kate, then to Hank and Pat. He ignored Talika.

'No one. Or all of us,' said Kate. 'Is there a problem?'

'I am afraid there is, Madam. It is against the regulations for anyone to pick flowers in the gardens, as I am sure you know. There are notices at all the gates. Your party has obviously picked a great many flowers.'

Kate shook her head, 'No, we haven't.' She laughed, 'Though I can see the evidence is a bit stacked against us. We—'

'Madam, I do not think this is a laughing matter . . .'

'But it is . . .'

He produced a notebook, 'If I may have your name and . . .'

'You see, we brought the flowers with us, to decorate the Easter bonnets . . .'

The man looked at her, contempt in his eyes. 'I am afraid that cannot be so.' He looked around, under the table. 'You have no flowers with you apart from those in your hats, no receptacles, buckets, boxes—'

Hank cut in. 'That's because we took them back to the car, so as not to litter your gardens. I'll show you if you like. We cleared—'

The official ignored Hank. 'Madam, I do not want to insult you, but I saw one of the children, with my own eyes, picking blue hyacinths from a border.'

Kate was suddenly angry. 'I don't believe you,' she said calmly, steel in her voice.

'This one,' he said, pointing at Toby. 'The one with the red, white and blue.' He said to Toby, 'You did, didn't you?'

Toby, eyes round and stricken, looked at the man without speaking. Pat put a protective arm round his shoulders, and Hank stood up.

'Look, fella,' he said, 'you're frightening the boy. You've got hold of the wrong end of the stick.'

Kate said, 'But why would Toby do that? Toby, you didn't—'

At that moment, Kate heard a familiar voice behind her.

'Kate McKinnon, what do we have here? Birthday party, am I right?' It was Oliver Stapler.

Kate jumped up, her face flushing. 'Oh, Oliver, hello, what are you doing here?'

Oliver introduced his wife. She did not look a bit as Kate had imagined her, which was overweight and tweedy. This woman was slim and attractive. Her skin looked almost transparent and there were blueish veins at her temples, tender and delicate. 'Ruth, this is Kate, I told you about her. She's the caterer who does all those—'

'Yes, I know who she is. You've told me more than once about her brilliant cooking.'

Ouch, thought Kate, that was not said or meant kindly. She

chipped in hurriedly, 'This is my mother, Pat, and her husband, Hank, and Talika my friend. She's the one who makes the cherry chocolates you like. And this lad here is Toby, my son.' She knew she was gabbling, but Oliver's sudden appearance had thrown her. And the Kew man was still waiting for an answer. 'It's Toby's birthday, but it seems we are in trouble here.' She indicated the official.

Oliver looked across the table and then quickly walked round it, arm outstretched. 'I'm Oliver Stapler, is there anything I can do to help?'

The man put out his hand, which Oliver shook, asking, 'And you are?'

'James Todhunter.'

Oliver looked directly into the man's eyes and smiled. 'What's the problem, Mr Todhunter?'

But Mr Todhunter had folded his tents. Kate felt sorry for him rather than satisfied. She would have persuaded him in the end about the flowers, but he'd been unfairly routed by fame and authority. Oliver's face was a familiar one, and even if he didn't know exactly what Oliver did, he knew when he'd met his match.

'No Sir, I think I'll just leave it. I'm sure it won't happen again.' And he turned tail and walked away, his back stiff.

'What was that all about?' asked Oliver.

Kate shrugged, her good humour restored. 'Oh, it was wonderful. The perfect misunderstanding. He took one look at all the Easter bonnets and concluded that the flowers had been filched from Kew. But I'd bought them in the flower market.'

Oliver looked at the various hats, some of which, after an afternoon of tree-top walking, were a bit bedraggled. He laughed. 'I do see. A natural enough conclusion. Poor chap.'

Kate said, 'Mrs Stapler, Oliver, I don't suppose you'd like to join us for a cup of tea? And a piece of birthday cake – Toby is about to cut it.'

To Kate's surprise Oliver said, 'What do you think, Ruth, shall we join the young man's party?' He bent to Toby and said, 'What do you think, Toby? Another couple of grown-ups at your birthday tea? Would you mind?'

Toby shook his head. Kate noticed that he still looked anxious. The unfortunate official had really upset him.

Oliver, sitting next to her, must have read her thoughts, because he said quietly, 'We watched you from over there, and you didn't look happy. I thought you were really going to take that fellow on. That's why we came over.'

'Well, it was funny until he decided to finger poor little Toby. Said he'd seen him nicking flowers.' She lowered her voice. 'Poor kid, it's his birthday, for God's sake.'

'And had he?'

Kate, confused, said, 'Had who what?'

'Had the Kew man seen Toby nicking flowers? And *had* Toby been nicking flowers?'

'Not you too!' Kate regretted the words as soon as she'd said them, but, really, what business was it of his? But he did not seem to have heard her and was talking to the children on the other side of him. Talking, thought Kate, with all the charm of a politician soliciting votes. Is it real, she wondered, or is he on automatic?

By the time Toby blew out his candles, he had forgotten the Kew man. He was excited and happy, and Kate had forgiven Oliver for daring to question her son's flower-picking behaviour. She watched with pride and pleasure as Toby, with Hank's help, cut the cake and solemnly offered a piece first to Ruth, then to his gran, then to Oliver.

*   *   *

That night, after Kate had read him his story, and tucked him in, Toby said, 'Mum, why did that man say it's wrong to pick flowers? We picked those yellow ones for Granny Pat's bedroom. Didn't we?'

Oh dear, thought Kate, hugging her son's pyjama-clad shoulders, I'm glad Oliver Stapler isn't here. Or the Kew man.

'We did, darling. Daffodils. And we picked snowdrops, do you remember, in the dark one night? I needed them to put on a table for a lunch I was cooking.'

'So it's not wrong then?'

'Well, it can be, if they are not your flowers. If, say, we just went next door and picked all their flowers, that would be wrong, wouldn't it?'

'They don't have any flowers.'

Too true, thought Kate. Only old mattresses and dead fridges and plenty of nettles.

'OK, but imagine they had a beautiful rose garden, full of roses they were hoping to use to decorate the church on their daughter's wedding day, and we came along and helped ourselves to the whole lot to make rose petal jam out of, do you think that would be wrong?'

'Can you make jam out of rose petals?'

'Yes, as it happens, but you need apples or something else too. The rose petals are just for the flavour and the smell. But you, clever young wretch, you are changing the subject!'

'What's the subject?'

'Whether it's wrong to pick flowers.'

Toby was silent, turning the pages of the book they'd been reading. Then he said, 'I guess it's wrong out of someone's garden. But why is it wrong out of a park?'

Good lad, thought Kate, he is getting there, slowly, with reason, not just confessing. 'There are usually rules saying no to picking flowers because they want everyone to see them, and if someone has taken them then someone else, who comes next day, can't see them.'

Kate thought, is this when I let him know I know, or do I give him a chance to tell me? She said, 'Did the man tell you that, or just get cross?'

To her relief, he took it in his stride. 'He asked me why I was doing it.'

'And what did you say?'

'Mummy, I . . . I wanted to tell him it was my birthday and that I wanted to give you a present too, but I thought Sanjay and everyone would think I was wet giving you flowers, so I pretended I needed more for my hat.' His words came out in a rapid stream, with no punctuation and no inflection.

He looked up at her, face full of anxiety, eyes full of tears. 'Mum, maybe that's why he thought we'd picked all the flowers. Because of what I said about my hat.'

Kate restrained the impulse to hug him to death. 'Oh, darling, thank you for wanting to give me flowers. I love flowers more than almost anything.'

'But did saying I wanted the flowers for my hat make him think we'd stolen the flowers for everyone's hat?'

'Yes, I expect so,' said Kate, releasing his shoulder. Her tone was light and matter-of-fact. 'He just jumped to the conclusion that all the flowers for all our hats were from his garden.' She watched the anxiety smooth out of his face, his childish confidence replacing it. 'Anyway,' she said, 'let's not pick any more flowers in public gardens, what do you think?'

'OK,' said Toby.

Kate put her lips lightly on his head, and breathed in that familiar and beloved Toby perfume, a mix of shampoo and boy, that never failed to move her.

Chapter Eight

Oliver looked at the message, perplexed. It was on his private email, not the one the office filtered before deciding what he should be bothered with. This one was only used by Ruth (rarely), his daughters (almost never), the PM and Cabinet colleagues (all the time). This was from the chairman of the House of Commons Ethics Committee:

> Dear Oliver,
> Could you give me a ring on the number below or on my private mobile, also below. We need a word.
> Jack

Oliver was struck by the tone. Jack Simons had been at Cambridge with him, and they'd entered the House the same year. They were not close – he was too right wing for Ruth – but they were friendly. 'We need a word,' was a bit peremptory wasn't it? And where had Jack got his private email address from?

He frowned with a fractional shake of his head. It made no sense, but he'd soon find out. He reached for the land line, changed his mind and dug his mobile out of his pocket. He stood up and walked to the window. He dialled Jack's mobile number.

'Jack, it's Oliver. What's up?'

'Ah, glad you rang, Oliver. Good of you. But I wonder if you could pop in to see us? We have a little problem we hope you can help us with.'

Oliver turned and walked back to the desk the long way round, skirting the sofa. 'Well, of course, but what is it? And is it urgent? You know how under the cosh we all are, budgets being slashed right and left while the work increases.' He slid back into his chair.

'Yes, and I do sympathise, but this is urgent too, and I think it would be in your interest to come in to talk to us sooner rather than later.'

Somehow the conversation had turned sinister. Oliver looked at the picture of Mattie and Andrea on his desk and his mind registered the fact that the state of their teeth had reversed since the photograph had been taken. Mattie, who was grinning gappily over the edge of a swimming pool in the picture, now had all her second teeth, while Andrea, with a full set of milk teeth in the photo, was now the one with a gappy smile and emerging new teeth.

Oliver pushed his fingers into his hair and rubbed his scalp. 'That sounds ominous. How extraordinary. Is something wrong, Jack?'

Jack's voice was noticeably brisker as he said, 'Oliver, I don't think we should discuss this on the telephone. If you could make room in your diary for a meeting tomorrow I would be grateful. Eleven a.m. would be ideal.'

Oliver's instinct was to tell him to go to hell, but within seconds he'd realised that he would not get a wink of sleep until he knew what was going on. He told Jack he'd do his best and then got Helen to cancel his eleven o'clock.

Oliver resolved to have a look at the Ethics Committee's remit before he went to bed to see if he had inadvertently broken a rule. If he remembered right, it was all about not taking brown envelopes, or giving jobs to friends or family, or asking questions in the house that would be helpful to some company on whose board you sat. Well, he was innocent of all those, and guilt free about everything else he could think of, but he would run down the code of conduct and see what crime he could possibly have committed.

In the event he never did. It was one o'clock in the morning when he finally closed his last red box, and he was exhausted. Bloody hell, he thought, it will be a storm in a teacup. I refuse to worry about it.

He hadn't mentioned it to Ruth when he'd made his usual evening call at the girls' bedtime. He'd told himself this was to spare Ruth anxiety, but he knew that it was more to do with him wanting to have answers before she fired questions at him. It was bad enough Jack suggesting he'd behaved unethically – and it had to be something like that, it was the Ethics Committee after all – without his wife piling in.

When he presented himself at the office in Great Peter Street the following morning, he was told that Sir Jack Simons was not in the office, but that Mr Struther was ready for him now. He had no option but to follow the woman down a corridor and into a meeting room.

There were two people in the room who rose as he entered. They had a thin file between them, which the taller of them, a man with thinning hair and spectacles, closed as he stood up. He leant forward over the table and took Oliver's hand.

'Good morning, Foreign Secretary. I am Alan Struther, and I do preliminary investigations for the Ethics Committee. Many thanks for responding so promptly. It is good of you.' He indicated the empty chair opposite him and they all sat down.

Oliver was tempted to ask them at once what this was all

about, but to his dismay his heart had suddenly started to thump alarmingly and he did not trust his voice. How odd, he thought, I have nothing to hide, but I'm nervous. So he said nothing and sat back, deliberately casual.

'This young man is my assistant, here to take notes of our conversation. If you would prefer, we can record the conversation instead. It is your choice.' He paused for a second but as Oliver did not immediately reply, he said kindly, 'We just need a record, you see. It is as much for your protection as for our work, but some people are unsettled by a note-taker, and others by a machine.'

'I have no preference, but I must say I'm surprised. This is beginning to look like a police interrogation, yet I have no idea what it's about.'

Alan Struther fiddled with his spectacles, taking them off carefully with both hands, then sliding them back, all the time looking over them at Oliver.

'Well, if you have no preference, I prefer a paper record. I find it easier to use than recorded evidence. So perhaps we can begin. The problem is rather delicate and concerns your wife.'

'My wife? What has she got to do with the Ethics Committee? I don't employ her, if that's what you think. She . . .'

'No, it is nothing like that. But you will remember your visit to the Yemen?'

'Yes, of course I do. It was only a few months ago. Ruth came with me.'

'Indeed, and she was given an antique necklace by the Yemeni president. Our information is that it is a museum quality artefact from the second century AD. It is priceless. As you know, under our anti-corruption code, Members of Parliament and their wives are not allowed to accept gifts worth more than one per cent of an MP's annual salary. And if it is diplomatically impossible to refuse them, they must to be handed in to the Treasury. Such gifts rightfully belong to the public: this necklace would have found its way to the British Museum.'

During this long speech Oliver's mind was racing wildly. First he'd felt relief. As a Foreign Office minister he was always being presented with gifts, which when the bowing and thanking was over, he always handed straight to Sean, who did whatever had to be done with them.

But then he remembered. There had been a small dinner with the president and his son, just the four of them, in a private room at the Sheraton in Sana'a. After dinner, the president had produced from his pocket what he described as a gift for the beautiful Mrs Oliver. It was an inlaid wooden box, of the kind you see in every Arab market, containing a beaded necklace. They had passed round the open box and Ruth had dutifully admired the filigree settings and orange and blue stones. Then the president had risen from the table, said, 'Allow me,' and fastened it round Ruth's neck.

Which was the last he'd seen of it.

'My God! Are you sure? Museum quality? We thought it was a bit of local craftsmanship. Strings of coloured beads and balls and dangly bits. Shiny gilt if I remember . . .'

'Coral, lapis lazuli and gold, actually.' Struther opened his file and shuffled through the few papers to find a photograph. 'This is, I believe, a similar necklace. This one is in the Athens museum.' He pushed the picture towards Oliver. The necklace consisted of an outer string of round gold bells hanging from a gold chain and interspersed with dangles, each consisting of half a dozen short strings of coral beads gathered at the top. The inner strings, six of them, were of lapis stones and gold beads, gathered together at the ends in ornamented triangular gold casings, studded with coral.

Oliver covered his forehead and eyes with his hand. He was frantically trying to remember what they had done with the thing. He was fairly sure he had never seen Ruth wearing it. She hardly ever wore jewellery, and when she did it would be the pearls he had given her on their tenth wedding anniversary. Oh God, he prayed, let her not have donated the necklace to a jumble sale or something.

Struther waited politely then said, 'Can you assist us at all?'

'Christ. I don't know what to say.' Oliver took a deep breath. 'Right, first, it was in one of those inlaid boxes that you see in all the tourist shops all over the Arab world. Second, the occasion was a private dinner and my PPS wasn't there. I usually hand all presents straight to him. And thirdly, I guess we just forgot about it. I haven't seen it since.'

'So you had no intention of keeping it?'

'Absolutely not. I'd no intention of receiving it, never mind keeping it. And nor had Ruth. It was totally unexpected, but of course these things happen, especially in the Middle East. I should have been on the ball, but I had no idea of its value.'

'It did not occur to you that a gift from the Yemeni president was unlikely to be fake?'

Oliver closed his eyes. 'No. I agree it's mad, but I just did not consider the matter. Of course, if someone had asked me that direct question then, I would have realised it must have some value. I suppose it didn't interest me – this sort of complicated shiny stuff is not to my taste.'

Aware that this was sounded limp in the extreme, he added, 'We'd seen so many of those necklaces in the shops and markets, and indeed in Morocco and all over the place, I suppose I put it on a par with being given a box of chocolates or a bunch of flowers.'

'Did you judge it, then, to be worth less than five hundred pounds, which would have been about the limit then?'

Oliver was beginning to get angry, but he made an effort to conceal it. 'No, I did not make any judgement at all. I don't go around calculating the value of presents.'

'If you had seen it, say, on your wife's dressing table the next day, would you have handed it in?'

'Yes . . . no. I'm not sure. I might not have noticed it. I might have thought it was a present Ruth had bought for someone back home. I might not have recognised it as the necklace she was given the night before. Of course we all looked at it then but I did not *examine* it.' Oliver's voice was rising. 'No, I doubt if I would have said, "This necklace could be worth more than we are allowed to receive as personal gifts under the Ethics Committee's parliamentary behaviour code, so we had better give it to Sean to deposit with Her Majesty's Treasury."'

Struther said peaceably, 'I'm sorry to have to ask you these questions, Secretary of State. I can see it is distressing, but I am afraid I must. So, where do you think the necklace is now?'

'I've no idea. Maybe sold at a jumble sale. Probably round the neck of some latter-day hippy.'

'That would be a pity, I must say. Well, I'm sure you will ask your wife if she can throw any light?'

Oliver, repenting his irritation, said, 'Yes, I'm sorry. Of course I will. I will ask her to hunt for it tonight and let you know in the morning.' He put his hands on the table, about to stand up, but Struther said, 'I'm afraid that's not all, Foreign Secretary.'

Oliver sat back in his chair in disbelief. 'What then?'

'There is the question of a set of Limoges china imported into the country. Ten years ago.'

'And?' Oliver said, baffled. 'What about it?' He remembered the china well. It was a full dinner service complete with serving dishes and coffee cups. It had cost a fortune. Somewhat depleted now, it was still their 'best' and, since they seldom entertained in the country, they kept it in the Lambeth house.

'I understand it was imported as part of the British Ambassador's goods and chattels, when he returned home after his tour in Paris,' said Struther. 'If that is so, import duty was probably not paid. Is that so?'

'Import duty? I've no idea. That was ten years ago, for God's sake. This is starting to feel like muckraking. Who's behind this?'

'I'm not at liberty to divulge sources, I'm afraid. You'll understand that, I'm sure.'

'Anyway,' said Oliver, 'I wasn't even in the Foreign Office, and only just in parliament then.'

'You were a junior minister in the Home Office, I believe.'

'But my job is nothing to do with this! Ruth and Marianne, the Ambassador's wife, are old school friends. We were having a private lunch at the embassy – I think it was Marianne's birthday, and Ruth admired her china and Marianne offered to get a set for us.'

'But you did not declare the transaction?'

'No, of course not. Why should we? It was between my wife and her old friend. What business is that of government's? The alarmists are right. We interfere too much in private lives.'

'The china was shipped home from the British embassy in Paris, was it not?'

'I can't remember, but that would make sense. As I said, Marianne ordered it. It wasn't a gift. We bloody paid for it!' Oliver sat back, pleased to be able to turn the tables.

Struther did not react except to say mildly, 'And how did you pay if I may ask?'

'Can't remember. Cheque, I would have thought.'

'Do you remember the cost?'

'No, but it was a lot. I remember thinking Ikea might have been a better idea.'

'And you cannot remember if you paid import duty on it?'

Oh God . . . Oliver suddenly remembered. Marianne had had the shipment delivered to the embassy so it could come into the country with their things and save the Staplers shipping costs. Ruth had collected it from Marianne and David's house in Regent's Park. Oliver had not at first thought about avoiding tax, but if he was honest, it had dawned on him that he would save, not just freight charges, but tax too. He had just chosen not to think about it.

But now he said, 'But there isn't any duty between France and England on personal purchases, is there?'

Struther said stiffly, as though he was reading from a rule-book, 'Travellers are permitted to bring gifts or souvenirs into the country up to a value of a few hundred pounds without paying duty. As I understand it, this was not a gift or souvenir and the value was greatly in excess of the limit on those goods anyway.'

Oliver opened his mouth to protest, then shut it again. The man was right.

'That brings us to the end of my questions,' said Struther, rising from the chair.

And to the beginning of a nightmare for me, thought Oliver.

CHAPTER NINE

Kate looked across the temporary kitchen at the frozen red block in the bowl. She hoped it would thaw in time. If she had to microwave it, it would lose that fresh raspberry colour. But then she noticed that it was already duller and deeper in colour than usual. There's something not right, she thought.

She walked quickly over to the dessert section, pulling a spoon from her pocket. Even before she'd tasted it she realised what she had done. This was beetroot, not raspberry. How could she be such a perfect idiot? She reached for the lid of the plastic box the frozen block had come out of. After weeks in the freezer the label was not easy to read, but she could make out Amal's writing: just the date and *Unseasoned Beetroot puree for borscht or risotto*. She was thawing the wrong one.

Oh God, she thought, her heart thumping in panic. We've got a hundred guests about to eat Pêche Melba, and no raspberry coulis.

She looked at her watch. Eight p.m. The starter would be going in any minute now. They were in the middle of the country, in a tent in her customer's garden. Even if she knew where the nearest supermarket was, she doubted it would still be open. And there was no way she was going to ask the hostess and ruin the woman's confidence in her.

She called to Joan. 'Joan, have you got a menu? I just need to check something.'

Joan hurried into the dining tent and returned with a menu. It said Pêche Melba, nothing more.

Good, thought Kate, most of the guests won't know that Pêche Melba has fresh raspberry in it, and anyway won't read the menu, and thirdly won't know the difference. She suddenly smiled to herself, thinking, this is disgraceful, but if it works it will have been an interesting gastronomic experiment.

The original idea was to serve each customer with two small meringue baskets, one filled with a stoned, poached white peach and one with a ball of vanilla ice cream. There was to have been a raspberry coulis lake all around.

Kate, thinking fast, rejected the idea of just sweetening the beetroot and pretending it was raspberry. The flavour would be too obvious if a customer took a mouthful of the sauce on its own. Could she leave the coulis out all together? Just serve the meringue, peach and ice cream? No, her customer was expecting raspberry coulis and she did not want her jumping up from the table to tell the kitchen they had forgotten it.

'Quick, Joan, can you get me some sugar? Have we any castor, or only gran?'

'Only granulated, I'm afraid.'

Kate put half a kilo of sugar into a pan with a cupful of beetroot slush and stirred fast over the heat until the grains had melted. Then she cooled it as fast as she could by putting the pan into a shallow bowl of cold water, and stirring. It did not take long. She had time: the first course was only going in now. Kate took about a litre of the softened but still-frozen purée and put it into a liquidiser with her cooled syrup mix and whizzed. She tasted it. Not a burst of raspberry flavour on the tongue, that's for sure, but perfectly pleasant.

'What are you doing?' asked Joan. 'I thought we were going to have the raspberry sauce poured round the Melbas by the waiters?'

Kate flashed her a smile. 'Trust me, sweetheart! I'll explain later. But if you could just tell the waiters that we are not going with the sauce, I'm using it to make the ice cream look like raspberry ripple, and I will put a few drizzles of it on each plate just before service.'

Which is what she did. She used a fork to ripple the beetroot purée into the rich vanilla ice cream, then she and two of the cooks used ice cream scoops to ball it into a hundred perfect portions and got them back into the freezer as quickly as possible.

When it came to serving, which wasn't until after ten p.m., the balls were firm but not rock hard. They quickly plated the puds, one cook adding a ball of red-streaked ice cream to one meringue nest, another putting a peach into the second. Finally, Kate added a few stylishly placed, but very small, blobs and splashes of purée to the plate.

And they got away with it. Nothing but exclamations of delight and congratulations. Joan was at first horrified, and then impressed. After the service, when they were packing up, relaxed and pleased with the whole event, they got the waiters and cooks to taste the unused ice cream and guess its flavour. The general consensus was raspberry, though a few said strawberry and one said cherry.

'It's beetroot,' said Kate, 'but don't any of you ever tell a soul!'

At the end of the month, as she made out the customer's bill, Kate briefly considered deleting the charge for the Pêche Melba. After all, she deserved to be done under the Trade Descriptions Act. But then she thought, hell no, the Melbas were delicious, and the woman wouldn't want to know that all her guests had beetroot ice cream. So she charged her full whack, feeling more amused than guilty.

Sending out bills was quite enjoyable, a lot better than paying them anyway, but doing her monthly accounts made Kate anxious.

She was OK on an Excel spreadsheet because the computer magically did the sums, but the VAT return still flummoxed her.

She frowned at the form, trying hard to remember the principle of the thing. Did she put her turnover in the Output or the Input box? And what did they mean by acquisitions from EC member states? She chewed on her pencil, making little indentations in the top inch of it.

When, last year, her revenue had breached the sixty-seven-thousand-pound barrier, she had had to register for VAT. But, her accountant had told her, no problem: she could simply reclaim it. Simply indeed! The thing was a nightmare.

Until very recently, she had regarded herself as a cook, hiring herself out for a fee. But in the past two years, more and bigger customers wanted her to take on the flowers, the staff, the marquee tent, the hire, even the photographer. So, though she personally earned less than forty thousand a year, her 'billings' had shot way beyond the VAT limit.

Of course she got a rake-off from suppliers for putting the business their way. But her customers – especially government departments – were slow to pay while her suppliers, mostly small businesses, needed their money at once. And they had a magic weapon to make her pay up: they didn't deliver if they had not been paid. Kate could not risk the non-arrival of a wedding cake or the agency not supplying waitresses.

She would have liked to use the same threat to her customers. But she feared they'd just hire her rivals instead. She didn't want to hand her hard-won contracts to Party Ingredients or Moveable Feasts.

Kate shook her head. She was owed nearly a hundred thousand pounds, and yet she was overdrawn to the tune of nearly twenty thousand, which was her agreed limit. How could that be? She'd have to start making unpleasant calls and hear the excuses about the bookkeeper being on holiday, the cheque being in the post, the computer glitch with direct debit. This was the only part of her job she truly hated.

The telephone rang. She hoped it was a client demanding something exciting, some gastronomic challenge that would take her mind off her finances, but it was the bank. Her 'relationship manager' would like a word. He would be with her in a minute.

Kate did not like the man. She hung on, vaguely apprehensive, and then irritated at the recorded message extolling the bank's savings rates. Finally he was on the line, his voice bordering on the smarmy.

'So sorry to keep you waiting, Miss McKinnon. Unforgivable I know.'

What a creep. She was tempted to say, so why do it then? I don't ring up my customers and then keep them hanging on.

'It's all right,' she said. 'What's up?'

'Well, there's something we need to discuss. Have you got a minute?' For goodness sake, Kate thought, just get on with it, will you?

'Sure. Shoot.'

'Thank you. Most kind. As you know you are applying to us for a loan to cover the new van and a . . . what is it? Some equipment, I believe?'

'A blast chiller. Yes, and you have agreed to it.'

'Ah, well, that's just the problem. I'm afraid there has been a hitch. We, at branch level, have been instructed to pass all prospective loans through our credit evaluation desk, which wasn't the case before. We used to be able to authorise these small loans.'

Kate's chest muscles seemed to contract. 'But you've already agreed. I have a letter.'

'I'm sure you understand that in the current banking circumstances—'

'No, I don't understand. What I understand is I asked you for a loan of thirty thousand pounds and you were delighted to give it to me. It's a done deal.'

'I know this is hard, Miss McKinnon, but as the monies have not yet left the bank, we are not obliged ... If the transfer had already been made, we would be less likely to reclaim it, that is true, but technically, we would be within our rights to call in the loan at any time. But as that is not the case, it is, I think you will agree, better to give you the bad news now, before you have spent the money ...'

He waffled on, while the meat of the matter slowly lodged in Kate's brain. She felt her face grow hot. Flushed and furious, she raised her voice to drown his polite patter, 'Are you telling me you will not lend me any money at all? You are welching on the whole deal?'

'I would not put it like that, Miss McKinnon, but yes, I am afraid our instructions are not to advance—'

Kate banged the telephone down and burst into tears.

A week later Talika and Amal were coming to supper. They had threatened to bring a friend of theirs, a single man, with them, but thank God he'd cried off. She didn't feel like yet another of her friends' well-meaning matchmaking efforts. It wasn't that the divorced banker, the single architect, the IT guru weren't interesting and presentable, but they ignited no sparks. Kate regarded all prospective mates as potential fathers for Toby rather than lovers for her, and inevitably they showed little interest in her darling boy.

She didn't feel like cooking, even for Amal and Talika. She was exhausted from crying after a horrible phone conversation with her mother, and she could not stop thinking about it.

Kate had resolved to ask her mother for help with money. She'd have preferred to speak to her face to face, but Pat and Hank had gone home ten days ago.

It had taken all her courage to make the call, but she had managed it, telling herself that if her mother loved her as she, Kate, loved Toby, she'd be bound to help.

But Pat had said, 'Darling, I can see you need the money but I don't think I can just give you the house. It just wouldn't be fair on Arthur, would it?'

'But I'm not asking you to, Mum. Of course it's your house, and it's wonderful you let me live in it rent free. I'm really, really grateful. But I desperately need a loan. I just thought we might raise a thirty-thousand-pound mortgage on the house. But if you don't want to put the house in my name, maybe you could do it? I know I can pay you back in three years, and pay the interest on the loan too. Interest is quite low at the moment . . .'

'Kate love, the thing you need to consider is that if the bank think you are a bad risk, is it wise to borrow the money? Or right to ask me to lend it to you?'

'Mum! The reason the bank won't lend me the money is because they're in trouble and don't want to lend to anyone! They admit I'm a good customer and reliable and that I will be able to pay it back. But they are just calling in all their loans, good, bad and indifferent.'

Her mother could not be persuaded. She'd said she'd talk to Hank and Arthur, but Kate was left with the feeling that she should not have asked, that her mother thought she was trying to steal a march on her brother. What had made Kate cry was her instinct that if it had been Arthur wanting a loan he'd have got it without question. Arthur, thought Kate miserably, had her mother's time, her attention, her love. But how could she complain when her mother provided a rent-free house?

That was the second time she'd been in tears in a week, the first when the bank reneged on her loan. And she'd had a couple of other bouts of blubbing recently. She told herself crossly she was falling apart. Why couldn't she pull herself together? But she was just so tired she wanted only to kiss Toby goodnight, watch mindless telly until she was sleepy, and then crawl into bed and oblivion.

But she couldn't put off her dearest friends, they were just too good to her, and she hadn't a decent excuse. She roused herself to get some sort of supper together.

She dug out some raw prawns and a couple of salmon fillets from the freezer and half-prepared a risotto. She would add the last of the stock, the seafood, and some purple sprouting broccoli a few minutes before serving it. Then she made a first course of fried chorizo, garlic and tinned haricot beans.

That would do. She had some nice cheese for afters, and she'd made good brioche that morning. It would be fine.

By seven o'clock she was sitting on the edge of the bath, persuading Toby to do more washing and less playing, and actually looking forward to Amal and Talika's arrival.

As soon as they were through the front door it was obvious that something good had happened. Amal was carrying a bottle of champagne and grinning with suppressed excitement. When Kate took the bottle from his outstretched hand and said, 'What's all this about, then?' Talika's shy smile widened into a happy laugh.

'Guess?!' she exclaimed.

Kate looked from one to the other and knew at once. 'You're pregnant!'

'Yes, yes, yes,' Amal shouted, putting his arms round Talika and dancing round in a clumsy circle.

Talika, laughing, extracted herself and hugged her friend. 'Oh Kate, I'm so happy, so happy. I thought I'd never...'

'When did you find out?'

'Now, just this minute. I didn't want to do a test too early. I was sure, but too-early tests are less reliable, at least I think they are. So I waited. I didn't tell Amal until now. Half an hour ago!'

'How many weeks, do you know?'

'Twelve, I'm sure.'

'And it's a boy, I bet you,' grinned Amal. 'Or maybe a girl.' He looked at both the women, laughing, aware he was talking nonsense. 'Whatever. I can handle...'

Their happiness lifted Kate out of the dumps, and it wasn't until they were eating the Roquefort and crackers that she told them of her financial plight.

'It's so crazy. The bank says I don't have enough of a history of borrowing. But that's just the point. I haven't borrowed before because I'm cautious. I'm the type that pays their credit card when they get the bill.'

'Not much of an earner for the bank, then,' said Amal.

'Not until now, I know, but I'm a good safe bet. Which they admit. Which is why they agreed in the first place.' She went on, telling them of her unsuccessful appeal to her mother, of the urgent need for a new van, which seemed a sensible alternative to sinking ever more money into keeping the old one on the road, the need for a blast chiller before summer made cooling food in a warm kitchen positively dangerous, the tickets for her and Toby for the States.

When she'd done, Talika was all sympathy, looking almost as worried as Kate felt. Amal was silent for a few minutes.

'Actually, Kate,' he said, 'I think the bank could have done you a favour. Manufacturers of big ticket items like blast chillers and transit vans can't be selling too many right now. They'll be desperate for a deal. I bet you could hire both as cheaply, or almost, as buying them off the peg. Anyway, I'll do some research for you.' He picked up his glass and clinked it with Kate's. 'Be happy, Kate. It will all be fine. Nothing to be frightened of.'

He looked so confident and pleased, Kate could not but respond.

'You're right,' she smiled. 'I'm being a wuss.'

'And I'll lend you the money for the plane tickets,' he said.

CHAPTER TEN

Oliver had a mountain of work to do, and no time to think. But all the week after his interview with the Ethics Committee, between meetings and briefings and trying to concentrate on a dozen matters, all international and all urgent, his mind kept gnawing at the question: who was behind these allegations? Who stood to benefit from his discomfiture or his disgrace? It had to be politically motivated.

He knew that both Government and Opposition did some enthusiastic muckraking towards an election. Any mud that stuck was a bonus. That was one of the least lovely things about politics: dog eating dog. But there were no plans to go to the country quite yet. Nowadays, thought Oliver, the spin and slander is no longer confined to the few pre-election weeks.

On Friday, Oliver arrived home at eleven p.m. He went up the stairs two at a time, panting a little. All this eating and drinking and hardly any gym is getting to me, he thought. He was tempted to slow down, walk up the stairs, after all it had been a long week. But he forced himself. Taking stairs two at a time was a sign of youth, and at forty-four he was hanging in there.

The children were in bed and asleep, Mattie with her earphones on. Oliver eased them off and put them on the floor beside the bed. He kissed both girls and then went in search of Ruth. He followed the sound of the radio into their bedroom where she was undressing. From the back she still looked like a boy and she was pulling her jumper off exactly like a boy would – grabbing it by the back of the neck and pulling it over the head.

He watched her, amused and affectionate. Any other woman, he thought, would struggle out of the arms first and then carefully lift the lot over her hairdo. But Ruth had always done it like that. If she had two or three jumpers on after riding in the cold, she would pull them all off together.

He waited for her to emerge, tousle-haired, and turn and see him. He didn't want to give her a fright.

'Hello. You're back. I hope you've eaten.'

'I have, don't worry.'

She wriggled out of her shirt, and then sat on the edge of her bed to yank off her socks, then her jodhpurs.

Right, thought Oliver, no welcoming hugs then. He went over to her, kissed the top of her head and said, 'I'm going to have a whisky. Will you join me? I need to talk to you about something.'

When she came down the stairs she was wearing her old dressing gown and slippers and her face was shiny from cream; her hair was scraped back in one of those Alice bands with teeth. He hated those bands, they dug into her hair to expose small triangles of scalp. It was not pretty.

Oh hell, he thought, I had a moment of feeling really close to her up there, but within minutes we are back to our just-cordial working relationship.

'So, what's up?'

He handed her a glass. 'Darling, something really irritating has come up. Do you remember, in the Yemen, the necklace the president put round your neck at dinner?'

'I remember him doing it. Yes. Why?'

'Because it turns out it's worth a fortune and we should have declared it, and handed it in to bump up the coffers of the state. I have no idea what we did with it. Have you?'

Ruth looked steadily at him, absorbing the information.

'You're in trouble, aren't you?'

'I could be. Depends if you've sold it for fifty pence in aid of the Pony Trust.' He had meant her to smile but she frowned. 'But on the other hand, if you . . .'

'I haven't sold it. It must be somewhere. If I can find it, will that take the heat off you?'

'Sure. We just give it back, explain that we thought it tourist tat. Game over.'

She sipped her drink, thinking. 'How did this come up? Who's behind the witch hunt?'

Oliver shook his head. 'No idea, darling. Could be the press, they're always ferreting for juicy bits of garbage. But they'd have published rather than shop me. Someone must have known about the necklace, and then established its worth with the president's office.'

'Someone in the Yemeni government? Isn't that a bit far fetched?'

'It's possible. When we were there, relations with Yemen were very cordial, but now they are not. And the president will have enemies within, extremists who want a more radical Muslim regime. I suspect this is more about embarrassing the regime for giving away national treasure to a Western country than about our failing to hand it in.'

'Politics looks the same the world over, doesn't it?' Ruth said, shaking her head. 'But who told you about it? How did it come up?'

'God knows. I had a call from the Ethics Committee. Summoned to answer for myself. Rather unpleasant really.'

'When was this?'

'Monday. I saw them on Tuesday. Told them I remembered the necklace but thought it was junk.'

'Why didn't you tell me about this before?' Her voice was steady, but Oliver knew at once she was put out.

'I didn't want—'

'You didn't want to worry me! God, Oliver, why do you treat me as a child? I'm in this too, much as I'd prefer to stay out of the political sewer.'

'Darling, come on. That's a bit strong. Political sewer!'

She stood up and put her glass down with more energy than it needed. 'Maybe. But if this gets into the press I will get it more than you – Cabinet Minister's wife accepts jewels from Arab president. Great. Thanks a lot.' She started to walk away, then turned. 'And anyway, why didn't you hand it in? You know the rules.'

Oliver sat back in his chair and closed his eyes briefly. Then he stood up and drained his glass. 'Ruth, I do not need this. I'm going to bed.' His voice was leaden.

Oliver took a discreet step back but the lank-haired woman promptly stepped close again, face up and head thrust forward. Back to square one. Why were these youngish females so damned earnest? You would think they had invented the Labour party. And why did this one have to stand so close? Her ill-cut hair hung in strands round a make-up-free face and lay on the collar of an oversized trouser suit. She was, he was fairly sure, in the House of Lords and a junior minister of something but he wasn't sure what. He had been told but hadn't concentrated enough for the information to stick. Maybe something to do with Overseas Development? She was banging on about India.

'But Oliver, if the Uttar Pradesh feeding scheme is relying on imported non-recyclable plastic it *should* be a concern of the

Foreign Office. All departments are signed up to the Low Carbon and Sustainability Inter-departmental Initiative, aren't we?'

'Yes, of course. But unless it's directly our responsibility, and I don't think it is, I really don't see—'

'That is precisely why the public thinks we're so useless – always disclaiming responsibility and passing the buck.'

Oliver edged back again, turning his head, looking for a way out. For a split second he caught Sean's eye, and his ever-watchful PPS got the message. He was fractionally taller than Oliver, the perfect height for discreet whispering, but he knew when to pretend to be discreet and yet be obvious. He came up close. 'Foreign Secretary,' he said, 'I wonder if you could have a word with . . .' He ducked his head closer to Oliver's ear and whispered so that no one else could hear 'the minister of rhubarb, rhubarb, rhubarb'. He reached for Oliver's empty glass as Oliver said, 'I do apologise,' to the woman. Sean put his arm out to direct Oliver through the crowd and to safety.

'Thanks, Sean,' said Oliver, 'that was smoothly done. Who is that ghastly woman?'

'Baroness Framer, junior minister in Defra. Ennobled in Tony's first onslaught on the Lords. Used to be in probation services. Now in charge of landfill sites, greening the construction industry, and Commonwealth environment matters.'

'What a horrible portfolio. But I can't say I care. Bloody woman harangued me non-stop. Who needs an opposition with fellow ministers like that?'

Oliver was tempted to leave the reception. It was being held in Admiralty House and was intended to improve relations between the top brass in government, especially now that they were all battling with the fall-out from the credit crunch and banking collapse. The only good thing about it, thought Oliver, was the food.

He looked around, noting that half the cabinet had not bothered to attend or had already scarpered. The PM had put in a
ten-minute appearance, and left with excuses about an early
start for the US in the morning.

But some instinct told Oliver to stick it out. The undeclared
gifts affair would probably break this week – Ruth had not been
able to find the necklace – and he was going to need all the
friends he could muster. Maybe he should have been nicer to
Lady Framer. It would be just his luck if she sat on the Commons
Ethics Committee or the Nolan Committee or some such. He
must check out the membership and start a discreet back-me
campaign.

Oliver was hungry. The necklace affair had made thinking
about anything else difficult, and today he had cancelled a
lunch to talk to his personal lawyer. Helen had ordered some
coffee and sandwiches, which were inedible.

He stopped a waitress who was passing with a tray of mixed
canapés.

'Could you just stand there while I have my lunch and supper?'
he said, popping two warm cheese tartlets into his mouth in
rapid succession.

She was very pretty and smiled brightly but did not understand a word. Polish or Russian, he thought. 'Ya ochen golodeyn,'
he said.

'Ah,' she said, 'you speak Russian! I from Belarus. Student.'

Oliver told her, in Russian, to keep him supplied with canapés,
and she laughed with pleasure at the attention. She said she'd
keep coming back.

He had a useful conversation with a couple of colleagues
from the Commonwealth desk and then the student from
Belarus was back. He took a little block of hollowed out
cucumber filled with crayfish mayonnaise and put it whole into

his mouth. He smiled at her. 'Delicious,' he said in Russian. Then he turned to Sean.

'Sean, who do you think the caterer is? This is a step up from the usual, don't you think?'

Sean looked at him blankly. 'I've no idea.'

'I bet you it's Kate McKinnon.'

'You like her, don't you?'

'Yes. She's good. And I trust her.'

'Trust her?'

'Well, you can leave menus to her and she won't come up with something ridiculous, like bacon-and-egg ice cream or blotches of sauce splashed about the plate, or calling strips of leek a tagliatelli. And she can cook, which makes a change for official functions.'

Sean looked slightly bewildered. 'You seem to know a lot about food, Sir.'

'I know the difference between good food and pretentious nonsense, yes.'

Oliver liked his PPS and would rather chat to him than most of the civil servants, ministers and quango bosses in the room, but duty prevailed and he launched himself back into the throng, giving Baroness Framer a wide berth. As he worked the room he conscientiously, and quite enjoyably, discussed the Congo, the latest revelations about long-dead spies disclosed under the thirty-year rule, a possible cap on MPs' expenses, and, inevitably, the economy.

After three, or maybe four, glasses of wine and a good few more exquisite canapés and some grilled asparagus rolled in grated parmesan, he was certain the cook in the kitchen must be Kate.

The crowd was thinning and he could decently leave. But he said to Sean, 'It would be nice to thank Kate. I usually pop into the kitchen and say a word.' Actually, he thought, more than a word, she's a lot more interesting to talk to than half my colleagues. 'But this isn't my show and I've no idea where the kitchen is, or even if there is one. Could you just do a recce and see if the caterer *is* Kate? And if she's back there somewhere with her troops?'

She was, and Sean came back and ushered his boss into a dining or meeting room, obviously commandeered as a temporary kitchen. The room was noisy with waiters dropping empty silver flats into heavy plastic crates and stacking dirty glasses into compartmented boxes. Kate was counting empty wine bottles.

'Hello, Kate, I knew it would be you. No one else does such delicious food.'

'Thank you! I wondered if you would be here. It seems the world and his wife are.'

'Well, yes, except no wives. Just the servants of the people.' He turned to Sean. 'You know my PPS, Sean?'

Sean and Kate smiled politely at each other. Sean said to Oliver, 'Will you be going back to the office or to Lambeth, Sir?'

'I'm not sure, but I'll walk. I'm getting fat and flabby. All this good food from, what's your company called? No Nonsense?'

'Nothing Fancy.'

He laughed. 'And you don't call rare duck breast tartlets with pomegranate fancy? I call it fancy and completely delicious.'

Kate dropped him a mock curtsey and said, 'Thank'ee kindly, Squire.'

Oliver turned to Sean. 'I think we are just about done here, Sean. Thank you, as always. Your mastery of who's who among junior ministers in obscure departments is second to none.'

'It's a pleasure, Sir. Shall I tell Debbie you won't be needing the car any more?'

'Please. And that I'm sorry to have kept her so long. I should have told her I would walk.'

'I think she's glad of the overtime.'

And, thought Oliver, I have just told everyone in the department not to waste taxpayer's hard-earned money. Oh dear.

When Sean had gone he said to Kate, 'This isn't my party tonight, as you know, so I can hardly offer you a glass of someone else's champagne, can I?'

She grinned at him. 'Can't you? I thought you guys were a law unto yourselves.' I wish, thought Oliver, his chest tightening at the thought of that wretched necklace.

She said, 'It's quieter in the next room. I'll bring a bottle. Fizz? Red? White?'

'Red.' Oliver walked through the door to what was obviously the outer office of the one used for the caterers. It had a door to the corridor outside. Good, he could escape without going through the reception room and being buttonholed by tipsy stragglers.

Suddenly he felt dog tired. He sat in a chair, put his elbows on the table and his head in his hands. I'm not quite sober, he thought. I should get up now and go home or I will regret it in the morning.

But he didn't move. It was pleasant sitting here, alone, without Sean minding him like a guide dog, without anyone wanting instructions or advice or to bend his ear. When Kate appeared with an open bottle of Rioja and two glasses, he looked up brightly and said, 'I thought you'd forgotten me.'

'Sorry, but everyone was ready to leave and I needed to finish counting the empties.'

'Why on earth do you do that?'

'So I know none of the booze has been nicked. If the empties and the full bottles equal the order, I don't have to check the waiting staffs' bags, which I hate doing. They know they can't go until the tally is done. Also, I can charge the client for the right number of bottles. Some savvy hosts check them with me.'

'Good Lord. I just assume you are an honest lot.'

'Well, I hope we are all straight, but we use a lot of agency staff and some of them have been on the bar circuit long enough to get wise to a million dodges. But knowing we always check probably keeps them honest.'

She poured them each a glass and handed one to Oliver. 'Mind you,' she said, 'the Foreign Office has its own cellar, so on your jobs the booze is yours, not mine, and it's Dennis's job to do the tally. I have nothing to do with it, I'm glad to say. Losing some of your top wines would bankrupt me!'

It was good sitting in this empty room, chatting to Kate. She looked as fresh as a daisy, though she must have been hard at it all day preparing for this party, then supervising it and being there to the end. She was dressed in chef's whites.

'Why don't you give your waitresses aprons with your logo on them? Like that?' Oliver asked, pointing to the crossed wooden spoon and cook's knife embroidered over Nothing Fancy on her pocket. It would advertise your wares.'

'I'd love to, and I do if I can. But most government departments, including yours by the way, frown on it. They want to give the impression that they do their own catering. Or maybe they just don't like advertising. Anyway, it's a no-no.'

They talked about Toby and his troubles at Kew, and about Mattie and Andrea, and then Kate stood up and said, 'I'd better get going. I have to start again at some horrible hour.'

Oliver looked at his watch. 'Good God, it's nearly eleven. I had meant to go back to the office, but I'm just too tired. So it will be an early start for me too.' He stood up and said, 'It's always good talking to you. I hope I've not made you too late. You don't have to drive a van back and unpack it or something nasty, do you?'

Kate shook her head. 'Not tonight. Amal left with it an hour ago. It will be unloaded and swept out and parked in my front drive by now.'

'So how are you getting home? Not by tube at this time of night? It's not safe.'

She smiled. 'And how would you know that, Secretary of State?' she asked. 'When was the last time you travelled by tube?'

'*Touché*,' he replied.

They walked downstairs together, and collected Kate's jacket from the coat rack, now empty except for hundreds of hangers.

'Don't you have a coat?' she asked.

'No, I walked across the river this morning in perfect spring sunshine, but April being April, it's now raining, or has been.'

Kate shuffled into her jacket.

'Seriously, Kate, how are you going home? I could flag you down a taxi.'

'I've a car outside. I hire one for big jobs. But you? I imagine you have a Daimler with a flag on the bonnet and a driver in uniform with a peaked cap.'

'Hardly. I do have a driver, Debbie, and she drives a pool car, a Jaguar mostly, sometimes a Range Rover or hybrid Toyota. No flag. She doesn't wear a peaked cap either. And what's more she's gone home, so it's Shank's pony.'

They walked to Kate's car, tailed by Jim the detective. The rain began to fall in earnest.

'I'd better run for a taxi. I've no umbrella. What an idiot. Goodbye Kate.' He waved cheerily and walked fast towards St James.

Kate sat for a few minutes checking her emails on her phone, and then set off for home. As she turned into Pall Mall she saw Oliver and Jim standing on the kerb.

She pulled up next to them. 'Can I offer you a lift? I don't think you are going to get a taxi.'

Oliver accepted. He couldn't face the walk down Whitehall, across Parliament Square, over the bridge and into the hinterland of Lambeth in the tipping rain.

Besides, he liked her company. He climbed in next to her and Jim got in the back.

When they drew up outside his house, Kate and Oliver were deep in conversation, but Jim got out quickly and made to open the passenger door. Oliver rolled down the window. 'Give us a few minutes, will you, Jim?'

'I'll leave you now, Minister, if I may. I see your security has arrived.' He nodded towards the policeman on the Stapler doorstep.

Kate and Oliver continued their conversation and Kate turned the engine off. They were talking about the MP's life, living away from the family in the week, weekends in the constituency. He told her of his daughters' obsession with ponies, which he found charming but inexplicable, and of Ruth's dislike of London and the political party circuit.

'It's an odd life,' he said. 'I can understand Ruth's charge that the Westminster village is immoral, unreal, obsessed with its own importance and with political manoeuvring.'

'It must be tough being a cabinet minister. So few people can behave normally with you.'

Oliver frowned. 'Don't you behave normally with me?'

'No, I don't. Or not usually, though at Lancaster House I guess I did, if losing one's temper and being so rude is normal.'

'You were quite right. I deserved it.'

'I'm glad I'm forgiven. But no, I don't behave entirely normally with you. I'd like to, but I can't. With anyone else, for example, I would ask, What are you up to at work? What's new? What's exciting? Tell me the gossip, but of course I can't. You might be dealing with state secrets or something.'

He was silent for a second or two, and then said slowly, 'Well, the answer to that question is that I'm not effectively dealing very well with anything right now because of an idiotic tangle, can you believe it, about a necklace.'

'A necklace?'

And then he told her the whole story as if it was an amusing anecdote about him being so crass he hadn't twigged that a president would not give street-market presents and that neither he nor Ruth could tell a two-thousand-year-old piece from one made in the Philippines yesterday. 'And the joke is that Ruth has never worn the necklace and hasn't a clue where it is. At least she didn't give it to the charity shop! So there's hope yet.'

He sensed that Kate saw through his jocularity and guessed just how concerned he was, and what the consequences could be. Her face was troubled. 'Oh, poor Oliver, and poor Ruth. You must both be worried sick. If you can't find it, the Tory press could try to hound you out, couldn't they?'

Oliver confessed that, yes, he was anxious, but he didn't think Ruth was. She was irritated with him for not obeying the rules and getting them into a potentially embarrassing mess, but she wasn't concerned for his political career.

'The truth is,' he said, 'I don't think Ruth believes in politics any more. I think she feels that however hard politicians try not to, they are corrupted by the power and the glamour, and that politics achieves very little. She sometimes says that business and charities achieve more than the state ever can, because the short-term need for popularity and votes prevents politicians ever doing the right thing. She's half right, I guess.'

'She's half wrong too,' Kate said.

Oliver shrugged, leant over to give Kate a quick kiss on the cheek, and opened the car door.

Later, lying in bed and replaying the conversation they had had, Oliver felt happier than he had for days. He did enjoy Kate's company, she was sympathetic and funny. Still, he was pleased with himself for resisting the temptation to invite her in for a nightcap. Cabinet ministers needed to keep their distance.

But in the morning he woke uneasy. He knew that he had had too much to drink, that he had been indiscreet, and maybe, he thought, even disloyal to Ruth. He hadn't meant to tell Kate about the necklace, but she was so easy to talk to.

God, he thought, what's the matter with me? I'm angry with Ruth for her lack of sympathy and solidarity, and then I go and blab our troubles to the cook. How solid and loyal is that?

CHAPTER ELEVEN

When Oliver leant over to kiss Kate goodbye, his cheek briefly brushed hers and she felt the quick peck of his lips. At once she felt her heart somersault. The blood rushed to her face so hotly she thought he must feel it. He climbed out, then ducked his head in.

'Thanks for the lift. And more than that, thanks for listening, Kate. You are good at it.'

Kate could not breathe, never mind speak. She could still smell his aftershave and feel the slight rasp of a day's beard. And feel his breath. It was as if suddenly all her senses and nerves were tuned to him and him alone. He closed the door quietly, and she watched him walk up the front step, exchange a few words with the copper, put in the key, open the door, then turn to give her a last quick wave before he went in and closed it.

Immediately she felt the loss of him. She wanted him to come back and kiss her again. And again. She fumbled with the car key, struggling to make the car move quickly so that if he looked out of the window he would not see her sitting there like a love-sick idiot.

Oh God, she thought as she swung out. Maybe I am a love-sick idiot.

She drove twenty-five yards to the end of the street and turned the corner. Then she stopped, turned off the engine and put her head down on the steering wheel, her heart thumping, trying to think.

She had so wanted to put a hand up to his cheek when he'd said Ruth did not care about his career. She'd wanted to pull his head down to her breast and let that thick grey hair slip through her stroking fingers. And then thoughts of his face in her bosom, his arms reaching round her back, were too much for her and she sat up abruptly, saying aloud, "Don't be such a bloody fool. He's married. Happily married."

She turned the car and headed back over the river (she hadn't told Oliver that Lambeth was seriously out of her way). She drove slowly, admonishing herself for her stupidity, for lusting after a man who was not hers and not available and anyway unobtainable. He was a politician, for God's sake, and a high-ranking cabinet minister. He was out of her reach for a dozen good reasons.

And yet, and yet . . . She loved the easy way he treated her. And the way he listened to her views, even on things she knew little about, like the massacre in the Congo or the new president of the US. And he was just so good looking: pale grey hair thick and shiny, face slightly tanned, eyes dark and deep. How had she managed to be so unaffected until now?

She knew the answer to that. It was because he'd come so close. She'd breathed him in. He'd added sex to the friendship mix and it was intoxicating. But she knew he had not meant to. He'd felt nothing, she was sure. He had not lingered for a minute over that goodbye kiss. He'd dutifully given it, as he would to any woman who had given him a lift. He'd told her some personal stuff because he'd had one or two glasses too many, and he would probably regret it tomorrow and be frosty to her.

She could not bear that. She wanted that closeness to go on

for ever. She longed to know everything about him: his child-hood, his ambitions, his getting into politics, the details of his marriage. It crossed her mind, of course it did, that she might be in love with him. Which was ridiculous of course. She'd had a couple of glasses too, and she was starved of male company, of proper conversation, of the dream of love. Fatal attraction, that's what it was. And it was dangerous, dangerous.

Kate had had no idea that a peck on the cheek could so undo her. It astonished her. She, who was such a control freak, so organised, so sensible. As soon as she'd thought it she knew it was true, and yet it surprised her. She said it to herself with a kind of wonderment. I'm lusting after the Foreign Secretary, that's what.

Amal had teased her, suggesting she fancied him, and at the time she hadn't. She'd been blind as well as stupid.

But it would not wash. Going round the Hammersmith round-about she sat up straight and shook her head vigorously, she had to be made of stronger stuff than this, surely? Your trouble, she told herself, is that you are a desiccated single female, with no love and no sex in your life. So you are clutching at straws. It's just because he is handsome, intelligent and nice to you. And he's there: who else is there around to desire?

She stepped on the accelerator and drove fast up Hammersmith Road, continuing her internal rant. You are infat-uated with a dishy guy who exudes power and fame, two great aphrodisiacs. Oliver has both and you are in the grip of an over-heated fantasy. Get real, Kate McKinnon.

A week later, on the Saturday afternoon when Toby was with Sanjay and Talika, she and Amal did the monthly Cash and Carry trip. This time they went in Kate's shiny new transit van, just delivered. Amal had been right: she'd managed to do a never-never deal which meant she'd hire it for two years, then buy it outright at a knock-down price.

They used the Anglo-Indian Emporium in Neasden, not because it was the cheapest or the nearest, but because it belonged to Amal's uncle and had a good stock of what they both needed: Indian spices and pastes and other specialities for the Taj Amal, and a good gourmet selection for the sort of stylish, mostly Western, food that Nothing Fancy cooked.

Kate enjoyed the Cash and Carry. She had to discipline herself to stick to her buying list and not be tempted by the mounds of cheap but good quality glass cloths, multipacks of discounted pepper grinders, and glass lily vases on sale at half price.

Amal and she took separate flatbed trolleys to prevent a muddle paying the bill and a muddle unloading. As quickly as she could, Kate stocked up on all the boring stuff: detergent, bleach, kitchen paper, J-cloths, a new bucket and mop, soft brown sugar, plain flour, bread flour, Uncle Ben's rice (scorned by chefs, but undoubtedly the best for caterers because it never stuck together however long you kept it warm) and tea lights.

She stacked all this on her trolley then started on the speciality section. She hunted down Maldon sea salt (expensive but the best: the fine flakes crumbled between the fingers and melted on the tongue with a burst of flavour); apricot jam (expensive smooth variety so she did not have to sieve it to glaze cakes or pastries); balsamic vinegar (she bought a standard brand which she'd boil down to thicken it and concentrate its sweetness); muscovado sugar (the only one with a deep treacly flavour); cape gooseberries in tins (for tartlets and clafoutis), and canned whole white peaches.

Amal arrived, his trolley less loaded than hers. 'I've pushed a drinks trolley through already,' he said. 'I've just got to find some coconut cream. They only seem to have desiccated, milk, or block.'

'The block works OK. You just melt it.'

'Yes, memsahib, so grateful for the advice, ma'am,' he said in an exaggerated Indian accent, bowing, hands together.

Kate cuffed him lightly round the head, 'Shut up, you idiot. I'm right. Just buy the block. Anyway, it's cheaper.'

'Are you done?' he asked.

'No, I've got to get some elderflower cordial. And could you get me tamarind paste while you're over there?'

'Tamarind paste? What do you want it for?'

'I'm going to make Vietnamese sweet and sour soup.'

'Really? Sounds horrible.'

'It's delicious. Clear broth with pineapple and prawns. It's for a hen party. The bride-to-be wants something spicy and healthy and of course stunningly pretty that no one has ever seen before.'

'And is it?'

'Actually it is. I float slices of star-fruit and leaves of coriander in it. Looks lovely.'

They were driving back, fully loaded, by four o'clock. As they were idling at a traffic light, Amal said, 'Kate, you remember I was asking you if our Foreign Secretary fancied you?'

Kate's heart jumped. But she kept her eyes on the road and her voice neutral.

'Yes. I do. And it's rubbish!'

'Well, some people don't think so. I was listening to a couple of Nothing Fancy staff gossiping the other day. I think you need to be careful, Kate. It could damage your standing with Government Hospitality, couldn't it?'

Kate found her palms clammy on the wheel. She said, 'But Amal, this is nonsense. Who said what? Oliver does not fancy me. Of course he doesn't. He's got a wife and kids. And anyway, he's the Foreign Secretary!'

'So? Foreign Secretaries are not normal men, open to the charms of—'

'Amal, just tell me what it is someone said, and who. I will kill—

'OK, OK, it was when we were doing that International Church breakfast in the Methodist Hall, remember? Anyway, the little one, Frankie, I think, said you were having an affair with Oliver Stapler.'

'What!' Kate was shouting now. 'What does Frankie know about it? It's not true. I'll . . .'

Amal put his hand on her thigh and said, 'Calm down, Kate. It doesn't matter if it's true or not, but you need to see the gossip stops, that's all . . . Kate, the light is green. Go.'

Kate drove on. 'What else did he say? Who was he talking to? What did you say? I hope you told them . . .'

'OK, well, here goes. Frankie was talking to Joan and her daughter. They were all polishing glasses. He said, would they like a juicy bit of gossip and that you were having an affair. Joan said bully for you: you worked too hard and you needed someone in your life, or something like that. And then she asked who it was. And Frankie said Oliver Stapler, at which there was a lot of "NO!" and "Really?" and Joan said you certainly liked him, and was about to expand I think, which was when I chipped in. I said they should stop gossiping and get on with the job, and that I had known you for ages and my wife is your best friend and if you were having an affair we'd know about it, etc, etc. I gave them a great lecture about damaging your reputation and they got the message. I hope.'

Kate sat silent at the next traffic light. She shook her head as though to clear it. 'Thanks, Amal. But what should I do?'

'I don't know. You can hardly not meet him. You work for him.'

'He's a good client too. Recommends me to all and sundry. And he's really friendly. He does come into the kitchen for a chat . . .'

Amal's eyebrows went up. 'Does he indeed?'

Kate felt the doubt and accusation and was immediately indignant. 'Why shouldn't he? It's a perfectly innocent thing to do.'

'But an unusual one for a senior cabinet minister,' Amal said coolly. 'Maybe you should tell him of the gossip, and suggest he doesn't.'

Kate answered at once, without thinking, 'Oh I couldn't do that. I couldn't.'

'Why not?'

'I don't know.' Kate's mind was whirling about. She couldn't speak to Oliver about that sort of gossip, he might guess how she felt. And she couldn't bear not to see him. She'd spent most of the last few days hoping he would come and talk to her after next Thursday's dinner party at Lambeth. She'd half decided she'd have her hair cut, and maybe splash her neck with Clarins Eau de Toilette . . .

Oh God what was she doing? Plotting seduction instead of planning escape.

She shook her head. 'It would seem so presumptuous to discuss that sort of thing with a client. Any client, never mind a grandee like him. I can't.'

'Well, you had just better avoid him then, make excuses and scarper. And maybe get Joan to squash any backstairs rumour.'

Kate knew it was good advice. She must try to follow it.

On Thursday she managed to prevent herself getting her hair done, or wearing perfume. But she spent the whole time she was in his kitchen cooking, thinking about him. She took inordinate trouble about everything. They had a plate of Iberian ham with a thin mustard dressing, followed by a risotto with langoustine and scallops, a chicory and pecan nut salad, and Chinese apple fritters for dessert.

The minute the fritters had gone into the dining room, she said to Joan, 'Joan, could you manage the rest for me? I'm sorry to leave early but I'm really tired and have stuff to do. Is that OK?'

Of course Joan agreed, administering motherly homilies about the need for beauty sleep. And yes, of course she'd do the coffee.

Kate carried her boxes out to the car, remembering how Oliver had helped her before, and went back for the rubbish.

'You'll have to just put the coffee grounds into his rubbish for once,' she said. 'I don't suppose he'll even notice. His cleaner will deal with it.'

Kate drove home, pleased with herself for running away, but feeling hollow inside.

Chapter Twelve

Oliver and Sean got to Hampton Court a little early. Oliver wanted to see for himself that all was ready for the Prime Ministers' Conference Dinner. His department was responsible, and it was an event for which they traditionally pulled out all the stops.

His communications people, terrified of the Downing Street Press chief, Terry Taughton, had banged on about the likelihood of journalists adding up the cost of Veuve Clicquot's Grande Dame, 1982 Chateau Latour and the like, and concluding that government ministers were living high on the hog while the rest of the country tightened their belts. But Oliver had insisted on doing the dinner properly or not at all.

'We own most of the wines, after all, bought them years ago comparatively cheaply to lay down,' he said. 'They are perfect for drinking now. And we're not having fireworks or giving the guests goodie bags stuffed with Rolex watches, for God's sake. This is Britain, Terry, not Dubai. Nothing ostentatious, just quietly excellent.'

To Oliver's relief, Terry had given in. If he'd really dug his heels in, the twin objectives – to fly the flag and to flatter the prime ministers of Europe – would have been lost in some mediocre event.

But as it was, Oliver was confident the evening would be a triumph. Hampton Court Palace's Great Hall looked magnificent. The famous hammer-beam roof, the stags' heads peering down from between the wide, leaded glass windows and the famous medieval tapestries, all spelt history, power, riches, class.

Oliver could not help a little buzz of pride on walking through the tables laid with gold damask cloths, gold-rimmed glasses, and huge yellow flowers the size of soup plates (tree peonies, according to Sean) in low vases with trailing ivy snaking between the objects on the table.

He said a few words to the Master of Ceremonies, a toast-master familiar from many a banquet, and to Dennis, who was in charge of the service. They seemed fine Dennis even refrained from disparaging Kate.

'Do you want to say a word to the chefs?' asked Sean.

'Not now. They'll be dashing around trying to get ready. I'll try to pop in afterwards.'

Just then Kate appeared, obviously searching for someone. She spoke to a waiter checking a table, and looked around. She was in pristine whites, wearing no make-up. She looks about fourteen, thought Oliver.

Oliver called her name before she had seen them. 'Kate. Over here.'

Kate moved swiftly through the tables, her stride surprisingly long for her height. She said, 'Good evening, Foreign Secretary. Hello, Sean.' She turned back to Oliver. 'I hope you're looking forward to dinner?' She spoke pleasantly, but formally.

'That rather depends on you, Kate. How are things back there? What's the kitchen like?'

'Well, it's not great, but at least it's a proper kitchen, not the usual temporary affair we have to deal with. We're not allowed open flames in case we set the place on fire, so no gas. But we'll manage. It's a great menu. Lovely produce.'

Kate was being very correct, her expression attentive, but

serious. Somehow he had expected her to be her usual lively self, a little jokey. I expect she's nervous before such a big event, he thought. Poor girl, it must be pretty tense back there.

'We'll leave you to get on, Kate,' he said. 'Good luck.'

'Thank you, Sir,' she said, and walked swiftly away, calling to Dennis. 'Dennis, could we have a word about the soup tureens?'

At dinner, Oliver sat between the astonishingly beautiful and charming wife of the French President, and Angela Merkel, the German Chancellor. He was enjoying himself very much. His briefing on Carla Bruni had of course mentioned her whirlwind romance with Sarkozy and her past as a model, but had not prepared him for her intelligence and charm. And he liked Angela. They all made an effort to stay off European politics and had a merry dinner discussing everything from conceptual art to football.

Oliver was pleased. Of course the food was excellent. He had asked for something British and Kate had produced extraordinarily elegant versions of soup, roast lamb and jelly and custard.

In a moment of quiet when both his neighbours were talking to the men on the other side of them, he looked across at his boss. The PM had come to office only a few years ago with a thick head of brown hair and a square full face, his whole body exuding confidence and a desire to get on with things. But already the deadly mix of economic collapse, the scandal of rigged expenses by MPs, and the continuing horror of Iraq and Afghanistan had taken its toll. He looks, mused Oliver, fifteen years older, his face thinner, hair dulled with grey. As the PM caught his eye and gave him a tired smile, Oliver thought, why do I want his job so badly? It's a killer.

The thought immediately provoked another, and he told himself that if the press exposed his necklace and Limoges china tax-avoidance troubles, he'd be lucky to have a job at all.

Wanting to shift his thoughts, he reached for the menu. As he read it, he remembered giving the dishes a thumbs up, and thought ruefully that since the disaster with the Lancaster House menu, when they'd nearly gone hungry, he had not dared fiddle about with Kate's ideas.

'And what are you smiling about?' asked Madame Bruni-Sarkozy.

'Well, as the host, I should not say this, but I was thinking the cook had done rather a good job.'

'Cook? Is he not a chef?'

'It's a she. Kate McKinnon. And she says she prefers to be called a cook because a chef has to be the boss of a big kitchen and she usually works on her own.'

'How astonishing!'

'Astonishing? Why?'

'I'm impressed you know so much about your cook. I don't even know our chef's name. Or the head gardener's for that matter. I only know the head of security. Oh, and my driver.'

Oliver looked across to the door where waiters came in and out, hoping to see Kate. If he had time, he must go and tell the team just how good the meal had been. She'd be more relaxed now, flushed with triumph, on a sort of happy high, like footballers when they've won a game. It would be good to see her.

When, the other night after his own dinner party, he'd gone into the kitchen as usual, bottle in hand, to congratulate and tip the staff and have a drink with Kate, she'd already left. Her waitress was still there, and he'd pressed a couple of fivers into her hand, saying, 'Kate not here?'

'No, Sir, I'm sorry. She told me to say that she hopes everything was to your satisfaction, and that she had to rush off because she has to be up early for a lunchtime job in the country.'

Oliver had felt a little cheated. Damn it, he enjoyed his ritual drink with Kate. Didn't she?

When the speeches were finally done (he only had to welcome the illustrious guests and introduce the PM who made a mercifully short speech with, unusually, a couple of not too leaden jokes) and coffee had been served, the top table led the walk-out to the Watching Chamber where more drinks were on offer. He went walkabout among his guests, smiling and clapping shoulders, shaking hands and bowing (he could not quite kiss a hand, but he was good at that formal duck of the head).

When the room was almost empty Oliver slipped into the kitchen to find Kate. She was busy wiping down a table and laughing at something one of the other cooks had said. She saw him, and her face immediately sobered. She put down her cloth, wiped her hands on the cloth tucked into the waist of her apron, and came over.

'Congratulations, Kate. That was a triumph.' He took her hand and pressed it warmly. He would have liked to give her a hug to emphasise his pleasure at her pulling off something so impressive but he restrained himself.

'Show me round, Kate, I'd like to meet the team,' he said.

'Of course. Certainly, Sir.'

She called the cooks and porters over.

'This is Jeffrey. He's actually a tour guide, but he moonlights as our driver and porter. He saves us a fortune on the scraping bench.'

Oliver, bemused, pumped Jeffrey's hand.

'The what?'

'If you aren't careful when scraping the plates, the silverware ends up in the garbage,' Jeffrey said.

'And these,' said Kate, 'are my most faithful cooks. Sandra is the pudding queen, she used to work for Raymond Blanc. Tom is meant to be the larder chef, doing starters and canapés, etc, but tonight somehow he was on sauces and veg as well. And this morning he was helping Grace make the rolls. And this is Grace, terrific baker.'

Oliver shook their hands and talked to them all, including the two apprentices from Westminster College. He asked questions, listened to the answers, and genuinely enjoyed it. He was good at small chat, he knew; it was one of the things that made him a successful politician, but he faked interest as often as really felt it.

When he had met them all he pulled his folded menu out of his pocket and consulted it.

'I thought the food was absolutely first class,' he told them. 'It can't be easy in an unfamiliar kitchen and for so many people. But it was perfect. You did us really proud. Thank you.'

There were gratified smiles all round, especially when he went through the dishes, discussing the samphire from Norfolk in the scallop soup, and where in Wales the salt-marsh lamb came from. He asked, 'How do you keep it so beautifully pink for so many people?'

Tom said, 'It's because we slow cook it,' at the same time as one of the apprentice lads said, 'It's the combi-oven. Brilliant piece of kit.' And then the plump baker, Grace, said in a thick Glasgow accent, 'It's because we rest it twenty minutes before we carve it.'

Oliver turned to Kate. 'All three,' said Kate. Oliver noticed with satisfaction that she had actually smiled. She was obviously proud of her team. Maybe, he thought, she was more relaxed now dinner was over.

'And I've never had parsnip fritters,' he said.

'Did you like them?'

'They were absolutely scrumptious. They were a hit with

Madame Sarkozy and with the German Chancellor too. And the elderflower jelly! Sandra, that was amazing. Gives a whole new meaning to jelly and ice-cream.'

He wanted to see how the kitchen worked and was pleased by Kate's obvious pride in her job. She'd looked severe, even frosty, when they'd arrived but she was cheering up. He commented on the orderly way she'd arranged the kitchen and asked, 'Where do you get all this kit? Surely you don't own it?'

'No, certainly not. Most of it, the heavy stuff, belongs to Hampton Court. But the Pacojet – that's the thing that whizzes rock solid ice-cream into a just-made airy texture – and a lot of the trolleys for shifting hired stuff and provisions, are mine . . .'

Oliver feigned interest in Kate's beloved ice cream machine, and in the mobile plate-stacks that allowed a hundred odd plates, all decorated and ready to go, to be stacked in a space that would only take three or four laid side by side.

But Oliver had seen enough now, and would have liked to sit down with Kate for a drink and a chat. He dutifully thanked the porters and then followed Kate back into the dining room to speak to Dennis and the butlers and waiting staff.

'That was excellent, Dennis. Were you happy?'

Of course he wasn't. He didn't exactly toss his head, but he managed, Oliver thought, to convey huge frustration, sacrifice on his part, and resigned tolerance about lesser mortals, all with a lift of an eyebrow and pursed lips. Really, the man should have been an actor.

'Shall I say we coped, Foreign Secretary, under difficult circumstances. I am glad you were satisfied. The Prime Minister conveyed his congratulations, I am happy to report.'

'But you have a problem with our performance?' Kate's head had come up, she'd turned squarely to Dennis, but her voice was neutral.

Damn, thought Oliver, now we'll be treated to the story of Dennis saving the day in the face of everyone else's incompetence. Sean, at his elbow, must have sensed his irritation.

'If there were any problems,' his PPS said briskly, 'I am sure you know the proper channels. Julian Hobhouse will let us know if the department can help in any way, but I saw him earlier, and he was delighted with the whole event.'

Mercifully, Kate's telephone rang and she took it from her apron pocket and looked at the screen.

'Would you forgive me?' she said, turning away to take the call.

Good, thought Oliver, as he once more thanked the waiting team, dismissed them with a firm thank you, and then turned back towards Kate, obviously trying to get a taxi, and failing.

'Forty minutes? But I need it straight away. No, that's too long. But thank you.' She put the mobile in her pocket and turned back to Oliver.

'Problem?' he asked.

'No. I'm fine.'

'I'll give you a lift.' Oliver found he was smiling. It would be nice to share the journey back to London with Kate.

'No, thank you.' She said it almost sharply. Really, what was the matter with the woman? He was not going to eat her.

'How did you come?' he asked. 'Didn't you bring your van?'

'I've got a new one now. A shiny new transit van. And yes, I came down in it, but one of the porters will be taking it home to Surbiton. He has to unload hired stuff nearby in the morning. But I'll be fine. One of the others will give me a lift.'

'Kate, don't be an idiot. I've got a driver and an empty car. Sean came down independently so there's room for you – and another one if they don't mind cuddling up with my detective.'

She shook her head, her curls bouncing with the vigour of the shake. 'No, honestly, Oliver, I'm OK.'

'Kate, I have an empty car. I told you.'

She looked round, as though trapped. 'But I don't want to hold you up. I'm not ready yet.'

'How long will you be?'

Oliver could see she was in two minds. 'Can you give me a second just to check where we've got to?' she said. 'I really don't think I can leave soon.'

Oliver was puzzled, and marginally annoyed. Kate was making a simple offer into a big deal. 'Kate, I just heard you saying to the taxi service you wanted a cab straight away.'

Kate didn't answer that, just frowned. 'I'll be back in a minute,' she said. 'I'll just see if there are any other stranded cooks or porters who would like a ride in a government limo. And I must fetch my knife box. I don't trust anyone with that.' She went back to the kitchen. Oliver thought, I bloody hope she doesn't round up any stray bods. I've done my stuff with the cooks. And the porters. I've been on parade all evening. It's enough.

Dennis appeared with Oliver's briefcase and raincoat. 'The car is outside now, Sir,' he said.

'Ah, thank you,' replied Oliver, taking the mac and case. 'I'm just waiting to see if Kate wants a lift. She's disappeared into the back somewhere. Do you think you could see if she's coming?'

Dennis face was a picture of distaste. Oh dear, thought Oliver, it's obviously well beneath his dignity to carry messages to a cook. Oliver could not resist baiting him a little. 'Dennis,' he said, 'is something wrong? You look as though you're chewing a lime.'

Dennis shook his head. 'No, Minister, nothing.'

'Well, in that case I'm sure you will not mind fetching Kate. There's a good chap.'

Dennis's struggle between outrage at this affront to his dignity and an equal desire to please a cabinet minister was wonderful to watch, but at that moment Kate reappeared. She had changed out of her chef's whites and was wearing a long coat over a short black skirt, her duffel bag over her shoulder and her knife box – actually it looked like a builder's tool box – in one hand.

'Are you sure?' she asked. 'One of the cooks says she can take me to Hammersmith. I can get a cab from there, easy.'

'Kate, it will be a pleasure. I owe you a lift home anyway. You drove me home after that Admiralty House drinks party, remember?'

Dennis wanted to carry Oliver's things to the car, but Oliver was suddenly sick and tired of the man. It was impossible to fault him on the job, the dinner had gone off like clockwork. But Dennis had his habitual bad-smell-under-his-nose expression, and Oliver gave him a brisk, 'Goodnight, Dennis and once again, many thanks.' Then walked fast to the car with Kate, his detective hurrying behind.

Chapter Thirteen

Kate, elated by the success of the dinner and thrilled by Oliver's interest in the kitchen, could not maintain the cool exterior she had been determined to arm herself with. With a real sense of relief, like taking off uncomfortable shoes, she leant back in the soft upholstery of the Jaguar, and smiled.

She was at first embarrassed by the presence of the detective and driver in the front. And she had a problem keeping her voice normal. It might tremble, she feared, or go breathy. The other problem was controlling her thoughts: she longed for Oliver to touch her. Even a tiny touch, a quick hand on her shoulder, a finger on her wrist.

Oliver chatted to his driver and detective – Debbie and Jim they were called – with a friendly remark to Debbie about her children and asking Jim to put a Schubert CD on the player, and then turned to Kate and talked of this and that, mostly the event tonight.

When he wasn't looking at her, Kate watched Oliver's profile, alternately lit and cast into shadow as the streetlights came and went. She was acutely conscious of his closeness, of the smell of the car leather, the cool May air from her half-open window.

Kate relaxed, *Die Winterreise* working its reliable magic through expensive speakers. She wanted to stay just as she was – well, maybe with his hand on her neck – for ever.

But too soon they were at Ealing Broadway, and for the first time in her life she was tempted to leave Toby sleeping at Talika's. She didn't want to explain to Oliver that she would now carry the sleeping, and increasingly heavy, child down the long block from the restaurant to home. Why not let Oliver take her to her house? She could collect Toby in the morning. Or when Oliver had gone home?

Once more she picked up the Kate vs Kate argument: Why wouldn't he go home at once? What was she hoping? Surely not for a one-night stand? He'd just drop her at the door and drive on. And quite right too. It's what she wanted.

They turned into the High Street leading to the old estate.

'Oliver, this will sound a bit mad to you,' Kate said, 'but I have to collect Toby from my friend Talika's, so can you drop me outside the Taj Amal Indian restaurant? On the right, past the lights.'

Oliver looked at her. 'It's gone midnight. Won't he be asleep?'

'Sure he will, but he's so used to me picking him up, he hardly wakes.'

'OK.' Oliver sounded hesitant, but he drew up outside the restaurant and Kate took her keys from her bag. 'I'll help you.'

'No. Please, Oliver, I don't want you to. He won't recognise you and he'll wake up. And honestly, getting him into the car and out again will be more trouble than carrying him. Truly. Please, just leave me here.'

In truth she was more anxious at the prospect of waking Amal or Talika and having to explain Oliver's presence to them.

He brushed her cheek in a quick kiss and Kate scrambled out of the car, anxious to get her goodbyes over with. She nodded and said a quick goodnight to the detective and driver in the front and let herself into Amal's flat. She shut the door and climbed the stairs.

She managed to carry Toby downstairs without waking him,

but it was a struggle, and certainly dangerous. Amal often carried Toby for her, saying she'd fall down the narrow stairs and break both their necks. When she got to the bottom she had to set him, grumbling on the stairs to free her hands to open the door. Then, holding the door open with her bottom, she reached in, picked up Toby, who immediately shut his eyes again and nestled into her shoulder. She sidled out of the door, letting the door lock behind her. He was really heavy now. This was getting ridiculous: she would have to get a babysitter so he could stay at home, or leave him all night with Talika.

'Kate, give him to me.' Oliver was suddenly there, his arms outstretched.

'But . . . No . . . Your car, you can't leave it . . .'

'It's fine. Debbie's in it.'

'But where's your detective? What will he think?'

'Don't worry about him. Here, give me Toby.' Somehow he put his arms under Toby's armpits and lifted him to his chest, hoisting him up to the same position, head on shoulder, that Kate had held him. Toby barely stirred.

They walked past the shops and down the street in silence, the detective following at a discreet distance.

Oliver's not speaking, she thought, because he thinks it will wake Toby. But I'm not speaking because I can't. Heart banging too much.

Kate opened her front door and Oliver carried in the sleeping child.

'Where to now?' he said.

'Upstairs, I'll show you.' Better be clear, she thought, and added, 'We share the bedroom.'

She led the way upstairs and opened the door to their bedroom. Thank God it's tidy, she thought. No knickers on the floor or anything shaming. She walked round to Toby's side of the bed, pushed off a pile of soft toys and pulled back the duvet. Oliver lowered the boy into the bed, taking care to ease him down gently, and Kate pulled up the covers.

They both stood up together and Oliver smiled at her. 'There, mission accomplished. One sleeping boy delivered safely.'

Then downstairs, another peck on the cheek, and he was gone. She watched him walk away down the street, his detective padding after him like a faithful hound.

That's two goodbye kisses tonight, she thought. How different from that other time, in her van, when Oliver's kiss had come with the smell of aftershave and the jolt of lust. That time she'd felt the shock of it run down her body, inflame her face, stop her heart. This time the lust was still there, but overshadowed by anxiety. Anxiety about waiters' gossip, about his driving out of his way, collecting Toby from above an Indian restaurant, of him seeing her house. Of what he might think of her sharing a bed with her son.

Kate was walking Toby to school when her mobile rang. She had to let go of the boy's hand to rummage in her handbag, and he bounced along ahead of her as she checked the display. No name came up and she didn't recognise the number so she cancelled the call. She didn't want Toby crossing the street without her and whoever it was would call again if it was important.

'Wait, Toby,' she called. He stopped obediently and transferred his attention to the contents of a litter bin on the kerb.

'Look, Mum, someone's thrown away a whole packet of Smarties.' He looked up at her, his face full of wonder and excitement. 'Can I have them?' He reached into the bin, but it was too deep.

'No, darling.' Disappointment flooded his face, instantly

replacing the childish triumph. Kate hated to see it, and put an arm around him.

'Sweetheart . . . no, it's dirty . . .'

But he wrenched free. 'It's not dirty. You're always saying not to waste things. That's a waste isn't it?'

'C'mon, Toby. We'll be late.' She took his hand and he walked along, sulky now, kicking at things: the railings, a crumpled Coke can. How quickly his moods change, she thought. It's because I spoil him. He needs a baby brother or sister, that's what.

But Kate knew it was she who wanted another child, not Toby. Ever since Talika had announced her pregnancy, Kate had had to hide her envy. In truth, I want the whole thing, she thought: a man, a husband, someone to share family life with. I certainly don't want another child on my own. And then, her mental will crumbling, she gave in and inwardly cried, I want someone like Oliver. Or maybe even Oliver.

She shook her head. Forget it. Just forget it. You cannot have him. Out of bounds. Not yours. Happily married to someone else.

But the ache was there. It assailed her constantly. She'd be doing something mundane like defrosting the freezer or checking her emails and suddenly the thought of him would hit her like a blast. It would make her gut contract, followed by a dull ache in the middle of her chest. Heartache.

By the time they got to school, Toby had forgotten the Smarties and was so eager to run and join Sanjay that she had to call him back for his lunchbox and a kiss.

Her phone rang again as she watched him and Sanjay run off and join a pack of boys who then ran together round the playground, shouting and laughing for no good reason. She waved, but Toby had forgotten her.

She pressed the green button, 'Hello.'

'Kate McKinnon?'

'Yes. Who is this?' She was still smiling at the boys, thinking how blissfully carefree a six-year-old could be.

'You sound happy!'

'Do I? Look, do I know you?'

'As if you are laughing.'

'Well, I'm watching my son running round the playground. Please, who am I speaking to?'

'I'm sorry. Of course. My name is Jarvis Stanley. I write for the *Evening Standard*. I just wanted to check a story with you, if that's OK?'

Kate's mind darted about. He sounded really nice. Probably wanted some gossip about the London Fashion Show party, for which she'd made wonderful tapas but the models and glitterati had mostly been too stoned to notice. She wouldn't give anything away, of course, she guarded her clients' indiscretions like a lawyer. Besides, she avoided personal publicity: it might be good for business but there was always the chance that if ever Toby's dad took it into his head to find his son, it would help him.

'How did you get my mobile number?' she asked.

'Oh, I'm so sorry.' He sounded genuinely worried. 'It was a bit of a run around, I admit, but I got it from a catering agency in the end. I didn't know it was private.'

'What's the story?' she said, frowning.

'Well, I'm sorry to be so blunt. But you see, we've had a tip-off that you and the Foreign Secretary, Oliver Stapler, are having a love affair. And we don't want to print if—'

'What! That's not true. It's nonsense!' Kate's mind darted about like a trapped ferret. This was what Amal had warned her about. How quickly a bit of kitchen gossip spread. She should have taken his advice, killed the rumour.

'It's not true?'

Kate felt the anxiety mount. 'No, it is not!' She looked round for somewhere more private than the public street to have this conversation. There was a low wall a little ahead. She could sit on that. He was talking again,

'So there is no truth in the allegation?'

'None whatever. And who told you that anyway?'

'I'm so sorry, Kate, I'd tell you if I could. But we're not allowed to reveal our sources, I'm sure you understand.'

Kate was trying to remain calm. 'What did you say your name was?'

'Jarvis Stanley.'

Kate watched people go by. She avoided the eyes of mothers she knew from the school gates. 'And which paper do you write for?'

'I'm the editor of Londoner's Diary, in the *Evening Standard*.'

'Well, Mr Stanley, I hope you believe me when I tell you that there is absolutely no truth whatsoever in your story. Someone is having you on, or has got it in for me. Or, more likely, for Oliver.'

'Oliver? You call him Oliver? So you do know him?'

'Certainly I know him. He's a client. I cook for him.' Kate's voice was robust, but she felt she had fallen into a trap. Why had she not referred to him as the Foreign Secretary or the Secretary of State or just plain Oliver Stapler?

'Kate . . .'

'I notice you call me Kate. And we have never even met, much less jumped into bed together!'

'Oops, I am sorry. I'll call you Miss McKinnon.'

'That's not the point!' Kate felt she was flailing about, like a fish on the end of a line. Innocent, but powerless.

And then, for the first time, she thought of the consequences for Oliver. No one was interested in an obscure cook, but the man tipped as the next prime minister? A story, even a false one, could ruin him.

'Are you dropping this story? I've told you it isn't true.' Her voice did not carry authority, it came out somewhere between a whine and a plea.

There was a pause before he spoke. 'Well. I can promise you that we will not claim you are having an affair. But, Kate, you should know that your link with Oliver Stapler is the talk of the press, and I can't say that all my colleagues are as scrupulous about checking stuff as we are. Why don't we meet and you can set the record straight? I promise I will print exactly what you say.'

'But there's nothing to say. We're not having an affair. Oliver Stapler is a happily married man. I'm his caterer. That's it.'

'So you did not leave the Hampton Court party together then?'

'I . . . I . . .' Oh my God, thought Kate, this could look really bad. Better not say any more. I must ask Oliver . . .

'No comment,' she said, and cut the call with a vicious jab of her thumb.

As soon as she got home, Kate hurried to her desk and telephoned the Foreign Office. She asked to speak to Helen, Oliver's secretary.

Helen had a grown-up, pleasant, voice and the sound of her 'Good morning, Helen speaking' calmed Kate.

'Helen, thank God you're there. It's Kate. Can I speak to the boss, do you think?'

There was a tiny pause, and then. 'Kate McKinnon? I'm sorry, but I'm afraid the Secretary of State is unavailable.'

Kate held the telephone in both hands, and was conscious of the clamminess of her palms against the plastic. 'But Helen, I must speak to him. The press have got hold of some daft story that—'

'Kate, the Downing Street press office is dealing with the matter, and we in this office are under instructions to say nothing to anyone. I'm so sorry. Goodbye.'

Kate heard the click, and sat there stunned. Helen had put the phone down on her. Why? She was not the enemy, surely? She, like Oliver, was innocent.

For a moment Kate sat there, telephone in hand, unmoving. Then slowly she replaced the handset, wrapped her arms across her chest and put her head on her desk.

Out of the corner of her eye she became aware of the flashing red light of her answering machine.

She reached over and pressed the 'play' button. The tape whirred briefly. At the sound of Sean's voice, Kate jerked upright. Thank God, a message from Oliver. Of course, I should have rung Sean, not Helen. It would not be his secretary, but his PPS who would handle this sort of thing.

'Kate, I'm sorry to tell you, but in the light of recent events the department must cancel all forthcoming catering that we've booked with Nothing Fancy. That means the dinners for tomorrow night, Friday week and the Durbar Court 12th June buffet reception, the summer cocktail party on the 23rd June at Lancaster House, and the working lunches on the 14th, 18th and 26th. I will confirm all these cancellations by email. I'm sorry, Kate, but I am under instructions not to have any further communication with you.' There was a pause, and then, in a more human voice, his real voice, Sean added, 'I'm so sorry, Kate. And good luck.'

She was still sitting there like a stone when Talika arrived. She did not get up, or smile, or say anything. She registered how pretty Talika looked. She'd begun to fill out a little, and her skin glowed pink beneath the brown. She was beautiful.

Kate noticed her friend's looks, but didn't greet her. The word 'fecund' came to mind. Talika looks fecund and happy, she thought. Well, she's pregnant, isn't she?

Talika said at once, 'What's happened, Kate? What is it? Is it Toby?'

Kate shook her head, slowly, almost as though she was in a trance. Talika crouched down beside her, her arm round her shoulders.

'Kate, talk to me. What's happened?' She gave Kate a little shake, 'Speak, Kate. Tell me.'

Talika collected the children from school and parked Kate outside in the warm May sunshine, ostensibly to keep an eye on them while shelling a load of fresh peas. While Kate podded peas, Talika countermanded orders for food, hire and staff for the various cancelled Foreign Office events, and dealt with demands for cancellation fees and explanations; there was outrage, too, at the late notice, especially from the prop company boss who had gone to a great deal of trouble to source Indian punka fans and artefacts for the Durbar Court party.

Normally, Kate regarded shelling peas in May as a pleasurable annual rite: she could not swear that by the time the peas had been through the London markets and then the wholesalers they were any more flavoursome than frozen ones, but they reminded her of peas from her grandmother's Scottish garden, eaten in soup plates with a dollop of farm butter and new mint from the trough outside the kitchen door.

These peas had been destined for tomorrow's dinner for Oliver, but now they would eat them for supper. Kate doubted that they'd enjoy them. Podding them was certainly providing little pleasure, just something to do, something to stop her trying yet again to ring Oliver, something to distract her from the horror of today's events.

All day she had expected a call from him. It was inconceivable that he would not ring her. And she didn't believe that he was behind the cancellation of the catering orders. Surely, since they were both innocent, they should just go on as usual, not be bounced into a reaction like this. It just made them look guilty.

But far worse than the loss of the catering jobs, was the feeling that she might have lost Oliver. Not that he had been hers, but they had something, she knew. He liked her, he sought her out for a drink and a chat, he'd insisted on driving her home. Of course he was not in love with her, but he would get in touch, she knew he would. Even if just to express a word of sympathy or solidarity.

Amal, instructed by Talika, appeared at six o'clock with the late edition of the *Evening Standard*. He had bought two previous editions, but there had been nothing in them. In this one the Londoner's Diary led with the story:

Foreign Secretary denies sex scandal

The Foreign Secretary, Oliver Stapler, this morning denied rumours of an illicit affair with Kate McKinnon, society chef responsible for many of the Government's high-profile dinners and banquets. The Downing Street press office statement said that the Cabinet Minister would have nothing further to say on the matter.

Neither the Foreign Secretary nor Ms McKinnon deny their friendship but Ms McKinnon has told our reporter, 'I hope you believe me when I tell you that there is absolutely no truth whatsoever in your story. Someone is having you on, or has got it in for me. Or, more likely, for Oliver.'

According to reports from those close to the couple, they frequently socialise and have twice been spotted going home together after dinners or events.

Oliver Stapler's wife, Ruth, lives in his constituency outside Birmingham with their two daughters. Kate McKinnon is a single mother, living in a council flat in Ealing.

Kate read the piece with mounting dismay. Every paragraph felt like another blow, another stab at her battered self. 'Society chef' had offended her, but any indignation was swept away by the graver consequences of the second paragraph.

That quote was exactly as she'd said it, wasn't it? But that use of his first name, her lumping them together made it look as though she was claiming a closeness that wasn't there. And the use of 'a couple', 'socialising' and 'going home together' could not be challenged. And 'dinners and events' made it look as though they were out together rather than he in the dining room and she in the kitchen.

Worst of all was the loaded description, 'single mother in a council flat'.

It wasn't a flat and no longer the council's.

It was horrible, all horrible.

'I've got to put this right, ring the editor or something!' she exclaimed. 'And I've got to explain to Oliver! Oh, why won't he speak to me?'

'I expect the press people have told him not to,' said Amal. 'And, Kate, there's really no point in talking to the paper. They'll just make another story out of it: "Cook at the centre of sex storm, denies . . . etc."'

Kate looked from Amal to Talika, her eyes filling with tears, 'But I can't just do nothing. What can I do?'

Talika put her hand on the back of Kate's neck. It was curiously comforting. Amal said, 'Do nothing, Kate. Just bear it. It will be a one-day wonder. You'll see. They'll be onto another story tomorrow, ruining someone else's day. Just take no notice.'

They went inside and Kate bathed the children while Amal cooked supper and Talika fielded calls. Kate's mobile was now going constantly, with friends and customers offering sympathy but really wanting gossip, to be on the inside, in the know.

The office telephone rang almost incessantly with the press wanting Kate to comment, to meet them, to give them her side of the story. Talika politely answered all enquiries with 'Ms McKinnon has no comment to make.' In the end she switched it to answerphone. She would have pulled the plug on it completely, but Kate wouldn't let her. What if Oliver was trying to get her?

The first photographer rang the front bell just before seven that evening. Talika opened the door to him, and was instantly blinded by his camera flash. She put her hand over her face and repeated the mantra, *Ms McKinnon has no comment to make*, and shut the door again.

After half an hour of constant bell-ringing, Amal took a screwdriver and disconnected the wiring.

Kate was grateful for the distraction of the children. She had to appear happy and normal for them, and while Amal and Talika dealt with the press, or rather refused to deal with them, she tried to explain to Sanjay and Toby what was going on.

'The people who work for the television and newspapers know Mummy cooks for famous people and they want me to talk about one of them so they can write what I say in the paper. But I don't want to.'

Toby frowned. 'Is it a pop star?'

'No, darling . . .'

Sanjay interrupted, 'But if you're on TV you will be famous too. It will be cool.'

She read them a story and tucked them both into her bed.

Then she, Amal and Talika had supper – mostly peas, with a bit of chopped left-over chicken and sweated onion in it, followed by defrosted banana loaf and custard. Amal and she drank a bottle of red between them (Talika wasn't drinking because of the baby) and then Amal stuck his head out of the top bathroom window to check if the paparazzi had gone, which they had.

'Kate, do not reconnect the bell. Don't answer the door or the phone. Talika will be back in the morning, early, to defend the fortress. And I'll do the school run.'

Kate thought she'd cry again. They were so wonderful; such great friends. She could feel her eyes welling up and she didn't dare speak. She nodded, kissed them both and watched them walk down the path, Amal carrying the sleeping Sanjay, Talika swaying slightly, elegantly, beside them.

Chapter Fourteen

When the piece in the *Standard* came out, Oliver was at home on his own in Lambeth. For once he had no engagements and was looking forward to an hour or two at his desk, the ten o'clock news, then bed.

But at six-thirty there was a call from the Downing Street press officer to tell him that the Press Secretary Terry Taughton was on his way to see him. 'It is top priority, Sir,' said the young man, 'and I am to ask you not to answer the door to anyone else, or speak to anyone else until you see him. He will be with you in ten minutes.'

Oliver felt curiously calm. He assumed that the Necklace Affair, or the Limoges Affair (as, rather dramatically, he thought of them) were finally out. Well, it was bound to happen. Terry will be coming to discuss tactics. Or maybe to ask for his head – Terry was very close to the PM. But no, Oliver decided, however much the boss might like his henchman to do the dirty work, he would have the good manners to sack him himself. After all he had been in government as long as the PM, and was, for all his secret ambition, a solid supporter.

Oliver climbed to the upstairs landing and looked gingerly down, but the porch roof was in the way and he could not see if there were any pressmen at his front door. As he stood there, tempted to climb onto the porch roof and peer over, with the risk of being photographed from below, the door bell rang, making him jump. He ignored it as instructed, and continued to scan the street. A taxi was stopping opposite. A man with a camera round his neck and a camera bag over his shoulder climbed out, hauling his tripod and a little ladder after him. As he paid the driver he turned his head, joshing with people already at Oliver's door. So the vultures were here in force then.

He still felt oddly detached, but expectant, waiting for fear or distress to kick in. He went downstairs and into the kitchen to make tea for his colleague. If his career was over, he would at least stick to the civilities. Personally he would prefer a whisky, and would probably have one, but Terry Taughton was teetotal. A legacy, Oliver suspected, of alcoholism.

He spilled a little boiling water as he filled the teapot. His hands, he saw, were shaking. Not so calm then. He wiped up the spillage, then held both hands out, stiffly, willing them to be still. But they continued to tremble. He carried the tray into the study.

Terry rang him from his mobile. 'Oliver, are you alone?'

'Yes.'

'Well, open the door, but stay behind it. Just wide enough for me to get through. I don't want the press to get a shot of you, do you hear?'

Oliver thought his tone unnecessarily peremptory, but decided to overlook it. After all, this is what press secretaries were for. It was the moment when they emerged from the background chorus and got to be, briefly, lead players.

'Sure, Terry. Will do.'

Taughton sidled through the door, his thin frame tall and bendy. Like the snake he was, thought Oliver. As soon as he was inside he walked ahead of Oliver towards the stairs.

'We need to go upstairs, and sit away from any window. OK?'

'Would you like some tea?'

'Forget the tea. I don't want them snapping you through the kitchen window.'

'I've already made it, and it's in my study. And the curtains are drawn.'

For the first time Terry smiled. 'Good man, you're learning. Let's go into the study then.'

Bloody cheek, thought Oliver. And what does he mean I'm learning? Closing the curtains is hardly rocket science. He poured the tea with his back to his guest, grateful to see that his hands were now steady – having the cup rattling in the saucer would be embarrassing, shameful even. It crossed Oliver's mind that his discomfort would be matched by Terry's satisfaction.

'First things first. I take it you have not seen the *Evening Standard*?'

Oliver shook his head. 'No.'

Terry took a newspaper clipping from his folder, which, Oliver noted, contained a lined notebook and a pen too. He passed the cutting to Oliver.

Oliver had trouble reading the text, let alone absorbing the information. His brain seemed to be on some sort of go-slow. His first feeling was confusion, or was it relief? There was nothing about the necklace or the Limoges dinner service. But then horror spread though him like blood in water. His first coherent thought was of the Prime Minister, what would he do? Then Kate: Christ, she would hate it. Then Ruth. Had Ruth seen it? No, the *Evening Standard* did not get to Birmingham. But some London friend could have rung her. He looked across at Terry without speaking. He wanted to sit down. Think for a minute. He sat on the sofa.

Terry sat opposite him and said, 'Right, now, first question. I need the truth. What actually is going on? Think before you answer, Oliver, because whatever you say now will become your story.' He put a hand up to prevent Oliver saying anything. 'No, hear me out. This is important. It is extraordinarily difficult to change a story once you've told it. And it will become your defence, or your explanation, the government line. So it needs to be sustainable.'

Not truthful, Oliver noted, but sustainable. The man was a creep. He said, 'I understand. But there's no problem. Kate McKinnon and I are not having an affair. I know her, yes, she's an acquaintance. She cooks for me. But there is nothing improper going on.'

Terry's eyes narrowed, and he nodded slightly. 'OK, so how come they have this story then?'

'I've no idea.'

'We'll find out. That won't be hard. It will be someone in your department, almost certainly. Who hates you, Oliver?'

'I don't think anyone. Anyway, the story is not true.'

'None of it? Not the going home together?'

'I gave her a lift back from Hampton Court, yes.'

'Why?'

'She couldn't get a taxi, and I offered.'

'Who knew about that lift?'

'Just about everyone. It wasn't a secret. I offered to take anyone else, not just Kate. I had an empty car. If you can call a car empty with a driver and a copper in it.'

'But you did not bestow lifts on any others?'

Oliver clenched his teeth at Terry's sneering tone. 'No, they were all sorted, I think,' he said. 'Only Kate needed a lift.'

'Was Sean with you?'

'No.'

'Why not?'

'God, Terry, what is this, the inquisition? He was in his own car. He lives somewhere south of the river.'

'If you think this is the inquisition, wait until you have to answer a pack of journos. Or a defending counsel in a libel court.'

The questioning went on, and Oliver began to see his relationship with Kate in a new light. According to Terry, a government minister who accepts lifts from a young woman late at night, who gives lifts to her in a government car, who regularly shares a bottle of wine in kitchens all over London with her, who goes to her child's birthday party at Kew, who defends her to a Kew official and gets her son off a charge of thievery, who even helps her load empty bottles and rubbish into her car, is either guilty or a complete idiot.

But, damn it, he had not done anything wrong. Just behaved like the friend he was. And yet, and yet . . . if he was so innocent why did he not tell Terry that the lift involved a detour through the streets of Acton, or Ealing or somewhere completely off his usual map. Or about carrying Toby along the street, or that he'd been into Kate's house, into her bedroom.

'Terry, for God's sake!' Oliver interrupted Terry's catalogue of his misdemeanours. 'You should know, being a master at it, that you can spin any innocent action into a crime.'

Terry raised a sceptical eyebrow. 'And if the cook in question had been male, ugly and old? Would you have been driving him home and sharing regular nightcaps with him? Grow up, Oliver. If you haven't actually screwed Ms McKinnon it's only because you're a bit slow and haven't got there yet. No one humps rubbish at midnight for people they don't fancy. Or dashes to the defence of the son of "an acquaintance".'

Oliver swallowed his anger. He shook his head, 'But no one knows about the birthday party or loading the van. I don't need to explain those. I only told you because you insisted on a catalogue of every minor interaction.'

Terry made a dismissive puff of the lips. 'No one knows? Want a bet? In my experience once one ministerial peccadillo emerges, it is swiftly followed by an avalanche of others. As we speak, waiters at Hampton Court and gardeners at Kew and little old ladies who just happened to be watching you kissing Kate at midnight, are reaching for their phones.'

'I have never kissed—'

'Careful, Oliver! Are you sure?'

'Yes! Or ... well ... depends what you mean ... I may have given her a peck. Everyone—'

'You see?' Suddenly Oliver did see.

'Shit.'

'Indeed, and hitting the fan in shovelfuls.'

'But surely if I just tell the truth ...'

'The great British public will back you? Well, that's our only hope. And only if you do what I say: lie low and let me handle it. And even then, my guess is ...'

'They won't believe me.'

'Unlikely to.' Terry was inspecting his manicured finger-tips. 'They think all politicians are dishonest, corrupt and devious and only interested in saving their skins. But your first hurdle is the PM.' He transferred his attention from his nails to his watch, delicately adjusting its position on his wrist. 'He's going to see you in forty minutes. If he believes you it makes my job marginally easier. He's hardly the most popular of prime ministers but his support might mean something. Of course if he doesn't believe you, you'll be out on your ear anyway.'

'I'm sure you'll get to know the result of the interview as soon as I do,' said Oliver, 'if you haven't fixed it in advance. Have you?'

Terry lips parodied a smile, but he didn't answer. God, thought

Oliver, I'd like to see him flat on the floor with a rapidly swelling lip.

Terry stood up. 'Just two more things,' he said. 'You're not going to like the first one. But needs must. I spoke to your wife this afternoon. I thought it best to get to her before the press does.'

'You what?' Oliver was half out of his seat. Terry, unconcerned, put up a hand. 'Steady on, Oliver. I had no choice.'

Oliver was now leaning over Terry, his fists clenched at his sides. 'You took it upon yourself to inform my wife that her husband is accused of adultery? Don't you think she might have preferred a call from me?'

'No time. Think about it, Oliver. That edition of the *Standard* hit the streets at about five-thirty. Which meant it would be on Sky News and BBC News 24 within the hour. And you are about to have an appointment with the Prime Minister. There was no time for me to tell you and then for you to tell her before the press pack would be upon her. So I told her.'

Oliver was forced to follow the man's logic but it did not pacify him.

'And what exactly did you tell her?'

'Don't worry, I said all the right things. How you were issuing a denial, and thinking about suing, and how the Prime Minister was issuing a statement of support. That it was just a malicious rumour and it would all blow over. But in the meantime you needed her, blah blah. The usual. And I said you would ring her as soon as you left Downing Street this evening and—'

Oliver cut in, his voice rising. 'For Christ's sake, Terry, stop. We haven't said anything about issuing a denial. I'm not thinking – or had not until this second – of suing. We don't know the PM is going to support me. I haven't even seen him . . .'

Terry waved a hand at him. 'Oliver, do sit down, I find your looming over me rather claustrophobic.'

Oliver sat down again, feeling stunned. He said, 'How can you prejudge . . .'

'Because the pattern is always the same. Always. The accused hotly denies the charge, the wife stands by him, the PM supports him, and the press go on ferreting. If they find nothing more, they give up and life goes on. Only usually they do find more, and that gives the PM an excuse to get rid of him and his wife an excuse to leave him.'

Oliver sat in silence, marvelling that anyone could be so casually, so smugly, unkind.

'Besides,' Terry added, 'if I'm wrong and the PM does not support you, then you issue a public letter of resignation, he issues a different statement about his regret, and only Ruth is confused. No real harm done.'

'But why tell her a pack of lies? Just because you enjoy lying?'

'Don't be childish, Oliver. I jumped the gun because I needed to brief her to keep her mouth shut. Besides, we need her here. Persuading her was not easy. She didn't seem to think "one of Oliver's muddles" as she put it, necessitated her presence.'

Oliver, beginning to feel beaten, said, 'OK, Terry, I can see you had to speak to her. You had better tell me how she reacted.'

'Rather well, I thought,' Terry replied. 'Took it pretty much on the chin. Said she did not believe a word of it. Said you'd often talked about Kate's delectable dinners or something, which did not sound to her like you were having a clandestine affair: talking about your lover to your wife was, she said, far too sophisticated a double-bluff for you. But she needed persuading that she did really need to come to London. She has a mare about to foal and a potential buyer coming to inspect a pony or something. She seemed to regard this as rather a storm in a demi-tasse.'

Oliver's stomach tightened. Ruth's reaction was entirely

typical. Stalwart and no-nonsense, unsentimental. Sometimes it would be nice to have a bit of sentiment, he thought.

'But she is coming? When?'

'Well, I left it that she'd speak to you. She did say she'd come if you asked her to. And she promised to speak to no one on the subject.'

'I will speak to her tonight, of course.'

'Good. If she's having second thoughts, Oliver, you must insist. I don't like to admit it, but it will make a lot more impression on the public than the PM's backing. And can you tell her that a car – actually it will be a local taxi so as not to arouse suspicion – will collect her tomorrow at ten in the morning. She needs to be in London for your dinner tomorrow night.'

Oliver found this whole conversation demeaning and over-familiar and he was in a state of fluctuating anger. But he was determined to stay cool. Terry was in control and he knew his sordid business, so Oliver had better let him get on with it.

'Of course I'll do my best,' he said, 'but I should warn you Ruth is very much her own woman. I know she will believe me, but she still may not appear for dinner. She hates the Westminster village and its petty gossip.'

'Well, this gossip is hardly petty. And she *must* be with you, you need her. Badly.' He bent down to flip open his folder, lay in it his pad and the *Evening Standard* cutting, carefully push the pen into its little leather loop.

'And what is the second thing? You said there were two.'

'Well, just as it is essential to have Ruth by your side, it is equally essential that Kate is nowhere near. Do not ring her, write to her, email her, text her, receive any communications whatever from her . . .'

For a second Oliver was more surprised than angry. He took a step towards the press secretary.

'Terry, don't be an ass. Of course I must speak to her. Poor woman, she's done nothing wrong! Neither of us has.'

Terry was leaning against Oliver's desk, one hand holding his folder at his hip. His lanky frame was both elegant and insouciant. 'Oliver, leave this to me. I will handle it. Just do not give it another thought.'

'But I need to speak to her. See if she's OK. It would be rude and unkind not to.'

'Out of the question.' Terry's voice was dry as dust. Not a grain of sympathy. 'It will get out and then you won't have a leg to stand on. I'm sorry, Oliver, you have no option but to cut her loose.'

'Cut her loose? God, Terry, you sound like a bad movie.'

Terry shrugged. 'It *is* a bad movie. But you wrote the scenario, old chap. I'm here to see that it has a happy ending.'

'Happy for whom? You don't seem to care what happens to Kate.'

'Of course I don't care what happens to Kate! She isn't my responsibility. I'm here to see that the damage to the government is kept to a minimum and – a secondary consideration I confess – to nursemaid you through this little drama so you can keep your job. You do want to keep your job, I presume?'

Oliver was now having trouble concealing his anger. 'I regard those comments as impertinent and out of order. But to answer your question, I'm not sure I do want to keep my job – not if the price is selling my friends down the river.'

Terry laughed, a derisive laugh with his head thrown back. Oliver watched his Adam's apple jump up and down in his long neck and for a second the desire to put his hands round that elegant throat and squeeze, gripped him. He closed his eyes and the moment passed.

Terry stopped laughing. 'Oh, Oliver,' he said, running his

hands down his face as if to prevent further mirth. 'What pompous nonsense. You're one of the most ambitious politicians in the House. For God's sake, you're in line to be the next PM. Don't tell me you'll throw all that away just to be nice to some little cook you want to get your leg over.'

The man needed punching. Oliver took a step towards Terry, who seemed to glide back, still chuckling. Oliver just managed to keep his hands by his sides as he snapped, 'You're enjoying this, aren't you? You get off on other people's miseries, don't you? But if you've finished having fun, perhaps you could take yourself off now.'

Terry looked at him, unperturbed. 'Mmm ... well,' he said, slowly, 'I admit this is a lot more fun than managing conferences where everyone knows everyone else's script. But I have no desire to see you busted, my dear Oliver. Indeed, quite the reverse. My reputation as well as yours is at stake here.' He drifted towards the door. 'And believe me, I'm your route to salvation. You may even get to thank me.' He shot an elegant cuff to look at his watch. A platinum Rolex, Oliver noted. 'Your car will be here in a few minutes. There's already a policeman outside, so running the gauntlet will be easy. The car will wait outside Number Ten to bring you home.'

'Unless I'm out of a job, in which case, you will cancel it?'

'Indeed. Politics is not for ninnies.'

Oliver went upstairs to put on his suit jacket. It was true that the administration liked to project an informal, hardworking, shirt-sleeves image, but he was too old-fashioned not to wear a suit for an interview with the Prime Minister. Especially if he was to leave that interview no longer a member of Her Majesty's government, and have to hail a taxi in Whitehall.

The interview with the PM was short if not sweet.

'All I want to know, Oliver, is, are you telling us the truth? I have just had Terry on the line and he says you are an idiot, but he believes you.'

'A fair enough summary, Prime Minister. I am not cheating on my wife, and indeed never have.'

'Good Lord. No need to protest too much. I don't expect complete marital fidelity from my ministers. Just that they are not stupid enough to give the press a story. Even an untrue one.'

'I'm truly sorry about that, Sir. But I'm genuinely innocent. What it amounts to is that I gave a friend a lift.'

'Is she a friend then? Outside of the official circuit, I mean?'

Oliver could see the trap. If he said she was he could be accused of improperly using his position to employ a friend. If he said she wasn't, then how to explain the lifts? He decided on the truth.

'I only know her through work. But I am interested in cooking, and she's a great cook, and I guess I have become friends with her as a result. Unwise, as it turns out.'

'Indeed.'

Oliver hoped the PM would not ask him to sever all connections with Kate, because he would not lie to his boss. And how could he be loyal to Kate and to him? But he didn't.

'Well, you will issue a carefully worded denial. Terry will write it for you. I will issue a statement of support. And then you must do what Terry says. He's deciding how best to proceed.'

The PM must have caught some dissent in Oliver's eye, because he went on, 'Terry is a difficult sod, but he is the best. If you get us into any more trouble, or it turns out there are more skeletons in your cupboard, then his job will be impossible and I will have no option but to throw you to the wolves.'

'I understand that. And thank you. I am very grateful for your support.'

'Mmmm. A public announcement of prime ministerial support for a colleague in trouble is often followed swiftly by his resignation. You're not in the clear yet, but as long as there are no more revelations we should be able to ride the storm. But I cannot pretend I'm delighted with you, Oliver. The last thing this government needs is to hand the Tories another muck heap to rake in.'

'There is no muck heap, Prime Minister. I promise.'

Except, thought Oliver, the little matters of a missing necklace and some smuggled china resulting in evaded tax. But he told himself the PM meant a sexual muck heap. And he was absolutely innocent there.

The car was waiting for him. Oliver ignored the questioning crowd of journalists corralled behind barriers across the street and got into the back seat. A policeman had opened the door for him, and a detective, one he did not know, slipped in next to him from the other side. Oliver looked, he hoped, relaxed and happy. Not triumphant, not solemn.

He fished out his mobile and rang Ruth. It went straight to voice mail, and for once he was relieved at this rather than annoyed. He left a message of much greater confidence than he felt: 'Hi, darling. I'm so, so sorry about all this. It's rot of course, but unpleasant, especially for you. Thanks for agreeing to come up. Terry seems to think it's important, and I would really like you here. They are sending a car for you at ten. We'll talk then unless you ring tonight. But don't worry, Ruth. I've just seen the PM and he's on side. So it will all be over soon, I'm sure.'

God, he was tired. And he needed a whisky. As soon as he got home, he poured himself a stiffish one, drowned it with water from the kitchen tap and turned on Sky News. Sure enough, there was footage of him entering Downing Street and a rolling headline at the bottom of the screen. 'Prime Minister issues statement in support of embattled Foreign Secretary.'

That was fast. Terry must have had both his denial and the PM's statement all ready to go, just waiting until the PM had seen him. So the interview was play acting.

Oliver waited for the story to come up again. There was nothing in the short piece other than a rehash of the *Standard* piece and some inane comment. He was relieved to see that there was no footage of Kate. Just a still photograph of her, head and shoulders only, looking rather plump and clearly taken some time ago. One of her friends had obviously made a little pocket money.

Nothing of Ruth, or their house either, thank God.

Once in bed, and before the Valium he had taken to ensure a decent night's sleep kicked in, Oliver's mind ran over Terry's crude analysis of his political ambition, and had to concede that what Terry had said was essentially true. He was in line for the top job, he did want it, he'd worked hard all his life climbing the ladder. Was he going to risk it all by being seen publicly to befriend poor Kate? Had he damaged his chances already?

And then Oliver suddenly saw the decision as perfectly simple, and, indeed, already made. He had to do whatever it took to overcome this idiotic crisis. Pompous as it sounded, there was a greater good than his moral comfort. Not just for his career, but for the Government, his Party, his Prime Minister. He could not let them all down by playing into the hands of the press.

He would have to find a way to contact Kate, to help her, but without openly championing her.

He would let the Downing Street press office manage the matter, while he stayed out of it and got on with his day job.

God knows, he thought, I haven't time for this nonsense. According to Terry, all tonight and tomorrow his office would be deflecting calls to the Downing Street press office and it would be a big story for maybe a week, for most of which he would be away in the Middle East anyway.

As long as he, personally, said nothing, absolutely nothing, it would go away.

Oliver wasn't sure the line Terry was thinking of taking – which was to threaten government legal action – was right, but then they were the experts. Terry had spent years in Fleet Street before joining the PM's team and he had a reputation for getting his way with newspaper editors by a mixture of carrot and stick; exclusives and access for the ones who behaved, outer darkness, even the law, for those who didn't.

He would do as Terry demanded and the PM ordered. Why employ a dog and do your own barking? And Terry was one mean dog.

CHAPTER FIFTEEN

Bone-tired from her horrible day, Kate had slept surprisingly well and was up next morning at six, anxious to know the worst. She would have to do her budget calculations for the summer without the projected income from the Foreign Office. They were by far her biggest customer, and she would not be able to replace them quickly.

She crept to the front door and peered through the spyhole. There was no one on the path or, as far as she could see, anywhere. So, she thought, the paparazzi are not early risers then.

When Toby was dressed and fed, she parked him in front of a sing-along DVD. She could hear him adding his small voice to the cartoon characters' rendering of *The Jungle Book*. The sound cheered her and she took her coffee into her office, with her shoulders back and her head up. Nobody died, she told herself.

But the first email she read was from her client at the Ministry of Defence, regretfully informing her that they would not be having the veterans' charity tea party in the Whitehall Palace crypt after all.

She didn't believe it. They were dumping her and getting another caterer, not cancelling the event. But the speed of it! They must have had instructions from Government Hospitality.

She rang her wine merchant. It was only seven a.m. but she knew he'd be there. Tim was not much more than a one-man band and he got to his business early to hump cases or deliver early orders.

'Tim, it's Kate. Can I ask you something? Are you still sponsoring the fizz for the MOD charity thing we agreed?'

'Yes, of course. I wouldn't let you down, Kate. You know that, surely?'

'They haven't told you it's cancelled?'

'No, is it? I haven't looked at my emails yet. Well, that's a relief, I was going to have to foot the bill myself because I can't get any champagne house to provide even one miserable case. Times are tough, they remind me.'

'Aren't they just? Well, the MOD have dumped me and told me it's cancelled. But of course it's not that.'

But Tim hadn't read the *Evening Standard* and knew nothing about the Oliver allegations. Maybe it had been a mistake to ring him, but she could hardly clam up now. So she told him the gist of the story and that it was not true. He was immediately on her side, indignant on her behalf, sweet and sympathetic. She was gratified when he said, 'Right, well, if they are shafting you they can whistle for their fizz. As far as I'm concerned I was doing you a favour, a thank you for all the wine you buy from me. I am not doing that for the government, and certainly not for some caterer who never buys a thing from me.'

Kate went back to her sums, now assuming she would lose all her government work. If she couldn't replace it she'd lose money this month and right through the summer. Her efforts to get paid by her slow-paying clients had not yielded as much as she'd hoped, she already owed Amal for the plane tickets for the trip to Arizona in August, and she had the new van hire and the blast freezer instalments to pay each month on top of the usual insurances, gas bills etc.

Cold panic was closing in as Kate did the sums. She reckoned she'd be in the red to the tune of fifteen thousand pounds by October – providing the bank let her run up her overdraft, which was unlikely.

She made a determined effort to think positively. If the worst came to the worst she could always get a job as a chef somewhere, give up the business, have the van and new chiller repossessed, turn her office into a bedroom and get a flatmate.

But she was nowhere near that yet. She needed to drum up some new business, that was all. Perhaps she should advertise? She never had, relying instead on word of mouth, which was free.

Perhaps she could get her existing City clients to give her a push with other firms in their offices, and perhaps her private dinner party customers would email their friends and recommend her.

Problem was, the City was catatonic over the credit crunch, just holding its breath and doing nothing, certainly not giving parties and dinners. And the Mayfair and Kensington women who employed her liked to pretend she was their personal cook, or that they'd cooked the dinner themselves, so getting them to divulge her telephone number to their friends might not be easy. And anyway it damaged her credibility: if she was so hot, she should have an order book crammed for a year, not be soliciting clients.

She would just have to borrow some money and wait for the business to regrow organically. But who from? Not her mother. She shuddered, thinking of how she'd been firmly rebuffed last time, and she could not bear to ask again. The bank. Again, she'd tried and been refused. Weren't there government loans for small businesses? She smiled at the thought of being lent money from the government to fill a hole made by the government.

Something would come up, she told herself, all was not lost. And today, she was certain, Oliver would ring her. She could bear anything, she thought, if he was on her side, which of course he would be. They were in this horrible mess together; it was neither his nor her fault and they would weather it with each other's sympathy and friendship. It would be fine.

Kate lifted her chin and went into the kitchen to make some coffee.

As Kate swung round the central work table in her kitchen, two large dark shapes moved abruptly against the window to the garden. Kate stopped stock still, terrified. As the first flash went off, followed at once by another she realised they were photographers, their lenses pressed against the glass.

Rage assailed her. How dare they? How did they get into the garden? She would kill them.

She flew through the larder to the door, a tirade forming in her throat as she prepared to yell at them. They were trampling on her flower-bed, and if Toby had come into the kitchen they'd have scared the life out of him. How *could* they!

In her fury she fumbled with the key and couldn't position it properly. And then suddenly she stopped, the fury draining out of her.

She must not go out. They'd just get pictures of her shouting like a fishwife.

Here, in the larder, she was out of their reach. If she went back into the kitchen they would get more pictures through the window. What could she do? She sat on a crate of mineral water, and looked at her watch. Eight-ten. She extracted her mobile from her jeans pocket and dialled Talika.

'Hi, Kate. Did you get any sleep?' The familiar voice calmed her. 'Are you OK?'

'Yes, I think so. But 'Lika, are you and Amal coming?'

'Of course we are. Just about to leave. We'll be with you in minutes.'

'It's just that I'm stuck in the larder . . .' Kate could feel the tears behind her eyes, in her throat. 'There are photographers in the garden, and I don't know what to do.'

'Stay where you are. We'll be there.'

As she waited, still sitting on the crate, someone rattled the door, trying to open it. She heard different voices shouting to her. The photographers had obviously been joined by reporters.

'Kate, we know you are in there . . . Why not come out and talk to us . . . I promise to report your side of the story . . . Kate, if you let us take one photo of you, a proper nice picture, then we won't use any of the horrible ones . . .'

And then a familiar voice, 'Kate, my editor says to offer you a really good deal if you will give us exclusivity. Just look on your mobile. We've texted you the details.'

She didn't answer. She was no longer furious, just trapped and distraught. The minutes dragged by while she tried to stop herself collapsing into tears or opening the door or answering their demands – she found it curiously difficult to remain silent in the face of the appeals from the other side of the door. To distract herself, she did read her text messages. There were three from friends, offering sympathy; they had seen the *Evening Standard* or picked up the story online. And there was one from Jarvis Stanley, the *Evening Standard* man:

Kate, I know it must be grim for you now. I'm so sorry. But you need to get your side of the story sympathetically told in a responsible paper. I won't let you down, I promise. Just ring or text and I'll be there. We can provide a protected hotel for you and Toby and keep the rat pack out. And pay you handsomely. How does £50K sound? Jarvis

This from a man who had twisted her words, who had broken the story, who used innuendo like a weapon. And he sounded so reasonable and civilised, even through the door. What a hateful profession, thought Kate. I suppose if you want to be a gossip writer you first have to be a conman.

And then, thank God, she heard the sounds of Talika and Amal coming into the house, calling to Toby, Sanjay chattering excitedly, the normality of their voices restoring her.

The next second Amal was with her, giving her a hug and a kiss, and helping her put on her hooded coat.

'Here, if you wear this and walk through the kitchen they won't get a picture worth using,' he said. 'Come, I'll shepherd you.'

And he did, one arm round her shoulder. They were through the kitchen in seconds.

Then Amal braved the reporters on the front steps again, this time with the two children in tow. Kate listened through the door to his firm and repeated 'No comment' in answer to the reporters' clamorous questions.

Talika made coffee, and the women drank it upstairs in the bedroom, out of range of press cameras. Or so they thought. Within ten minutes of getting her hooded coat off and sitting down with a cup between her hands, Kate looked up to see the top of a wobbly ladder weaving about outside the window as someone tried to put it in place.

Once again, anger ripped through her. Without a thought she ran to the window, flung it open and gave the ladder, a heavy metal one, a mighty shove. It fell back and sideways, and crashed to the ground. A tiny moment of satisfaction was quickly doused by the thought: Oh Jesus, it might have killed someone.

She peered through the window and was relieved that all the ladder had crushed was a big camera. There were broken bits of black plastic and glass lying on the stone flags. As the enraged photographer dashed to inspect the damage, Kate yelled, 'Serve you right! Now get off my property!' And then she slammed the window.

She and Talika sat on the bed again and started to laugh.

'I shall remember his furious face for ever!' said Kate.

'And I will remember yours!'

'I bet the other chap got a good pic of me yelling at him,' said Kate. 'I'm going to regret this, but it was fun while it lasted.'

When they'd calmed down and drunk their coffee, Talika said, 'Kate, I think you and Toby had better come to us for the duration. You can't live in a goldfish bowl.'

'No.' Kate shook her head. 'I'm damned if I'll be driven out of my own house. I've got a business to run, and we have that cocktail thing for Battleby and Partners tonight, remember. Everything's here, I can't decamp to you.'

Kate spent the morning working as normally as she could. She cooked and stacked, sorted and tidied. The difference was that Talika manned the phones, saying 'No comment' to the press and taking messages for the rest. Then Kate would ring customers and suppliers back, and ignore pleas from TV stations, radio or the press. But on the whole it was productive. She concentrated on getting the Battleby party done, and there were moments when she forgot about the press altogether.

She never forgot about Oliver, though. Every time one of the phones went she hoped it would be him. Every time the bleep of her mobile alerted her to a message, she'd silently pray. But nothing.

At lunchtime she and Talika listened to the news. There was

a short piece about Oliver's statement and the Prime Minister's support.

They flicked on the TV in time to see the end of a discussion about public morals, with one pundit saying what ministers did in their own time was their affair and the press should stay out of it, and a second saying politicians should be role models for the nation and the press had a duty to hold them to account. Up flashed a head and shoulders picture of Oliver and one of Kate, looking young and pretty with a background of trees. The presenter covered the station's back with a reminder that the allegations were not proven, and then it was over and they were on to the next item.

'Where did they get that picture from?' asked Talika.

'No idea. It looked like a family snapshot or something, didn't it? I've never seen it before.'

'Maybe your brother? Or mother?'

'They're in Arizona.'

'It could be emailed in seconds.'

Kate shook her head. 'No. They wouldn't do that without asking me. And that looked like a picture taken fifteen years ago, when I was in catering college. Could have come from anyone.'

Talika put her hand on Kate's, her eyes soft with sympathy. 'Are you OK?'

'I'm fine. Really, 'Lika. Let's get back to work. I want to be done before Amal gets back with the boys.'

'They won't be here till four. He's taking them to Uncle Rashid's Cash and Carry, remember? They can run riot in the aisles and be fussed over by Rashid.'

They worked on, hardly talking, Radio Three in the background, for a couple of hours, and then Talika went to make some supper for them all while Kate checked through her lists to make sure she had everything. Nothing infuriated her more than leaving stuff off the van and having to go back for it. It meant an inevitable panic.

When she was ready to load the gear, Kate decided she'd brave the door stepping journos and do it herself. After all, what could they really do to her? And anyway, surely they could not interfere with her going about her lawful business? It would be outrageous.

Carrying two crates of wine glasses, she propped them against her hip and opened the front door. She glanced around and was relieved to see only two photographers, sitting on the low wall by the gate. They scrambled to their feet and ran to her, but she kept her head down and walked calmly to the van. She put the boxes down and unlocked the van doors.

'Kate,' called one, 'this way, Kate. Look here, Kate.'

She refused. She knew her longish mop of curls would obscure her face, preventing them from getting a usable pic.

As she turned and bent to pick up her boxes, one of the men suddenly leaned down and grabbed her hair by her fringe. He yanked her head back while the other man pushed his camera into her face and clicked away.

'Ow,' Kate screamed, 'let me go! How dare you?'

One of them laughed, and said to the other. 'Thanks, mate. I owe you.'

Kate now stood, trembling but furious. She repeated, 'How dare you?' She held her forehead in both hands. 'That hurt.'

'Sorry, sweetheart.'

He didn't look sorry and Kate, her voice calmer, said, 'Right, I will do you for assault.'

'No witnesses, darling,' he said, 'and I could do you for busting my camera. I've got a witness for that.'

His mate said, 'Calm down, love, we just had to get a picture.

We've got a couple or three now, and since Barney here hasn't got a camera any more, we've come to an agreement we'll share these. So you'll be glad to hear we'll love you and leave you. No harm done, is there?'

They took themselves off and Kate leant against the van, her head on her crossed arms, eyes shut. She was conscious of the metal against her forearms, warm from the afternoon sun. She could still feel the ache at her hairline. She wanted to run inside and weep on Talika's shoulder, but she fished in her pocket for a tissue, blew her nose loudly, and then got on with loading the van.

Thank God there was no one else there. Maybe the press machine had already moved on to the next story, she thought. Maybe things would now return to normal.

She must have made five or six trips to the van, and had loaded all the last-minute cooking utensils, the glasses, linen, ice, paper napkins, rubbish sacks, etc at the back, when Amal appeared with the children.

Kate found her eyes filling with tears as Toby ran to her, flinging her off balance with the violence of his affection. She staggered back, laughing, then picked him up for a hug. He flung his arms round her head and buried his face in her neck. Then, within seconds, he was struggling against her grip. She put him down reluctantly and watched him run after Sanjay who, looking for his mother, had gone into the house.

Amal said, 'No paparazzi then? That's good news.'

Kate wanted to explain the events of the afternoon, but she looked at her watch and decided she didn't have the time. Talika could tell him tonight.

'Yup, and I've decided to just get on with it. I need to get the food out and I can go.'

Amal followed her into the house and went to say hello to

his wife, while Kate fetched the first refrigerated box. It wasn't heavy, but it was awkward. She hitched her skirt up and climbed into the van. Then she knelt on the floor and pushed the box into place. She needed to pack the van tightly or she wouldn't get everything in.

It crossed her mind that if Amal reappeared he would be horrified at the sight of calves, maybe even a bit of thigh, visible from behind as she clambered about. She should really have worn her chef's pants. This skirt wasn't particularly short, but kneeling on it was awkward. Talika would never be so indelicate as to display her calves, or even her well-clothed bum, to the world like this. She smiled at the thought. Amal was such an old fashioned, lovely guy.

Suddenly she heard his voice behind her. She turned round and saw him put his hand over the lens of a movie camera while trying to push the cameraman away. He was speaking loudly but not quite shouting.

'Will you please stop that? You are on private property and no one has invited you to film here. Besides, have you no decency?'

'Give us a break, mate, we're only doing our job . . .'

She realised there were two of them, one holding a boom. Amal reached into the van and helped Kate out, saying, 'Go inside. I'll do the rest.'

Kate ran inside, pursued by the sound man. She shut the door in his face, her heart pounding, and looked through the spy hole. She could not see the TV people, but she could see Amal, shaking his head. Then he turned, put his key in the lock and slipped in.

'What do they want?' she said. 'They can hardly think Oliver is going to pop out of the front door, can they? A TV crew is expensive. They must think they're on to something.'

'I doubt it. They just need some pictures, vaguely relevant, to go with their non-news story. But if the back view of a woman loading a van is relevant, I will be very surprised. Don't worry, I doubt if they'll use it.'

But he didn't sound exactly convinced.

'I wonder how long they were there for?' said Kate. 'I was in the back of the van for ages, moving stuff to get the cold boxes in.'

Kate was thinking of Oliver. She couldn't bear the idea of him seeing her on television, crawling inelegantly around her van, displaying her bum and bare legs.

She found herself cringing at the thought.

'Have they gone? I've got to get on. It's four-thirty.'

'They've gone as far as the street, but we can't stop them filming from there. So, if they want to see me loading a van, I am happy to be a telly star.' He smiled broadly, obviously to cheer her. Which it did. He gave her a quick kiss on the forehead and said, 'Come, where have you got to? I'll load the rest, drive it to the client, and Joan can take over from there.'

'But I have to be there. The Battleby secretary is a dragon.'

'No, you don't need to be there. If necessary, I'll stay and cope with the dragon, then leave Joan to it. It's only a cocktail party isn't it? She can do it on her head.'

'I can't ask you . . .'

'You're not asking me, I'm telling you. When I'm through at Battleby's I'll go on to the restaurant. I've got to be there tonight, but you need supper with the boys and a soppy DVD with Talika.'

Kate grinned. 'Goodness, Amal, you're a star. A Bollywood hero rescuing tearful women with masterful authority.'

'Any more of that, woman, and I'll abandon you to the rat pack.'

Chapter Sixteen

At four o'clock the day after the Kate thing broke, Sean arrived with the speeches Oliver was to give over the next week on his Middle East tour. They were basically the same speech, about the necessity for Hamas and the Israelis to stop killing each other, but there were several versions. One was clearly for American and Jewish consumption and one for Arab/Palestinian ears, but since he was going first to India and Pakistan, local sensitivities and leaders' egos had to be catered for as well. Sean fed him a lot of background information, and gave him a clutch of reading which he would somehow have to absorb between dinner tonight and arrival in New Delhi tomorrow.

He would be flying in a private jet from the Queen's Flight, leaving from Northolt. Normally this was a privilege and a pleasure. There was no hanging around, no customs, no passport control to speak of, and a private cabin with a proper bed and a lot of saluting and 'Yes, Minister'. This time, however, he'd be up most of the night working and arrive completely knackered.

He had proposed chucking the dinner, but Terry had been adamant. Right now he needed to show that it was business as usual, and pictures of the Foreign Secretary with his wife on his arm, arriving or leaving a dinner with colleagues just before flying off on Government business, would help.

Oliver was not looking forward to seeing Ruth. They had still not spoken. He had left for the office long before she was due at the Lambeth house. He had tried the land line at lunchtime but there was no reply, and her mobile, as usual, was off. He told himself he was right not to cancel appointments to be with her; he was innocent, so why behave as though there was a crisis? Besides, he had work to do. But he knew, too, that he was avoiding her.

He would have to have a few minutes' private conversation with her, maybe at home when he picked her up. It would be OK. She was a sensible woman, and she'd said she believed him.

Right now he was more concerned about Kate. It was twenty-four hours since the *Evening Standard* piece had appeared, and now all the papers and news bulletins were covering the story. And he had not been able to say a word to the poor woman. Last night, Terry had made it crystal clear that he should not contact her. Not that he'd have obeyed if he'd been able to ring her.

The very fact that he didn't even have her number on his mobile, or anywhere at home, thought Oliver, was proof, if proof were needed, that she was not his lover. Maybe, he thought grimly, I'll end up having to produce Vodafone records to clear my name.

All today he'd wanted a moment to get Kate's number from Helen, or even to ask Helen to get her on the line for him, but it had been impossible. He'd kept all his morning appointments and there had been no space between them. Then Terry had again been with him this afternoon, updating him on the investigation: irritatingly, it looked as though Terry was right that the source of the story appeared to be a government butler or one of Kate's people; they were not sure yet. Terry had stayed a good hour, and then there had been the Middle East briefing with one of their experts and Sean. It was nearly six-thirty before they were done, by which time Helen had already left the office.

It was completely ridiculous. He was Foreign Secretary and he couldn't get hold of a woman he wanted to speak to. He couldn't do as he normally would and just tell Sean to download her contacts onto his BlackBerry, or even send his driver to Kate's house with a message for fear of worsening the situation. Even if Helen was here, it would probably not be wise to involve her.

He would be away a week and almost never alone, so if he was to speak to Kate he must do it now. He walked through to the outer office and found the telephone book. He sat on one of the black leather sofas and looked up both McKinnon and MacKinnon. But where did she live? Somewhere west, Ealing or Acton. It was mad – he'd been to her house, indeed *into* her house, yet he had only the vaguest idea where it was. He'd sat in the back of the car, exhausted as always, but enjoying talking to Kate and glad of an excuse not to be doing his boxes. He hadn't noticed where they were going, although he remembered crossing Hammersmith Bridge. Debbie had been following her sat nav – he remembered Kate giving her the postcode – but of course he couldn't remember what it was.

There was no Kate or Katherine in the book, only a Kevin and a Keith and a couple of plain Ks living in unlikely places, none of them in Acton or Ealing. Kate had once told him that she didn't have a website or phone book entry in order to make it difficult for her ex-partner to trace her. He'd thought at the time such measures in today's electronic age would be futile, but her smokescreen was certainly impeding his efforts.

He put the directory back on its shelf and went through to Helen's little office. He riffled through her trays, searching for an invoice or letter or menu from Kate. He opened her cupboard and peered at the neat rows of box files, looking for something that would lead to his caterer. But nothing jumped out as likely. That chap Hobhouse in Government Hospitality was responsible for caterers so presumably any files would be with him.

He considered checking Helen's computer. Kate's number would be sure to be on there somewhere, but he didn't know where and couldn't remember the name of Kate's catering company – he remembered she'd said she'd changed it from Kate's Kitchen, but to what? Something silly, Fancy Footwork? Fancy Handwork? No, he couldn't remember. And he didn't know Helen's password, and it would be too embarrassing if someone found him snooping in his secretary's files ... And anyway he had to get to his house, talk to Ruth, go to dinner.

He had a hasty shave in his private bathroom, and was surprised, on emerging, to see Sean had returned.

'What's up? Not more papers, please.'

'No, Sir. But the press are outside both the King Charles Street and the Whitehall entrances, and so I came to take you through to the Ambassador's entrance. I've asked Debbie to pick you up in the courtyard and drive straight through if the rat pack appear there too.'

'But she'll have gone home. I told her I'd walk, and she was to pick me up from the dinner to go to the airport.'

'I know, but she figured she'd be needed, so she came back. The paparazzi are everywhere.'

There was a small clutch of photographers and journalists outside the Ambassador's entrance. Oliver, trying to look cool, made some trite remark to the detective beside him as a policeman, suitably burly, held his arms wide to clear a path and Debbie drove deftly through the gap.

The whole manoeuvre, thought Oliver, was efficiently handled and over in seconds. Poor Kate would have none of that protection. No one to guide her through the door steppers, no back route, no assistant, no copper, no detective, no driver – all of them trained in press evasion. He refrained from looking back as the car slid off. He was damned if he'd give them a shot for tomorrow's paper of him looking cornered and anxious. He was neither, he told himself.

Sean, sitting next to Debbie, had the good sense to say nothing on the short run to Lambeth. Oliver was preoccupied: it occurred to him that maybe he should take the frightful Terry into his confidence about the Necklace and Limoges affairs. They could, singly or separately, undo him, since it seemed he was guilty on both charges. The irony that he was more likely to be brought down by a charge of which he was entirely innocent was not lost on him.

And he couldn't help fretting about Kate. She must think he was a complete shit. She couldn't know that he wanted to contact her, that the political machine had taken him over, that he had no option but to ignore her plight. She did not know about his conversations with the all-powerful master of government spin. His thoughts went back to this afternoon's conversation with Terry, when he'd renewed his arguments for contacting her. It must be much worse for Kate, he'd said, since she would have none of the protection afforded him.

'They must be door stepping her as we speak,' he'd said.

'I am sure they are. Indeed I know they are,' said Terry. 'There's a clip going out every few minutes on both ITV and BBC news of her trying to load her van. She was forced to retreat inside and some Indian fellow, an employee I assume, finally loaded the van for her and drove it away. Wise guy, he would not be drawn.'

'Oh, God, poor Kate. Can't we do anything?'

'What do you have in mind, Oliver?'

'We can give her some protection, surely? Put a couple of bobbies outside her house to keep them at bay?'

'Don't be daft. Of course we can't. The first assumption of any self-respecting journalist will be spot on: that you are protecting her and, what's more, spending public money doing so. So, not a chance.'

'I can't believe it! Are you saying we are to just leave her to her fate then?'

'Precisely.'

Ruth was ready, looking elegant in a green silk dress with a low neckline. It was a long time since he had seen her wearing make-up and her pearls. And she'd had her hair done, also her nails, which were painted a soft apricot. Her fingers held a small gold bag he had brought her from India.

She didn't smile or walk towards him, but met his gaze steadily. He returned the look, unsmiling, put his hands on her shoulders and looked into her eyes. 'Darling, I am so, so sorry. This is a complete fiasco, and all about nothing.'

'Are you sure? I need to know, Oliver.'

'Ruth, I promise you. I absolutely promise you. There is nothing between Kate McKinnon and me. Nothing.'

'There must be something, Oliver. Something for the press to latch on to. I have been hearing endless comment on the news all day. Some of it I know is rubbish. But giving her lifts in your official car? Surely that is not nothing?'

Oliver realised that this was not going to be a quick conversation. 'Come into the study,' he said, guiding her with an arm. 'I need you to understand the situation exactly as I do. Know everything I know. I understand your desire to avoid politics if you can, Ruth, but we're in this together.'

Of course he could not be quite open with her. He did not

tell her about the long conversations, about sitting in Kate's car, about the disloyalty of discussing the necklace affair with her. But he did cover all the bases. Confessed to his practice of taking a bottle of wine in for the kitchen staff (plural, he implied) by way of thanks after events, admitted to accepting a lift from Kate one night when he'd sent Debbie home and found he was too lazy to walk, owned up to offering an empty car to bring home stranded caterers from Hampton Court, told her he had helped load her stuff into her van one night.

'I've told that serpent Terry Taughton everything I can think of. Even that you and I ran into Kate at Kew, remember? At Toby's birthday party.'

'Toby? You know he's called Toby?'

Oliver winced internally. He knew a lot about Toby. Even how heavy and warm he felt at midnight, sleeping on his shoulder. But so far, at least, neither Debbie nor Jim had said anything. It would never look as innocent as it was. 'Yes. I think it's Toby,' he said. 'Isn't it?'

She looked down, shook her head slightly. 'Now you remind me, yes. But it's just that knowing her son's name implies some intimacy. As does being prepared to go to Westminster from Hampton Court *via Ealing*. As does the amount you talk about her. I know the names of almost none of your department, but I know your favourite cook's name. Why is that?'

Oliver felt genuinely sorry for her. She was trying to be calm and reasonable, but she must feel threatened, unsafe.

'Ruth, you know why! I love food, I'm interested in cooking, and Kate is really good at it. I tell you about meals because I cannot tell you much of what goes on in the department, and anyway, you don't want to know about politics. I talk to you about food because I want to talk to you about something, have you share my life a bit! If I was having an affair with her, I'd hardly talk about her to you, would I? You talk to me about your vet. It doesn't mean – at least I hope it doesn't mean – that you're having an affair with the man, that he's not inspecting or injecting ponies but bonking my wife!'

She looked at him then, and smiled a rather weak and watery smile. 'OK,' she said.

'What do you mean, OK? OK, you believe me, or OK you love me? Because I love you, Ruth.'

Ruth was silent for a minute, thinking, her fingers idly picking at the stitching on her evening bag in her lap.

'All right, I'll try to tell you where I am in all this. I don't think you do love me, certainly not as you used to. I don't just mean in quality – of course love changes in time – but I mean I don't think you love me much at all. And I'm not sure I love you either. Although there must still be something there, because I have discovered over the last twenty-four hours that you still have the capacity to really hurt me . . .'

'Darling, I did not, do not, want to hurt you.'

'I know. I believe that. And I believe you are not having an affair with this woman. So, whether we love each other or not, the next thing is to clear this nonsense up. And possibly the other things – the tax on the china and that bloody necklace.'

'Nothing further has come up about those.'

'I've been thinking. It seems that both those things were really my fault. I lost the necklace, and I wanted that wretched dinner service and contrived to get it on the cheap. So I owe you. I think you've been foolish and indiscreet and probably got too close to the famous Kate. I think it could have turned into an affair if it had not been rudely interrupted, but let's stick together, shall we? At least for the moment.'

Oliver pulled his wife out of the sofa and put his arms round her. 'Listen, Ruth,' he said into her hair, 'not just for the moment.

We do love each other. I know I love you, and I think you love me – you are just understandably hurt by all this.'

Ruth had stiffened at the embrace and now she pulled back and shook her head. 'I don't think so,' she said. Her face was serious as a judge's. Oliver would have preferred it if she had ranted and raved, or broken down and cried. This stiff rational coolness was hard to bear.

'Please, Ruth,' he said, 'give it a chance. Give us a chance. Political marriages are famously difficult to sustain, but we're doing OK. And yes, I need you now. Your being with me will make all the difference. Not just to my career. But to us. You are right, darling, let's stick together.'

CHAPTER SEVENTEEN

Within a week the crowd of photographers and reporters outside had gone. At least, thought Kate, I no longer have to clench my teeth and square my shoulders to run the gauntlet of taking my son to school, or walking to my van.

It was true that hardly a day went by without some little paragraph appearing somewhere. But they were only snippets, jokes, innuendos in the gossip columns. Nothing serious. But she was very tense.

And then, in the first week of June, she had an email from the *Evening Standard* journalist, Jarvis Stanley. When she saw his name in the sender's box she was tempted to delete the email unread, but curiosity overcame her and she clicked it open:

'Have you seen the piece about you and Oliver S in today's Scandal Sheet? We need to talk, Kate. I can help you.'

Her heart banging, Kate Googled the magazine and the on-line version came up. The header read,

Scandal Sheet – the satirical weekly that pulls no punches

She tapped in Kate McKinnon and immediately the piece was there:

So, how the mighty have fallen. The expensively elegant Oliver Stapler – yes, him with the designer grey hair – is in trouble. The

apparent heir to Labour's leadership and currently – but for how long? – Foreign Secretary has been following his predecessor's example and tupping the hired help. Robin Cook made an honest woman of his secretary. Will Stapler do the same for his cook?

Or will we see the brave little wife stand by her man, and the delectable Kate McKinnon disappear back to the kitchen? Scandal Sheet's money is on the cook. Why? The Sheet's spies tell us Kate brings flowers from her garden and home-made chocolates to garnish the great man's table when she cooks his lunch. At government functions Stapler spends more time with her in the kitchen than with the guests. And he celebrated her son's birthday with them at a party in Kew gardens.

Besides, if you are choosing between a wife besotted with horses and a mistress who cooks like a dream, we think it's a no-brainer.

Kate sat at her desk, motionless. Then her resentment at Oliver's treatment of her came flooding back and she had a moment of cruel satisfaction at his discomfiture. He would absolutely hate this. And so would Ruth.

She went back to the top and read the piece again. 'The satirical weekly that pulls no punches', she read. Too right they didn't. Surely this was libellous?

The innuendo stung her. She'd only once taken flowers from her garden – the snowdrops she and Toby had picked in the dark – and they were not a gift for Oliver. She'd done that before she'd even met him. It was her first job for him and she wanted the lunch to go well, that was all. And the 'home-made chocolates' were hardly a labour of love. Talika had made them and the Foreign Office had paid a pound each for them.

But how did they get the flowers and chocolates story? Only she and Toby knew of the flowers and only Talika of the chocolates. And who knew about Oliver and Ruth being at Toby's birthday? Surely Kew officials were not ringing the press? Maybe that piece of tittle-tattle came from Oliver himself. He must have given a full run-down of their relationship to some investigating official. And once in the department, anyone with access could have leaked it. What a nest of vipers.

Kate closed the computer with the dull realisation that the media circus would now start again. The camera lenses so thick at her car window they looked like a honeycomb, the dependence on Amal and Talika to protect her, the constant calls and emails.

Somehow she would have to find the strength to battle through again without saying a word. She certainly wasn't going to talk to Jarvis Stanley. That would only add fuel to the fire.

By mid-June Kate was doing odd agency jobs to keep body and soul together: a day's work in a confectioner's, cheffing at the weekend for a hotel, even covering for a sick sandwich hand in Pret a Manger.

It was easy work. The other staff were generally friendly, she didn't have to think, and she could go home when her time was up. It made her realise just what a lonely business being a small caterer was: doing all the thinking, planning and selling single-handed, and then doing nearly all the cooking alone.

It bugged her that so many of the kitchens she worked in were, to her mind, unprincipled: using cod from unsustainable fisheries, never trying to buy veg locally or in season, not bothering to recycle anything, employing illegal immigrants and underpaying or overworking them. She was slightly ashamed of her ability to simply shut her mind to such issues. And on the whole, she enjoyed the work and the temporary holiday from responsibility.

She was offered a permanent job in a conference centre

kitchen in which she'd helped out, and for a moment she was tempted. She knew she could do a better job than most of the cooks there, but the pay was appalling. She knew she couldn't have survived on a nine-to-five cooking job unless she got to the top and became a head chef or something. And then she'd be back to working fifteen-hour days.

Survival was her only objective right now. The Oliver scandal had put paid to all her government work and the recession had pretty well halved the rest. It was astonishing to think that two months ago she was doing so well she was barely able to cope. Now she was no longer even earning enough to be registered for VAT. In some ways this was a relief because filling in the VAT returns was a pain, but it meant no reclaiming VAT on anything.

Kate had had to ask the hire company to repossess her brand-new van because she couldn't afford the payments on it. She was without a vehicle of any kind, though Amal lent her his van when he could. Sometimes she had to hire a taxi to take food and equipment to jobs, which meant adding the cost to her prices. But there was no other way.

She had kept the new blast chiller, because the penalty for default was almost as much as the price of the thing. At least she'd been able to renegotiate the terms – the supplier didn't want the chiller back anyway, since no one was buying, and he'd have to collect and store it.

There were still some loyal customers, and they still had parties, but they drank supermarket cava, not champagne, and ate fish pie, not lobster. But she was grateful. With thousands more out of work every month she knew how lucky she was to have a rent-free house, and to work in an industry which meant she and Toby would never be hungry; indeed they could eat really well.

Not that her molly coddled young son thought so. One day he said, 'Mum, why can't we have food like everyone else? Mary's mum gives us ice-cream from the supermarket and white bread and proper sausages. Not home-made stuff.'

Not for the first time, Kate explained the benefits of healthy food. 'I know,' said Toby, 'but I like proper food from the shop. So does everybody.'

'Is that really true, darling? You like fruit, don't you? And vegetables, and the curries that you have at Sanjay's house.'

'They're OK. But I like chips better. And burgers.'

One Saturday, Nothing Fancy was doing the sort of job that was now extremely rare, a no-expense-spared wedding in a magnificent country house near Esher. It had been booked a year before the banking collapse and Kate had feared it would be cancelled, or that Lord Suskind would decree that he could no longer afford such extravagance. But no, it seemed the Suskind riches were beyond the reach of recession and Kate hoped to make enough money on this one day to get her through the month.

It had rained all night and the ground was so soggy they could not set up tables in the open air as planned. The chair legs would have sunk deep into the lawn as soon as anybody sat down, and so would the high heels of the female wedding guests. The best Kate could do was have the porters roll up the sides of the big marquee. It had stopped raining now and at least the guests, safe on the matting floor of the tent, would be able to see the dripping peonies and roses in the garden, and beyond that, the manicured lawns, the park, the woods and fields. It was a magnificent setting, surrounding a perfect Georgian mansion. No wonder Lady Suskind wanted her guests outside.

Kate was running late, but forced herself to behave as if they had all the time in the world. Nothing upset a client more than the caterer panicking: the whole point of caterers, she reminded herself, was to take the stress out of the occasion.

She walked fast into the kitchen tent. 'Joan,' she said, 'why isn't the buffet laid up?'

'Nearly there,' said Joan. There was something in her tone that alerted Kate to a problem.

'What's up?' she said. 'It's nearly two. We need to be ready before they go to the church or the poor woman will spend her daughter's wedding wondering if we know what we're doing.'

'I can't find the tablecloths for the buffet. The ones for the round tables, thirty of them, were there OK, but no long ones. Are you sure you ordered them?'

'Of course, eight three-metre cloths plus undercloths, and slip cloths for the tiered back. And a smaller one for the wedding cake table.'

'I've got the undercloths. Tommy is putting them on now. But no linen.'

'Hold on, I'll look.' Kate hurried to her briefcase, fished out the papers and found the hire order. 'Yes,' she called, 'they're on the order. Didn't you check the order?'

Joan closed her eyes briefly. 'I'm so sorry, Kate. Of course I should have, but the rain meant the hirers dumped everything in the garage at the front of the house. It took ages to lug it all over.'

Kate's mind was racing. 'If the cloths are not in the linen box, they're not here. We'll have to get others from somewhere.'

'We could ask the client. She must have some in a big house like this.'

'Absolutely not,' said Kate. 'We don't want her knowing we've screwed up. You'll have to drive into Esher and see if you can beg, borrow or steal some. A hotel might lend us a few, or you might have to buy them if you can find a department store. Or get sheets, or curtain material. Anything. Preferably white or cream. OK?'

Joan said, 'I'll have a go. Don't worry, love, I'll find something.'

Kate pulled a fat roll of ten pound notes – the cash with which to pay the casual staff – out of her handbag, and thrust it at Joan. 'Quick. Go,' she said. 'We need a total of about twenty-five metres of cloth.'

Suddenly Adrian, the florist, was at her elbow. Oh God, she thought, we are now going to have histrionics from the artist. Adrian was hugely talented but he considered himself a genius, and he had a temperament to match.

He didn't waste time on preliminaries. 'For God's sake, Kate, how am I meant to decorate four buffet tables and a backdrop in ten minutes?'

'Hello, Adrian,' said Kate calmly. 'The tables look sensational, well done.'

'Fuck the tables, how am I to do the buffet if you can't have a few trestles ready?'

Kate looked beyond him to see Lady Suskind, now in a pink silk suit and feathery hat, teetering across the wet lawn towards them. Kate looked squarely at Adrian.

'Adrian,' she hissed through clenched teeth, 'if you say one word of complaint, or contradict me in front of the client, if you give the tiniest indication to her that we have a problem, then this will be the last job you do for me.' She didn't wait for an answer, but moved swiftly through the tables to inter-cept Lady Suskind on the other side of the tent, far away from the unmade buffet tables.

'You look wonderful, Lady Suskind,' she exclaimed, 'such a pretty colour.'

'Thank you, Kate.' Lady Suskind looked round the marquee,

at the thirty round tables for ten, covered with cloths of cream and silver brocade; at the swags of orange blossom and ivy round their skirts; at the arrangements of white lilies, jasmine, and cream roses exploding from the top of tall silver stands, variegated ivy and silver ribbons trailing to the table; at the silver-painted chairs with silver and white cushions and huge white bows at their backs, and at the sparkling glasses and carefully laid places.

It was, thought Kate, as traditional as you could get. But it was certainly pretty.

Lady Suskind exclaimed over the little packets of sugared almonds, tied with silver ribbon. 'It looks very nice, doesn't it?' she said, 'but what about the buffet? I particularly want to check the buffet.'

Kate could not stop her. Weaving between the tables, she walked straight to where it had been agreed the buffet would be. She stopped in consternation. 'I thought you said everything would be ready before we left for church. We leave in fifteen minutes.' She surveyed the bare trestle tables and the littered floor in dismay.

God, it looks like a war zone, thought Kate. On the ground around the long tables were a mass of polystyrene blocks out of which they were to build the tiered back to the buffet. The wedding cake, still in unassembled tiers, sat in three boxes. The boxes of flowers and greenery were stacked to one side, and the tools of Adrian's trade (wire, secateurs, ribbons, pins) were waiting in a shallow tray. An aluminium stepladder lay on its side, a full watering can next to it.

Kate's voice, she hoped, was steeped in confidence. 'Don't worry, Lady Suskind, it's all under control. We never put the food out until the very last minute. I like everything to stay in the fridge, covered up. Food dries out so quickly, and besides, we need to keep it cool. We'll do the buffet while you're in church.'

'Kate, that is not what you told me when we went through all this. Is something wrong? Has the food not arrived, is that it?'

'No, everything is fine, I assure you, Lady Suskind. The food is here, in the fridges, ready to go.'

'But surely you could get on with the flowers and decoration before you bring the food out. How long will it all take?'

'Please, Lady Suskind, don't worry. It will take us at most half an hour to add the cloths, flowers and food, and you will be gone well over an hour. We'll be fine. Don't give it a thought.'

'But surely the florist needs more time. He took all morning . . .'

'Truly, Lady Suskind, *we* are fine. But how about you? I would be a bag of nerves if my daughter was getting married. Would you like a quick glass of fizz before you set off?' Kate caught her head waiter's eye and he nodded.

Lady Suskind persisted. She turned to Adrian, 'Are you under control, young man? You have certainly done a lovely job on the rest.'

Kate stared hard at Adrian, willing him to toe the line.

'Thank you very much,' he said. 'And yes, it won't take a jiffy to get this lot done.' He gave a dismissive wave towards the buffet and the gear on the floor.

Lady Suskind did not look entirely reassured as she took the glass of champagne from George, but she nodded and said, 'Well, I must leave it to you.' Then she accepted Kate's suggestion that she inspect the food before she set off for the ceremony.

Kate had the driver lower the tail lift of the refrigerated truck so Lady Suskind could get in. But fear for her wedding finery and the icy blast of chilled air cut the visit short. She admired the two towering gâteaux St Honoré, made from caramel-covered choux, filled with whipped coffee and vanilla flavoured cream. Talika had assembled them early this morning in Kate's kitchen, using silicone moulds to get a perfect witch's hat shape. Kate had been nervous that the damp weather would soften the caramel, but it was fine, thin and brittle.

While Lady Suskind made her hurried inspection of the trays of lobster and crab, the terrines and mousses, bowls of salads and platters of meats, Kate sneaked a glance at her watch. Joan had been gone twenty-five minutes. The wedding was at two-thirty and they'd be back sometime after three-thirty. It was getting a lot too close for comfort.

The minute their client hurried off to round up the wedding party, Kate rang Joan on her mobile.

'Any luck?'

'No. Nightmare. There's a stationer's with thick paper cloths, not too bad, but they are out of cream and white. I've tried the hotel – duty manager too junior to dare give them to me, and a restaurant, but they use runners not full cloths. Am looking for a store now, but the traffic isn't brilliant.'

'OK, but if you can't find anything in the next ten minutes, come back. As soon as they've left for the church, I'm going to raid their linen cupboard.'

Kate cut the call and dropped her mobile into her apron pocket. She found the wine waiter. 'Have you got any napkins?' she asked, 'I know we ordered two or three dozen extra for tray-cloths and so on.'

'Sure, how many do you want?'

'All of them. Your chaps will have to pour the champagne from unwrapped bottles and fold tea towels over your arms. I'm sorry, but the linen for the buffet hasn't arrived and I need everything I can lay my hands on.' She did not wait for an answer, but picked up the pile of napkins and hurried back to the buffet.

'Adrian, come and help me. We need to pin these round the boxes.'

Adrian was boiling up for a tantrum. 'But they are all wrong! The background is supposed to be plain white. My design—'

'Tough,' said Kate. 'No option. And silver brocade won't kill you. The alternative is coloured paper. So be grateful.'

'I cannot work with this sort of—'

'Just shut up, Adrian,' she snapped. 'Do you want this job or not? Decide now.'

Adrian rolled his eyes but he did help. And he was much quicker than she. He had the boxes neatly wrapped and pinned in the big brocade napkins, their edges sharp, the pattern the right way up. Together they lifted the tables into place to make two long wide service stations each side of the smaller square table for the cake.

Kate made sure the cake table was slightly in front and separated from the others so the bride and groom could get round to cut the cake without presenting their backs to the guests, or, more important, to the photographer.

Then they were stuck again. They couldn't continue assembling the tiered backdrop until the tables were covered.

Kate ran across the lawn and through the house. All of the Suskind staff had gone to the wedding so there was no one to ask permission from, or even to ask where the linen cupboard was.

But Kate found it almost at once. A small room on the landing outside the first floor bedrooms. It looked like a bed-linen shop, stuffed full of sheets, blankets, duvets, everything you could think of.

But there were only two white tablecloths and both of them were round, with deep lace borders.

Most of the bed linen and towels were coloured or patterned, in separate shelves marked *Pink Room, Green Room, Peach Room, Lilac Room.* Each shelf had different piles, all in matching colours, over stickers on the shelf edge: towels; duvet covers; flat sheets; fitted sheets, etc. This is one organised housekeeper, thought Kate.

The *Master Bedroom* had white linen sheets. Kate simply pulled all the flat sheets down. No duvet covers. *Cream Room* was out of flat sheets but had two duvet covers, which she added to her pile. She started for the door, then turned back and added the round tablecloths, and all the white pillowslips. Just in case.

She raced down the stairs, across the lawn and into the tent. Joan was back, empty-handed, and everyone fell on the linen and got to work.

Suddenly it was fun. Maybe I'm a crisis junkie, Kate thought. Her spirits lifted as the buffet tables swiftly materialised. She found herself even grinning at Adrian, who had forgotten his sulks in supervising the others.

They folded the heavy linen double sheets so that the deep embroidered edges ran along the front drops each side of the cake table in the middle. Adrian used the Suskinds' lace cloths for the cake table, one on top of the other and artfully, apparently casually, draped, ruffled and pinned to disguise the fact that they were round and the table was square.

Once the cloths and back tiers were in place, Adrian arranged the flowers and pinned the garlands in no time at all. And then the waiters brought out the food, and positioned it under Kate's direction. Joan and Adrian assembled the cake between them and everyone helped clear up the debris. It was exactly three-thirty.

Kate clapped her hands for silence.

'Thank you, all of you. I honestly believe Nothing Fancy has the best team in the world. And Adrian, you have excelled your-self. This is beautiful.' And then they all clapped, relief and pleasure and pride combined. It was a good moment.

The party went wonderfully well. As always, a good many guests got completely plastered, among them, to Kate's amuse-ment, the elegant Lady Suskind. After her daughter and new son-in-law had cut the cake, she was standing next to Kate by the buffet, now full of pastries for tea. Suddenly she turned, wobbling a bit and smiled broadly.

'Kate,' she said, 'you are just so good! There was I thinking you would never be ready, but you were of course.' She peered down at the front of the buffet cloth. 'And how did you find tablecloths with our family monogram on them? So clever!'

Kate smiled and opened her mouth to tell her the truth. But then she thought, No, I'll tell her tomorrow. Just for today, I'll leave her thinking we are miracle workers.

By nine o'clock that evening it was all over. The guests had gone to a post-wedding ball at the golf club, and Kate's job was nearly done. The wait staff were paid, the vans were packed, the marquee and kitchen tent picked clean of litter. The chairs were stacked and the tables dismantled, and the hired gear was checked and ready for collection.

Kate was folding the pilfered linen and stacking it into her car to take to a good laundry, when Adrian, who had come back to collect his vases and stands, said, 'Well, Kate, are you going to marry this government chap? I hear he's mad about you.'

Kate looked at him astonishment. 'Who told you that?'

'Isn't it true? It was all the gossip in the kitchen today. Even Joan thinks it's true, and I met some friends of yours at dinner a few nights ago and they said—'

'Stop, stop. What friends?'

'A couple you used to work with in some restaurant. Carole something. Says she read it in the paper . . .'

Kate dismissed this with a shake of the head, 'But Joan? She cannot believe it. She knows better than anyone . . .'

'She does. Ask her . . .'

Kate, exhausted though she was, was galvanised into action. She left Adrian abruptly and rushed into the kitchen to find Joan.

She was pulling on a waterproof anorak, and looked really tired. Kate had a second of regret that she was about to challenge her. But she had to.

'Joan, Adrian says you believe this rubbish about me and Oliver Stapler. Do you?'

'I . . . er . . . Well, yes, I think I do. Unless you tell me differently, of course. But he obviously seeks you out, and you seem to . . .'

'Well, none of it is true. None of it, do you understand?'

'OK, OK, Kate. But it's not just me. Even Lady Suskind . . .'

'Lady Suskind? Good God, what has *she* said?'

'Well, some of the guests were talking about it. She said she hoped when you were a grand cabinet minister's wife you wouldn't give up Nothing Fancy . . . And she knows the Staplers. She said she'd asked them to the wedding and she assumed they'd said no because his wife would not want to meet you.'

Kate felt utterly deflated. It had been such a triumphant job, and she'd not given the Oliver matter a thought for hours.

'Oh Joan, it's not true. And I hope you'll do me a favour and scotch any rumours you hear.'

Joan said she would, and put a motherly arm round Kate. 'It's all Dennis's fault, you know. He was the one that told the paper that you drove home together, and that you and Mr Stapler often shared a bottle of wine and sent the rest of us home.'

Kate was silent, trying to absorb this information. She nodded slowly. 'Dennis, of course. Of course it was. I should have guessed, he's such a snake. I don't know what I've done to him to make him so dislike me, but he does.' She shook her head, then looked directly at Joan and said, 'But Joan, how can you say I "sent you home"? You make it sound as if I let you go because I wanted to be alone with Oliver. Well, I did – in the sense that I enjoyed a drink with him. But I let you go because if the work was done there was no reason for you to hang around.'

'I'm sorry, Kate, I didn't mean . . .'

'I was thinking of you, not me.'

But Kate knew this was not quite true. As far as Oliver was concerned she thought of little but him, and her, all the time.

Chapter Eighteen

Oliver could not believe how fast things were moving. He seemed to have no control, or even any say, in any part of his life.

Ruth, once she'd done her bit, standing beside him outside their Lambeth house to be photographed and hear him publicly declare that he was innocent of adultery and that he loved her, had gone back to the West Midlands and resumed her cool distance. Far from being gratified, she'd hated the whole performance, and the pictures showed her looking either glum or disdainful.

Of course he'd not enjoyed it either; it was against his nature to talk to strangers about such personal matters. He'd longed to order them all to stop muck raking and go away and do something worthwhile with their lives.

He had telephoned Ruth twice during his Middle East trip: once from Tel Aviv, and two days later from Cairo. She had failed to return his first call, and was cool on the second. They had a rather formal exchange about the press trying to make something of the fact that he, a Labour minister, sent his daughters to a non-state school.

'If that's all they can dredge up,' said Oliver, 'it must mean the Kate story has run out of steam. Just as long as the other stuff doesn't surface.'

'Why should it? They questioned you months ago and you've paid the duty on the china, haven't you?'

'And a fine. But both matters are on the public record, if anyone cares to look.'

'I doubt if anyone is interested.'

'I just feel uneasy. It would be a load off my mind if we found that necklace. You have really looked, haven't you?'

'Of course I've looked.'

He had waited for her to say something encouraging, however banal: ask him how the trip was going, wish him a safe flight home. But nothing.

He'd said, 'All right, darling. See you at the weekend.'

'Yes. Goodbye then.'

In the ensuing days of little sleep, strange food, air-conditioned hotel rooms and long meetings that ended in bland and meaningless statements, Oliver realised he had never felt more lonely.

His political career hung in the balance, his wife was cold, his children indifferent. Unused to self-pity, the thought that he had no real friends surprised him. But it was true. There was no brother or old mate he could discuss his troubles with – all his closest friends were politicians or civil servants and he could hardly embroil them in his troubles.

The one person who might have lent a sympathetic ear and said something sensible was Kate. And she was the one person he couldn't speak to.

He'd still have liked to lift the phone, commiserate, and discuss their joint problem, but it was too late now. He had not done it at once, when he should have, and now he dare not. Terry was right: he must give no ammunition to the press or the Tories. Anyway, he had behaved like such a cur he doubted if Kate would talk to him if he did call.

Two weeks later, after a weekend in the country which he had spent in his study catching up on work while his family were off competing in some horsey event, he arrived at his office to find Terry sitting at his desk.

The press supremo didn't apologise and he didn't get up. 'I asked Helen to let me in. Hope you don't mind?'

Oliver dropped his red briefcase on the sofa and sat down beside it. He didn't answer. He did mind, but what was the point in saying so?

'Why are you here?'

'Ah. Yes.' Terry took his time opening his briefcase on Oliver's desk and extracting a file, which he did not open.

Oliver swallowed his irritation. He could not believe they were to have a conversation with Terry occupying his desk while he sat halfway across the room on the sofa. But he was damned if he would take the chair opposite the desk, like a supplicant for a job. Terry can come over here, he thought. But Terry looked up and said, 'We have decided to sue *Scandal Sheet*. That piece was without doubt libellous.'

Oliver's heart sank. They had discussed taking legal action endlessly, and Oliver thought he'd won the argument. Apparently not. 'But why?' he asked. 'What good would that do? If we aren't going to sue the *Standard*, why sue a one-man-and-his-dog outfit? They won't have any money, they'll just fold.'

'Probably.' Terry gave the slightest of shrugs. 'I'd rather have gone for the *Standard*, since they do have money, but according to the lawyers we have less of a case. They could argue that the *Standard* was asking legitimate questions in the public interest – and that goes for everyone who reported on the stories in local rags and elsewhere. But *Scandal Sheet* is different. The piece is not hedged about with "allegedly" and "according to our sources", etc. If you are telling the truth, then their account is straightforward lies.'

As always, Terry had the knack of making Oliver angry. 'If

you are telling the truth' indeed. How dare he? Terry knew damn well it was the truth. To give himself time to cool down, Oliver stood up and filled a glass with water from the jug on the corner of his desk. He did not offer Terry one, but returned to the sofa wondering sourly why the man bothered to come and discuss anything with him. If the past weeks had taught him anything it was that Terry was not going to listen to anyone who didn't agree with him.

But Oliver challenged him nonetheless. 'Terry, this is mad. It will just start the press hare running again. Apart from some comment on the *Scandal Sheet* piece, everyone has pretty well dropped it. The story is on its last legs, surely?'

'That's not the point. The point is to teach the bastards a lesson. It's a good opportunity for the Government to rein in the press a bit. We will undoubtedly win, and that will give the rest of Fleet Street something to think about.'

'And in the meantime my poor wife has to endure having her job as a breeder and horsewoman ridiculed, and Kate McKinnon has to put up with new attentions of the paparazzi.'

'Yup. I imagine you are right, Oliver. But I presume, since you protest your innocence and both the ladies' good names, you would prefer all three of you to be exonerated, would you not?'

Oliver knew further argument would make him furious and achieve nothing, so he changed tack. 'Does that mean, I hope it does mean, that you will join Kate's name to the petition?'

Terry smiled, a quizzical curl of the lip. 'Absolutely not. If Miss McKinnon wants to sue, the courts are open to her. She might even get legal aid. Who knows? But we will certainly not complicate matters with a joint petition.'

'But why ever not, Terry? Her defence will corroborate ours, and it will show the world that the Government believes her to be as much a victim as I am.'

'Why would we want to do that?'

Suddenly Oliver had had enough. He stood up, walked to the desk and leant over it, forcing Terry to look up at him. 'Because the public might think that you lot had a heart, which of course you do not, and because Kate has been appallingly treated by all of us. She's had her contracts terminated, her life turned upside down and her good name muddied. If we are to sue and get what damages there are, Kate needs the money. That's why.'

Terry stood up, put the unread file back in the briefcase, slowly clicked it shut and shook his head.

'No dice, Oliver,' he said, making his languid way to the door. He turned with his hand on the doorknob, holding the pause like a bad actor in a play. 'You are sounding like a lover, Oliver. The less concern you show for your little cook the safer you will be.'

Oliver went to see his old friend Lord Brampton in the House of Lords. Brampton had been a peer for the last twenty years and was now in his late seventies. He had been a friend of Oliver's father for fifty years, since Durham University where they had both played in the squash team. Brampton was a crossbencher, admired by both sides of the House. He was also formidably clever, the premier Queen's Counsel on intellectual property rights. Oliver could not claim to be on intimate terms with him, but he knew Brampton would be straight with him, neither telling him what he wanted to hear, nor revelling in doom.

It was a Friday evening and neither Lords nor Commons were sitting. As he stopped in the middle of the echoing, history-soaked lobby, he could see down the wide passages into both chambers. He looked through the open doors to his left at the familiar green benches of the Commons with the Speaker's dais to the end, and then to the right to the gilt and red of the Lords, with the woolsack under the throne.

The likes of Salisbury, Wellington and Palmerston had spoken from those red branches. This was the chamber where distinguished, erudite, interesting, big achievers from the law, the church, business, government and charity, ended up. Plus, he thought, a few rogues and hereditary peers to leaven the mix. The best club in the country.

The thought that he might now never be a member hit him like a sudden punch. It had not occurred to him before. While fighting for his current job he had not, until this minute, thought he was also fighting for his future seat here. Having successfully made it to one of the most senior posts in the cabinet, his right to a peerage was pretty well automatic. The only proviso (unwritten, of course, just as his right to the Lords was unwritten) was that he not be disgraced.

Oliver straightened his shoulders and walked on up to Brampton's cramped office, shared with two other peers. Brampton, still lean and athletic looking, rose and came round his desk.

'How good to see you, young man. I follow your rise and rise with admiration and interest.' He didn't wait for a reply, but put a hand on Oliver's shoulder, 'Shall we go to the bar?'

When they were seated in a corner, insulated by the steady buzz of talk, Oliver said, 'I imagine you have been following my travails. Likely to bring an abrupt halt to my rise and rise as you put it.'

'I doubt it. But, yes, I've been reading the gossip. I sent you a note, you remember, of the chin-up, play-on variety.'

'Of course you did. I'm sorry. Actually the only heartening things about this horrible business are messages like yours. I've had mail from friends like you, but also from hundreds of constituents and complete strangers.'

'So, how can I help, Oliver? Where have you got to? Is Terry still threatening to sue?'

Oliver told him everything: his unease at abandoning Kate, his conviction that to sue was a mistake. He also told Brampton about the necklace and the china, and his anxiety about the stories being made public. Brampton listened carefully, like the lawyer he was, seldom interrupting, and making a few indecipherable notes in a little Moleskine notebook done up with an elastic band.

When Oliver had finished, Brampton stood up and picked up their glasses. 'Right,' he said, 'let's have another whisky and I'll tell you what I think.'

He started with the Necklace and Limoges affairs. 'I don't think there is anything more you can do about the tax on the dinner service. They will have your statement that it was a long time ago, with rules less clear, and that you had simply not thought about it; that you admitted you should not have done it, that you later paid the tax, the interest on the tax, and the fine. If a journalist goes digging around and discovers it, they will try to make something of it, probably accusing you also of using public funds to transport your goods, but it won't run for long. The public will see it as trifling. Foolish, but not drastic.'

'God, I hope so,' said Oliver, 'and it may not see the light of day. As far as the Inland Revenue is concerned the Limoges file is closed. The one that worries me is the necklace. We still haven't found it.'

'OK, well, here's what I think. You should get a letter into the Foreign Office files that states your case very clearly, apologises, and offers to repay the value of the necklace.'

'I couldn't afford it. It could be worth half a million.'

'Really? Good God.'

'Yes. My suspicion is that the tip-off about the necklace was somehow prompted by discontents in the Yemeni administration. When Ruth was given it, relations between the two countries were good. Now they tend to lump us in with the US, and they don't like us at all. Could be a way of embarrassing us, but I think it's more likely to be a stab at the present regime. The president has recently been re-elected but with more opposition. You know the sort of thing. How could our leaders be giving away Yemen's priceless heritage to infidel westerners? Maybe one of their museum people ferreted around our national museums and discovered it was nowhere and asked a few questions.'

'Interesting. I guess the only way we will know is if some journalist thinks it worth his while to pursue. Getting info under the Freedom of Information Act is time consuming to say the least.'

'Well, that's one thing in my favour. But won't the letter you're suggesting, even without an offer of repayment, just spark a mole to leak the story, especially if they know the value. It's too good a story to pass up, surely? "Foreign Secretary in Half a Million Fraud" will sell a few papers. Wouldn't I just be hastening disclosure?'

'There is that danger, but it shows that you are proactively concerned about the matter and not waiting like a frightened mouse for it to surface. You could write to the head of whoever collects such things – is it the Treasury? – and simply say that you are very sorry to report that you and Ruth have been unable to find the necklace, and remind them that neither of you thought it was valuable so regret you did not take proper care of it.'

'And what about the repayment?'

'Best to say nothing about that, I'd say.'

They turned to the central question of the adultery allegations. Brampton thought Terry was playing a slippery game, one that would enhance his standing, but do nothing for Oliver's or Kate's. 'He cannot lose. It's cut and dried. It will give the press a bloody nose, but it will drag you and Kate through the mud for months more. True, you will have proved your innocence, but the public won't really believe in it. "No smoke without fire", is how they see all sex stories.'

'What would you advise them to do, if you were Terry?'

'God forbid. Appalling man.' Brampton gave a theatrical shudder. 'What they should do is settle the thing as quickly as possible, asking for a complete apology printed prominently on the front page of the next issue and on the home page of the website. And they should insist on costs and a small sum for damages, which they should give to charity. Not enough to bankrupt *Scandal Sheet* – bankrupting small businesses, even unsavoury ones, won't go down well in this climate – but enough for Terry to be able to say they have won on all counts.'

Oliver agreed with all this, and was pleased when Brampton offered to see the Prime Minister or Terry and see if he could persuade them.

'That is really good of you. If anyone can make them see sense, it's you.' Oliver took a slow sip of his whisky, and looked steadily into the older man's eyes. 'Can I ask you to make the case for including Kate in the petition? It is so unfair on her, and she can't afford to sue. The fact that she won't be challenging *Scandal Sheet's* allegations in court surely weakens our case, doesn't it?'

But Brampton was shaking his head. 'Not as much as photographs of you walking side by side into court, and testifying one after the other will. No, Oliver, not a good idea. You have to drop her.'

Oliver ran his palm over his head, eyes shut.

'Would you at least ring her and explain why I cannot help her?'

Lord Brampton again shook his head. 'No. I'm sorry, Oliver.'

Oliver sat still, looking into his whisky. He knew that what had just passed was his last, feeble, unsuccessful parry on Kate's behalf. And it had failed. He had a momentary image of her sinking fast in deep water, drowning, hands reaching for his ... He looked up to see Brampton's eyes, soft with sympathy, watching him.

'Brutal, I agree,' Brampton said. 'But that's politics.'

CHAPTER NINETEEN

Kate was in the downstairs bathroom looking for a decent-sized safety pin to hold her chef's pants up – she'd lost a good bit of weight recently and she didn't have time to alter her trousers – when she heard the thud of the mail hitting the hall floor. She pinned the trousers, checked her image in the mirror and thought how much better she looked when slim (well, slim-ish), then went through to sort the mail.

As usual it was ninety-five per cent junk. Most real communication came by text or email these days, but that did not diminish the post-bag. She swiftly sorted through it, binning a lot and keeping the few items of interest – a couple of postcards from friends, her subscription copies of the *New Statesman* and *The Week* and a catering mag.

There was only one proper letter for her. Kate looked at the Foreign Office logo on the back of the envelope for a long while, hesitating to open it. For a split second she'd thought it was from Oliver and her heart had leapt. But of course it wouldn't be. If he had wanted to communicate with her officially, he'd had six weeks to do it. And if he was writing from home, he wouldn't use a government envelope. She thought, he's a bastard or a coward, that's what. Either he does not care what is happening to me, or he is ignoring me on orders from above.

She slowly inserted her paper knife and slit the envelope.

Inside was a smaller envelope, addressed to Kate McKinnon, Kate's Kitchen, c/o the Foreign Office, Whitehall, with a big blue handwritten message across it: *PLEASE FORWARD*. The writing was vaguely familiar. Probably from an old customer from the Kate's Kitchen days who has lost my address and doesn't know of the change of name, she thought. Well, good, I could do with any new work right now. She slit the smaller envelope and unfolded the letter.

Dearest Kate,

I hope so much this gets to you. Over the last six months I've tried to track you down through places we both worked, or friends we had in common, but either they had not heard of you or had no idea where you are now. Even internet search sites, and Facebook etc came up blank.

But tapping your name into Google five weeks ago suddenly brought up the Evening Standard *story, and then a lot more like it. So I discovered that you are still cooking, still single, that you have a son, Toby (who must be our child) and that you are embroiled with a government minister.*

It will be nothing to you I know, but I cannot tell you how much jealousy I feel for this Oliver Stapler, and sadness for you. I have thought about you so much over the past seven years but until recently I've not tried to contact you because I know you must hate me. You have every right to. I behaved like such a shit, running away. And now it looks as if this Stapler chap is scuttling back to his wife and abandoning you. Poor Kate, you must think men are a complete shower.

You will not be surprised to hear that my marriage fell apart. I am obviously lousy at relationships. My ex-wife has got the kids, and makes access to them as difficult as she possibly can. She also got most of my money – I had to sell my half share in a successful restaurant, so now I work for my ex-partner as salaried chef. Not great.

But the reason for this letter is to say how truly sorry I am for the way I behaved. I would give anything to see you again and to get to know my son.

I long to know if you love this Stapler guy, if there is any point in my coming to see you?

I feel as if I'm putting a message into a bottle and tossing it to the waves. But there must be some chance of this reaching you. If it does, have mercy, and contact me.

Chris

At the top of the letter was an address and telephone number in Melbourne.

Kate sat quite still, conscious that her heart rate was up and that the letter was trembling in her hand.

For nearly seven years, ever since she'd announced her pregnancy and lost Chris as a result, she had cut him out of her mind. If she thought of him at all it was as something evil to be kept away from Toby at all costs.

She started to read the letter again, and then realised there were two pages. She lifted the top one to reveal a picture of Chris, looking very much as she remembered him but tanned, and with slightly gingery designer stubble giving him an outdoor look. He was smiling, crouched on the beach with his arms round two little girls.

As Kate studied his open, carefree face, she remembered how much she'd loved him, how much fun they'd had, how they had talked and dreamed of owning a restaurant together. Tears came into her eyes for that lost time. He hadn't been a villain, just a coward. Maybe most men were cowards . . .

She looked intently at the children. Both were blonde and

pretty, one – she was about three or four – looking seriously at the camera, her plump little legs covered in sand, a beach bat in her hand. The smaller one was sitting on Chris's muscled thigh, his arm round her middle. She was twisting towards him, both hands reaching up to his face.

It must be appalling to have your wife take your daughters away. She thought of losing Toby, and immediately her stomach contracted with a visceral pain and she shuddered. Losing your children was worse, perhaps, than having your lover run away at the prospect of one.

Poor Chris, she thought. He's lost his children, his wife, his business, his money. He's desperate for love and family, and maybe harbours hopes of breaking into this one. For a moment Kate let a little fantasy run like a movie through her head: a fantasy of falling in love with Chris again, of running away from Oliver and her business troubles to Australia, of realising those old dreams – a family restaurant in the country, with children, chickens and pets underfoot; tables in the garden; food from the veg plot. Then she dropped the letter in the wastepaper basket and stood up.

She would not reply to him. She could not have him messing up her life again.

Kate was in the bathroom when she heard Oliver's voice. For a wild second she thought he was in the bedroom. Her heart, treacherously forgetting her weeks of anger, leapt with a mixture of excitement and alarm.

But almost at once she realised it was the *Today* programme. Careless of the window to the street, she hurried naked into the bedroom and sat on the bed, staring at the radio, her towel in her hands.

It sounded as though the Government had won their case

against *Scandal Sheet*, But surely that could not be? It couldn't have come to court so soon. But something must have happened because Oliver and the presenter, John Humphrys, were debating the case. Oliver's voice sounded full and relaxed. Kate's chest contracted, almost with pain, at the sound.

'I know, Minister, that you cannot speak about the rights and the wrongs of the case.'

'No, sadly the terms of the settlement agreed between the government and *Scandal Sheet* forbid me to comment, much as, I'm sure you understand, I would like to.'

'Precisely. We're to draw our own conclusions, and they are pretty obvious. We're told that the satirical magazine *Scandal Sheet* is to issue a front page apology, admit there was no substance in their allegations that you had an affair with Kate McKinnon and pay a substantial sum in damages. So that's pretty clear: if it had come to court they would have lost.'

'John, I'm saying nothing!' Oliver was smiling, Kate could tell. She found herself, against her will, smiling too. But her smile quickly turned bitter. So Oliver was to get a shed-load of money, whereas she, who was the only one in this sorry tale to have lost money because of it, was to get nothing.

'Well, can you tell us what you will do with the money?'

'Yes. First of all, it won't come to me. The government sued *Scandal Sheet*, I didn't. But I am, I believe, to choose a charity to benefit from this unfortunate business. At least some good will come out of it.'

'And what charity will that be?'

'I'm not sure yet, but it will be a local one in my Queensmead constituency.'

Kate heard Oliver say, 'I'd like any money to go ...' but Humphrys overrode him.

'We need, Minister, to move now to a wider issue. It was

the *Evening Standard* that started this rumour and led the chase. A false rumour, as has now been shown. But they, a big rich corporation, are to escape any penalty while *Scandal Sheet*, a tiny magazine run on a shoestring, might well be bankrupted.'

'I don't think there's any danger of that. I don't want to see any business go bust. Radical, unreliable, sometimes unlikable, publications are the price we pay for freedom of the press. We just require that they be honest.'

'So you're saying that *Scandal Sheet* was dishonest, in effect telling lies?'

'John,' said Oliver, amused, 'you don't catch me that easily. Everyone knows I denied, and do deny, the charge that I had an affair with Kate McKinnon. But I cannot comment on the recent legal settlement. I'm talking of the press in general, not any specific publication.' Kate squeezed her eyes shut at the mention of her name in Oliver's mouth. His voice was beautiful, deep and resonant, and for a moment it produced an image of him talking, his eyes alive. It stopped her listening to what he was saying. She frowned and forced herself to concentrate.

'OK, Minister, I accept that,' said Humphrys, 'but what about the *Standard*? Why did you not go for them?'

'*I* did not go for anybody. The government took up the case and sued *Scandal Sheet*, because this sort of coverage is damaging to the government and to the reputation of politicians in general.'

'So why not sue the *Evening Standard*? They must have been far more damaging to the government, and certainly to you?'

'Well, yes, I had a horrible time at their hands, as I am sure Kate McKinnon did, but, according to the lawyers, because *The Standard* hedged its allegations around with words like "alleged" and "supposed" and "according to our sources" none of that innuendo and rumour was actually libellous. I'm sure if they'd been less clever – remember big newspapers have very good lawyers checking copy before they print it – the government would have been able to sue them too.'

'So the giant gets off scot-free, while the minnow pays the price?'

'Not quite scot-free. Inevitably, the *Standard's* reputation will be damaged by this case. Readers aren't stupid. They, like you, will draw their own conclusions and I couldn't possibly comment!'

Kate found her heart was thudding uncomfortably in her chest. She wrapped the towel tightly round her body and bent towards the radio. She could not help but warm to Oliver. He was just so *grown-up*. So humourful and confident. She could never have spoken about this thing without getting indignant, or tearful, or tongue-tied.

But then, she thought, he's a politician. He knows who matters to his career, so of course he puts on a show for them. The *Today* programme matters, and the listeners matter. But what about her? She did not matter, so no point in expending energy, or sympathy, or kindness, on her.

'Blah, blah, blah,' Kate said, as she silenced Oliver Stapler, Foreign Secretary, with a stab of her finger on the Off button.

The door stepping by the press resumed at lunchtime: the honey-comb of paparazzi lenses pressed to her window, the photog-raphers standing in her flowerbeds, the papers re-raking the story. For two days she was emailed and telephoned constantly, not least by the ever-civil Jarvis Stanley from the *Standard*. He seemed to see no conflict between his polite wooing of Kate (to talk to them, sell her story, 'put the record straight') with his paper's long pieces of self-serving justification of its actions in breaking the false story in the first place. She refused all his overtures.

One evening Kate returned from a shift in a French restaurant in Chelsea to find her back door open, the door jamb splintered. Oh my God, Toby, she thought and hurtled upstairs to their bedroom, her heart pounding, fear propelling her. She reached for the light switch and for a second was bewildered by the sight of the room, flooded in light, empty, neat, the big bed with the duvet unruffled and innocent as she'd left it this morning. She leant against the door jamb, her legs too weak to support her, her brain slowly coming to its senses and translating the scene before her from child kidnap to orderly, welcoming bedroom. Of course, Toby was with Talika. What was she thinking? That she'd left him in their bed alone? She'd never left him alone in her life. She sank down to the floor, puzzled that she had come home instead of going as she usually did to collect Toby first.

Then suddenly she leapt up and ran down the stairs to see if anything had been stolen. Everything was as it had been, but something felt wrong. She sat at her desk and automatically leant down to switch the computer and printer on at the wall. They were already on. She always, always, turned them off at the wall. As she did the TV and DVD player. It saved a lot of energy.

She pressed the button to boot up the computer and a message immediately came up: 'Your computer was not closed down properly. It is now being checked for problems. Please wait.'

But she *had* closed it properly! Someone had been using it. Or snooping. But why? Surely they must know that the victory over *Scandal Sheet* meant there was nothing in the story of the Minister and the Cook. Everyone must now know it had been a tissue of lies. So what did they hope to find? Pictures of her in bed with the Foreign Secretary? Emails declaring undying love?

There was a time when she'd have loved the story to be true. Now she just wanted the whole horrible business to stop. Why were they hounding her like this? There was nothing to gain.

She knew she should call the police but, she thought wearily, what is the point? They'll not come for ages and then they'll not bother to look for the culprits. No one was hurt, nothing stolen. The police had better things to do.

I'll ring them tomorrow, she thought. She stood up to go and get Toby, but found her legs were shaking, and now she felt the sting of tears. She went through to the sitting room, her hand to her mouth, trying not to cry. She rang the Taj Amal.

'Amal . . .' Her voice was high from the effort to sound normal. 'I'm so sorry, but . . .'

'What is it, Kate, what's happened?'

And then she'd blubbed in earnest, and Amal brought the sleeping Toby over and they put him into bed. Amal secured the splintered door by nailing a plank down it, made them both tea and then stayed the night on the sofa. To Kate's protests he replied that Talika was fine. Both her brawny brothers were down from Bradford for the weekend and were camped in the sitting room.

Kate had never been frightened, living alone or with Toby, and life soon returned to normal, at least on the surface. But the incident had unsettled her. Sometimes now, her neck and shoulders ached with tension and she would find her nails digging into her palms for no reason.

She kept going, tried not to think of Oliver Stapler. Thinking of him no longer made her tearful. Just angry. She had heard nothing from him of course. He really had proved himself uncaring, selfish, hard as nails. Kate was tough with her thoughts, frog-marching them out of her head, regimenting her mind to remain focused on the essentials: caring for Toby, getting the jobs in, cooking food, paying what bills she absolutely had to. Valium helped.

Chapter Twenty

Oliver had a backlog of work that would kill a mule, and was already irritable. Ruth had spent the day in London and was put out that he had cancelled lunch with her. She seemed to have little understanding of just what being the Foreign Secretary entailed. He did the same slog as his colleagues in preparing for cabinet meetings, running a huge department, dealing with day to day crises, and sitting in the House. But in his case, on top of all that, he was constantly abroad. International meetings and conferences, with their attendant dinners, were infinitely more wearing than those at home, conducted exclusively in English.

And now he and Ruth were on a train to Solihull. On a Tuesday, when he badly needed to prepare for a statement in the Commons about Pakistan.

But Mattie's headmistress had been adamant that it could not wait till Friday. The school was worried about her progress and she wished to see both Mattie's parents. Oliver was not used to being summoned, except perhaps by the PM.

Suddenly Ruth pushed her *Evening Standard* under his nose, preventing him seeing his BlackBerry. He looked up, frowning at the interruption. Ruth said 'Look,' indicating something he should read. Oliver sighed, turned his BlackBerry off and dropped it into his shirt pocket.

He took the paper from his wife without looking at her.

There was a picture of him and Ruth coming out of their Lambeth house. He registered it as one taken the night he'd flown to the Middle East, the evening Ruth had been summoned by Terry to come to London and do her wifely duty. They both looked washed-out by the cameraman's flash. Underneath the picture he read:

STAPLER IN MORE HOT WATER

The Foreign Secretary, after the capitulation of *Scandal Sheet* over the rag's allegations of his adultery, its grovelling apology and payment of substantial damages in compensation, must have thought he was home and dry and back on the yellow brick road to the premiership.

But it seems he's back in the soup. He has been fined by the Inland Revenue for failing to pay duty on some fancy goods he imported from France. Bad enough. But we are now told he also failed to hand in a priceless antique necklace given to his wife. The museum-quality bauble was given to her on a diplomatic visit to the Yemen by the President of Yemen. It should have gone to the Treasury, if not to the British Museum. The Minister's wife claims to have 'lost it'.

One storm is damaging, three might prove fatal. Have our rulers no morals at all? The Hon Member for Queensmead has some explaining to do.

Oliver felt his face go lifeless and rigid. He looked at Ruth, and hers was the same. A bloodless mask. 'God, Ruth. I'm sorry.'

'The bastards.'

'That's that, then.'

'What do you mean?'

'I'll have to resign.'

Ruth eyes widened and she shook her head. 'No you don't. You can't.'

'I must.'

Ruth's face was recovering its colour and becoming fierce. 'You cannot wimp out now. Not after all we've been through over that bloody woman. It would be ridiculous for you to fold because of this nonsense.'

Oliver realised her voice had risen and looked across the compartment to meet the eyes of the couple on the other side of the aisle, sitting opposite Jim the detective. They had the *Evening Standard* open between them and could make the connection at any second. He stood up. 'We have to get off this train, I need to get back to the office.'

'Sit down, Oliver.' Jim, who was about to stand too, sank back in his chair as his boss sat down again.

Her looked at her. Ruth had not moved and her voice, now controlled and low again, was nonetheless charged, intense and adamant. Suddenly Oliver's irritation blossomed into hostility. She was hissing, he thought, like a witch in a pantomime. She was a stranger, a merciless stranger.

'We are going to Mattie's school because her teachers are worried about her,' she said. 'That you are in trouble again, and that it looks as if I'm to take the blame for that fucking necklace, is nothing to do with Mattie. It can wait.'

Her eyes were furious, hard as glass. He looked down and held one hand like a visor across his forehead, shielding him from the sight of her and allowing him a moment to calm down and think. He couldn't blame Ruth, and he knew she was right. But her lack of sympathy, her reaction of hard fury, shook him. And how could he have an intelligent conversation with his daughter's teachers when his world was crashing about his ears?

The meeting with Mattie's housemother and headmistress

went by almost without input from Oliver. He listened in silence as the two teachers and his wife talked in concerned tones about his daughter: perhaps all the unfortunate publicity about her father had unsettled poor Mattie; her grades had slipped, she was unwontedly truculent and rude, she was frequently half asleep.

Oliver marvelled at how calmly Ruth handled herself. She agreed that Mattie should have a conversation with the school psychiatrist or counsellor or something, and expressed her and Oliver's gratitude that the school was so supportive and caring. She looked to him for corroboration, willing him to pull himself together and say something. Oliver's forehead furrowed as he tried to get a grip on the conversation. Then he nodded and said, 'Yes, indeed, Mattie is lucky to have you. As we are.' Ruth looked slightly mollified by this, but Oliver felt as though he were in a dream. Thank God for a strong wife, he thought, but he knew he didn't mean it.

As soon as they got home, Ruth went up to check on the girls and did not come down again.

Meanwhile, Oliver sat at his desk and composed a careful letter of resignation to the Prime Minister.

The morning after the news of his resignation broke, Oliver was again in the BBC's *Today* studio, feeling curiously buoyant. He enjoyed his cup of indifferent coffee and slice of bendy cold toast in the glass-walled ante-room to the studio. The huge news room visible through the glass was almost empty; a solitary cleaner worked between the rows of desks, almost all unoccupied.

He flipped through the morning's newspapers, gratified to see that even the Tory press gave him credit for doing the decent thing, and the *Guardian* went so far as to say he'd be sorely missed. Well, he thought, from now on I'll not have to worry about the press, I'll be a matter of no interest to them. He felt a tiny tinge of regret, and reflected ruefully that losing power and privilege and a degree of fame would probably be painful, but good for him.

After ten minutes the young man who had collected him from the reception lobby reappeared. He ushered Oliver through the heavy sound-proofed door into the studio and indicated a chair opposite the two presenters. His half of the big baize-covered table between them was covered with wires, fat head-phone sets and the half-drunk water cup of a previous victim of the *Today* interview. Both presenters were half hidden behind their computer screens and desk lights but John Humphrys said a brief hello before waving to Oliver not to answer: a fat, domed light bulb embedded in a wooden block had turned from green to red and they were on the air.

'Good morning, Minister . . . Oh, I'm sorry, I should now call you Mr Stapler . . . Thank you for coming in. I must say, I'm delighted to have you in the studio so soon after your last appear-ance. Wednesday, wasn't it? But I'm also surprised. Resigning ministers usually go quietly.'

Oliver smiled. 'Well, I'm not trying to go loudly. As you know I made a statement in the House yesterday afternoon, but since the story is all over the airwaves, papers and internet, I thought I should tell the public the truth as quickly as possible so the government can get back to work.'

'We're eager to hear what you have to say, but before we get to that, when you were in this studio two days ago you were fresh from trouncing your detractors and delighted to have been vindicated on the matter of adultery. It's rather a different picture now, isn't it?

'Not as regards the imagined adultery, no. As you know, the terms of the settlement forbid me commenting on that, but it's true my star was rather higher on Wednesday than it is today.'

'All right, so what is it you want to add to your announcement in the Commons yesterday?'

'Mainly that I accept I needed to go. I resigned, it's true, but the PM could as easily have asked me to go.'

'So you jumped before you were pushed?'

'Yes. If I had not left the job of my own accord he'd probably have sent me packing. It's hard enough running a country in the middle of a recession without the distraction of press speculation about one of your team. I hope it will now die down and stop.'

'So, for the few people who have not heard or read about it, what exactly did you do to warrant your sudden departure?'

Oliver found he was rather enjoying himself. It was strangely liberating to speak openly and frankly, not in the mealy-mouthed fudge that members of government generally had to use.

'I did two very stupid and thoughtless things, one of which turns out to have been criminal.'

'Criminal? Let me understand this. As Secretary of State for Foreign and Commonwealth Affairs you committed a criminal act?'

'It happened before I got my present job, but yes, I failed to pay some customs duty on a set of china that my wife and I bought in France. What happened was that the Ambassador's wife and Ruth—'

'Ruth is your wife?'

'Yes, sorry. They went shopping together, and bought a dinner service, quite an expensive one . . .'

'Limoges, I believe?'

'Yes. Limoges. And the Ambassador and his wife were coming back to England after six years in the job and they offered to bring our crate of china back with their goods and chattels, on which of course there is no duty.'

'So you were in effect smuggling luxury goods in the diplomatic bag?'

Oliver sat back, but a gesture from John reminded him about the microphone on the table and he leant forward to his previous position. 'Well, certainly that's the shorthand your press colleagues have chosen to use. It's not strictly true. But we did fail to pay any duty. That is true.'

'And, in effect, the taxpayer was paying your freight?'

'I'm afraid so.'

'When was this, exactly?'

'Ten years ago. I was a junior minister of state in the Home Office.'

'Forgive me, Minister ... er, Mr Stapler ... but I must ask: how could you have been so careless? I hesitate to use the word dishonest, but how could you, a minister of the Crown, have done such a thing ... I see you are nodding?'

'Well, yes. It was certainly careless, even stupid, but it was never intended to be dishonest. I was just pleased not to have to pay the expensive carriage – a twelve-place dinner service is very expensive to pack and post – so I was delighted to put it in with the Ambassador's things. I was certainly glad to save money, but I'm afraid no thought of import duty or smuggling or the taxpayer paying the transport costs entered either of our heads. Ruth and I went home and a few months later our china turned up.'

'And that's the truth?'

'Absolutely.'

'And you've paid up?'

'I have, plus a fine for late payment.'

'But that still leaves the matter of the necklace.'

'Indeed. I'm afraid that incident was even more stupid. On a diplomatic trip to the Yemen, my wife was given a necklace by the president. He fastened it round Ruth's neck himself. I assume – it was some months ago, and I genuinely cannot remember – that we went back to the hotel with Ruth still wearing it.'

'According to the reports, it is a priceless antique piece.'

'This is what's so shaming. We thought it was, well, if not exactly a cheap trinket, certainly a modern necklace of no value. I do remember Ruth and I discussed it that evening in the hotel and we agreed we'd seen necklaces very like it in the street markets. I suppose it was a traditional design. And to make matters worse, we now can't find it.'

'You've lost it?'

'It looks like that. My wife has never worn it since that evening, and has no idea where it is. We have, as you can imagine, turned the house upside down.'

'So what happens now? Will they let you off?'

'I don't know. I don't think anyone, except perhaps the donor, could put a price on it, but I'm told it could be worth a lot of money. Certainly I'm unable to compensate the government for it.'

'Will the government pursue a claim against you for the value?'

'I don't know. Of course I hope not.'

'What a sorry tale. One more question, if I may?'

'Sure,' said Oliver.

'Who shopped you, Mr Stapler?'

Oliver laughed. 'I've no idea. Someone looking for mud to sling at the government, I suppose. It must have taken a while to go through the cumbersome business of getting at the records under the Freedom of Information Act, claiming public interest, etc. But they struck lucky. The gift was recorded as received in a Foreign Office note on the dinner, but there is no Treasury record of receipt of the necklace. The first I knew of it was when the Ethics Committee called me to account. They had been alerted by the enquirer, I guess.'

'So, what happens now? Is the necklace insured?'

'No, sadly. As I say, we didn't know its worth, and if we had we'd have handed it in, not kept it and insured it.'

The conversation then turned to Oliver's resolve to revert to the back benches.

'To spend more time with your family, or more with your golf clubs?'

'Certainly the former, but not the latter. I'm still an MP, so I hope to spend more time in my constituency.'

As Oliver crept from the studio, ushered out by an assistant signalling silence so as not to spoil the sports report, he wondered if he really wanted to spend more time with the family. And more to the point, did they want to spend more time with him? The girls became more distant every day, and he wasn't sure he even wanted to see more of Ruth . . .

He stepped out of Television Centre and looked round for Debbie and his car. Then he remembered that he didn't have a ministerial car any more, and presumably Debbie was already working for someone else.

As he climbed into the minicab hired by the BBC, he thought, well, at least it's not the bus.

He did not go straight home. He had intended to return to Lambeth, spend an hour in his study, then catch a train for Birmingham to join the family for the weekend. But as the car turned into Piccadilly he suddenly said to the driver, 'Stop anywhere here, I want to walk a bit.'

He stood on the pavement, feeling distinctly odd. He couldn't remember when he'd last had nothing to do. It made him faintly anxious. Parliament had already broken for the summer recess so he couldn't even sit on the back benches or gossip in the Commons bar. Should he cross the road and have a stroll in Green Park? Or wander down to Hatchards and browse around the bookshelves? Or see what was on at the Royal Academy? He had done none of these things for years.

In the end he walked back to Hyde Park Corner and took the tunnel that led to the centre of the circus. It was only nine o'clock but the sun was bright and warm and Oliver took his jacket off, hooked a finger through the loop at the neck and slung it over his shoulder. The gesture, such a time-honoured young-man-in-a-movie gesture, immediately lightened his mood. There was a forgotten pleasure in walking about a public place without a fixed purpose and, most of all, without any officials or minders, without being recognised (only tourists here) and without feeling he was on parade.

He approached the newest of the sculptures that occupied the patch of grass around which ceaseless traffic stop-started. He had often wondered, as he sped up Piccadilly in his ministerial limo, what the new brutal sculpture of several girder-like posts planted in the grass, was all about. It looked, he thought, like the remains of a shipwreck sticking crookedly above the water.

He soon found it was a New Zealand War Memorial with shallow reliefs on each post – rugger ball, kiwi, Maori inscriptions, etc. But he was unmoved by it. He preferred the Victorian grandeur of the quadriga on top of Wellington Arch, or the romanticism of the naked David, his idealised bronze back and bum facing Park Lane. But the sculpture that drew him up short, that made him stand immobile, was the massive work by Jagger of young soldiers round a First World War howitzer and the bier of a fallen comrade. He could not take his eyes from the exhausted face of a standing soldier, so young, so lost, so stoical, his world so utterly bleak.

Against that generation's shattered dreams, Oliver thought, what exactly do I have to complain of?

He walked slowly back down Piccadilly, cheered by the thought that he had spent his first hour of real freedom from government discovering something new. He settled his mind to be positive: he would mend relations with Ruth and the girls; spend a lot more time in the constituency; be a better local MP.

He stopped at the restaurant in St James's Park for breakfast. It struck him as unusual to be in a roomful of people who didn't know, or care, who he was. They consulted their guides and maps, ate their croissants, drank their lattes and cappuccinos, without so much as a glance at him. He ordered eggs Benedict and enjoyed them, feeling happily anonymous and confident that the famous Westminster 'Post Power Depression' would not get him.

Oliver's optimistic mood lasted while he caught a bus to Lambeth, collected his briefcase and set off by taxi for Euston. He now had an almost euphoric sense of freedom. Not to have a detective in tow, not to have to chat, or at least be civil to, his PPS and his driver, felt like an unimaginable luxury.

But on the train he felt strangely tired, and arrived home to find Ruth grumpy and out of sorts.

'Why didn't you ring me?' she said, barely looking up from her desk. 'I'd have fetched you from the station. We can't afford taxis all the time now, you know.'

'It was only ten pounds. And I knew you'd be busy.'

'And why are you so late? I thought you were coming down straight after the broadcast?'

'I said I'd be home for lunch. Which I am. Actually, Ruth, I had an hour in the middle of Hyde Park Corner, and I . . .'

'You what?'

Oliver tried to describe the Jagger sculpture, but Ruth wasn't listening. Annoyed by her lack of interest, he asked her the question he suspected she would not like answering.

'Darling, did you listen to the programme?'

'No. I knew what you were going to say, and you know I don't think you should have resigned.'

'Is that why you didn't come to the House yesterday, either?'

'Of course. What is the point of sitting in the gallery to hear you say something I don't think you should be saying and then have to listen to everyone telling you – or worse, telling me – how noble and principled you are.' She assumed a pompous voice. 'Not since Carrington resigned over the Falklands have we seen such self sacrifice . . .'

Oliver frowned. Why was she being so vitriolic? He really did not want to have the resignation conversation again. He remembered his resolution to build bridges with his family, and decided to overlook her outburst. He said mildly, 'Well, it's done now. And do you know, I feel rather good about it. It's a horrible time to be in government. Everyone thinks you're a crook, bumping up expenses . . . and useless to boot.'

'You're still an MP, still a politician. You'll still be tarred with the expenses brush.' To Oliver she seemed to say this with a kind of relish, but maybe she didn't mean to.

'At least we didn't submit any dodgy claims,' he said. 'Not that it makes any odds. In the eyes of the press and public there's no difference between what we did ten years ago with a set of china plates and falsely claiming for hundreds of thousands.'

She didn't answer and Oliver, anxious to placate her, was grateful.

'Do you know,' he said, 'I walked down Piccadilly and had breakfast at Inn the Park. It was really nice. Just so good having nothing to do. It must be twenty years since—'

Ruth interrupted. 'Oliver, I'm sure it's very nice to be free as air, but you will forgive me if I don't share your delight. We've still got school fees to pay, and if you think my father will just stump up . . .'

He sighed. Was there no subject they could discuss peaceably? He knew he was being baited, but he couldn't stop his temper rising. 'Ruth, you know as well as I do that the school fees were taken care of with an insurance plan we bought years ago.'

'Oliver, your salary as Foreign Secretary is – was – a hundred and twenty thousand on top of your MP's salary. Now we are to sacrifice that and live on sixty-four grand, all because you lacked the balls to weather the storm.'

Oliver felt his anger turn to icy calm. 'Ruth, you are obviously highly dissatisfied with me. Is it permanent, do you think? Or is it worth our trying to be civil to each other in the hope of avoiding more damage?'

Ruth stood up and faced him, her expression hard and set. 'I don't know. You asked me a while back if I loved you and I said I wasn't sure. Well, I am now. I don't. But lots of marriages survive without love. The problem for me is that I'm so angry with you, Oliver. Not just because you have resigned over nothing, but because of that bloody cook! And because—'

'But you know the truth.'

'I know you spent a lot of time with her, yes, and it got us into hell fire. But if you want to know what has really made me angry, apart from the mess you are making of your career, is your decision to dish out *Scandal Sheet's* money to a music charity! Why could you not give it to my Pony Trust? Didn't it even occur to you to consult me? Don't you think you owe me anything for standing there like an abused little wife and backing up your pious denials? I work my guts off for that charity, for free, and have for years. I raise just about every penny we spend. And you get a bloody great windfall and casually dish it out to a charity you hardly know.'

Oliver listened to her in dismay. He tried to stop her a couple of times, but she was not to be brooked. She went on and on, about his absence of loyalty, the way he took her for granted, his lack of interest in his daughters. She fired any arrows she had to hand.

When she stopped, Oliver turned and left the room. His face burned hot and he did not trust himself to speak. The long and the short of it was that, as usual, Ruth was fed up with him, and her reasons were many and various.

He walked out into the stable yard, through the home paddock, and fast up the hill. It was still clear and hot with only the slightest of breezes: a rare perfect English summer's day. As his body warmed with sun and exertion, his anger dissipated. When he got to the top of the path, he sat down on a grassy patch and looked back down the valley. It was laid out like a map. Pretty stone house, bright lawn and garden to the left, and to the right Ruth's meticulously kept yard, with loose-boxes, feed and tack rooms to one side and riding school shed to the other. He could see Ben the saddler sitting on the step of the old hay barn he rented from them, and behind the yard ponies grazing in one paddock and brightly coloured show-jumps in another. The trailer and the great horsebox were neatly parked behind the shed, the muck heaps carefully piled and the surrounding concrete scrubbed clean.

Random thoughts came and went in his head. Ruth ran a tight ship, no doubt of that. But if it wasn't for her father subsidising her, she would have realised years ago that horses don't pay.

I really don't like the brutes, he thought. They look good, but they're dangerous, demanding and expensive. He thought about the things Ruth had said. Maybe he should have discussed the charity money with her. If he were honest, he *had* briefly considered Ruth's pony rescue charity but had seen at once that giving her the money would look like nepotism. He'd named Musical Instruments for Kids because he'd been impressed with what they'd done for local schools and he knew no one would grudge them the money.

That she had not come to hear his resignation speech in the Commons yesterday – she was in London and could easily have done so – or listened to the *Today* programme this morning was insulting, an indication of how little he interested her. But he found he didn't really care. He had no desire now to go back and heal any rifts. He lay down in the warm grass and closed his eyes.

Maybe this is it, he thought. She doesn't love me, she's quite clear about that. Do I love her? God knows . . . But I think not.

On Monday, after an uneasy ceasefire and a calmer discussion, Oliver rang an estate agent friend and asked her to find him a cottage or a flat nearby.

They had agreed on a trial separation. Oliver had winced at the time-worn, mealy-mouthed phrase. But Ruth wanted him out of the house and he wanted to be near his daughters.

Chapter Twenty-One

In the end, leaving Toby in Arizona had been much easier than Kate feared. He was in seventh heaven, excited at seeing his cousins, sleeping with them in a tent on the lawn, and being spoilt and fussed over by everyone. Far from him weeping and wailing at her departure, he'd hardly seemed to care. She'd felt a little tearful on the flight home, but she was exhausted too, and soon fell asleep.

She did miss him, and counted the days to his return like a schoolgirl. Meanwhile she tried to pretend she was fine. 'I'm fine' had become a sort of mantra, something she was saying all the time: to her mother on the telephone from Arizona; to suppliers worrying about the woman upon whom their payment depended; to the dwindling band of customers who'd read the gossip columns and wanted confirmation she'd manage their order; to Amal and Talika who knew what she was going through. But mostly she lectured herself: I'm fine, just fine; I'm fine about leaving my darling son thousands of miles away to be monopolised by my mother; I'm fine that he's so happy that he's not giving me a thought. I'm fine: I'm not going bankrupt; I can sort out my ex trying to muscle in on the family; I'm not in love with Oliver Stapler; I'm not lonely. I'm fine. I'm fine. I'm fine.

But she wasn't sleeping well. Knowing there'd be no sleeping boy beside her, she dreaded waking without his merry eyes willing hers to open. She avoided going to bed, and worked until her brain went on strike and she could not do the simplest sums. Then she crawled into bed, slept soundly for a couple of hours, fitfully for a couple more, then took a Valium which kept her under until six a.m. or so. At six-thirty she rose, groggy and sad, and doggedly started the new day.

One morning she found an email from Jarvis Stanley, and opened it. Normally she deleted his emails unread, as she did all messages from journalists and radio or TV stations.

She knew very well it was Stanley who'd started the hare which had pretty well ruined her life, but Kate also recognised that he was a cut above the rest of the rat pack. He would never have held her by the hair to let a colleague get a picture of her; he would not have broken into her study; he didn't climb ladders to peer into her windows. And on the few occasions when he had got her on the telephone, he had been decently spoken and respectful. He never called her 'Darlin'.'

For all these reasons, or for none of them, maybe just on a whim, Kate opened the email:

Kate, I really think we should meet. You have a great story to tell, and it should be told. You are the victim in all this and yet you are the one person who has behaved well. Besides (I hope this is not impertinent) couldn't you do with a few grand? We pay well and we would not stitch you up, I promise. We would agree the shape of the story with you in advance. I'm on your side, Kate.

PS, If you agree, or even want to discuss it, you should get someone to represent you. Max Clifford is the best. But Rake Jones is good too. www.rakejones.com You need someone to negotiate with my bosses, and to do any media deals you will need someone to advise you.

Kate pressed the delete button. But even as she switched off the computer she thought, well, if I need the website I can always get it out of the deleted folder.

She went back to the kitchen where she was in the middle of a massive clear-out, embarked on in an attempt to banish the blues.

One of the enormous fibreglass wheeled bins she used for chilling wine at parties was already full of black bags of rubbish. She'd enjoyed cleaning out the equipment cupboards and throwing away redundant attachments for long-dead machines like a cumbersome yogurt maker which did nothing that a bowl and spoon would not do; or old ice-cube trays and useless gadgets she was never going to use. She'd also successfully thrown out past-their-sell-by-date spices and condiments, and cleaned her storage jars, shelves and drawers.

But finally, she had to tackle the freezer. Kate found throwing away perfectly good food impossible and small packages of left-overs tended to collect in the domestic freezer. She always told herself that one day she'd use up the cake, raw pastry, mashed potato, icing, pea purée, risotto or whatever.

But somehow, if she and Toby didn't eat these things before they got to the freezer, they seldom got eaten. She'd sooner make a quick stir-fry or an omelette than defrost anything. So today she was determined to do something about the overstuffed freezer and steel herself to junk her carefully labelled packets and tubs.

She took everything out of the freezer and piled it on the table, with a couple of thick towels over the top to slow thawing. She knew most of it should go in the bin and she should get on with sorting good from bad, but she must defrost the encrusted freezer first. She switched it off and busied herself putting roasting pans of boiling water on each shelf. She had just shut the door on them when Talika arrived.

'Good Lord, Kate, what are you up to?' she said, looking at the upheaval all around.

'As you see, the annual great chuck-out. I thought it might be therapy for the glums.'

'And is it? Are you coping?'

Kate smiled. 'I'm fine,' she said. 'Really. But you are just beautiful, 'Lika. Pregnancy suits you.' Kate hugged her friend as she admired the pink blush to her brown skin, the clarity of her eyes and the new fullness to her cheeks and neck. She looked like a model for a Visit India brochure.

Suddenly, she had no idea why, Kate felt her eyes fill with tears and she turned away, but Talika's arms were around her at once and Kate gave in, unable to stop herself crying.

Talika didn't ask why. She just waited for Kate to stop. Then she said, 'Can I help?'

Kate knew she meant would it help to talk about her troubles, but she chose to misunderstand.

'Well, you can do what I'm incapable of, and chuck that lot out,' she said, sniffling and waving a hand at the towel-covered pile.

Talika removed the towels and examined the packages. 'You can't chuck all this out.'

'I know, but I must. There's just no room in there. But how can I dump the beetroot and sweetcorn from the garden?' She picked up a package. 'Or the stewed apple. That comes from that apple tree out there.' She rubbed her eyes with the tea towel and smiled. 'I'm so hopeless. I can't chuck this fruit compote, or that elderflower syrup. Toby and I made those after pick-your-own sprees last year.'

'Mmm.' Talika started sorting packages rapidly into two piles, the bangles on her wrists flashing and clinking. 'We could make brilliant chutney. Why not? It will be fun.'

And so they did.

With the cleaning session turning into a cooking one, Kate cheered up. She put her iPod into its stand and turned the sound up so Beethoven's Pastoral Symphony swelled and swooped through the kitchen. She collected her biggest pan (actually a fish kettle) from the garden store and put it on the range. The women chopped onions and garlic, and tipped them into the pan with everything else. The beetroot and berry fruit turned the mix a vibrant pink, and the apple and parsnips gave the mixture body.

Talika patiently grated orange zest and fresh ginger. Kate blitzed a handful of coriander and cardamom seeds in the coffee-grinder and added everything with a pint of vinegar.

'I know,' said Kate, 'let's add these.' She reached for one of the storage jars, containing hard dark discs.

'What are they?' Talika looked sceptical.

'Believe it or not, they're apricots. Only God knows how old. They've dried to leather.'

She tipped them into the mixture and set the pan to simmer, stirring slowly. They'd judge the amount of brown sugar to add when everything else was cooked down to chutney thickness.

Why, she wondered, was cooking so calming, so uplifting? Her mother, who hated cooking, thought her daughter liked it because she wanted to be in control: of the food, of the diners' diets, of the family timetable. But her grandmother, who had cooked wonderful old-fashioned Scottish fare, had understood. She'd seen that cooking gave one the chance to care for people you loved, to give friends a good time.

'Talika,' she said, 'do you think cooking is an act of love? My gran thought it was.'

Talika looked up. 'Of course it is. Or should be. My mother liked feeding the goats, or mixing the scraps for the chickens in the same way as she liked making the dhal for the family. There's satisfaction in being the provider.'

Kate nodded. 'I think the pleasure also comes from the ritual of the process: turning good ingredients into something important and wonderful. We lose that ritual at our peril. Microwaving a TV dinner somehow doesn't do it.'

Talika smiled, 'How about microwaving pea purée? Is that allowed? We could eat it with eggs on top. I'm starving.'

She thawed the bright green purée, and reheated it with a dollop of butter. Kate fried some rashers of bacon (also rescued from the out-of-date pile) and poached two eggs.

They carried their plates into the garden and sat on the bench in the shade.

Talika, grinding black pepper over her egg, said, 'Tell me now why you were so upset. Is it because you want another baby too?'

Kate nodded without looking up. 'Partly, yes, but I'm just in such a mess, Talika.'

She told her friend about missing Toby, about Chris resurfacing, about her cash-flow crisis. She just stopped herself from blurting out her ridiculous longing, and occasional hate, for the monstrous Oliver and managed to remain on safer ground.

'I can't even pay you back for the flights to Arizona. What am I going to do, 'Lika?'

'Forget about that. Amal hasn't even mentioned it. One day you will pay us back, but it doesn't matter if you never do.'

'It does, it does. I can't bear it.'

Talika changed the subject. 'More important, what are you going to do about Chris?'

'Nothing. Just hope he stays away.'

'Are you sure? Is that fair on Toby? Chris *is* his dad.'

Kate was comforted by the long conversation and Talika's concern and good sense, and when her friend left, she went back to her desk cheered. She sweetened the chutney, gave it one last boil and filled twenty-eight jars with the ruby-red mix. It smelt wonderful and looked beautiful. With a few months' mellowing and covered with pretty gingham or paper tops they'd raise good money for Toby's school.

Mum was right, Kate thought. She could hear her mother's brisk answer to her teenage groans and moans. 'Stop complaining, darling, and do something. Physical activity, young lady, is what you need.'

And cooking, Kate thought, is the best.

But the next morning she had a letter from her bank telling her that as she had gone beyond her authorised overdraft of twenty thousand, she would now be paying two per cent a month on both the unauthorised total of £392 and the agreed overdraft of £20,000. In addition, since she had breached the overdraft limit, they had the right to call in the whole loan, which they were now doing. She had thirty days to settle the debt.

Kate stared at the figures. She could not make sense of them. She unconsciously held her breath while her heart banged loudly in her chest. How could they insist on cancelling her overdraft?

She read the letter again. And then she understood. Two per cent a *month*. On the lot. She had been paying six per cent *a year*. Suddenly it was twenty-four per cent. Kate gasped air back into her lungs and swallowed, nausea and despair competing.

Why were they pursuing her for repayment? It wasn't that much money for the bank, surely? And where was she to get twenty grand, plus interest, in a month? Her business, if it ever recovered, would not do so that fast.

Kate knew she must get rid of the overdraft. Even if the bank could be persuaded not to call it in, she would be paying five grand to borrow twenty. Every year. It was criminal.

She rang Jarvis Stanley. And immediately she regretted it. Banks might be sharks, but so were journalists. Was she jumping from the fat into the fire? She felt her whole life heaped on top of her. But was she really reduced to doing deals with a newspaper?

She put the fingers of both hands into her thick curly hair and clutched at it in a frantic gesture of panic and indecision.

Almost for the first time in her life, Kate longed for a partner to share her troubles with, to talk money to, to help her through the woods and tell her it would all be all right.

And then she sat up and said to herself, so, OK, you want the dream husband. Well, forget it. He doesn't exist. Grow up and make decisions for yourself.

Jarvis Stanley would worm all sorts of tiny details out of her and blow them into a scandal. He would make it a sort of kiss and tell piece, even though there'd been no kissing, no real kissing anyway, and there was little to tell. But what could she do? She had to get out of debt.

And what would Oliver think?

But then she thought, what do I owe Oliver? Precisely nothing. Damn his eyes, he's screwed up my life and he doesn't give a toss. I have to live. I cannot end up bankrupt, on state benefit.

All day Kate was on a roller-coaster of indecision. One minute her hand was on the telephone, about to cancel. The next she had bolstered herself with the thought that she would tell the truth, and how could the truth hurt Oliver? And even if he didn't like it, so what? He'd not given a thought to her suffering. He'd got her into this hole, with her business down the drain and the world thinking she was a tart. Time for him to suffer a bit.

* * *

Jarvis Stanley and Rake Jones arrived together at four p.m.

Kate made tea and they sat in the kitchen. Jarvis was all avuncular concern. 'I brought Rake with me, because I don't want you feeling I've bounced you into anything. If he says not to talk to me, then no harm done. My editor doesn't even know you rang me, so there will be no pressure on my side.'

Kate didn't quite believe this, but she wanted to. She didn't challenge him, just nodded. He went on, 'Of course I want to tell your story, and I'd be sick as a parrot if you sold it to someone else. But why don't I go away for half an hour or so while you talk to Rake. I'll go have a fag in the street. Or maybe I could talk to young Toby? Is he in the garden?'

'Arizona. With my mother.' For once Kate was glad of this, she would not have wanted him talking to Toby.

When Jarvis had left, Kate said, 'Is Rake your real name?'

He grinned, 'No. Made it up. But everyone calls me Rake now.' He reached for a biscuit and stayed sitting forward, looking at Kate.

'Let's start at the beginning. Why do you want to tell Jarvis your side of things?'

'I'm broke. I need the money.'

'Good reason. You do know that if you hire me, I will take thirty per cent of anything you get?'

She didn't, and it seemed a lot, but before she could object, he said, 'But I do promise you that I will get far more for you, even after my commission, than you would get on your own. I am very good at this.'

Kate nodded. 'Fine. I just want to clear my debts, and get enough money to rebuild my business, which has gone pretty much belly up because of this Oliver business.'

'Have you totted up how much you need?'

'Urgently, about twenty-five thousand. But I really need twice that.'

'No problem. They'll easily pay a hundred grand for a double page spread. But they *will* want pictures, some that they take when Jarvis does the piece, some of you and Toby . . .'

'No, not Toby.'

'They needn't be taken now. They could be family snaps.'

Kate frowned, hesitating, and Rake came in quickly. 'It will make all the difference, Kate. We need the reader to sympathise with you, and a picture of you and Toby will put them on your side before they've read a word.'

Kate shook her head. 'I'm not sure.'

'Well, let's leave that for the minute. How do you feel about television interviews, magazine stories? The truth is I can make you a celebrity, which will help rebuild your business. You do want to rebuild the business?'

'Yes. Or I suppose so. I have to. But to be honest, I wish I could just run away and forget the whole thing. Oliver, the business, everything.' Kate could feel the emotion welling up, and she stood up and walked away to the window. Then she turned. 'I'm sorry. Could we just talk about what happens next? If I allow the interview, will I be able to vet it, change it if I don't like what he has written?'

'No, they'll not agree to that. But I know the line he will take is that you are innocent and that you have been damaged unfairly. You will need to be careful to tell him only what you are prepared to see in print.'

'OK. I understand. I've never done this before.'

'You could make a lot of money, Kate. And if it's a good story and creates interest, it could lead to other things. Which will set you up, make you known and sought after.' Kate shook her head, and he said quickly, 'But that's all for a later discussion. Shall we just agree I will do a deal with Jarvis's editor?'

Kate consented and Rake went to find Jarvis. She cleared away the tea things then wandered into the sitting room from where, through the window, she could see the two of them sitting side by side on the garden wall, Rake talking animatedly on his mobile. Once or twice he broke away to speak briefly to Jarvis, then went back to his call.

Kate stood with her forehead against the window pane, knowing that the die was cast and soon Jarvis would come inside to tell her the deal was done. He'd start questioning her, a photographer would arrive, and she would betray Oliver.

She turned away from the window, straightening her shoulders. Tough, she told herself; and he cares so little it will be water off a duck's back. At least I'll be able to pay the bank.

CHAPTER TWENTY-TWO

In the end Oliver took a flat in a converted stone barn on a neighbouring farm. It wasn't ideal – rather cramped and facing north – but Ruth wanted him out of the house and he was in no mood to traipse round a succession of cottages and flats. At least this was only two miles from the house and his daughters could bike there.

One Saturday morning he heard the sound of horse's hooves coming up his garden path, followed by a shout, 'Dad, are you there?' With Obi-Wan Kenobi yapping at his heels, he walked to his open study window to see Andrea sliding off her pony. Oliver felt an unexpected flood of love at the sight of his daughter.

She was wearing what looked to him like a petticoat, or perhaps fancy-dress for a sprite. Her hair, long, straight and blonde, draped her shoulders in windblown hanks. She was wearing flip-flops.

As she landed on the ground, she looked up. Her pale, still-childish face, so open and eager, broke into a wide smile at the sight of him, 'Oh Dad, I'm so glad you're here.'

'Andrea, you idiot, you cannot ride bareback on public roads without a riding hat or boots. It's probably illegal. And where are you going to put Toppy?'

'I don't know, but she's good as gold.'

Oliver opened the front door to let the near hysterical Jack Russell leap into his daughter's embrace. He noticed that not only was the pony without a saddle but she had no bridle. Just the halter she wore in the field and a rope. I suppose I'm lucky she has that, thought Oliver: Andrea frequently scrambled onto her pony for a canter round the field with nothing but a handful of mane to hold on to.

They hitched the cob to a wrought-iron lamp screwed into the stone wall. Securely, Oliver hoped.

As Andrea followed him inside, he said, 'Does your mum know you're here?'

'No, why?'

'We'd better tell her.'

But there was no answer from the house phone or Ruth's mobile. Oliver put the phone down. 'Where's Mum? Do you know?'

'No. She's probably at Ben's.'

'Who is Ben?'

Andrea rolled her eyes at the extreme stupidity of her father. '*Ben!* You know who Ben is. He's only your *tenant*. The man who sells the saddles and stuff, who rents the old hay barn.' She tapped her father's temple with a finger, 'Hello? Anyone at home?'

Oliver said, quite sharply, 'Don't be rude, darling.' Then he softened. 'And don't be such a smarty-pants. OK, I know Ben, but what makes you think Mum is in his shop?'

'She's always there.'

'What for?'

It occurred to Oliver that he was pumping his daughter for information about her mother and he found the thought distasteful.

But Andrea had lost interest and didn't answer. She just gave an exaggerated shrug and said, 'Can I see my room?'

'You can. But it's Mattie's room too, remember. And it's not finished yet.' They went upstairs and Andrea bounced about on the bean bags Oliver had bought online, approved the huge cork boards for sticking posters and photos on and staked a claim for the top bunk for when the furniture arrived.

They had a Coke and a biscuit and then Oliver tried Ruth again. This time she answered at once and Oliver said, 'Darling, just thought I'd tell you that our mad daughter is here. She came on Toppy.'

Ruth's only response was, 'OK. But don't call me darling.'

He felt the now familiar flick of irritation, but quelled the desire to snap at her. 'So sorry. Habit of a lifetime. Must try to break it.' Immediately he knew that his tone, which he had meant to be merely cool, sounded sarcastic.

He snapped his phone shut and turned to see that Andrea's face, which a moment ago had been a vision of childish happiness, was now clouded with anxiety.

'Why are you being so horrible?' she asked.

Oliver bent down to hug her. 'Oh darling, I don't know. We just seem to get on each other's nerves at the moment.'

Andrea struggled out of his grip so she could look at him. 'Are you going to get divorced?'

'I don't know. I just don't know. Would it be terrible if we did?'

'Yes. Samantha's parents are divorced and she never sees her dad now.'

'Sweetheart, that will never happen to us, I promise. That's why I've got this flat. So I can be with you in minutes, and you can bike over here to see me whenever you like.' He stroked her head, her hair silky and slippery under his fingers. 'Though I don't think coming on the pony is such a hot idea. If she gets a fright she could pull that lamp out of the wall and set off down the road by herself. Or eat the plants in my landlord's garden.'

Andrea wanted to watch *Saturday Kitchen*, and Oliver, less engaged by the programme than his daughter, went to get his camera. He wanted a picture of her in her ridiculous dress, which he now saw had pink and purple sequins and pearly buttons all over the floral semi-see-through material of the bodice. Her arms and legs, spread over the sofa with the gawky grace of childhood, were thin and tanned. Obi was tucked in beside her, his head on her ankle. Andrea's toenails, he noticed, were painted deep purple.

He pressed the button to bring the picture into close-up and waited for it to focus. He'd already noticed the traces of lipstick round his daughter's mouth, but now he saw the bracelets and rings and a necklace, obviously one of Ruth's. He wondered where the line between a little girl dressing up and a ten-year-old wearing unsuitable adult things came. He thought crossly that Ruth should not let Andrea wear her jewellery, she might lose it.

And then it hit him: Andrea was wearing THE necklace! The lost Yemeni necklace! He was sure of it.

He lowered the camera and hurried to her, 'Andrea, where did you get that necklace?' The child, absorbed by the television, did not respond. Oliver put his hand briefly over her eyes to get her attention and then said, 'Darling, where did you find that necklace? Mummy and I have been looking for it for ages.'

Andrea put her hand up to feel the necklace. 'Oh!' she said, 'in the dressing-up box. With this dress. Mummy bought it in a jumble sale and I wore it with big wings to be a fairy in that school . . .'

'But the necklace . . . In the dressing-up box? Are you sure?'

'Yes, I'm sure. Why, Dad? What's the matter?'

Oliver's hope that this was indeed the missing necklace was rapidly turning to relief. There was no question, this was it. He found himself laughing. 'Sorry, darling, but that necklace belongs to someone else. Do you mind if I take it off you?'

After a while, Oliver began to worry that Toppy would get restless so he hoisted his daughter onto the cob's back, led her across the road, and opened the field gate for them. He picked up Obi to prevent him following Andrea, who kicked Toppy into a trot. 'Bye, Dad,' she called, waving her free hand above her head. She looked, he thought, absolutely at one with the horse, her shoulders relaxed, her bottom planted deep into the animal's back with no danger of bouncing, her long hair flying. Andrea settled Toppy into a canter and Oliver watched the pony's rotating bum and his daughter's almost immobile back. Those girls of ours sure can ride, he thought.

Back inside, Oliver picked up the necklace and turned it over in his hands. On closer examination, he could see that the gold bells were old and buffed, the intricate raised pattern slightly worn, the hook at the back of the neck large and unusual, the coral beads differing in size and shade, the flat lapis pieces worn and shiny with age. It was obviously not modern. But half a million? Amazing!

He rang Ruth again.

She picked up the phone with, 'Have you still got Andrea there?'

'She's on her way. I sent her back by the fields since she has no saddle, no bridle, no hat, no boots.'

'Don't be pompous, Oliver.' Ruth's voice was tired and patient, maddening, in fact. 'That child could ride anything. She'll be fine.'

'All the same, she's only ten . . .'

'Oliver, butt out. Andrea, we agreed, is in my care. She and Mattie are my responsibility. Unless you want to argue for custody? Do you?'

'Ruth, please, let's not go there. What I rang about was to say that Andrea was wearing the necklace, the famous lost Yemeni necklace.'

There was silence for a few seconds, then Ruth said, 'Good Lord, how did she get it?'

'She found it in the dressing-up box. I thought you said you had looked for it, Ruth. I have been going through merry hell about that wretched necklace, and all the time . . .'

Ruth's voice rose. 'Don't blame me, Oliver! OK, maybe I didn't look in the dressing-up box, but did you? Did you look anywhere at all?'

Oliver resisted the temptation to remind her that she'd said she would turn the house out.

'Look, it's found now,' he said wearily. 'I just rang to tell you. At least we won't have to recompense the Treasury for the value of it. Though I bet they'd rather have the money than the jewellery.'

That night, half-watching television on his own, Oliver made a decision. Not a big one, like whether to go for divorce, or resign as an MP, or write a book. But one that might help him think about these things.

He would go away. Book a cottage somewhere warm. The summer recess still had six weeks to run, he had no government job to occupy him, the children were off to pony camp so he'd not see much of them anyway, and he was hardly welcome at home.

He'd go for a good long stretch, maybe a month, somewhere far from here; somewhere pretty and quiet, on his own. Completely on his own. No work colleagues. No children. Above all, no politicians.

And no wife, he thought, with a small stab of guilty satisfaction.

*   *   *

Ruth had been furious.

'You're so bloody selfish, Oliver,' she'd said. 'When the going gets tough for all of us, you take off on a nice little retreat!'

'Ruth, you wanted me out of the house. I'd have thought out of the country was even better.'

'I'd not mind if you were out of the world,' she'd barked, 'but what about the girls? You're their father. Shouldn't you be there for them?'

Oliver had felt his temper rising, but told himself Ruth was having just as grim a time as he was and was just mouthing off. He answered coolly. 'The girls are fine. They are both going to pony camp, and then Mattie is going somewhere to play polo, remember? Anyway, I've spoken to them both. Separately. Their attitude was pretty much, "Go for it, Dad, you need a break." And anyway, I'll talk to them every day, as always.'

'And what about me?'

'If you want a break, let's find a time when I can have the girls. Maybe at half-term? They could come up to London. I would love that, and so would they.'

Ruth said, 'Mmm' in a manner that managed to convey both non-commitment and dissatisfaction, and ended the call.

Oliver's *gîte* was on a tributary of the Loire, very pretty and cheap, and he found it oddly satisfying to be on his own. The absence of company, obligations and family, and his decision not to open emails and to keep his mobile switched off, meant he had finally been able to start writing.

He had been thinking for a long time, but more pressingly since his troubles, of a book (or perhaps it would just be a pamphlet) on how the pressures of public office dehumanised politicians; how the desire to do good is corrupted by the need first to get elected, and then to stay in power, and above all not to make mistakes. It made you so risk averse that you could no longer do the sensible or honourable thing. He had wanted to stand shoulder to shoulder with Kate over the allegations of an affair, but the risk of being thought too close, the danger of innuendo and gossip losing him his job, had made him a coward, and worse, a poor friend.

He wished he could talk to Kate. Not just to apologise and try to explain his powerlessness in the face of the spin machine, but he wanted her thoughts on this book. There was a time when he could talk to Ruth about ideas or politics, but she was no longer interested. Poor Ruth, she had realised early on that being an MP was compromising his principles, and she'd become critical of all politicians. On the other hand, she'd been pleased at his every promotion and she'd been as ambitious as he, maybe more so, about the top job. It was odd. Maybe he just did not understand her. Maybe he had not tried hard enough to understand her. Now, he thought, I don't even want to.

He remembered a conversation with Kate late one night after a dinner in the crypt under Whitehall Palace. Kate had been frothing at the mouth over an article in the paper about the myriad checks that a school had to do before putting children into a mini-bus.

Oliver had said, 'But it's sensible to ensure the driver has a licence, the bus has good tyres, that the parents are content their children should go, isn't it?'

'Yes, but it's the documentation that goes with it, the need for volunteers who go with the children to have criminal record checks, the pages of boxes to tick. It's a miracle schools still take children anywhere. And who is assessing the risks of *not* taking them to a play or concert, or to play football in the next town, or to the Science Museum?'

Oliver smiled at the memory. Kate, when she was angry or excited, coloured up like a child, with shiny eyes, her chin slightly lifted, cheeks aflame. Damn it, I miss her, he thought.

She might approve of his ideas for common sense in policy making. He'd been shocked to discover that the latest rules governing workers in charities had led to services closing down for lack of volunteers prepared to go through the clearance process. Who was that helping? Regulation, and codes of practice, should only be there, he thought, to ensure a better service, not to cover the back of the provider while making things worse for the recipient.

The trouble was that if anyone responsible for the spending of public money took any risk at all and something went wrong, they got crucified by the same papers that fulminated about bureaucracy.

Oliver had planned the shape of the book, written a synopsis, and made himself a reading list of books and speeches he thought he might research. He had even written to two left-wing think-tanks asking if they would be interested in publishing his work, if it ever came to fruition. One of them had replied that his thesis sounded more Tory than Labour to them, so no. The other was interested, but only if it could be published while his notoriety made him newsworthy. But Oliver was determined to stay away from the personal. He'd had enough of the press to last him a lifetime.

Early in the morning, when the dawn had barely broken and the mist was still on the river, he would walk along the water's edge, or late in the evening after a day's solid writing, he would sit on the river bank idly watching leaves chase each other down the stream in eddies and swirls. He marvelled that he had not, until now, valued time by himself. He thought perhaps his interest in the political tension between doing the right thing and in taking risks might be more to do with his own life and career than in propagating ideas that were hardly new. The simplicity of this self-imposed exile seemed to give him licence to think about himself in a way that would have seemed indulgent, even shameful, to the pre-scandal Oliver.

He rang Ruth and the girls every day as promised, but it was never satisfactory. Ruth was full of suppressed anger and would not understand how, when they were going through the hell of separation and possible divorce, he could take himself off to France. She complained of having to look after Obi. She resented Oliver wanting the dog in the flat at weekends when he was there, yet minded him 'dumping' Obi back with her in the week or when, like now, he was away. Like the children, Obi seemed to be a bone to be quarrelled over.

Andrea and Mattie seemed broadly indifferent to him. He wondered if they would notice if he disappeared altogether. But then he remembered Andrea's anxious face when she'd asked him about divorce, and he'd remind himself that children, above all, had to be cool: Mattie could no more express concern for him than she could admit to anxiety.

One lunchtime, when he'd had a demi-carafe of good red in the village café, the desire to talk to Kate crystallised into action. He would ring her up.

But then he remembered. That had been one of the blockers all along: she wasn't in any phone book and he didn't have her number. He'd tried Googling her and all he got was painful press stuff about their alleged affair. Nothing Fancy did not have a website. They had no friends in common and he was reluctant to contact his old office for her number. It would only start the rumour machine spinning again. He walked home, determined to find a way.

And at last he did. He remembered that at the height of the media interest he had refused the Suskind wedding invitation because Kate was doing the catering and he had to avoid being in the same room as her. He didn't have the Suskind home number either, so he tried *Service de Renseignement* but was told they were ex-directory. He rang David Suskind's office, spoke to his secretary and got their home number.

He hesitated. He liked Susan Suskind. But she was a gossip, no doubt of that. And then he thought. So what? Why should he care?

'Oliver, how lovely to hear you! . . . Where are you? I do hope you are all right . . . It must have been so ghastly . . .' She prattled on with Oliver saying almost nothing, until she ran out of steam and said, 'But what can I do for you?'

'Actually, I would like Kate McKinnon's telephone number if you have it,' he said evenly.

'Good Lord, don't you have it? I mean . . .'

'No, I've never had it. But I would like it now if you've got it.'

The woman was desperate, he could hear, to draw him into juicy revelations. But he would not play, and finally she went to her address book and read out Kate's mobile number, her home number and her email address.

Of course she might gossip, but, thought Oliver, so what? Let her. At least, at last, he had Kate McKinnon's contact details.

He toyed with the idea of emailing her. That way he could say what he had to say in a measured way, and get the tone right. Or he could ring her.

He hesitated, and then suddenly picked up his mobile and dialled.

He heard the ringing tone, but when it stopped he was not sure that she had answered. The reception was terrible. 'Hello . . . Kate?' he said. 'Is that you? Kate?'

'Who is it? I can't hear you, I'm sorry.'

He heard that, clear as a bell, and his heart lifted at the sound of her voice. 'It's Oliver,' he said, 'Oliver Stapler.'

But she still could not hear. 'You're breaking up. I'm driving. Rotten signal. Who is it?'

He cut the call, paced round the living room for five minutes then called again.

This time she answered at once. 'Hello,' she said, brightly, 'was it you just now? I'm sorry about that, no signal, but it's OK now. Who is speaking?'

'It's Oliver.'

'Oliver?' Her voice sounded dead.

'Oliver Stapler. I wanted—'

'No,' she stopped him short. 'No. I can't speak to you. Sorry.' And she put the phone down.

Oliver held his mobile in his hand, staring at nothing. For so long he had thought of speaking to Kate, of trying to explain, of somehow being forgiven. It had never occurred to him that she would refuse to talk to him.

Chapter Twenty-Three

Kate pulled into the service station and stopped at the petrol pumps. She turned the engine off and pulled her key out of the ignition. Her hand was trembling. She held it up in front of her face, willing her fingers to hold still. But the car key and house key jingled together with the violence of her shaking. She dropped them into her lap and held the steering wheel tight.

She did not understand the shaking hands, red face, knot of horror in her gut. She'd thought she was done with Oliver. How could it be otherwise after his callous indifference to her? Of course he had never loved her, but he was supposed to have been a friend. Well, now he'd seen the article he would not even be a distant acquaintance. He would hate her, of course. And scorn her. Her stomach contracted in shame. Why, oh why had she admitted to Jarvis that she'd been in love with Oliver? Why give him the satisfaction?

He must want to talk to her because he'd read the article. To berate her for telling her story to the press. Kate pushed her fingers into her hair, clutching it to drag it down over her face. She was mortified at having been so indiscreet with Jarvis. And she was alternately miserable at having cancelled Oliver's call and glad she'd had the courage to put the phone down on him. She told herself he deserved all he got.

She still had her head in her hands when she was startled by a bang on her window, right next to her head. She jerked up to see a burly biker, tattoos on his neck and a shaven head, grinning at her through the window. He was gesturing at her to lower the window.

Oh God, she thought, road rage. That's all I need now. She shook her head, fumbled with her keys, trying to find the ignition. And then suddenly she was crying, great out-of-control sobs which made it difficult to get the key into the ignition and turn it. But she managed it, and the car, still in gear, jerked forward. As she jammed her foot on the clutch she was conscious of the leather-clad guy jumping clear. Horrified, she watched him in her rear-view mirror. He stumbled and righted himself.

Relieved, but still desperate to get away, Kate drove the car round to the far side of the filling station, and stopped again. She must pull herself together. She looked in the mirror over the windscreen and saw great mascara streaks down her cheeks. God, she was a mess. She had to rummage in her handbag for some cream to remove the mascara and then open her brief-case for her spare pack of tissues. As she did so she saw the edge of newsprint sticking out of the back pocket of the case.

Kate had tormented herself half a dozen times with reading the article and she knew it almost by heart. Now she pulled it out again. The headline yelled across the double-page spread:

'I WAS A FOOL. I LOVED HIM,' SAYS KATE

And then in smaller letters:

Jarvis Stanley meets the woman at the centre of the Minister and the Cook Scandal

There was a blurry picture of her and Toby ducking photographers on their way to school, and a much larger one of them both looking happily into camera. It was captioned, 'Kate and son Toby in happier times'. Rake (now her 'media manager') had persuaded her it was better to use a good photograph from her album than another one of the stolen ones that made her look furtive or angry or frightened. And there was a picture of Oliver and Ruth all dressed up for dinner, captioned 'Ruth Stapler stands by her man'. Kate's eyes ran down the familiar text:

Six months ago, Kate McKinnon had everything. She was a confident, good-looking woman with a successful, fast-growing business, a job she loved, a private house with a garden in which she felt safe and happy, a circle of friends that included the rich and famous, and a young son, Toby, doing well at school and the apple of her eye . . . But she also had a secret passion which was her undoing.

Today she is still good looking, but she is drawn and thin: she has lost a stone and a half. Her business is in ruins, her former colleagues either avoid her or blame her for the loss of their jobs, and she has been abandoned by her friends in high places. Only six-year-old Toby is as he was.

'I cannot let Toby see the wreck I am,' she says, blinking to hold back the tears. 'He is only six. He still thinks his mother is perfect and wonderful.' She smiles a hesitant, wobbly smile.

Kate has agreed to an exclusive with the *Evening Standard* and she is obviously nervous. 'I'm not good at this,' she says. 'I don't like talking about personal stuff.' I ask why, then, has she agreed to speak to me? After all, I am the journalist who first broke the story of the suspected affair between her and Oliver Stapler, the then Foreign Secretary. She replies that she wants to set the record straight, that although the settlement paid by *Scandal Sheet* appears to exonerate them both, she still feels a victim, punished for something she did not do.

'I've lost most of my business,' she says, 'and not one government department has booked a single job since this all started. And not one of the people I dealt with all the time, the secretaries who booked the dinners, the facilities managers who agreed the costs, the party organisers who worked with me to plan the events, not one of them has texted or emailed or rung me, never mind booked another job.'

We are sitting in Kate's enormous kitchen, made by knocking two ground floor rooms together to accommodate her then-thriving catering business. But today the huge oven range is cold, the hob bare. The place is spotless, ordered, but apart from the kettle used to make our coffee, there is no action. More than half Kate's business came from government departments – everything from small business lunches for ministers, to grand international events at Hampton Court Palace. All contracts were cancelled at the first whiff of scandal.

The house was once a council house, but her parents bought it in the Thatcher years of council house sales, and, since they now live abroad, Kate has made it her own, converting it to efficient business premises and a cosy family home for a single mum and her little boy. The old garden shed has become a storeroom and larder, the downstairs bedroom is her office. But upstairs the big bed, which she and young Toby share, is covered with cuddly toys, the bedside tables piled high with children's books and games.

Kate is very proud of Toby. He is doing well at school, and has lots of friends who come to bounce on his trampoline in the garden. He is mad about any ball game, loves music, reads fluently at six years old, and he will play or read by himself for hours.

'He's such a well-balanced happy child,' she says. 'I like to think he's living proof that what matters is love and attention, not how many parents you have.'

I ask her what happened to Toby's father. 'Oh, he took fright when I announced I was pregnant. Hot-footed it to Australia.'

She smiles as if this was a joke, but then admits she was desperately unhappy at the time. 'But I have mellowed since then. I'm more understanding I suppose. We were young. We had no money. We weren't planning a baby. It was all just too scary for him.'

Her parents left soon after, to live near her brother in Arizona. I ask if she did not feel abandoned.

'Well, yes, I did, and in a way I still do. You have to wonder if there is something the matter with you when your entire family goes to Arizona, and your boyfriend scarpers to Australia.' She looks rueful, making light of her woes, and then says, bitterly, 'and then the man you think of as a friend hangs you out to dry.'

I ask if she means Oliver Stapler, and she nods.

'I just don't understand it. I still don't. We were not lovers, but we were very close friends. I never did a catering job for him when he didn't come into the kitchen with a glass of wine for me at the end of the evening. And we would talk. He was so kind to me, and interested in Toby. I guess he was lonely in London without his family.'

When the story broke Kate had an email from Stapler's office cancelling all the jobs she was to do for them. His PA refused to let her speak to him, and indeed said she herself was under instructions not to speak to her. Overnight Kate McKinnon had become a pariah.

Kate still cannot believe that Stapler could be so hard-hearted as to ignore her calls, and not ring her up himself. 'And why, when the government decided to sue *Scandal Sheet*, could they not include me? I was as injured as Oliver. More actually. And if he is innocent of an affair, then so am I. The government suing to clear Oliver's name but not mine makes it look as if somehow he was the victim, and I don't count.'

How, I wondered, does she feel about Oliver now? 'Well, I don't feel anything. Except disillusion. I had really thought he was wonderful. He seemed so honest and sincere. I was so proud to think that the next prime minister (because back then I believed that's what he'd be) was a friend of mine. And he was a real friend. He liked my company. He would tell me all sorts of things . . .'

I ask her what sort of things, but Kate is uncomfortable. 'It's true he is no friend of mine now, but he was then. I can't tell you things he told me in confidence.'

Kate protests she feels nothing for Oliver, but she is very bitter. 'While he was protected from the press by switch-boards and secretaries and officials, with policeman preventing the press getting near him, I could not get out of my house for the newsmen outside the front door. The photographers used long ladders to peer in the bedroom window. They would invade the garden and take pictures through the windows. They hounded me when I took Toby to school. Poor boy, he found them really frightening.

'Once they broke into my house and copied files on my computer. Of course I can't prove it but it's obvious from what was copied – emails and a file called Personal

Correspondence – that they were hoping for evidence of an affair. And this was *after* the court settlement so they obviously think there is no smoke without fire, even though they invented the smoke.

'People I thought of as friends gave the press snaps of me and Toby, and one of the butlers at the Foreign Office – no, I can't name him: that would make me as low-life as him – leaked everything he could to the press: that Oliver had given me a lift home; that he'd been at my son's birthday party; that he chatted to me after dinners – all things that could look bad but were in fact totally innocent.'

Kate was weeping now and said through her fingers, 'I could have shrugged it all off if Oliver had not been such a bastard.'

I ask her directly, 'Kate, are you in love with Oliver?' and she says, 'No. No. I hate him.' Then she looks up and says, 'But maybe. Maybe I was, just a little bit. I was very drawn to him. Attracted to him, I admit. I'd have done anything for him. Was that love? Anyhow it doesn't mean we did anything. We didn't. And I certainly don't love him now.'

She had never told anyone, not even her closest friends, how she felt about the Foreign Secretary. I ask her why she is telling me, a journalist, now? She says, 'I don't know. I don't know. I just want to tell the truth. I want people to understand. I did not do anything wrong. I wouldn't have. I didn't even tell Oliver.'

'You never told Oliver?'

'Good God, no! I'd have died of shame. He's happily married, kids, wife, ponies, position, the lot. Why would he want me?'

Kate wipes her eyes and looks out of the window. 'I feel such a total idiot. To me his friendship was a big deal. To him it was obviously nothing. A cat looking at a king. "Stupid cook falls for the boss". Big deal.'

Kate folded the paper and tucked it back in her briefcase. And here am I, blubbing *again*, Kate thought. What the hell is the matter with me?

The pictures were bad enough, but the text was worse. She recognised that Jarvis had not invented anything, that he had recorded her remarks and faithfully reproduced them. But almost every paragraph made her cringe in mortification. All that stuff about love. How could she have said those things? She'd made it clear, she knew, that she was not in love with Oliver. But Jarvis had only used the bits that made it look as if she was. The headline was the worst. She'd never said 'I loved him.'

The truth was she bitterly regretted agreeing to the article. She had crucified Oliver, and found that revenge was no consolation. Even paying down her overdraft had not relieved the guilt.

She climbed out of her car and headed for the Ladies at the back of the building. It was mercifully clean and tidy, and she splashed her face under the tap and dried it on loo paper.

She was walking towards her car when she saw that the man heading for the Gents, and yards from crossing her path, was the biker man – the chap she'd almost knocked down at the petrol pump. Her heart in her mouth, she kept on walking, deliberately looking away from him.

But as they drew level, he stopped. 'Good, you look a lot better,' he said. 'I'm sorry I gave you such a fright. I just wanted to see if you were all right.'

Kate, dismayed, turned to look at him. He was smiling. Kind. Solicitous. Not out to berate her, or attack her, or rape her. Just an ordinary citizen, who happened to have a lot of tattoos and a few earrings and necklaces.

'I'm so sorry. I thought . . .'

'Don't worry, love,' he said, grinning. 'Happens all the time. I know I look a bit scary to some. But I'm harmless really.'

She shook her head in apology, 'I don't know what got into me.'

He touched her shoulder briefly. 'Anyway, you've stopped crying which is the main thing. But if you want a good blub,' he patted his leather jacket, 'I've got a broad shoulder. We could have a cuppa? You shouldn't drive when you're upset, you know.'

Smiling now, Kate refused the invitation with more thanks and apologies and made it back to her car, distinctly cheered.

She sat in silence behind the wheel, thinking. Then she shifted her bottom purposefully in the seat and turned on the ignition. When she got home she would dispense with Rake Jones's services. She would not make a career out of being a victim.

Kate's positive mood stayed with her. She rang Rake and gave him the bad news. She followed it up with an email asking him to cancel his planned interviews in two magazines and a talk show on Sky, and she told him to send her an invoice for whatever she owed him.

'Right,' she thought, 'now for the big decision. Change of career.'

She emailed the Head of St Thomas High School in Ealing, an acquaintance whose daughter was in Toby's class. Kate liked her, she seemed bright, forward-thinking with a sense of humour.

Dear Judy,

I saw you were advertising for teaching assistants last term. Have you filled all the places?

I didn't apply then, because at the time I was in a bit of a mess – you will have read about the Oliver Stapler nonsense – but since then I've done some thinking and would like a change of career.

My catering business has done me well over the years, and I love cooking, but with recession and one thing and another it is no longer giving me the pleasure or the security I'd like.

I'm attracted to the idea of teaching because I'm good with children and young people, I think, and of course it would suit me to have school holidays with Toby while he is still in primary.

I know teaching assistants are paid very little, but maybe there is a route towards professional teaching qualifications I could follow at the same time? Food Technology or whatever?

I would love a job with you, but I know it is a long shot. Even if there is nothing you could offer me, could I come and see you, do you think? I need someone to give me the low-down on school life and an honest assessment of whether I would ever make a teacher. And who better than you?

Kate McKinnon

The next afternoon Kate was sitting in the living room, eating yogurt with a squirt of maple syrup, and flicking through the TV channels. She'd done little all day, just put in a couple of hours this morning for Amal, making sweet Indian desserts. She was filling in for one of his cooks who was off trying to sort out his immigration status. All day the absence of Toby had oppressed her. She missed him all the time. It was silly really. When he was at school, she hardly thought of him, just got on with her work knowing she'd see him within hours. But it was different now. The ache seemed constant.

It would be another week before he returned. Pat and Hank would be bringing him back and they would stay a fortnight. Kate had mixed feelings about this. Of course she wanted to see them, and it was handy, and cheaper for her, that Toby was coming with them rather than her having to fly out to fetch him. But she would have liked him to herself for the little that was left of the summer holidays.

When the telephone rang she jumped up, relieved at the distraction.

'Kate, it's Chris. I'm here.'

For a split second she could not place the voice. And then her heart leapt into her mouth. Chris. Toby's father.

'Kate? That is you, isn't it?'

'Yes ... yes. Chris. Where are you? I thought you were in Australia.'

'I was. But since you didn't answer my letter I thought I'd better come in person.'

'You are here? In England?' Kate could not keep the distress out of her voice.

'Yes. I'm here. In London. I want to see you, Kate. Will you give me a cup of coffee?'

She swung her head from left to right and back again. No, no, no. She didn't want, didn't need this.

'Kate, I'm on my way. You'd better say yes, because I'm coming anyway. I've got to see you.'

Kate made a conscious effort to gain control of her emotions and her voice. 'Chris, this is a really bad time. I don't think I can handle—'

'Kate, that is why I've travelled ten thousand miles. I know you're going through the pits. I want to help you.'

'Help me? How can you help me?'

'Look, sweetheart, I'm on my way.'

'No, no, Chris . . .' But he'd ended the call. How had he found her? And he'd called her sweetheart. What right had he to call her sweetheart, or to offer her help?

But some deep instinct to be in control, not to give anyone cause to think she was incapable, or going to pieces, galvanised Kate into action. She had no idea where Chris was or how long he would be, but she ran upstairs and straightened the hastily made bed, rearranged Toby's soft toys on the pillows, threw her towels into the laundry basket and replaced them with clean ones. Then she dashed down to the kitchen. It wasn't too bad, but Kate liked things to be perfect. She stacked her lunch things in the dishwasher, wiped all the surfaces with a J-cloth, polished the swished-out sink with a dry tea towel. Then into the living room to plump up the sofa cushions, polish the glass coffee table and sort the newspapers and books: out of date mags and papers into the recycling bin, current ones in a neat pile, books back on the shelves.

So far so good. Still no Chris. It was nearly six o'clock. She brought out the Hoover and ran it over the living room floor.

The house now looked immeasurably better. Looking round, Kate was suddenly ashamed of herself. She had always been so organised, tidying stuff, dusting and polishing as she went, automatically cherishing her home. And that was when she was working long hours. But now, when she had hardly any work to do, there had been smears on the coffee table, crumbs on the carpet, the bed only just made. What was the matter with her?

She opened all the windows to air the house and, feeling calmer, went into the garden and picked a bunch of Michaelmas daisies to stick in a vase. They looked good.

She went upstairs, changed her T-shirt and pulled a comb through her hair. It was too long, and the dark curls round her head and over her forehead made her face look small. She examined herself in the mirror for the first time in weeks and noticed how thin her face was and how pale her skin, the freckles dark and numerous. Her eyes looked huge and shadowed, and her cheeks had lost their plumpness. I look old and washed up, she thought. Good thing too. Don't want Chris getting any ideas.

CHAPTER TWENTY-FOUR

For four or five days now, Ruth had not spoken to Oliver on his nightly calls. Mostly one of the girls answered, but if his wife did, she said at once, 'I'll call the children,' and left the phone without another word.

This time, as Oliver put the phone down after talking to Mattie (Andrea was in the bath and declined to get out of it) he realised that he had ceased to mind about Ruth. Technically, intellectually, he knew that he should understand her anger, resentment, or whatever her problem was. But in fact he no longer cared. He knew he was responsible for a lot of her troubles, but he'd begun to think maybe not all of them.

And then one day when he came back from the village with his baguette and croissant, there was a thick envelope from her on the mat. He slit it along the top and pulled out a letter. It was short and to the point.

Dear Oliver,

I want a divorce. There seems no point in trying to keep a marriage going that is giving neither of us any satisfaction.

I expect the girls will have told you about my relationship with the saddler in our yard, Ben. But in fact Ben has nothing to do with it. He's on the spot, he's sympathetic, and he thinks the world of me. But I am not such an idiot as to think it will last. I see

*my affair with him as essential therapy to help get over the failure
of our marriage.*

*I have spoken to Sargeant and Roberts and, if you agree, they
can represent us both. I cannot see any point in worsening things
by haggling over who gets what while two sets of lawyers get rich.*

I have not told the girls. I imagine we should do that together.

Ruth

Oliver read the letter twice, surprised and hurt at its
brutality. He knew Ruth, underneath, was not cold, and he
told himself that she was unhappy too, that her defence was
an icy front.

And Ben the saddler! He realised now that he probably knew
about Ben all along. The children had included him in ever
more of their bulletins, and he now remembered Andrea saying
something about Ruth always being in the man's workshop.

He should feel outraged. Outraged that she was having an
affair. And with his tenant. Outraged that Ben should dare to
touch his wife. Outraged that Ruth was conducting their affair
on home ground. Maybe even in their bed.

But oddly, all he really felt was shock that Ruth could express
herself so collectedly, so cold-bloodedly. Maybe that was a bluff.
Maybe she loved the guy. Maybe he could make her happy when
Oliver could not. He pushed away the thought.

Did he want his marriage to end? Was this the call that should
have him on the next plane home, to beg for forgiveness and
a new start?

He did not know. He felt panicky at the thought of separation from the girls and he didn't like the thought of Ben and
Ruth together. But he felt strangely indifferent to the word
divorce.

He still held the envelope in his left hand, and now he

extracted whatever it was that Ruth had enclosed. It was a fat newspaper clipping, folded tightly.

As soon as he saw the headline: *Exclusive: 'I was a fool. I loved him,' says Kate,* he sat down at the kitchen table. He was conscious of his heart beating fast. He spread the two pages out and read the article, top to bottom.

At first he couldn't concentrate on its content. His mind kept demanding why Kate would do such a thing. How could she have agreed to talk to the press? It wasn't like her. Of course the head-line was nonsense – he'd been around the press for long enough not to believe much what they printed, especially headlines. But why was she doing this to him? *He*'d never said anything at all, beyond his official denial, written by Terry and issued by the Downing Street press office. He had obediently done as Terry had demanded: dutifully got on with his day job. He had refused, polite and smiling, to say anything beyond 'No comment'. It wasn't until he was exonerated by the court settlement that he had spoken in public at all, and then only for a few minutes on the *Today* programme. Why on earth had Kate reopened a can of worms?

He felt no resentment, only dismay and disbelief. Why? Surely it could not be for the money?

And then as he read the body of the piece, and began to understand for the first time Kate's feelings of abandonment and betrayal, saw how he had shattered her opinion of him, grasped the fact that while he was smugly 'doing his day job' protected by all the resources of the state, she was on her own, fighting to keep her business going, to protect her boy, to go about her work, to survive.

How utterly feeble his efforts to protect her had been. How supine his obedience to Terry and his spin machine. How blind to just how bad it was for her. God, he had been an unthinking fool.

It was only on the second reading that the more important message got through to him, and he was mortified. Poor Kate had really cared for him, maybe even believed herself in love with him.

How could he have been so insensitive? To have enjoyed her company, abused her confidence, revelled in her enthusiasm and good sense, and yes, in her youth and attractiveness, without realising what he was doing. He had encouraged her by attention, by affection, by admiration. And then expected her to treat the relationship as though it were nothing unusual.

Oliver stood up and poured himself a large whisky. He thought back through all the occasions that they had sat talking, sometimes into the small hours, drinking wine in a kitchen somewhere. But he had never laid a finger on her, had he?

The negative answer to this did not fool him. He might not have touched her, but that did not mean he had not wanted to. He thought back to the ride in his car from Hampton Court, when he had given her a lift home. He remembered noticing how smooth and shapely her legs were under stockings that glinted in the sudden light of street lamps. He had forced his eyes away as she crossed her legs.

He felt guilt creep over him like fog. He'd been stupid and unthinking. At best. But the truth was worse than that: he had employed his grown-up charm to captivate her. He had used his sophistication, his position, his fame and power to seduce her. He had *made* Kate fall for him just because he liked the feeling of being adored, and because he could. He had wrecked her life to satisfy his ego. Terry's words came back to him: *If the cook in question had been male, ugly and old? Would you have been driving him home and sharing regular night caps with him?'*

Oliver seldom swore, even inwardly, but now he said aloud, 'Oliver Stapler, you are a first class shit.'

For the second time in less than a week, Oliver rang Kate's number. This time, as soon as she answered, he said, his heart pounding, 'Kate, don't hang up. It's Oliver.'

There was a fractional pause, an intake of breath and then she said, very fast, as if she had learnt the speech by heart, 'Oliver, I cannot speak to you. I don't want to. If you want to give me grief over that article, I probably deserve it and I'm sorry. I mean it, I really am so sorry. But I can't talk to you. There is nothing to say.' And she hung up.

Chapter Twenty-Five

Chris appeared at her door at six-fifteen, a bunch of roses in his hand, like a shy suitor on his first date.

'Hi,' he said.

'Hello, Chris.' And then they stood there, silent.

He was looking very good. He had shaved off the stubbly beard and his tanned open face, candid eyes, one chipped front tooth and nervous smile had taken her right back to seven years ago, when he could make her gut melt with a look. They shook hands, a trifle awkwardly.

He seemed genuinely sad not to meet Toby. But Kate thanked her stars that neither Toby nor her mother was around. She needed, she thought, to send him packing before they even knew he'd been here.

They sat at the kitchen table, Chris with a beer, Kate drinking tap water. She wanted to know why he'd tracked her down.

'I've wanted to, oh, for years. But I felt guilty, you know? For what I did? And I'd try every now and then. I couldn't believe you wouldn't turn up on Facebook or Friends Reunited. But nothing. So, although I would occasionally Google you, I more or less gave up.'

'But why now, Chris? What is the point? We have different lives now. I don't understand.'

Chris shook his head, 'I dunno, Kate . . . Maybe my wife getting custody of my daughters, you know? I miss them so much?

Maybe that made me think ... realise what a dreadful thing I'd done, what a fool I'd been? I couldn't stop thinking about you Kate, and what a bastard I was.'

Kate had forgotten how he ended his sentences on a rising note, making all observations a question requiring confirmation. It was very Australian and she'd found it attractive. It had made him sound a touch diffident and unsure, a nice counterpoint to his confident Aussie directness.

She said nothing, just watched him gather his forces to continue. He said, 'You know, you were always a cloud, always sort of *there*, in our marriage? My not being able to forget you, and wanting to know if I had a son or daughter, you know? It was a real issue, for Jolene more than for me. She hated it, and after a while, kind of hated me for it too?'

Chris had rubbed his big hands roughly over his face and had shifted on the sofa to look directly at her. 'Kate, you have no idea how grateful I felt when I knew that you had gone ahead and had the baby. I was crying, you know? Like a kid.'

Kate had seen that he was near to tears, but she'd said nothing. She didn't trust herself to speak. 'Anyway,' he said, 'the publicity over the Stapler affair answered some questions at last. I knew you were alive and had had the baby and he was now six-year-old Toby. But knowing that made me want to see you more, you know?'

'How did you find me?'

'One day I Googled you, expecting to draw the usual blank. But up came all this stuff about Oliver Stapler. I feel so sorry for you, Kate. What a shit! Anyway, I wrote to you at the Foreign Office, and when you didn't answer, I went on standby and came here. Of course the bastards there would not tell me anything, so I just trawled our old haunts, looking for chefs we knew. Struck lucky today.'

'How?

'You know Gerard at Le Trou Normand?' he said. 'He told me you sometimes did casual shifts for a mate. And the mate gave me your address.'

They talked for nearly two hours in the house, then walked along the High Street and had supper in Odile's. It wasn't great, not a patch on the Taj Amal, but Kate was careful to choose a restaurant on the nearer side than Amal's. She didn't want to risk Talika or Amal spotting them through the window and popping out to say hello.

Chris talked a lot about his marriage break-up and how he missed his daughters, and Kate sympathised. 'I know, I could not bear to lose Toby,' she said. 'I'm neurotic about it.' She hesitated, wondering if she should say what she wanted to say. Why not, she thought? 'The reason I've no website, am not on Facebook etc, is because I didn't want you to find me, in case somehow you'd make a claim on Toby.'

'But Kate, that's crazy,' he said. 'I would never want to take him away from you, even if I could.' He reached across the table and took her wrists. 'You must know that? Anyway, I'm the bastard that abandoned him, remember?' Kate looked into his eyes, searching for any false note. But he was, she knew, absolutely sincere.

She told him something of her financial troubles, the hurt she felt at being closed out by her old government colleagues, by the lack of contact from Oliver.

And then, somehow, after a bottle of Pinot Noir, they were walking back with their arms around each other. It felt comforting and familiar, and when he stopped her at the gate and kissed her, Kate knew that they would go to bed together. They did, and it was wonderful, both exciting and familiar. Most of all it was deeply, wonderfully, satisfying: it was so long since she'd made love she found the sheer physical release, the crashing pleasure of it overwhelming. She lay on his shoulder, tears running down her face, but laughing.

The next few days reminded Kate what it was to be happy. Chris was with her almost all the time, and they spent a lot of it in bed, marvelling at their easy resumption of the old magic, and how seven years seemed to have somehow vanished.

Chris helped her with two small catering jobs and it had been fun working with him again. She felt alive for the first time in months.

'Chris,' Kate said, as they were finally unpacking his back-pack and stowing its contents into a cleared-out couple of drawers in her cupboard, 'I've asked Amal and Talika to supper tonight. I want you to meet them. It's going to be so difficult with my mum, and we need them as allies.'

'Sure thing, babe.' Chris knew Amal from their old agency cheffing days before he got his own place. 'He's an amazing cook, and not just Indian tucker. He was sous-chef in that French joint with the Michelin star.'

'I know. If I get this school job, I want him to take over my clients. He'd have to cook mostly French and Italian, often very stylish and modern. But most still want Country House British – you know, salmon fish cakes, beef Wellington, upside down apple cake.'

'Yeah, that posh woman we did the gallery opening for was bending my ear about how much she hates fancy food with foams and drizzles and micro-leaves etc. She called it television food.'

Kate laughed, 'Yup, that's Lady Suskind all over. But she's used me for years. We did her daughter's wedding in June. The gallery belongs to her son, though I suspect it's her husband's money. She's a good client, pays on time, but she's not exactly adventurous about food and she'll need some persuasion to accept an Indian caterer.'

'How many are there? Clients, I mean? I thought they'd mostly gone?'

'No, only the government ones went really, which admittedly was most of my business. The private ones have all stayed loyal though they spend less than they did. There's maybe thirty or so. I don't want to leave them high and dry. We've got thirteen forward bookings and if the worst comes to the worst I could probably manage them: get up early, go to bed late, get someone to stand in for me if the job's in school time. Wouldn't be the first time, but I would rather make a clean break.'

Kate was folding crumpled T-shirts and putting them into a drawer. Chris came up behind her and wrapped his arms slowly round her body and covered her breasts with his hands. He said into her neck, 'Kate, don't take the school job. Come back to Melbourne with me. Bring Toby. Leave all this crap behind. Let's start again, Kate.'

Kate turned round, shaking her head, but almost at once she felt desire creep into her like melting honey. She lifted her arms round his neck and in doing so her T-shirt came out of her jeans and his hands slipped under it, round her back on her bare skin. She could smell the sharp clean smell of his aftershave and she let her mouth and nose rest lightly on his neck, breathing him in. She felt her bra tighten round her breasts as his hand pushed under the back strap and held her steady. He slid the other hand round under her bra.

She put her fingers into his hair and pulled his head up to look into his face. She felt dreamy with desire as she said, 'Can we discuss this later?'

*　　*　　*

'Who was that?' asked Chris, without looking up from his newspaper as Kate came in from the study.

'Oh, nothing. Just someone I don't want to talk to. Cold caller.' Kate hoped her voice betrayed nothing of her agitation. She walked through the sitting room into the kitchen, touching her ex's springy hair with her fingers as she passed. 'Do you want some coffee?'

She had said nothing to him about the *Evening Standard* article. It had come out before he arrived from Oz and with luck he'd never hear about it now. She didn't want him to know that she had been infatuated with Oliver, any more than that she had talked so candidly to the press. Chris believed, had chosen to believe, that she was as pure as the driven snow, an innocent twice wronged: first by him when she was pregnant; now by a bastard politician called Stapler.

Oh, why did Oliver have to start ringing her up now? She'd spent months longing for a word from him, but now she wanted to be free of him; free even of the thought of him.

Kate put the kettle on and felt a now familiar rising tide of panic. What on earth was she doing? She had let Chris back into her life, and had been both excited and horrified at the speed with which he had re-established himself.

And now Toby, her mother and Hank were due back. Of course she longed to see Toby, but she absolutely dreaded the arrival of her mother and stepfather. Her mother had not approved of Chris the first time round, and then when he had abandoned her and the embryonic Toby, she had seen him as the devil incarnate.

Pat would never understand. Indeed, Kate hardly understood herself. She could not believe that it was only a week ago that Chris had arrived, that, after all the years of fearing he might just reappear to claim his son, she had let him into her house, and into her bed, within a couple of hours of reunion.

The next morning, Judy telephoned to offer her the teaching assistant's job. Or almost.

'I'm ninety per cent certain you will get it,' she said, 'but we have to go through the formalities. You can start at the beginning of term anyway, as a temp. And apply for the job at the same time.'

Kate took a Coke out to Chris, who was trying to tidy the garden on Kate's instructions. It was an attempt to forestall criticism from Pat. 'Things are looking up,' she said. 'First you appeared. And Toby's coming home. Then Amal agreed to take on my customers. And now I've got an interview with the Head of St Thomas's. And she says the job is probably in the bag.'

She grinned at him, waiting for the praise. But he frowned.

'Look, Kate, if you want to teach, you can do that in Australia. Have you given the idea any thought at all? Just think how much better it would be for Toby to grow up in that climate. Kids in Oz don't spend all day in front of the telly, or sitting in the park in the sodding rain. And the schools are probably better? Less bullying, and more sport, and teachers getting some respect, you know?'

For a second Kate allowed herself to be carried along by this picture. Of Toby with a father, his real father, of her having a man to look after her. Of an open-air life, trips to the beach, she teaching well-behaved kids, helping them cook the vegetables she had helped them grow.

But it was a pipe dream. 'Chris, I can't work in Australia. And you haven't got a job. And you already have one family to support. How would we live?'

'You could marry me. Then you could work. I can get another job.'

I don't want to marry you, she thought. I've no idea what the hell I want, but I don't want to marry you.

But she didn't say so. She just smiled and gave him a quick kiss. 'Too far! Too fast! How about we decide nothing yet? You've not even met Toby.'

For the first fifteen minutes after Toby, Pat and Hank walked through the automatic sliding doors at Arrivals, Kate was so happy she didn't give Chris a thought. Toby had ducked under the barrier and leapt into her arms, his tanned face alight with the purest happiness. He had clung on like a monkey, while Pat fussed and clucked like a mother should about Kate's loss of weight and pale, drawn face. Hank had been his usual good, solid self. It was wonderful.

Kate had refused to let Chris come to the airport: she wanted to tell her mother about his reinstatement before they got home and found him there. She had had a vague idea that she could do this on the Gatwick Express to Victoria, or in the taxi from the station to home. But Toby was so excited, telling her about the desert, the caves, and going to Waterworld it was impossible. There was no opportunity to get her mother away from the others and anyway, she did not want to leave Toby. She also began to think she should talk alone to Toby too, explaining his father to the child, before they met.

She walked down the train, ostensibly to find a loo, and rang Chris from the next compartment.

'Darling, I'm sorry, but I just cannot tell Mum about you now. Toby's so happy to be with me, so excited. I don't want to disappear into a corner with Pat and leave him. Do you think you could . . .'

'Kate, you've got to tell them sometime.'

'I know, but now is not the moment. You have to trust me, Chris. Please? Could you just disappear for tonight? Would you? I will tell them, I promise, after Toby has gone to bed, when it's peaceful and we can have a proper conversation.'

There was silence from Chris, and Kate found anger mounting. He was obviously unwilling, which he should not be. After seven years of absence, you'd think he could stand one more single night.

'Are you OK with that, Chris?' she said, her voice hard.

'He is my son as well as yours, you know . . .'

'Yes, Chris, I know. Which is why we have to get this right . . .'

'Right. *We*,' Chris jumped in. 'You just said it. *We* have to. I should be with you. I have a right as his dad . . .'

Kate erupted, 'No, Chris, you don't. You've no rights at all, not with me, not with Toby. Nothing. If you want rights, go to court for them. One thing is for sure – you have no right at all to stay in my house tonight if I don't want you to. And I don't. OK?' She snapped her phone shut, breathing hard. She stood for a moment, watching the bleak environs of Clapham slide past the window. What would she do if Chris was there when they got back?

She was almost back at her seat when Chris rang back. She pressed the button without speaking. He said at once, 'All right, all right, I'm sorry, babe, I'm over-reacting. It's just that I was excited at seeing Toby too. I've been thinking of nothing else all day. I'm so sorry, darl.'

'OK, I'm sorry too,' Kate said, pacified. 'I'll ring you tonight after I've told them. And thank you, darling. It will be nice to have one night with my boy in my bed too. Before we banish him to the study.'

Kate finally got her chance when Hank was in front of the television and she and her mother were doing the washing up.

'Mum, I need to tell you something.'

Pat looked at her sharply, 'You are not going to marry this Oliver chap are you?'

Kate shook her head. 'No, Mum, no chance of that.'

'Then you've found another man.'

Kate smiled, a bit wobbly. 'You are psychic, Mother! But it's not another one. It's the same one. Chris.'

She watched her mother's face, which had lit with pleasure, suddenly shut fiercely, like a door slamming, 'No, Kate. No. No, you cannot be such an idiot. Don't tell me that. I cannot bear it.'

Kate felt the old indignation engulf her. 'OK, I won't tell you,' she said childishly, 'since you cannot bear it. I should have known it would be all about you.' Dropping the tea towel on the worktop she walked into the sitting room and threw herself into the sofa next to Hank. Stony-faced, she stared at the TV, pretending an interest in the football.

Her mother followed her, strode to the television and pressed the Off button.

'Hey, folks, what's up?' said Hank. 'Am I in the dog house or something?'

'Sorry, honey,' said Pat, 'but Kate has just dropped a bombshell. She's back with that idle layabout who fathered Toby and then beat it. That's about the sum of it, isn't it, Kate?'

Kate was silent, trying not to lose her temper. And then, quite suddenly, she was trying not to cry. She bit the insides of her cheeks until they hurt, and said nothing.

Hank moved up close to her and put his arm round her. 'Look, your mother is wonderful, and she loves you like crazy, but she isn't the most tactful woman in the world. I don't know what happened in there, I was too busy rooting for Arsenal, but mothers and daughters shouldn't scrap on their first evening together, surely?' He gave her a hug and a little shake, trying to make her look at him.

Pat said, 'I'm sorry, pet. It was just such a shock, and you know I cannot forgive Chris for what he did to you and Toby. But Hank is right. The last thing I want to do is quarrel with you.'

Kate, her voice unsteady, said, 'It's simple, Mum. If you can't accept that I'm back with Chris, you'll have to go. Stay in a hotel or something.'

'Where is he now?' asked Hank.

'He's living here with me. I just asked him to make himself scarce tonight so I could talk to you, and prepare Toby for meeting his dad.'

As she said this, Kate felt a clutch of fear. What if they didn't like each other? And then she thought, Oh God, I'll have to share Toby. I don't want to share Toby. He's mine, no one else's.

As if reading her thoughts, Pat said, 'Kate, just tell me, are you sure about this? Do you really love Chris or are you looking for a dad for Toby?'

And then the questions followed thick and fast. What about Australia? What happened to the wife? Were there kids? What did Chris do for a living? Could Chris afford two families? She wasn't thinking of going to Australia was she?

Kate felt as though she were twenty again, being interrogated by her parents about some new boyfriend. But she told herself Pat had a right to know, and her beady questioning testified to her concern as much as to her hostility to Chris. And it ended in tearful hugs and Pat's insistence that she and Hank sleep on the sitting room sofa-bed so Kate and Chris could keep the bedroom.

But the session left Kate feeling unsure and anxious. It would never be really right with Pat. Sometimes she seemed to love her mother more in absence than when she was around. Maybe Chris was right. Australia would be a new start for all of them.

When she was in bed, trying but failing to shut her thoughts out with a book, Pat knocked gently on her door and came in with a cup of hot chocolate. 'When you were little and ill I used to give you Horlicks, but I couldn't find any.'

'I remember. It was the most comforting thing. You used to tell me it would make me sleep, and because I believed you, it did.'

'Hot chocolate works the same magic,' Pat said, smiling. Kate sat up and took the cup.

'Mum, the truth is I have no idea what I should do. I change my mind by the hour.'

Pat bent to kiss her forehead. 'Then do nothing, darling, just keep going and wait for the answer to come. It will.'

As her mother left the room Kate had a childish desire to call her back. Mummy, can I have a drink of water? Can't I have another story? I want the light on in the corridor . . .

In September Toby went back to school and Kate started at St Thomas's. She was only temping as a teaching assistant but she loved it. Mostly she helped with practical classes in the food rooms. St Thomas's was a big school and Food Technology was popular. The government's new enthusiasm for giving every child cooking lessons had meant a lot more work for the department. As well as after-school cooking sessions for the under-sixteens, there was a 'Student Survival' cookery club for the sixth form and a mothers' and toddlers' food group.

Kate seldom stayed to help teach in these clubs because she wanted to get back to Toby, but she did most of the shopping and preparation for them, weighing out ingredients, hunting down equipment, photocopying recipes, filling in forms.

But what she really liked were the food lessons in the curriculum. The senior food teacher, a large no-nonsense Jamaican woman called Elizabeth, was a survivor from the Home

Economics days and thought it was a sad day when the subject became Food Technology.

'Until very recently,' she'd said, 'if you really wanted to, you could teach the whole Food Tech curriculum on a computer. All marketing plans, packaging design, nutritional labelling, distribution channels, etc. Now, thank the Lord, or maybe Jamie Oliver, we have to get our hands in the flour. And children love that. I've been teaching for thirty-five years and I've never met a child who didn't enjoy cooking. Seems to me the best way to get them to come to school is to teach them to cook.'

Elizabeth had quickly recognised that Kate was not only a good cook but a natural teacher, and she gave her half the class to supervise. This still meant fifteen or sixteen children to worry about, but, used to a team of chefs, Kate found it exciting and satisfying rather than stressful.

At home they had settled into a kind of routine. She dropped Toby at school early, and he went to the breakfast club. This saved her having to make him breakfast and it gave her time to get to St Thomas's. Chris, Pat, or Talika collected him after school.

But things were far from ideal. Having Pat and Hank's open cases in the sitting room irritated her, though she tried not to show it. She missed the intimacy of Toby in her bed, but Toby had declared that even after everyone left, he wanted to sleep in the office, which from now on, he said, had to be his new bedroom.

'I had my own bedroom in Arizona,' he'd said. 'And I am six and nearly-a-half, and no one else sleeps with their mum any more.'

Having Chris around all the time irritated Kate too. She could not understand why – after all, he wasn't doing anything that she could accuse him of. But, because he was Australian and over thirty, he could no longer claim to be a student or on work experience. He needed a work permit to do a regular job, which would be near-impossible to get.

He worked when he could, temping illegally for kitchens not too fussy about the law. Kate secretly disapproved of this, but told herself she was being po-faced. What else was the poor chap to do? She had refused to give him a 'yes' about Australia and was taking her mother's advice to just keep going and let the decisions make themselves.

Chris, she admitted, was more than willing to do the shopping, cook the supper, dig the garden, generally carry his weight. And Kate was grateful. But he took up so much *space* – sprawled on the sofa, legs apart and stretching halfway across the room. In their previous life together Kate had never been irritated by beer cans on the floor, clothes all over the bed, crumpled tissues everywhere, wet towels on the bathroom floor. I guess, she thought, the years of being a caterer, where being organised is more important than being able to cook, have changed me into a control freak.

But there were moments when she thought Chris blowing back into her life would somehow save her. He seemed to want her so much, to be so determined to persuade her to marry him, go home to Oz with him, let him back into her life as if he had never left.

And the sex was good. They had to be quiet because they were directly above Pat and Hank, but somehow the need to bite her lip and be silent was something of a turn-on. Chris could be a wonderful lover, demanding, sometimes forceful, but able to feel by instinct what she wanted. The only time it did not work was when she was reluctant – too tired or anxious – and then he would be offended, and roughly turn his back to her. And then she would feel bad, and stroke his back, and work doubly hard to make things better, and finally they would make love and everything was fine.

But it wasn't peaceful. If we went to Australia, she thought, maybe we would have more room, less stress, and all these niggles and doubts would just disappear. I'm thirty-five, damn it, what do I want? A fairy tale prince?

The October sun still had some heat in it and one day Kate was sitting with her mother outside, drinking tea. 'Darling,' said Pat, 'I want to talk to you about something.'

Kate was instantly wary, 'What about?'

'OK, it's like this. The reason we have stayed on in London this week is because I needed to see your dad's old lawyer. Your brother and I have agreed that you should have this house, now, rather than have to wait until I kick the bucket. I'd always intended to leave it to you, darling. Arthur doesn't need it, he's doing well.'

Kate was so astonished, she could not absorb the information. She stared uncomprehending at her mother's face. She noticed how delighted her mother looked, and she started to smile back. 'I don't understand. You wouldn't even borrow any money on it for me. Why would you? Why would you want me to have it? The whole house?'

Pat put her hands, one of them warm from her mug of tea, each side of her daughter's flushed face and just held them there.

'Darling, I have a good reason, and I don't think you'll like it, but I can't help that.'

Kate frowned at her and Pat took away her hands. 'So, hear me out, no interrupting, OK? Promise.'

Kate, still frowning, nodded. Pat took a sip of tea. 'It's like this. You know I don't approve of Chris, and I don't think Toby likes him. But I sense that you are being drawn to this idea of going with him to Australia because your business has foundered and a teaching assistant's salary will not give Toby the life you want for him.'

Kate wanted to protest that of course Toby liked Chris, he was just not used to a second parent and it was hard for him to adjust. But she had promised to hear her mother out, so she just shook her head slightly and said nothing.

Pat continued. 'I accept that if you really love each other then you should get married and either live here or in Australia. Giving you the house just loads the dice a bit in favour of England, though not much. But your friends are here, like Amal and Talika, and the security of the house might make you feel less inclined to decamp with Chris.'

'But, Mum—'

Pat put her hand up. 'Hey, you said you'd hear me out. If you decide to stay together and in England, Chris could, once he was married to you, get a legal, decent job and you could stick with training to be a teacher. You could borrow some money on the house to tide you over. Either way Toby would not be uprooted.'

Kate was still more puzzled than pleased. 'But Mum, I still don't see why you're doing this. If you want me to dump Chris, surely this just helps us stay together?'

'Sure, it's a risk. You might sell the house and still go to Australia. But I'm banking on your good sense. And making it possible for you to take your time.'

'Oh, Mum.'

Kate looked into her mother's face, and saw in her something she recognised. Poor Mum, she thought, she loves me exactly like I love Toby. She'll put up with anything, do anything, to make me happy.

Chapter Twenty-Six

In October, the parliamentary recess over, Oliver faced what he hoped would be a final hurdle. He must return to the House of Commons as an ordinary backbencher, knowing all eyes would be upon him.

He had hoped his resignation in July and the subsequent interview on the *Today* programme would lay the Limoges and Necklace affairs to rest. But the *Daily Telegraph*, which for months had been running a gleeful series of revelations about MPs cheating on their expenses, had had a ball with his misdemeanours while skilfully glossing over the time-lapse and his lack of evil intent. When Oliver had been in France, he'd followed the story on the *Telegraph* website and the temptation to respond was almost irresistible. But he *had* resisted, and ignored the messages on his mobile phone. Since then, the matter had resurfaced periodically when journalists needed padding to buttress some other MP's expenses scandal. He flinched at the thought of commiserations to his face and gossip behind his back.

But in the event it was fine. He'd managed to get a reasonable office on the top floor and he spent his first morning working in it on constituency business. The rooms were nothing like as grand as he'd had at the Foreign Office, of course, but his former status still seemed to cut some ice with the Serjeant-at-Arms and he had not been confined to a shared cubby-hole.

At noon his telephone rang. It was Lord Brampton, whom Oliver had not seen since he'd consulted him about his troubles.

'Oliver, glad you are in. Do you want some lunch?'

'How very nice of you. Is there a reason?'

'I thought you might like to escape your colleagues, for whom you will be an object of too much interest for a day or two.'

'Well, that is kind, and it's tempting.' Oliver was indeed tempted, and he hesitated. 'But I think I'd better stick around to be stared at, and get it over with. But how about a drink? It would be good to see you.'

He ate lunch alone in the section of the canteen reserved for MPs. Colleagues nodded and smiled, a few who knew him said welcome back, and he found himself discussing the dire quality of the catering. No one mentioned his resignation or the expenses scandals.

That evening he and Brampton had a drink at the bar of the Athena in Millbank. Oliver nodded to several people among the crowd of politicians, civil servants and journalists.

The double whisky Brampton bought him was very welcome. As was his non-Westminster chat: Brampton reminisced about student days with Oliver's father, and Oliver told him of his pending divorce from Ruth. He was, Oliver thought, a wise old bird. Non-judgemental, interested, reassuring.

At seven-thirty Brampton had to go to a dinner and Oliver decided to stay on and have something to eat. He walked to the bar, consulted the menu on the wall, and tried to order his supper.

The barman had his back to him, and seemed determined not to turn round. Oliver tapped his glass on the counter, politely trying to make his presence known, but without result.

There was something familiar about the man, thought Oliver. 'Excuse me. Could I order . . .'

The barman turned round. It was Dennis, the Government Hospitality butler. His expression was a mix of surprise and dislike.

'Good Lord, Dennis,' said Oliver. 'Are you moonlighting?'

'Certainly not, Sir.'

Something's wrong, thought Oliver. The man has changed. Where is the obsequious, almost fawning, creature he was used to?

And then he realised. Of course. He was no longer Secretary of State. Not worth fawning for.

'You've left the service then?' he asked. 'I'm astonished.'

Dennis frowned. 'Of course I've left. I had no option, thanks to you.' His tone was petulant and rude.

'Thanks to me? What do you mean, Dennis?' Oliver was more puzzled than angry. 'What on earth is the matter?'

But Dennis was rapidly becoming angry. 'I got the sack, that's the matter. And all because of you and that cook you could not keep your eyes off. Or your hands, I bet.'

Customers at the bar were staring in horror and fascination, and Oliver realised that they were heading for just the sort of scene he had been dreading all day, only infinitely worse.

'Dennis, I am sitting in the corner over there,' he said, his voice icy calm and very quiet. 'I would be glad if you would order me a plate of hummus, taramasalata and olives. And I would prefer it to be brought by another waiter, please.'

He strode back to his seat, through the throng of customers. Fortunately the noise was such that the extraordinary exchange with Dennis had not been heard by many. But he felt unsettled by it and waited a little anxiously for his food to arrive.

Unfortunately it was Dennis who brought it. Oliver, with sinking heart, watched him mincing through the crowd, the oval platter held with professional skill high above his shoulder. He put it down, almost tossed it down, with disdain.

'Just because you lost your job,' he said, his hands now on his hips, 'you need not have blamed me, and cost me mine.'

'Dennis, I do not know what you are talking about, and if you have a quarrel with me, make an appointment and come and see me. This is no place for a discussion.'

'I don't want a fucking discussion,' said Dennis, his voice now high with indignation. 'I want to know why you had it in for me.'

'But I didn't. To be blunt, Dennis, I have never liked you, but I've certainly not wasted my time thinking about you or plotting your dismissal. I had better things to do.'

Dennis tipped his head on the side, lips pursed, 'I bet you had. Like cheating on your wife and robbing the taxpayer.'

Oliver looked round. He could either let this ridiculous scene escalate into a full-blown show for the bystanders, or he could walk out and leave his supper. Or make Dennis see sense.

'Dennis,' he said, his voice low, 'I can see you are upset. I don't understand why, but again, this is not the place. You have customers to serve and I have supper to eat. Just go away.'

But Dennis's voice was again on the rise and Oliver was conscious that the neighbouring tables had fallen silent. 'What do you mean you don't understand?' said Dennis. 'Don't pretend that you don't know I've been blamed for the press stories about you. As if the whole world didn't know what you were up to – closeted in the kitchen with Kate McKinnon, driving her about in a Government car ...'

Suddenly Oliver understood.

'It was you who tipped off the press! I should have known.' What a slimy bastard the man was.

'What if I did? It was my duty!' Dennis was rapidly losing

control. 'It's right to blow the whistle. That wine you were drinking with her was government property.'

Oliver stood up as the manager elbowed his way out of the crowd round the bar and into the restaurant area. He said, 'I apologise about this, but your barman here . . .'

'I know, Sir. It's for us to apologise, not you.' He took Dennis by the arm and said, 'Dennis, you're fired. Come with me.' He signalled to two waiters. 'Give him his things and chuck him out.'

'Christ!' shouted Dennis, now completely out of control. 'First he gets me the sack from a job I've done for twenty years, and then he—'

But he was not allowed to continue. The waiters bundled him through the crowd and out of sight.

Oliver sat down again, and bore the manager's apologies. He really wanted to abandon his supper and leave, but almost everyone in this room would know who he was, and he was not going to run away. He sat back, assured the manager there was nothing to worry about and asked him for half a bottle of the Australian Merlot.

When the man returned with the wine, he explained that he had occasionally used Dennis to do odd shifts on a casual basis and had felt sorry for the man when he lost his job, and had hired him to run the bar.

'But why was he sacked?' asked Oliver. 'I had no idea he had been. Was it for speaking to the press?'

'Not exactly, though I guess that was a part of it. Government butlers must hear stuff all the time that's secret, and they're not meant to go blabbing. And he didn't deny he got paid for it. But when he was summoned to a disciplinary hearing he lost his temper with the boss. Julian something? Like now, I guess.'

As Oliver ate his supper he began to feel a tiny shaft of sympathy for Dennis. But really, the man was a snake. He deserved what he got.

It was weeks since Kate had last put the phone down on Oliver and it puzzled and annoyed him that he couldn't put her out of his head. Specifically, he could not forget the bitter tone of her remarks in that newspaper piece.

Maybe he just wasn't used to people not liking him, or thinking he had wronged them? Up till now I've led a charmed life, he thought: happy marriage, wife with money to pay for the good life, great political career, enough celebrity for people to be honoured by my attention. So when someone feels I've done badly by them – no, when I know damn well I've done badly by them – I can't handle it.

Poor Kate. He would have one more go at reconciliation. He rang her home number. Almost at once a male voice answered.

'Hello. Chris here.'

Oliver frowned. Who was Chris? 'Oh, I'm sorry. I think I must have the wrong number.'

'No problem, mate.'

The voice was Australian. But he was sure he'd dialled the right number. Oliver said, 'I was looking for Kate McKinnon.'

'Right, well she's not in. Can I help? I'm her partner.'

Partner? What kind of partner? Oliver said, 'Could you ask her to give me a call? It's really important.'

'If it's about a catering job, I can probably help? We work together.'

Ah, business partner. Oliver said, 'No, it's private. Could you just ask her to ring this number?' He had to wait while Chris found a pencil and wrote it down.

'What's your name, mate?'

'Oliver. I'm Oliver.'

There was silence at the other end so Oliver said, 'Thanks, that would be great.'

'Oliver? Not Oliver Stapler?'

'Well, yes. I need to speak to her.'

Oliver heard the intake of breath and then suddenly the man was shouting. 'Oliver bloody Stapler. What makes you think she'd want to ring *you* back, shithead? You're the guy who couldn't pick up the phone for, what is it, six months? When she was going through fucking purgatory? When she thought you were a *mate*? Some bloody mate. I'm not giving her any messages from you. Take a hike, Oliver Stapler.'

Oliver stood stock still by the phone, listening to the silence. Then he slowly put the handset back in its cradle and sat down.

He pulled his laptop towards him and told himself he would forget about Kate. What was the point of apologising or explaining? She'd not change her view, and speaking to her would be painful or embarrassing for them both.

He would concentrate on dealing with constituency emails and correcting the proofs of his booklet for Civitas.

But the conversation with the Australian bugged him and two days later he just pulled out his mobile and texted Kate:

I know it won't change your attitude to me, but I want to say I'm sorry. Can we have lunch? Or supper? Any day, anywhere. Oliver

He had a reply ten minutes later.

Can't do supper. And lunch would have to be at half term. Oct 26-30 this month? Kate

Wonderful. Shall we say Tuesday 27th. Wolseley in Piccadilly? One o'clock? Oliver

Yes. Thank you. Kate

Three weeks later, Oliver was early, determined to be there before Kate. He waded through a wall of restaurant noise, nodding at customers he knew, returning the smiles of waiters and feeling the old glow of satisfaction at being in the thick of it. The Wolseley had that perfect atmosphere of buzz and fashion upheld by serious service. The place looked like a Paris brasserie with gleams of silver and glass, white cloths, high ceilings, dark wood, waiters in long black aprons. But the clientele was modern, mostly under forty and tie-less, the woman polished and chic. The food was unpretentious, good and generous.

Oliver was gratified to see that he'd been given his usual table in spite of his fallen status. It was one of the quieter corner ones where you could sit diagonally across from your guest on a roomy banquette rather than opposite on a chair, or side by side. In his glory days he'd eaten a lot of good food at that table, hosted a lot of VIPs, drunk a lot of fizz.

He positioned himself so that he could watch the door. But almost immediately Kate was at the table. She'd come from the back of the room.

Oliver half stood. 'Kate! You look wonderful. But where did you spring from? I've been looking out for you.'

She slipped into her seat. 'I arrived early. I've been skulking in the loos.'

'You mad woman. Why didn't you sit here and have a drink?'

'I don't know. I've never been good at being on my own in posh restaurants. I think everyone's feeling sorry for me because I've been stood up or something.'

'And you so independent, and in the catering trade!'

'Feeble, isn't it? I can just about manage Carluccio's, but even then I'd probably prefer a coffee bar.'

But Oliver noticed there was no trace of shyness when it came to ordering. Kate questioned the waiter about the food with cheerful confidence and his professional coolness melted under the warmth of her interest and knowledge. She spoke to the man, not like a pedantic foodie, but like a fellow enthusiast. How did they make the steak tartare? At the table or in the kitchen? Where did the beef come from? What breed? Within seconds the two of them were nodding and chattering like old friends.

As she alternately lifted her face to the waiter or bent her head to the menu, Oliver examined her. She was much thinner, and her skin was pale. Her thick curls made her face look small and her freckles were more noticeable than he remembered. He noticed that her eyes were subtly made up with soft smudgy browns. They had that frank, almost merry, gaze he remembered. When she smiled her teeth were bright against her dark red lips. She was wearing some sort of lipstick but it wasn't thick or shiny, more like a rich stain. If I touched her mouth, he thought, it would feel soft and dry and leave no trace on my fingers. He pulled his gaze to the menu.

The ordering over, there followed a few minutes of conversation about nothing: the traffic, the weather. Oliver took the plunge.

'Kate, I told you I wanted to apologise . . .'

'No, Oliver, really . . . I should . . .'

He put his hand on her knee, hard. 'Kate, just hear me out.'

She shifted back in the seat. 'OK.'

'Until that article in the *Evening Standard*, I had no idea how horrible it must have been for you.' He paused, frowning. 'No, that's not true. I did know. I saw footage of you being doorstepped by the press, and I did nothing. I behaved disgracefully, Kate. I'm so sorry.'

She returned his gaze, her face solemn. 'All the same, I should not have talked to the press. My excuse was that I needed the money, but I think I wanted to hurt you too.'

Her hand was on the table, curled into a fist, tense. He put his much larger hand over it, with the sensation of holding still a small animal. 'You had every right. I did not even ring you. I did want to but I let myself be talked out of it. I was leaving for the Middle East and I didn't have your number and didn't want to ask around for it in case that lent credence to the story . . .'

'It's over now. It's OK.' Kate pulled her hand away, not fast, but firmly. Oliver's hand felt the loss of it.

Maybe she would never say 'I forgive you', but Oliver, still seeking absolution, told her of his tussles with Terry and the refusal of the Government to join her case to his in suing the paper, of Brampton's refusal to help, and his advice to steer clear of her.

Even to his own ears it all sounded like the feeblest of excuses and he ended by saying, 'The truth was I was more concerned with my career than with yours, or, I'm ashamed to say, with damage to you.'

Neither of them had touched their food.

'Some of the damage was the recession,' Kate told him. 'But your cutting me off so fast did hurt. You seemed not to have given me a thought, or not to care . . .' She tried to smile but her lip trembled and she put her hand to her mouth and ducked her head.

He wanted to put a hand on her arm or an arm round her shoulder. 'Maybe we should eat,' he said.

He applied himself to his fishcakes, and, giving her time to recover, he did not speak for a few mouthfuls. Then, nodding at her eggs Benedict, he asked, 'Any good?'

'Delicious. Spinach gritty though. Still, it proves it was grown in sand and didn't come in a pre-washed packet.'

'Is that good?'

She smiled, 'Well, it means the chef is probably buying British and local.' She took another mouthful. 'Oliver,' she went on, 'won't you be unhappy as a backbencher?'

'I don't think so. The fall from grace was nothing like as painful as I expected.'

'Really?'

'Really. I spent a month on my own in France and somehow settled a few things in my head. Finally rumbled that being constantly busy, forever on the move, always in demand is not the same as doing something important. A lot of that constant round of meetings, late night discussions, those endless papers, papers, papers, achieves precisely zero. And it certainly distanced me from the things that matter, like family and friends, and walking along a river bank or reading a book. Sounds trite I know, but it's true for me.'

He looked across the room, wondering if he was being wholly honest. He knew he'd never get the top job now: did he really not mind? On the whole he thought he didn't.

They talked on, and Oliver found he was slipping back into the comforting groove of confiding in Kate. He told her of his separation from Ruth and his worries about damage to his daughters. He talked of his ambitions to write, and his new life in the rented cottage, living like a sort of appendage to the family, close in case of need, but not central to it.

'Things at home seem to be progressing inexorably to divorce,' he said. 'These days Ruth and I communicate almost exclusively through intermediaries: our lawyer, the children, occasionally stiff emails.'

Kate reached over and rubbed his forearm. With real concern in her eyes, she said, 'Poor Oliver. Poor Ruth. It must be horrible.'

'Ruth says she's happy. I don't think she really is, but she's having an affair with a brawny young saddler who rents space in our yard. That must boost her ego a bit.'

'Oh, Oliver, how awful for you.'

'I mind less than I ought, I think. I ought to froth and fume as the wronged enraged husband, ready to kill the man, but you know what? I'm not sure I even mind now. Not sure I even want to get back with Ruth.' He was silent for a while, frowning at the table. Then he looked up at Kate. 'But all the years of loyalty and love must count for something. I'm sure one day we will rub along OK.'

He reached for the water and poured them both a glass. 'I expect it's vanity,' he said, 'but what I find tough is the loss of my reputation. For a politician, I used to be moderately well thought of. A bit aloof maybe, and the press made great play of what they thought of as my grandee air. Now everyone thinks I'm a corrupt thieving politico, a philanderer and a cad. Your partner, for example. Chris . . .'

'Chris, how do you know Chris?' Kate interrupted.

Oliver explained he'd telephoned before resorting to text but got short shrift from Chris. 'Don't worry,' he said, in a bid to soothe Kate's anxious face, 'it's understandable. Presumably he knows how I failed to help you, so naturally he's cast me as a villain. He's probably right, don't worry about it.'

He picked up the menu. 'How about pudding?'

She shook her head, almost impatiently, her mind obviously caught by the talk of Chris. He went on, 'I didn't know you had a business partner. That must mean the business is recovering, which is good, isn't it?'

'No, it's not like that. Chris is Toby's father.'

'What? The Aussie who ran away when . . .'

'Yes, that's right. He came back. He's living with us now.'

So that explained the hostility. He was the low-life who had abandoned Kate when she was pregnant with Toby. And Kate had taken him back.

The news made Oliver uneasy. More than uneasy; indignant, almost angry. But he said, 'That's wonderful, Kate. So you are together again. Young Toby must be thrilled to have his dad back.'

'Yes, it's good. I think.' She stared at her wine which she had hardly sipped. 'But I'm not sure. My mother says I'm with him for the wrong reasons. You know – security, he's Toby's dad, et cetera. She's been wonderful. Before she went back to Arizona she told me she's going to give me the house I live in – it's hers, not mine, you see – so that I will have the security to kick him out if I want to.'

'And do you want to?'

She had been looking deadly serious but now she suddenly lifted her head and laughed. 'God knows, Oliver. I certainly don't. I think maybe at my age you don't marry for the right reasons. Any reason will do.'

'And what would be the right ones?'

She looked at him steadily. 'Love?'

Then she straightened up and smiled. 'Can we get back to you, do you think? I don't want to talk of my love-life, or lack of it.' Oliver's heart went out to her. She wouldn't want to revisit her confession to that journalist about her feelings for him. They'd obviously changed now, and he didn't want to get into that either.

He signalled for the waiter and asked for some cheese and

more bread. 'No,' he said, 'we've been here two and a half hours and talked of almost nothing but me. Now it's your turn.'

She ran her eyes around the still full restaurant. The other tables were as full of women as the lunch-time ones had been of men. They were drinking tea and eating cake. Kate looked at her watch.

'God, Oliver, it's ten past four.'

'You're not in a hurry are you?'

She shook her head. They ordered two more glasses of red to go with the cheese, and she told him, reluctantly at first, how she'd turned down Jarvis and Rake's ideas of making money from her notoriety, and how her mother and brother had been so generous with the house, how she was working as a teaching assistant, aiming to be a fully fledged food teacher. And how she could not make up her mind about Australia.

As she talked he watched her. Sometimes, when she was talking of Chris or her mother, of the catering business that was bumping along under Amal's direction and with help from Chris, her eyes would lose their life, and it was as though she was just imparting neutral information. She stirred her coffee cup absentmindedly, the sugar long since dissolved, or ran her fingers up and down the stem of her wine glass.

But when she talked of the children she taught, of Toby and her friends, of Talika's impending baby, her eyes would light up, and the pace of her speech would quicken. She would push her hair off her forehead with an impatient gesture, and look intently into his face, seeking understanding and approval. He liked watching her.

They finally stood up to leave at five-thirty. While they waited in the lobby for their coats, Kate suddenly pulled his sleeve and ducked her head against his chest, whispering, 'Oliver, that's Jarvis Stanley. He's the journalist who wrote the story. Quick . . .'

Oliver looked up at the moment that the man recognised them. 'Kate,' he said, 'good to see you. And with Oliver Stapler!' He put his hand out to Oliver. 'Jarvis Stanley, *Evening Standard*. Don't think we've met. Kate, you know Rake.'

'Jarvis, please, this is not what you think.' Kate sounded desperate, but Oliver felt perfectly calm.

'Hi,' he said coldly but politely, 'good to put a face to the words at last.' He shook Rake's hand too.

'Would you like to join us for a drink?' asked Jarvis. 'I'd enjoy that. Professionally, of course. But also privately. You know I've always been a fan of yours, Kate.'

Oliver said calmly, ''Fraid not. But for the record, we are old friends, as you know, and we've been having a long lunch together to compare notes and catch up on how each of us has survived the damage that you and your like have done to us. And you will be pleased to know, I'm sure, that we are both just fine. Kate is doing well, and I am very happy as a backbencher.'

The coats arrived and they shuffled into them as Jarvis persisted, 'Do you lunch together often, Mr Stapler?'

Kate cut in, 'Jarvis, please. Leave us alone.' But Oliver said affably, 'None of your business, old chap.'

Jarvis smiled at Kate but again addressed Oliver. 'Were you not concerned that to lunch with Kate at such a fashionable place could start the rumour mill again?'

'Not at all,' said Oliver, putting a couple of coins into the coat-check girl's hand. 'I deliberately chose the Wolseley. I will not pretend that Kate is not a friend, and since there's nothing between us to get you guys excited, I'll lunch where I like. Good day, gentlemen.' And he ushered Kate out of the door and into a taxi. Jarvis, he noted, at least had the decency not to follow them out of the restaurant.

Oliver didn't feel the slightest anxiety about Jarvis seeing them. He knew that the story, once he'd left government, was very small beer, and even if they carried a paragraph, he doubted that any other paper would pick it up.

He turned to Kate and at once saw that she was shaken. He put his arm round her and drew her to him a little. She did not resist, but her eyes were troubled.

'Kate, you mustn't worry about that journo. He can't hurt us now, though I could kill him for spoiling a good lunch. It was supposed to make you feel better.'

She smiled then and said, 'I enjoyed it. And thank you. It was good. I don't mean just the food. It was good to talk.'

'Talking to you has always been easy. I've missed it.'

He withdrew his arm and shifted a little to look into her face more directly. 'Kate, why did you accept lunch so suddenly, after resolutely putting the telephone down on me for weeks?'

She smiled. Sadly, he thought. And then she shrugged and looked directly back at him. 'Couldn't resist,' she said.

CHAPTER TWENTY-SEVEN

Kate picked Toby up from Talika's on her way home. Talika pressed her to stay. 'Amal will be up in a minute, and we both want to hear all the details of your lunch.'

'I know, and I want to tell you, but Chris is at home and I'm hugely late and not entirely sober.'

Talika stood with one hand on her tight round belly, the other on the door jamb. She looked, thought Kate, like an advertisement for pregnancy. The baby was due any day now, and yet she still looked so vital: slim and fit, eyes clear, hair glossy, skin aglow.

'Sometimes I'm jealous of Chris,' Talika said. 'We hardly see you now he's back in your life. And you don't even employ us as kitchen hands since you have your own live-in chef!'

She was half-joking but what she said was true. Chris didn't like her to go anywhere without him, and was generally negative about Amal and Talika, and indeed about any of her friends. He wasn't going to approve of her rolling home at six-thirty after a lunch date.

Kate had not told Chris who she was lunching with, and was aware that such secrecy, right at the beginning of a renewed relationship, did not bode well. But since he had been so violently on her side and placed Oliver firmly in the role of arch-villain, she could hardly confess to lunching with him.

She and Toby walked home, Toby chattering about a DVD

Sanjay and he had watched about a baby being born into a family who already had a child. 'Sanjay went on and on about his new baby sister or brother. He's so lucky, Mum. I want a baby brother. Why can't you have a baby?'

Kate was a little thrown by the thought, but she said, 'Would you like that? For Mummy and Chris to have another baby?'

'Why does it have to be Chris's too? I don't want Chris to be the father.'

Kate's heart missed a beat but she said calmly, 'Why not, darling? Chris is your dad. It would be good if you and a new brother or sister had the same dad, wouldn't it?'

Toby was silent, his head down. Then he said, 'I suppose so,' with obvious reluctance.

Kate stopped walking and took his hand. 'What's the matter, darling? Don't you like Chris?'

Toby looked up at her, his face solemn. He shook his head.

'Why not, darling? He's always nice to you, isn't he?'

Toby, dropping his eyes again, aimed a kick at a drifting plastic bag. 'No, he's not. He's only nice to me if you're there. When it's just me and him he says he's too busy to bother with me.'

Kate winced inwardly. 'Well, sweetheart, he has a lot to do, you know. He can't play with you all the time.'

She saw her son's face set into what she called his Churchillian look: grumpy and determined. He muttered, 'Well, I don't like him. I don't care if he is my father.'

They walked on a few paces. 'He says I have to call him Dad, but I won't. I don't have to, do I? Do I, Mum?'

'No, darling, not if you don't want to.' Kate felt oddly pleased by this. The truth is, she thought, I don't like sharing Toby.

Chris's coat and the small back pack he used for carrying his chef's kit around were in the hall but he was nowhere to be seen. No sign of supper on the go either. Kate left Toby to lay the table, and went upstairs in search of him.

He was in the bath, reading a car magazine. The bath was so full it was running gently into the overflow and a corresponding stream of hot water dribbled into it from the tap. He was surrounded, she noticed, by bubbles smelling suspiciously like her expensive Givenchy, a present from Amal and Talika. Forcing herself to bite her lip on these matters she sat on the loo seat, leant over to give the top of his head a kiss. 'Hi,' she said. 'What sort of day?'

'Pretty bloody,' he said. 'I've been turning the garden shed into an extra room for both of us. Hefting fridges and freezers is heavy work. Also the place was so full of junk . . .'

'You were doing *what*?'

'Well, you need somewhere for all your school stuff and recipe books, etc, since Toby's in your office. And I've nowhere to put anything.'

'But you can't just . . . Chris, the catering stores and the blast chiller, everything for the business is in there.'

'Not any more, it isn't. I've managed to get most of it outside. We can probably flog the chiller through a small ad in *The Caterer*, and the council or some charity could maybe collect the rest.'

For a moment Kate sat there, open-mouthed, thinking that this was ridiculous. She was sitting on a loo seat, Chris was stark naked in the tub, and they were about to have the most almighty row. She said, deliberately calm, 'Let me get this straight. You have decided to rearrange my house without consulting me? Is that it?'

Chris swivelled in the bath the better to look at her and a wave of soapy water sploshed over the edge and onto Kate's foot. 'Well, yes. I hoped I'd have it finished before you came in and it would be a surprise. But it turned out to be a massive job.'

'And how are we meant to manage the catering without the stores and fridges, etc?'

'Don't sound so bloody frosty! It's not a problem. We can talk to the clients and persuade them that Amal will do as good a job, if not better. It's stupid, Kate, continuing in this half-hearted way with a catering company that is going nowhere. Either Amal should have the business, or I should. For me to be footling around with only the rump of the customers, those too stuck-up or prejudiced to have Amal cook for them, makes no sense.'

'So you decided it was time to put an end to my business?'

'Well, you'd already done that, hadn't you, in giving up in favour of teaching?'

There was some truth in that, but Kate was too angry to concede the point. In fact, she thought, I am too angry to speak at all. She stood up and walked through the bedroom to the window overlooking the garden. The first thing she noticed was that Chris had left the shed light on and the door open. Typical. Then she registered the shapes of fridge, freezer, blast chiller and several black bags lined up on the concrete apron outside the shed.

She marched downstairs, intending to investigate further, but was intercepted by an excited Toby.

'Mum, Mum, it's wicked.' He pulled her by the arm into his room, until this morning still serving as a sort of ancillary office space for her files.

She stopped at the door, amazed. The camp bed, her filing cabinets and stationery cupboard had all disappeared. In their place were brand new bunk beds, each covered with a *Dr Who* duvet and pillow. The steps to get up to the top bunk doubled as storage boxes accessible from the side and were neatly filled with Toby's clothes. At the end of the room was the bookcase she recognised from the sitting room, and on it were arrayed Toby's books and toys.

On top of the old beige carpet was a bright blue rug, perfect for playing on.

Toby was jumping up and down. 'Thank you, Mum! Thank you. It's so cool. I can have Sanjay to stay, but I'm having the top bunk. And . . .'

Kate forced herself to be pleased for Toby, and to tell him that this was Chris's doing, not hers. She could not spoil it for him, and she sent him upstairs to thank his father.

She inspected the rest of the revolution that Chris had visited on her house. Her filing cabinets and cupboard were now in the shed. So was her desk, which had been taking up too much of the sitting room. Chris had arranged one half of the shed as her office, and had put her desk under the only window. He had left the shelves in place and put some of her office kit on them. It didn't look bad. Only brown and bleak and cheerless. She did not want an office in a garden shed, thank you.

But she had to admit that he had tried. This must all have taken backbreaking effort. And planning. He must have ordered the bunk beds in advance. And she should be pleased and touched by his wanting it all to be a surprise.

But she could barely contain her fury. How dare he make major decisions without consulting her? Even if he were her husband, which at this rate he never would be, he'd have no right . . . She stood in the shed, shivering. For God's sake, it's nearly November. How does he think anyone can work in here? She went outside to inspect the freezer and fridge and found them still full of food, but now, of course, unplugged.

Successive waves of indignation and anger engulfed her. How did he think he was going to earn his living if not by cheffing?

And how on earth had he paid for Toby's bedroom furniture? Probably on the never-never and she would have to pick up the tab. Had it not occurred to him that the blast chiller might belong to a hire company and not be hers to sell? And what a criminal waste of food.

And worst of all he was lying in that bath upstairs, smug in the belief that she would be grateful.

But she was wrong. It appeared he was now out of the bath and extending his energies to her kitchen because Toby was shouting, 'Mum, Chris says you have to come in now. It's supper.'

Chris says? Kate wanted to retort *Tell him to go to hell*, but she called back that she was on her way. On her way to a blazing row, she thought. But at least the presence of Toby would delay the inevitable. Maybe by the time they'd eaten she would be calmer.

But in the event they were saved by a phone call from Amal. Talika was in labour. Would she come to the hospital and look after Sanjay?

'Of course. Oh Amal, how wonderful. I'm on my way.'

'There's no hurry. The baby seems very reluctant to appear. Probably won't come for hours. Sanjay's here with us in the ward. But when she goes into the delivery room . . .'

'I'm on my way,' repeated Kate.

She didn't tell Chris there was no hurry. She just said to Toby, 'Darling, Talika is about to have her baby. Isn't that good? I'm going off to look after Sanjay while the baby is being born. You'll be OK with Chris, won't you, sweetheart?'

'Can't I come? I want to see the baby too.'

But the thought of getting into his new bunk quickly reconciled Toby to being left with Chris. How easy it is to win a child's affection, thought Kate. A mixture of bribery and attention, and bingo.

*   *   *

It was a relief to Kate to transfer her thoughts to Talika. Of course she looked wonderful, just as she had a few hours before, radiant and relaxed. Amal, on the other hand, kept getting up from his chair beside his wife's bed and prowling the ward.

'C'mon, Amal, relax,' said Kate, 'you've done this before.'

'He hasn't, you know,' said Talika. 'Sanjay was born in Delhi, at my grandmother's house. And there childbirth is women's work. Amal was not allowed anywhere near.'

She stopped talking as her belly muscles gripped her. As the contraction faded she said, 'We've hours yet, so now you'll have to tell us about lunch with Oliver.'

So Kate explained how they had had a four and a half hour lunch and how all her indignation and resentment had evaporated. 'I'd no idea how little choice he had. He is convinced he behaved badly, but when you think how busy cabinet ministers are, and how ruled by their diaries, it's understandable, isn't it? If someone says, "You do the job the taxpayer pays you for, we'll take care of Kate," it must have been a big relief. He'd little idea what I was going through, and . . .'

Amal interrupted, 'And he didn't want any more links with you to get in the way of his climb to the top.'

Kate opened her mouth to defend Oliver. But then she said, 'Yes, there is that as well. He said as much.'

They talked on about Oliver, and the Wolseley, punctuated by Talika's contractions. Kate told them about meeting Jarvis Stanley and Rake. 'Oliver was just great. Polite, but relaxed and somehow in control. He's wonderful. He really is.'

Talika said, 'I think you *must* be in love with him. Probably have been from the start. You've forgiven him everything. Did he mention your confession in the public prints about loving him?'

Kate laughed. 'Talika, I've told you. I never said I loved him.

That was the newspaper sub adding a sensational headline. But no, thank God. Oliver was the soul of discretion. Not a word.'

Another contraction mercifully let Kate off that conversation, and then they were talking about Chris.

Kate told them of his taking over the house, reorganising Toby's bedroom and her study. Trying to be the husband and father, unasked. As she spoke she found her resentment returning.

'Half the time I don't know what I feel. I suppose it's good for Toby to have his dad back, though he didn't seem to appreciate it until tonight, when he got a new bedroom out of it. And I like having a man about the place, most of the time. And a lover. He's a great lover. But he does drive me mad. He's so bloody untidy, and thoughtless. Even when he does things with the best of intentions, like this study in the shed, it infuriates me.'

'It would infuriate me too,' said Talika, 'but the bottom line, Kate, is does he go or does he stay?'

'Oh, God, I don't know! He wants us to go to Australia, new start and all that. Either that, or get married so he can work in England. I'm tempted by Australia. I'd be less grumpy and territorial if we had a place that wasn't mine, I'm sure. But workwise, why should he do any better with me and Toby in tow than he was doing before, which was not well? And he's already got a family to support. It's mad.'

Amal had his watch in his hand and was studying Talika. 'Shouldn't the contractions be speeding up by now?'

'Stop fussing, darling. Mother Nature knows what she's up to, I'm sure.' To distract him, she said, 'Kate needs your advice on Chris, Amal.'

'That's easy. All I've heard in favour of Chris is that he's Toby's dad and good in bed. It's not enough, Kate. Chuck him out!'

'Wow! That's a bit brutal,' said Talika.

'Well, I see a woman at best lukewarm about the man. Meanwhile, her mother, her son, and her best friends are not even lukewarm. They think he's a disaster.'

Kate turned to Talika. 'Is that true, Talika? Do you think he's a disaster?'

Talika said, 'Hold on a sec,' and puffed her way through another contraction, Amal breathing with her and Sanjay joining in. Then Talika relaxed and smiled her serene smile. 'If you marry him I will discover he's the best man on earth, Kate. But if you don't I'll think you have been very wise indeed.'

Kate looked from Talika to Amal and decided that she would veto Australia. These were such wonderful friends. A lot more important to her than Chris.

Talika's contractions were increasing in frequency and depth, and conversation became more disjointed. Talika caught Kate's eye and Kate said, 'Sanjay, suppose you and I go and explore this hospital and see if we can find a drink and a biscuit or something. Then we'll go home and get some sleep, and come back to see Mummy and the baby in the morning. Shall we?'

Talika, whose brow was beginning to have a fine sheen of sweat upon it, said, 'Sanjay darling, give Mummy a hug and a kiss. Next time you see me you'll be kissing your new brother or sister too. So I want a proper kiss while I can have you all to myself.'

Sanjay half climbed onto the bed and wrapped his arms round Talika's neck and kissed her. 'Yuk,' he said, 'you're all sweaty.' He put his ear to his mother's belly. 'Hey, baby,' he said, 'see you soon, OK?'

Sanjay fell asleep in the taxi back to Amal and Talika's house. Kate pulled his trainers, jacket and trousers off and tucked him, floppy as a rag doll, into bed without benefit of pyjamas or washing. She looked at his face, innocent and vulnerable as all sleeping children are, and thought, poor little chap, you've no idea of the serious competition for your Mummy's attention you are going to have to put up with.

She lay, still dressed, on top of Amal and Talika's duvet with the coverlet over her, and stared at the invisible ceiling. She so badly wanted another child, but not with Chris. She wanted the father to be someone like Oliver. No, not *someone like*. Oliver. She wanted Oliver's child. Would that not be the answer to everything? If Oliver loved me, I would surely love him.

She felt a tear slowly running across her temple into her hair, and then another on the other side, while she gave in to longing – longing for Oliver. She let herself, for the first time, simply dream the impossible: that Oliver would fall in love with her, leave Ruth, marry her, have a baby with her and live happily ever after. It was the most trite of fantasies, the most banal of ambitions. Unworthy and impossible, but how could she help it?

In the morning Kate shook her head in disbelief at her tears and dreams of the night before. Oliver did not love her. The best she could hope for was that he'd stay her friend. If he and Ruth divorced, he would need a friend, a hand to hold, a shoulder to cry on. Maybe she could go on being his confidante, his understanding mate. It wasn't what she wanted, but it was something.

As she woke Sanjay and dressed him to meet his new-born sister (her arrival announced by text sent at three a.m.), she knew she would not settle for marriage to Chris, not even for Toby's sake.

When Kate got home from delivering Sanjay to his family in the hospital, Chris had his coat on and was champing at the bit.

'Christ, Kate, I'm meant to be in the City, cooking for Roger. I'd forgotten and he's going ballistic.'

'Roger?'

'Yeah, that Aussie guy with the gastro pub. Anyway, I'm off. Bye.'

'When will you be back?'

'No idea. See ya.' He gave her a grin and a hug and rubbed Toby's head, and he was gone.

It was as typical as it was irritating. He was all over the place. He was hopeless at communication, seldom told her where he was, or what time he'd be back. No news is good news, he said, don't worry about me. I'll be fine. He gets blown about by wind or whim, she thought. It's sad, but I'm about to blow him right out of here too.

In fact Chris was back in two hours. And in a filthy temper, thought Kate, as she heard him slam the door and throw his backpack against the wall.

She and Toby were cuddled up on the sofa, watching children's TV, and Toby was so absorbed he didn't look up. Kate went out to Chris and closed the door behind her.

'Arsehole,' he said, 'that bloody Roger sent me home. Said I should have been there at eight. Wouldn't even cough up for the taxi fare.'

'You took a taxi? When you're barely on the minimum wage?'

'Had to. I was late.'

'Why didn't you tell me you were working today?'

'Because I bloody forgot, woman. I told you. Do you want to hear it again?' He gave his backpack a kick. 'I forgot. I forgot. I forgot.'

Kate felt dismay more than anger. She shook her head and turned away.

'Anyway,' said Chris, quieter now, 'I had to babysit your precious son, didn't I?'

'Not your son then, Chris? Well, I'm glad of that, because this isn't working.'

'What do you mean?' She saw the flash of fear in his eyes. God, she thought, this is going to be horrible.

'Come into the kitchen, Chris. We have to talk.'

She walked ahead of him. 'Do you want a cup of coffee?' Delaying the inevitable. He shook his head.

She went up to him thinking he might put a hand on her shoulder and they could do this with affection. But he stood before her like a chastened schoolboy, his arms hanging by his sides. She took his wrists in her hands and looked into his face. 'Chris, you have to go. I'm sorry.'

'For Christ's sake, Kate, why? We're great together. It's wonderful.'

'In bed, yes.' She didn't tell him that now even that only worked because she pretended he was someone else. She said, 'You're a terrific lover, Chris. But we don't love each other. You don't really, really love me, do you?'

'I do. Of course I do.' He had a trapped look, which triggered a memory of this very conversation, many years ago. He doesn't know how to love, she thought. 'And I think you love me,' he went on, 'as much as anyone—'

'Maybe you're right,' she cut in, 'and maybe I'm a fantasist. But I want much more than sex and affection. Maybe it's a female thing. Women, I think, want their men to be stronger than they are, better at everything than they are. They want to respect and admire their men. They want to trust them. They want them to be *better people* than they are. They want to idolise them. Most of all they want to be looked after.'

Chris yanked his arms out of her grip and swung away from

her, then back to face her. 'That's such bollocks, Kate. You are always going on about equality and women's rights and all that feminist crap, and now you sound like some simpering romantic. If you don't want me, have the courage to say so.'

'I didn't say it was reasonable. I don't think women are always reasonable. In fact I think most marriages hit the rocks because of women's unreasonable expectations. They want equal rights, they want to be the boss in the office, they want the top jobs, but they are far too picky about a mate. Men have no problem marrying the air hostess, or the cocktail waitress. They're always marrying their juniors or underlings. They quite like having non-competitive stupid wives. But women want to marry the boss. They don't want a tasty bit of beefcake with a six-pack and a nice bum and nothing between the ears. They want equal rights AND they want to marry Mr Darcy or Rhett Butler.'

Chris's voice was very bitter. 'So I'm brainless beefcake, is that the problem?'

Suddenly Kate realised how much too far she had gone. In expounding her little theory she'd almost forgotten she was talking to a man she was in the process of dumping. A man with a heart, and feelings.

She shut her eyes. 'I'm so, so sorry. Of course I didn't mean that. I was just banging on about something I've thought a lot about. This is far more about my unreasonable demands than any inadequacies of yours.'

'Yeah,' said Chris with a little snort, 'I bet. So let's have your list of my inadequacies.'

'What is the point, Chris? Let's just say I want more, in the way of responsibility, money, seriousness, looking after, than you can give me or Toby.'

'Well, that's pretty clear then.' He looked at her and she

saw his eyes were wet and his face flushed. She steeled herself and said, 'And I want you to go because your presence will prevent me ever finding that chap, if he exists, which of course I doubt.'

Chapter Twenty-Eight

Relations between Oliver and Ruth were a little less strained since the terms of their divorce were now agreed and the world knew that they were separated. The Londoner's Diary had carried news of the petition and a few lines of speculation, with a mention of Oliver's long lunch with Kate, but his hide had been toughened over the last year and he shrugged it off.

One Saturday afternoon, towards the end of November, Oliver and Ruth took the girls to the National Theatre to see *War Horse*. A pre-Christmas panto was a family tradition and Oliver was determined not to abandon the ritual now he and Ruth were no longer together.

The children were mesmerised by the giant horse-puppets, and genuinely interested in the First World War. Oliver and Ruth spent most of the interval explaining about trenches and barbed wire, about the transition from horses to tanks, about shell shock and the numberless dead on both sides.

'Aren't they taught *any* history?' asked Ruth.

But they all loved the play, and Oliver was glad of the improbably sentimental ending. He'd feared realism, and consequently tearful daughters.

Ruth and the girls went to get their coats from the cloakroom, and Oliver waited for them by the lifts. He felt a tentative tap on his shoulder and turned to see Kate and Toby.

He felt a flush of pleasure. He'd been meaning to ring her.

'How wonderful to see you, Kate. Have you been somewhere hot and sunny? You look brown.'

She shook her head. 'Straight out of a bottle,' she said.

'It smells horrible,' volunteered Toby. 'She puts it on her legs too.'

They both laughed. Kate said, 'What a coincidence to see you here. I sent you an email today. But maybe you haven't read it yet?'

'I did, and thank you. I thought we might—' He was interrupted by the arrival of Ruth and the girls.

There were slightly awkward introductions all round. Ruth said, 'Yes, I remember. We met at Kew,' as if there had been no other connection, and Oliver was embarrassed for Kate. Oliver asked Toby if he remembered him, and Toby turned shy and shook his head in silence.

Oliver was aware that poor Kate was bewildered. Her email, which he had read just before leaving to collect the family from the station, was a brief condolence.

Just seen the *Evening Standard*. Damn Jarvis Stanley. Divorce is such a brutal word. But I know you love the girls too much to let it affect them unduly. Don't fret. It will all come good. Kate. P.S. And I owe you lunch. Any day during the school holidays?

The next day, Oliver telephoned her. The phone rang and rang and he was about to abandon it, when Kate's voice answered with a slightly breathless Hello.

'Kate, it's Oliver, I was about to give up.'

'Yes, sorry. I was making apple crumble with Toby and we both had sticky hands.'

'Mmm, delicious, I love crumble.'

'Oliver, I'm so sorry about my email. I thought you and Ruth were getting divorced. I felt such an idiot. Ruth must have . . .'

'Kate, that's why I rang. We *are* divorcing, but we're trying to do family things. Like the theatre.'

'Ah.' There was a short silence, then she said, 'It was good, the play, wasn't it?'

They talked briefly about *War Horse* and then Oliver said, 'Kate, you said lunch in the school holidays. Are you still up for it?'

'Of course I am. I can't take you to the Wolseley or anything half as grand, but . . .

'You could make me apple crumble. I miss your cooking. And if it was supper or at the weekend it could be in term time and I could see young Toby too.'

She said, her voice a little higher, excited. 'You could come to lunch today if you like. But I guess you're in the country?'

'No, in fact I'm not. Ruth has taken the girls to her parents and I guess she thinks I had my ration of seeing them last night, so I stayed in London. I've been Christmas shopping. There are all sorts of things I'm learning. Christmas shopping is one, and I don't like it. I've retreated to a coffee joint in the Westfield shopping centre. This place is heaving. It's horrible. And on a Sunday in the middle of a recession.'

'Would a rather late Sunday lunch help? It won't be ready till two-thirty. That might give you time to go back into the fray and buy those presents.'

Oliver felt his spirits lift immediately. Lunch would be perfect. He wanted to see Kate, but didn't want it to feel like a date. He would not have to eat on his own in one of these sterile trendy cafés. He could stop shopping. And he could give Toby the kite he had bought for Andrea. He'd loved kites as a child and this was such a beautiful one, like a bird with a long swooping tail.

Only one problem, the Aussie partner, Chris, would be there. But if Kate didn't see a problem, why should he?

Oliver arrived precisely at two-thirty, and was relieved to find another couple and their children already there. Chris could hardly be aggressive with other guests in the house. The couple turned out to be the Indian pair he remembered Kate talking about, her best friends who had taken over her business. Their new baby was the centre of adult attention, while Toby and their son hung about waiting to be released.

Oliver gave Kate the white poinsettia he'd bought in the shopping centre, and handed the huge kite to Toby. The lad's excitement, and that of the other boy, Sanjay, was gratifying, but he quickly realised he'd made a mistake. The boys were desperate to fly the thing, but there wasn't time before lunch to go to the park, and it would be dark by the time they were finished. Kites should be a summer present for flying on long warm evenings.

Kate ruffled Toby's hair and said, 'Darling, we will fly it next weekend, I promise.' The boys, clearly disappointed, were persuaded to play tennis on the Wii in the shed, bequeathed to them by Chris who had bought it in one of his bursts of extravagance with Kate's money.

'Oh Kate,' said Oliver as soon as they were out of the room. 'I'm so thoughtless. Kites need an adult, at least if you're learning. You'll have Toby badgering you for weeks, but you'll not be able to do it. Maybe Chris . . .?'

She looked directly at him before she answered. 'Chris has gone back to Australia. It didn't work out.'

'Oh, I'm so sorry . . .' But he didn't feel in the least sorry.

'Don't be.' She flashed him a grin. 'There are no secrets here. Amal and Talika did not approve of Chris. Nor did Toby, though I'm keen he should have a good relationship with his dad. As for me, I think I was mad to let him back in my life at all. In fact this lunch – we don't have good roast beef every Sunday, I assure you – is by way of a celebration. Two actually. The first visit of baby Aliana to the house, and the departure of Chris from it, though I have not said as much to Toby. Chris going is, I must say, a huge relief.'

Oliver was slightly taken aback by her frankness, but impressed by the way she said it all with such lightness and charm.

'The kite will be great fun,' she said. 'It will get me out to the park, and I could do with that. Not that I have ever flown a kite. If I follow the instructions, will it work?'

Amal was examining the kite. 'This is an absolute beauty,' he said, 'and I know about these things. I grew up with kites, mostly made out of bamboo and brown paper on the kitchen table. Although I confess we have a bought one now. Not as good as this, though.'

Oliver said, 'I used to make them too. That was half the fun. I'll challenge you to a making-and-flying contest, Amal.'

Kate suddenly said, 'Look, is anyone absolutely starving? If we can all hold out for another hour, you could fly the kite now, and we could have lunch when you get back. It's a perfect day, and I can see you two are itching to fly the thing. More than the boys, I suspect.'

'But won't the dinner be ruined?' asked Oliver.

'Ah,' said Kate, 'you are forgetting you're talking to a caterer. We have ways.'

Oliver had not had so much fun for years. Amal had ducked back home to fetch their kite and he and Sanjay flew it with great confidence. Toby learnt fast, and quite soon could keep the great blue bird from its tendency to suicidal plunging.

When they got back, cold and hungry, they sat down at once. The baby slept in a sling at Talika's side.

'This is delicious,' said Oliver, 'I'd forgotten what an expert you are. I was sure we'd get overcooked beef and rock-dry Yorkshire pudding as the price for being an hour late.'

'Well, you've got luke warm beef instead. It's been out of the oven for an hour and a half. But I comfort myself in the knowledge that lukewarm food has the most flavour. I read somewhere that the nearer to our body temperature food is, the better taste buds operate.'

'It's perfect, but so is the Yorkshire, and the spuds, and the veg. All as if just cooked. Explain please, ladies.'

Kate grinned at him, amused and pleased with herself. 'Tell him, Talika,' she said.

'The Yorkshire hadn't gone in yet when you arrived. So it didn't go in until half an hour ago,' said Talika. 'And those are sauté potatoes, which stay happy for ever, not roasties which go leathery, and Kate pre-cooked the veg and dunked it in cold water to set the colour. Then nuked it in the micro at the last minute.'

'OK, OK. You are brilliant, Kate.'

Oliver looked across at Kate, confidently carving the beef into neat slices, scooping up the juices, instinctively arranging the food attractively on each plate: two slices of overlapping pink beef, shiny from its libation of boiling hot gravy, a clump of bright cabbage and carrots, a slice of Yorkshire pudding, a crunchy potato, crumbly at the edges. She worked fast, but it seemed without needing to give the job her full attention. Her focus was on the children, on Talika, on him. No doubt about it, at home Kate was a softer, more relaxed and happy woman. He hoped the departure of Chris had something to do with that.

Oliver spent the Christmas holiday in his flat in the country. He offered to buy and cook the Christmas lunch for the family in the house, which would allow the girls and Ruth to go riding in the morning.

It worked well. It was a glorious clear morning with a hard enough frost to keep the mud at bay and the girls came in glowing from two hours of hard riding.

Oliver produced roast beef à la Kate for six (Ruth's parents were there) and it worked a treat. He'd made a mock Christmas pudding with good quality bought vanilla ice-cream, mixed with mincemeat and flavoured with brandy, turned out from a pudding dish and topped with holly.

No one quarrelled, Ruth was friendly and the boyfriend, Ben, had obviously been banished for the day. The girls were delighted with their presents – a replacement kite for Andrea, sequinned top for Mattie. Even Ruth's parents, whom he'd feared might be hostile, were civil. No one mentioned separation or divorce.

But at six p.m. Oliver left with relief, glad to have survived the day. Even, he admitted, to have enjoyed it. Maybe, he thought, we will manage this divorce with consideration and good sense, stay friends and love our children.

Over the holiday period he did a good deal of reading, worked on his Civitas book, and saw the girls often. But he found himself thinking a lot about Kate, and in the end he rang her.

'What are you doing on New Year's Eve?' he said without preamble. 'How about a date?'

She didn't answer, but he could hear her breathing. 'Kate?'

'I'm here. Hello, Oliver.'

'What do you think?'

'I think that would be lovely. But aren't you at home with the girls?'

'No, they're all going to a big bash at Ruth's father's place, and frankly, I couldn't stand it. Ruth concurs: better I'm not there.'

'I would need to check with Talika about having Toby. It might be too much for her with New Year frolics in the restaurant below, and a baby to look after.'

But it was fine. Oliver managed to book at the fashionable Boca di Lupo in Covent Garden after a cancellation. The menu was full of the sort of traditional Italian food he knew Kate loved.

She looked unbelievably glamorous. Her dress was a sort of crushed purple velvet with a low round neckline that revealed the soft swell of her breasts and the very edge of a lacy black bra. She was perhaps over-dressed for the informality of the place but he was flattered at the trouble she'd taken. She was wearing more make-up than usual; her hair was obviously professionally done, scraped back from her face and piled on top of her head with a few escaped curls brushing her left cheek. Her nails were bright with polish. Oliver felt stunned by her beauty.

'Kate, you look wonderful.'

'Thank you.' She smiled, but looked embarrassed. 'Well, have to make an effort. It is New Year.'

'And here was I thinking it was all for me.' As he said it, he thought, why am I flirting?

'It's just that you're so used to seeing me in chefs' whites.' She looked so sophisticated, but seemed self-conscious and nervous, not the Kate he knew.

He wanted to reassure her, as he might Mattie in circumstances too grown-up for her. 'Believe me, Kate, you are a beautiful woman, always. But such glamour is disconcerting, I admit.'

She looked at him, her eyes somehow smiling and troubled at the same time. 'Let's look at the menu,' he said.

Watching her dithering over ox cheeks or pork belly was a delight. But the place was too noisy to talk without shouting, and once the ordering was over conversation was difficult.

He didn't feel right either. Up till now he had been able to tell himself he was behaving like a mate, or a family friend, a recently separated man who needed a bit of female company and succour. Tonight felt too much like a date, with the expectations that dates carried.

Maybe Kate hoped for more than friendship from him. Neither of them had ever mentioned her bitter admission to that journalist that she'd fallen for him. That love, if it had ever been love, had been killed by his behaviour, he knew. She'd obviously forgiven him but was she now just a good friend? And is that what he wanted?

He was attracted to her, no doubt of that, but it was only a few months since his separation. He must not get into an emotional entanglement now. Perhaps he was *using* Kate, as he'd always used her, regardless of the effect on her. He needed her to listen to his troubles, to soothe his anxieties, to provide good sense and a bit of laughter. He mustn't hurt her again. Must not get in too deep . . .

The effect of good food and wine had relaxed the atmosphere by the time he paid the bill, and when he insisted on accompanying her home in a taxi, she was her old feisty self.

'Oliver, don't be daft, I'll go on the tube.'

'No you won't. I will escort you home like an old-fashioned gent,' he said.

'It's right across town! A round trip will cost a fortune.' She was right. The taxi meter clocked up inexorably: twenty-three pounds by the time they got to Ealing, and the return journey all the way to Lambeth would be even longer.

So this is what it's like without an official car and a driver, he thought. But, hell, it's worth it. Kate's hair, always unruly, had resisted the hairdresser's combs and some escaped curls lay on her cheeks and neck. He could smell her perfume – unfamiliar but delicious. He was tempted to put an arm round her, but resisted.

She confessed what an immense relief it had proved to be when Chris went back to Australia. 'I was mad,' she said. 'I spent seven years hoping never to see him again and then fell straight back into his orbit the minute he arrived.'

But when they were on her doorstep, some of her stiffness returned. Her goodbye kiss, on his cheek, was quick and final. She seemed to scuttle inside.

Well, he thought, as he returned to the taxi, we are both damaged goods. And do either of us know what we want, never mind how to get it?

Over the next week, Oliver often thought of ringing Kate, but didn't, but then the perfect opportunity arose. He had agreed to visit a secondary school in his constituency the day before term started, when they were having a big 'Adventure Day' for Year Sixes from surrounding primary schools and the local press were to cover it. The idea was to raise the profile of the school, and woo families whose children were due to go to big school in October. Oliver was to hand out certificates to children who had taken part in the day.

Oliver's constituency chairman briefed him the week before. 'The Head wants you to know of a slight hitch, in case you get complaints from the kids or parents. She's got Year Sixes coming from six different primaries and they'd lined up different activities for them to choose from, you know the sort of thing – making a rocket in science, visiting a farm, photography, cooking, five-a-side, steel band, etc. The most popular choice, can you believe it, was cooking. The TV-chef effect, I guess. Anyhow, now she's lost her food teacher and has no one to lead the class. So no cooking. Just so you know.'

Oliver said nothing at the time, but later he picked up the phone to Kate.

'You wouldn't like to do me a favour in my constituency?' He explained the problem. 'I think they have teaching assistants and it will be well organised – I know the school. But they don't have anyone with the personality and ability to control twenty excited ten-year-olds.'

Kate said she'd love to if her own Headteacher at St Thomas's would let her off. 'It's the day before the term starts and the staff are all in getting their classrooms ready. And I've only just joined the staff. But maybe if I do my stuff before . . . Anyway, I'll ask.'

She rang back to say that Judy, her Head at St Thomas's, was easy about it. She'd asked Elizabeth, Kate's immediate boss, who'd said it would be good professional development for her.

Oliver found himself excited at the prospect of seeing Kate again. He usually did a school visit in an hour but he'd blocked off the whole morning so he could observe her lesson. But first he had to glad-hand a line-up of teachers and parents, and then endure the inevitable, and seemingly interminable, tour of the school, conducted by a sixth-form boy and girl who had given up their last day of holiday to do it.

He made an effort to show interest in them and the school. He vividly remembered being told by Prince Philip at some VIP function that the only way to enjoy his job was to use the time to understand everything that anyone wanted to show him. And the sixth formers were bright kids. The boy wanted to be a chef and was going on to catering college. The girl was hoping for a place at Stirling University to read marine biology.

When they got to the food rooms an hour later, Kate was just starting her induction. Oliver's heart missed a beat. She looked so ridiculously young: no make-up, her round cheeks pink, her chef's jacket immaculate, her apron doubled at her waist, a tea-towel tucked into her apron strings. She came across to them quickly, and shook his hand formally.

Then she turned to the class and raised her hand. The children shushed. 'This gentleman is Mr Oliver Stapler, and he is your MP,' she said. 'Does anyone know what an MP is?'

Several children chorused, 'Member of Parliament.'

'Excellent. Shall we ask him to tell us a bit about what he does as an MP?'

Oliver gave the children a few minutes on the duties of political representation and then said, 'But, Ms McKinnon, I'm sure cooking is much more interesting. Can we watch for a bit?'

Kate was halfway through the standard Health and Safety preamble, warning the children to wash their hands between tasks, not to run, push or shove, that knives were sharp, hobs and ovens hot, to ask if unsure, etc, etc, when Oliver noticed one little boy with his name sticker – labelled KYLE and meant for his apron – stuck across his brow. Small and slight, he was standing directly under Kate's chin, his face tipped up, pulling faces. Little monster, thought Oliver, he's going to be trouble. Indeed Kyle then raised his arm and started to click his fingers at Kate's face while chanting, 'Boring, boring, boring . . .'

Oliver stood transfixed while the child continued his mantra, his clicking fingers getting closer and closer to Kate's nose. Poor Kate, what would she do? She could not, he realised, take the little devil's arm and force it down to his side and tell him to belt up – his parents would probably do her for assault. If she took a pace back she'd have lost and the monster would have won. There were twenty-odd children in the room and if she lost control it would be bedlam. If she stood her ground and he tweaked her nose, it would hurt like hell.

Then the child paused to draw breath, and Kate said, quick as a flash, 'Now, Kyle, I agree this bit might not be fascinating, but if you will just be quiet I will be able to get it over with and we can all get on with the exciting part – the cooking. OK?'

Kyle thought about it for a second, his eyes narrowed in his pinched young face. Then he resumed his finger-clicking chant.

'Boring, boring, boring.'

Oliver's instinct was to wade in there and get the little sod's arm up behind his back and march him out the door.

Suddenly a chubby girl, a lot larger than most of the class, took a swing at Kyle, punching him hard in the ear. 'Shut your face, Kyle,' she said.

Oliver could have kissed her. Kate immediately held her hand up and said with great emphasis, but without shouting, 'Quiet everyone, please. Not a word.' The children stood in shocked silence, the only sound Kyle's whimpering, 'Oh Miss, it hurts, Miss. She hit . . .'

'Shush, Kyle, and take your hand away. Let me look . . . Yes, well, your ear is a bit red, but it's not bleeding. You sit over here.' She led him to the teacher's desk at one end of the room. 'Just sit quietly and I'll see you in a minute.' Then she turned to his assailant.

'Michelle.' Kate peered at the girl's name sticker. 'It is Michelle, isn't it? I'm quite sure you know that hitting people is wrong. You will have to leave the class.' Kate turned towards Oliver and he thought for a second she was going to appeal to him for help, but she said to his student guides, 'Would you two be good enough to take Michelle to the Head's study? She probably won't be in it, but I am sure her secretary will be. Explain what happened and ask her, or any teacher you know, to take charge of her. OK?' Then she said to Oliver, 'Are you happy to stay in our cooking lesson, Mr Stapler, until these young people get back and rescue you? Or are you meant to be somewhere else by now?'

'No, this is the end of the morning tour, Ms McKinnon, so if you don't mind, I will watch the rest of the lesson.' Oliver smiled inwardly, thinking how well they were both playing their parts.

He watched the lesson with fascination. Kate divided the class into four groups, each group clustered round a table of prepared ingredients, and each with a grown-up (teaching assistant or parent volunteer) to help. One group made fresh pasta, first rolling the dough by hand then feeding it repeatedly into a small but sturdy little machine that rolled it thinner and thinner. Then they cut it into tagliatelli. The children draped the ribbons of pasta over rolling pins to dry and then chopped and ground pinenuts, basil, parmesan and garlic for pesto. It smelt delicious.

The second group made dough for pizza, rolled it out, and added toppings of their own devising. They favoured cheese and tomato, but Kate managed to persuade a couple of them to risk a few olives, anchovies or spicy sausage.

One group watched Kate fillet and skin a large trout then each child wrapped a piece of fish with a dab of butter and some tarragon leaves in puff pastry. The final team made a chicken stir fry, starting with a whole raw chicken. Oliver wondered why Kate had not specified fillets of fish and chicken breasts. So much quicker and less messy than the whole animal. But as the lesson progressed he realised that Kate wanted the children to understand where chicken nuggets and fish fingers came from.

Oliver kept half an eye on Kyle. Kate, he noticed, once she was satisfied that no damage had been done to the boy, studiously ignored him. After a bit more unproductive muttering and rubbing of his ear, he left his chair and wandered round the classroom, grimacing and making sick noises. 'Yuk', 'Urggh',

'That's gross'. Oliver thought Kate should fling him out of the class: he was getting in the way, and contributing nothing. But apart from a sharp reprimand about his language when he declared, 'Only my Nan eats that fish crap. It's shit, that is . . .' she left him to his own devices.

And then, about halfway through the class, when it was obvious how absorbed and happy his classmates were, Kyle suddenly approached Kate. 'I'm sorry, Miss. Can I make a pizza?'

Kate smile was genuine. 'I'm afraid the pizza ingredients are all used up, Kyle. But you can make a fish parcel. Why not?'

Kyle looked doubtful. 'But it's horrible, Miss, fish is.'

'Does your Nan think so?'

'Nah. But she's old, Miss. She's . . .'

'Does she live with you?'

'Yeah.'

'Is she good to you? Do you like her?'

'She's all right. S'pose.'

Oliver wondered what on earth Kyle's relationship with his grandmother had to do with anything, but by now he'd realised that there would be a purpose to Kate's questioning.

'Well, what about making her a little fish parcel for her supper? Wouldn't that give her a buzz? To think you could do anything like that. Make something like a proper chef?'

Kyle turned out to be rather good at it, though he did try to resist including the tarragon, 'Urggh, Miss, I hate green stuff. It's cr—'

'No swearing, Kyle. Does your Nan hate green things too?'

'Well . . .'

'This is for your Nan, isn't it? I think we'll include the tarragon.' Kate's voice was kind, but firm.

Kyle made a neat little parcel, decorated on the top with his pastry fish, complete with scales marked with the tip of a knife, and a large eye, carefully cut out of the pastry with scissors. Oliver was amused to see that when he painted the parcel carefully with egg yolk, he stuck his tongue out of the corner of his mouth, a cartoon image of concentration.

When they were waiting for the last of the pizzas (charred round the edges and dripping with cheese) and little trout parcels, brown and crisp, to emerge from the oven, Kyle resumed what was obviously his default persona.

'It's not proper food, this shit,' he said to the others. 'Why can't we make real stuff, like sausages and chips, and burgers and pot noodles? Something what's nice to eat.' Pointing at the wok full of chicken with broccoli and mange tout, he said, 'You aren't going to eat those vegetable things, are you? They're gross, they are.'

Once again Kate took no notice. But when Kyle's parcel came out of the oven, she held it over the bin, and called across to Kyle, 'Kyle, I'm binning this, am I? I think you said it was rubbish. So I guess you don't want—'

Kyle's face clouded with alarm. He hurried across the room. 'No, Miss, no. I said I'd give it to my Nan. She eats that cr—'

'That what, Kyle?'

'That food.'

So Kyle's fish parcel went into a little cake box like the others.

Oliver was enjoying himself. When the children were released, each proudly and excitedly clutching their creations, he helped Kate and the assistants clear up. He was impressed that Kate had them wiping out the ovens, mopping the floor and polishing the taps before she thanked them and let them go.

She tied up the rubbish bags, handed the recycling one to Oliver and took the composting one herself.

'Let's get rid of these and go and find some lunch,' she said. 'And then it will be my turn to watch you perform, doing your

VIP bit. I wish the press had been here to see you wiping down tables. It would make a much better story.'

As they walked down the corridor, rubbish sacks in hand, Oliver whispered in her ear, 'Kate, look over there . . .'

Kyle stood, on his own and facing the wall, scoffing his fish parcel.

Oliver looked into Kate's face, expecting to see triumph there. But her eyes filled with tears. She shook her head, 'Poor little chap. What chance has he got?'

Oliver suddenly knew, with the full force of belated realisation, that he loved Kate. The knowledge silenced him completely.

They walked past Kyle, averting their eyes so as not to embarrass him, and dropped their rubbish into the wheelie bins.

'Well, Oliver Stapler, MP, did you learn anything?'

'I did,' he said. He put the back of his hand against Kate's cheek. 'More than you could possibly guess.'